THE
CINDERELLA
EFFECT

Miriam Morrison used to live in Cumbria, where she was a journalist, teacher and hotelier, though not all at the same time. She now lives in Kent with her daughter, Emily (a genius in the kitchen) and a cat, Poppy (a genius at getting her own way). Miriam Morrison is also the author of *Recipe for Disaster*, which was published by Arrow in April 2008.

Praise for Miriam Morrison

'This clever and funny novel is great as a Sunday afternoon read' *The Sun*

'A clever little tale' *OK!*

'Morrison has an easy wit which also reads nicely – rarely does a page pass without a decent quip. This is a fun, absorbing debut that doesn't take itself too seriously. Morrison is onto a winner.'
City AM

Miriam Morrison

THE CINDERELLA EFFECT

arrow books

Published by Arrow Books 2009

1 3 5 7 9 10 8 6 4 2

First published in Great Britain in 2009 by Arrow Books

The Random House Group Limited
20 Vauxhall Bridge Road, London, SW1V 2SA

www.rbooks.co.uk
Addresses for companies within
The Penguin Random House Group can be found at:
global.penguinrandomhouse.com
The Random House Group Limited Reg. No. 954009

A CIP catalogue record for this book
is available from the British Library

ISBN 9780099517481

The Random House Group Limited supports The Forest Stewardship
Council (FSC), the leading international forest certification organisation. All our
titles that are printed on Greenpeace-approved FSC-certified paper carry the FSC logo.
Our paper procurement policy can be found at www.rbooks.co.uk/environment

Typeset by Palimpsest Book Production Limited,
Grangemouth, Stirlingshire
Printed and bound in Great Britain by Clays Ltd, Elcograf S.p.A.

For Mike and Beccy

Prologue

Lila

Silently, I begged Tony to drop the gravy in my lap, but of course he didn't. He poured it neatly onto the roast lamb, just the way I liked it, and then stood up.

'Oh, and I got you that CD you've been wanting – I'll just put it on.'

I stared down at my plate and inhaled the intoxicating scent of garlic and rosemary. This was my favourite meal. Feverishly I cast around for something, anything, that we could have an argument about. Politics always seemed to work for people on television. I tried to drum up a controversial opinion about Parliament and failed. My hands twitched.

'Dig in, darling. There's heaps more where that came from!' said Tony tenderly, dropping a kiss on the top of my head before sitting down. He smiled at me lovingly, and he had every right to – he was my fiancé.

I smiled weakly and pushed my fork around on the plate. But my throat had dried up completely and the ring on my finger was winking out a coded message. It was telling me what an idiot I had been, again.

'Mmm, the scent from those roses is just wonderful, isn't it?' he said, sounding pleased with himself.

He had cooked my favourite meal, put on my favourite music, and even remembered how much I loved yellow roses. I stared at them, bobbing slightly in the breeze from the open window, and shuddered. Everything was perfect. And suddenly I was so miserable I couldn't bear it any longer.

'I can't do it! Tony, I am so sorry but I can't marry you!'

He stared at me aghast, his kind brown eyes full of shock. 'What?' he managed to whisper eventually.

I gulped, but knew I couldn't back away from this. 'I don't deserve you. You are a wonderful man, but I am not the right woman for you.'

'But I haven't done anything wrong.'

I nodded and a tear of pity for him plopped into the now congealing gravy. Poor Tony. He was right. But then he probably hadn't put a foot wrong in his life. Vicar's son, head boy at school, Duke of Edinburgh Gold Award winner and now a conservation worker – Tony could fix just about anything. He frowned and I could tell he was thinking about ways to fix this.

'I've gone overboard with the flowers and all this food, haven't I? I know you don't like fuss. I will back off and give you some space.'

'No, it's not that at all . . .'

'Maybe I haven't been giving you enough attention. Do you want to go out more? Is this all too staid and middle-aged, just sitting at home and having dinner?'

'I'm not yearning for wild parties and bags of cocaine and the likes of Pete Doherty, if that's what you mean,' I said wildly. 'It's just that . . . well, I . . . you see . . . oh, Tony, I am so sorry but I just need to be on my own!' I blurted out. I knew with an unshakeable conviction that we had to break up – I just couldn't explain why. I felt like I had led him up the garden path to our 'roses round the door' future and then slammed it shut, leaving him out in the mud and the pouring rain. At least he had found out the truth about me before I led him up the aisle.

He slumped. I couldn't bear to look at him. But then I didn't have to; I knew every inch of him off by heart. Tony was tall and very fit. He ran every morning and he didn't just belong to a gym – he actually used it, three times a week. He had a square dependable-looking face, the sort of face that said, I won't let you down. Oh, how I wished mine could say the same thing.

Then his eyes sharpened. 'Is there someone else?' he asked hoarsely.

At least I could meet his gaze unflinchingly. 'I would never do that to you,' I said.

'Look, I know things haven't been going right for you recently: your home, your family . . .' He paused and then realised that was too big a subject to tackle now.

'I know your career isn't really taking off either,' he began.

'That's because I haven't got a career. Or even a job,' I finished for him bluntly, determined to call a spade a spade, even if he couldn't. My hands twitched again.

'But honestly, darling, things won't stay like that. And even if they do, I don't care. I love you as you are. I don't want to change you one bit. I will support you whatever happens. That's why we're getting married – that's my vow to you!'

I felt like a surgeon starting the operation without the anaesthetist. 'Tony, I am very, very sorry, but there will be no wedding. I don't think I can really explain it properly, but I am absolutely certain that I cannot marry you.'

He stared at me. 'I don't believe you are doing this!'

'I know. It must seem like I don't know my own mind, but I assure you I do. You see, it's –' I began.

'I don't mean that. I mean that we are in the middle of the most momentous and life-changing discussion of our relationship. I expected – I hoped – you would at least concentrate. But you –' he pointed a shaking finger at me – 'you're doodling on the napkin.'

I looked down, horrified. I wasn't, was I? Yes, I was. Any other woman breaking off an engagement would have taken off the ring and put it quietly on the table, a mute gesture to signify it was over. But not me. My hands had other ideas. They were busy scribbling a sketch of me taking the ring off.

I stood up and clasped my hands firmly behind my back so they wouldn't get me into any more trouble. 'You are quite right. At least this will show you that you deserve someone far better than me.' I turned, tears welling, and blundered towards the door. 'I'm sorry, I'm sorry, I'm sorry, but I think it would be better if I just went home . . .' I babbled, and ran out.

As I unchained my bike from the railings outside Tony's flat, keeping my head bent because I knew he was at the window staring down at me, I realised I was still wearing his ring. But I knew I couldn't go up there again now. I would have to send it back. I shoved my hand in my pocket in case he saw it glittering in the lamplight – it was rather a big diamond – and cycled – or rather, wobbled – off, because balancing was difficult with only one hand. I was still sniffing and sobbing, so as soon as I was round the corner, I stopped to blow my nose and mop up. I took the ring off and put it in my pocket. Instantly I felt better.

As I cycled home soberly, I reflected that out of all my admittedly numerous engagements, this had probably been the most unsuitable. I'd known Tony all my life – we'd gone to the same school, but then hadn't seen much of each other until the day he turned up at our house. In his capacity as council heritage officer, he was talking to Ma and Pa about a grant to shore up what he called 'the east wing', but what we called 'those mouldy old bedrooms round the back that never get any sunlight'. He stayed on to fix a floorboard – he has a passion for mending things – and it all started from there. There were many lovable things about Tony, and I did still love him, actually, but there was no spark between us, never had been really. Oh, I was such a fool for agreeing to marry him in the first place.

My route home took me past my first fiancé's flat. There were plenty of sparks between Greg and me then, and even more during the break-up. Greg was passionate, with flaring nostrils, and I thought the break-up would go more smoothly if we did it in a public place – a restaurant, to be exact. This certainly meant that we kept our voices down, but Greg flung his arms about quite a lot and knocked over the candle, setting fire to the tablecloth. Greg was an English teacher and I can still remember him declaiming a Shakespearean sonnet about lost love and broken hearts in his deep, melodic voice, over the crackling of the flames. One table thought it was a floor show and applauded.

Greg wrote to me six months later to say that our relationship, though painful, had inspired his lessons on *Wuthering Heights* with his Year Ten students, who had then gone on to pass their English Literature GCSE with flying colours, so at least the engagement hadn't been a total washout.

My bike skidded to a halt beside the park railings and a wave of horror washed over me. How many engagements did a girl have to break off before she became, well, a serial fiancée? Was that what I had turned into?

I glanced over the railings and shuddered. Everywhere I looked, my shameful past rose up to haunt me. Just over there, by that exact park bench, was where I had fallen over fiancé number two's legs. Richard was an architect and he was sitting in the park while going over the agenda for an important meeting. I was in my all too brief jogging phase, but had stopped looking where I was going because I had suddenly noticed how the sun was shining on the leaves of a tree. It would be quite a challenge mixing the right shade of green, I thought, as I fell over him.

Richard was such a gentleman, even though my nose bled all over his very important papers and he ended up being twenty minutes late for his meeting. He mopped me up with his handkerchief, sat me down on the bench and arranged to meet me for coffee later. He was very kind, but terribly bossy, I later learned. He was always telling me what to do – which dress I should wear to the restaurant, what to order when we got there, whether we should have sex before or after dinner.

For his birthday, I drew a sketch of him sitting at his desk. He said he loved it, but I could see him looking at it doubtfully.

'Darling, I think you've made my nose a little too big,' he said.

'I haven't,' I said firmly.

'Darling, I do know about proportion and accuracy, and this nose is . . . it's . . . positively gigantic.'

I laughed and kissed him on the offending honker. 'You know what they say about big noses,' I giggled.

'You will have to draw it again,' said Richard, stubbornly. There wasn't even a glimmer of a smile on his face.

'I won't,' I said, louder. Suddenly, defending that nose became the most important thing in the world. We stared at each other and I had an awful vision of our future together, with Richard always insisting he was right.

Later, and obviously I didn't explain it very well because I was still very upset, I said that the engagement was over because Richard and I couldn't agree as to the size of his nose. My family clearly thought I was bonkers. Sometimes I agree with them.

Chapter One

Lila

'Everyone's talking about us again,' said Ma gloomily, two days later. 'I was in the post office this morning and I heard someone say it should be a regular item in the parish magazine. Or a competition. Something along the lines of: "Guess how many engagement rings Lila Barton has given back this year!"'

I winced.

'Someone else said you were better entertainment than the television,' she continued, drying the dishes with such gusto a handle fell off a teacup. 'Well, that's the last of the Minton tea set.'

'That cup was chipped anyway,' I offered consolingly, but my mother was looking at Will. Maybe she was hoping he would instantly produce a twenty-five-page analysis of my condition, along with a list of treatments, all of them cheap.

But Will was doing the crossword. 'There must be another word for arboretum, because this one just doesn't fit,' he complained. He saw us staring at him and tapped his pencil impatiently, eager to get back to the puzzle. 'She's just a romantic dreamer and I am sure at some point, probably when she has run out of steam, or men, she'll grow out of it,' he opined. 'Ah ha! That's it! Arboretum is right and gravy is wrong,' he said triumphantly, and bent his head again. This was one of those times when it was hopeless trying to get any sense out of him.

Will is much older than I and already starting to go bald, which annoys him, as Pa still has a full head, though penury and deprivation have turned him completely grey. Will has earned so many psycho-therapeutical qualifications that anyone writing to him needs an extra large envelope to fit in all the letters after his name. He is as familiar with the thoughts of Freud and Jung as you and I are with the contents of *heat* magazine.

He once said it was unprofessional to analyse members of his own family, to which Pa replied he wished he had known that before forking out all that cash to send him to university, and anyway, no one needed analysing except me.

Brothers can be really quite silly sometimes, even psychotherapists like Will. He'd got it all wrong, anyhow, because I considered myself to be the least romantic member of my family. But even so, there was no escaping the fact that I had made rather a habit recently of collecting and disposing of fiancés.

'I am no psychologist, but isn't it the current

trend to blame the parents for everything?' Ma asked hesitantly.

'You and Pa had three children. Statistically one of them is bound to turn out a bit off,' chortled Will, and ducked when I threw the dishcloth at him.

A sudden gust of wind hurtled a sheet of rain at the kitchen window.

'Which one of us is on bucket duty?' asked Ma.

'I'll go,' I offered, even though it wasn't my turn. It was the perfect excuse to escape the firing line of family criticism, so I set off upstairs to my attic bedroom.

Being on bucket duty was an activity peculiar to those of us who call Barton Willow home. Usually houses are described as, oh, a four-bedroom bungalow or a two-bed flat, for instance. Barton Willow has lots of bedrooms, actually, but I preferred to describe it as an eleven-bucket house. This was the number currently required to catch the rain that dripped through the holes in the roof, a figure that had been growing steadily for the last few years. If the family fortunes didn't change for the better soon, we would be all buckets and no roof. But how could things get better? There didn't seem any way to reverse the downward spiral of our fortunes. And if they didn't . . . No, I definitely wasn't going to think about that right now.

I love my attic bedroom even though the ceiling is so low at one end I can't stand up. But the other end is practically all window, and when I look out, it feels like I am looking halfway across Kent. I stood for a few minutes admiring the view and daydreaming, and then remembered I was here to empty those bloody buckets before the water overflowed down through the floorboards and into Ma and Pa's bedroom.

It also made one less job for Jeeves, our faithful and desperately over-burdened retainer. Poor Jeeves, he could barely lift the silver teapot, his hands were so gnarled and twisted with arthritis . . .

I'm sorry, I made that last bit up. That whole last bit, actually.

We didn't have an old retainer. We didn't have any servants at all, not even a cleaner, and, boy, could we have done with one in this mouldering mansion, with all its bedrooms, reception rooms, anterooms, stables out the back and a drive so long you'd need a cup of tea and a sit-down long before you reached the front door. Yes, we had all that. We just didn't have any money, or the possibility of getting any.

Barton Willow was sometimes more like a monster than a house. It sucked up every bit of money you threw at it like an enormous vacuum cleaner that you couldn't switch off. My sister, Anna, who is good with figures, did a rough calculation of how much it would cost to put Barton Willow right.

'I sort of knew it was going to be seven figures, but even I didn't know it was going to be those particular seven,' she said, and gulped.

Our mood was damper than the clothes drying above the Blessed Aga. To make us laugh, I demanded to look into Pa's wallet. I shook it and out fluttered an ancient one-pound note.

'Oh, Pa, how long has that been there?'

'Since I was eight,' he admitted. 'I got it for my birthday. It was the first time anyone had given me any money and I was so excited. There were so many things I wanted, I decided not to spend it until I was absolutely certain. In the end it became a sort of talisman and I couldn't bear to part with it . . .' He trailed off into silence.

'And now it's not even legal tender,' said Will mournfully.

Really, I thought poverty and perpetual damp had sent us all slightly mad. No wonder I was tempted every now and then to make up stories about servants. It also took my mind off the fact that I was in a tiny bit of boyfriend bother at that moment. Again. I was just fed up with getting it wrong all the time. If falling in love was an exam, I would have been on my third resit by then. Maybe I should just have awarded myself a double F for my failure to be a proper fiancée.

I started emptying the buckets. It was all going well until bucket number ten, which was so ancient that the bottom fell out when I picked it up, and instantly my socks and trainers were drenched in icy cold water. I tore into the bathroom to find a towel for mopping up, but by the time I found a dry one it was too late, the water had seeped away through the floorboards. I upended the waste bin, which was plastic and would serve nicely to catch the drips, but which left rubbish all over the floor. Really, that should have been an incentive to tidy up!

But then I caught sight of my reflection in the bottom of the broken bucket and groaned. I really wasn't up to a critical analysis of my features just then.

'You have a lovely smile,' Ma says, but this is the sort of thing a mother has to say. I tried a quick smile but I have such a large mouth, I just looked manically cheerful and certainly not sexy, like Angelina Jolie when she smiles. No, my smile was just big. When I was ten, for a dare, I got a whole pork pie in my mouth without losing a crumb, which I suppose is an achievement. Angelina looks like she wouldn't know what a pork pie was.

By the way, I only did the pie thing once, though cash was offered for an encore. I discovered there are some things even I wouldn't do for money.

I had been wearing a blanket draped over my shoulders like a cloak while I did the bucket thing and even though I had changed out of my soaking wet socks and trainers, and into slippers, I was still shivering. Now, because I had once timed it, I knew that it took exactly three and a half minutes of icy cold corridors to get from my attic to the kitchen and the Blessed Aga, but if I took the blanket with me to keep warm in those three and a half minutes, someone was bound to swipe it, and then I would never see it again and I would die of hypothermia, which might be one way out of my current troubles, but rather a drastic one.

What better sign that the family fortunes had hit an all-time low than the fact that we were reduced to scrapping over a mouldy old blanket with a red jelly stain in one corner, I mused, as I made my way quickly down the rickety staircase from the top floor and along a wood-panelled corridor. Was that woodworm I could hear or a deathwatch beetle? No, the heel of my slipper had come loose and was clicking on the bare boards. This part of the house wasn't important enough to merit a carpet. I turned right into another corridor, lined with bold squares where pictures had once hung and where now only rusty nails remained. At the top of the stairs leading to the ground floor I paused, even though I was so cold my teeth were chattering. These stairs demanded style and elegance. I should really be wearing something long and floaty, and as I wafted down, there would be a man waiting at the bottom, hand held out chivalrously to take mine, which in my fantasy was manicured and dainty, not spattered with old ink stains. But then my imagination refused to work another minute in this frigid cold, and I ran down the rest of the stairs quickly.

I opened the kitchen door and got an unexpected view of Ma's bottom, which, despite her advancing years and the hideous brown corduroy trousers she was wearing, was still in very good shape – better than my own, I suspected.

'Why are you trying to climb in the oven? Has Pa been beating you up again?'

'Don't be silly – you know your father wouldn't do that.' Ma's face emerged, rather flushed. 'Actually I was looking for the knives. I simply cannot remember where I hid them last night.'

'Why did you hide them in the first place?' I said, bewildered.

'Tony. I saw his face reflected in the hall mirror when you were giving the ring back. And then, when he asked to use one of the knives, I didn't want him doing anything silly.'

'Oh.' I was engulfed in depression. Tony had insisted on coming to the house the next day to see if we could talk things over. We had then endured an excruciating hour while I'd tried to explain the unexplainable, which was that I was totally convinced we weren't right for each other, I just couldn't explain why. 'He wanted a knife to cut away that bit of loose carpet before someone tripped over it. He wasn't going to do anything else with it,' I explained.

'Well, I wasn't going to take any chances. You have such a volatile love life, dear.'

Tony deserved someone far better than me, someone who didn't heap even more worries on her already over-burdened mother, for instance. 'Ma, I really am sorry.'

'I don't know how I can make dinner without a knife – not that I have much appetite, because afterwards I must phone Graham and Sylvia for a very uncomfortable conversation.'

I winced. Tony's dad, Graham, is our vicar and our families have been friends for ever. Who could blame Sylvia if she wanted to heap insults on my head?

I started opening and shutting cupboards, hoping to locate the knives. They were nowhere to be seen, but I did come across Anna's latest donation, a packet of custard creams. As I fumbled with the pack (why are they always so bloody difficult to get into – do they not want you to eat them?), I scrabbled around in my head for something, anything, to mitigate my poor behaviour. But there was nothing. Tony was a perfectly nice guy. He had no annoying habits, strange fetishes or psychological defects, which was probably why I had fallen for him in the first place.

I sat down miserably next to Will. Could I tell Ma the truth? I wondered. No. It sounded ridiculous even to my own ears. The truth was I had leaped into this relationship as I had into all of them, madly impulsive, sure that this was what I had been searching for, and then, well, it was like becoming instantly sober after a prolonged period of drunkenness. I would look around, my eyes focused now, and discover I didn't want to be with him at all.

'If you keep saying you want to be on your own, why do you persist in getting engaged?' asked Will. 'You're practically salivating for an engagement ring, and then when you get one, you run off like a frightened rabbit. Your auntie's an idiot, isn't she, darling?' This bit was addressed to my niece, Emma, who was lying on the kitchen table having her nappy changed.

I blew out my cheeks in a gusty sigh. Will was absolutely right – I was an idiot.

But then he turned round and gave me a quick grin. 'Cheer up, sis. I have every confidence you'll get your life sorted . . . eventually.'

'Then you are probably the only one around here who does,' I said gloomily.

'Console yourself with the fact that you are providing the village with gossip fodder,' said Will.

'Why would that be a consolation?'

'Well, it's one of the things a Barton has to do – it's a sort of family tradition – and you are doing it almost as well as Pa's great-great-great-grandfather Quentin. You know the one.'

'Er, no . . .'

Will sighed. 'You really should mug up your family history a bit more,' he grumbled. 'Quentin Barton was one of the first people to experiment with talking to plants to see if they would grow better. The villagers were perfectly happy to let him loose in their gardens, but unfortunately he insisted on conducting these botanical chats in the nude. Even then the village didn't mind too much – it gave people something to talk about on those long winter nights – until he tried to persuade the blacksmith's wife to join him – lying down.'

'I've never heard of Quentin,' I said suspiciously.

'Yes, you have, and you've seen him. It was his ghost you saw running through the kitchen garden last year.'

'I told you I had seen something suspicious but you all blamed it on Ma's sloe gin,' I said triumphantly, and then saw the look on his face. 'Liar! You just made all that up!'

'You are so easy to wind up, post engagement break-up,' he grinned.

If I stuck my tongue out at Emma, she stuck hers out right back and sometimes she even blew bubbles. She was obviously a most advanced baby and destined to be the genius that would turn our family's fortunes round, though by then it would probably be too late. Genius had clearly skipped my generation, or at least me, I thought. The drawings I had done of her the previous week didn't do her justice at all. They didn't capture the uniqueness that was Emma; they were just a bunch of rather dull drawings of possibly any baby in the world.

'Well, you do seem to start things and then not finish them – boyfriends, pictures . . .' Will continued, pointing to a drawing I had done of Anna, which still lacked ears. Actually, I think I could have passed it off as meaningful art, you know, made the earlessness a statement about modern life. Or maybe it could have been an homage to Van Gogh. But the truth was it lacked ears because I couldn't get them right and had tried so many times with this particular set that there were now two small holes in the paper.

19

Ma gave a shout of triumph, which made us all jump, when she finally found the knives in the washing machine.

'It was a kind thought, Ma, but I am certain you needn't have bothered. Tony wasn't remotely suicidal. He is far too considerate to put people out like that, and anyway, I am sure he will get over me very quickly.'

I ruminated on the fact that he always seemed to laugh more at Anna's jokes than at mine and that they had been friends for ages, while Ma set to work on the rabbit that was to become tonight's supper. It was lying in a depressed way in the sink, well out of Emma's view in case it frightened her. On top of the rabbit, so he looked like he was wearing camouflage, was a pile of potatoes and a bunch of herbs, all fresh from the soil. In other words, they were covered in muck and needed vast amounts of effort before anyone could eat them. Oh, how I yearned sometimes for those little meals you shove straight in a microwave. When they come out, you don't even have to transfer the contents to a plate. Being poor is such hard work.

I picked up a potato and examined it. I was sure it had the same shape as Tony's father's head, but this obviously wouldn't be a good time to go round with it and check.

'Peel it and don't even think about drawing it!' Ma waved her knife at me threateningly. It was a good thing none of Will's colleagues were round – they would have had a field day. 'Are you sure she hasn't got that attention deficit thingy?' Ma looked at Will hopefully.

'Um, I'm right here, Ma. You can't talk about me behind my back when I'm right in front of you,' I complained.

'Tell your sister I have decided not to talk to her until she sorts herself out.'

'Sort myself out? What do you mean? You make me sound like a pile of dirty laundry!'

'For the love of God, what she means is, just start something – anything, really – and see it through to the finish, the bitter end, if necessary,' translated Will, inserting Emma into my old high chair.

'I did. I finished with Tony, didn't I?' I pointed out. I put down the half-peeled potato, sat, and began giving Emma her tea. 'I just haven't found my métier yet.'

'Yes, we know that. It is quite obvious from your bank statement,' said Pa, poking his head round the door from the garden and pulling a silly face so Emma would smile.

'Hey! Why were you going through my mail?' I demanded.

'Well, I have this recurring fantasy that you have actually left home, Lila, so any mail that comes through the letterbox is either for me or your mother. I'm sorry, I just opened it. I certainly wish I hadn't. It was not heartening to discover that you have an overdraft the size of the national debt.'

'Are you going to come in or are you deliberately

leaving the door open to let that Siberian draught in?' demanded Ma. She feels the cold terribly, though judging by her size I reckoned that today was a three-jumper day.

'I am checking that I can walk into my own kitchen without coming face to face with blubbing or naked bodies,' said Pa.

'Oh, don't be so silly,' I said, but I squirmed uncomfortably. I had put Pa through the mill a bit, though some time had passed since the awful occasion Pa had barged in, right in the middle of me dumping Peter, who was almost my first fiancé, but I broke up with him just before he proposed. But he has had the last laugh, because look at him now: he is the most sought-after plumber in the whole of Kent, it seems. He has his own house, which never leaks, anywhere, is married to a gorgeous girl and the father of twins. And then look at me: jobless, penniless, single. Again.

Pa sat down rather heavily at the big kitchen table. I knew he wasn't going to make any more comments about my overdraft, because we all know his is much, much worse and Pa is nothing if not fair, though he does bellow a bit every now and again, just to let off steam.

I went over to the Blessed Aga to make him a nice comforting cup of tea and also to lean against its lovely warmth. I wished I had one of those all-in-one things that Emma wore. I could line it with rabbit fur, I thought idly, watching Ma skinning ours with a speed born of much practice. Her hands were red with cold. Poor Ma, I reckon the Blessed Aga is the only reason she has stayed in this decrepit house for so many years.

That's not true, of course. My parents would never criticise anyone for being impetuous, seeing as theirs was a whirlwind romance. They met in Norfolk, where Pa was learning about estate management, and they were married within the month at the local registry office because they were in such a hurry.

After the service they came straight here, travelling through the murk of a wet and foggy November evening.

It was a very good thing Ma met Pa before she saw Barton Willow. If she hadn't, she may well have run screaming for the nearest two-bedroom maisonette. From the outside it looked, well, fabulous – like something out of a fairytale. But once inside, with the crumbling walls, mouldy carpets, draughts and the family of mice that had set up home in one of the sofas, it turned into a nightmare.

When Ma and Pa arrived home after their wedding, there wasn't a single fire lit in the entire house because Pa was so excited he forgot to lay any. Ma always claimed that the fires of passion kept her feet warm that night, but the reality was that, at six the following morning, frozen beyond belief, she staggered downstairs, past all the huge, empty fireplaces, which seemed to be giving out hollow, mocking sounds, the chimneys unswept for years, until, like a pilgrim reaching Mecca, she stumbled into the kitchen and heat.

'Oh, bless this Aga,' she is reputed to have said.

When the milkman arrived later that morning he saw Ma curled up, fast asleep, on the warming plate, while Pa made tea and gazed at her adoringly. There is a rumour that Will was actually conceived on this Aga, which is always worth bringing into the conversation when he is being particularly annoying.

Actually, although we all laughed about it, we had all had occasion to bless the presence of the Aga. It hardly ever went out, and was the only part of this crumbling house you could absolutely guarantee to find warm.

'Here, a lovely cup of tea and, look, some delicious biscuits Anna must have bought specially for you!' I said.

Pa looked at me over the top of his glasses and we grinned at each other in a complicit way.

'Stop that!' warned eagle-eyed Ma, even though we hadn't said anything. But then, Pa and I didn't have to. I take after him in temperament as well as looks. We are both tall and skinny and find things funny that other people don't, usually.

Anna is curvy and beautiful, like Ma. She has a brilliant way with clothes so she always looks fabulous, confident and bang on trend. But underneath that, she is an emotional volcano. Anna sees disaster looming round every corner. She can spot catastrophe so early on, it is still in bed, scratching its head and wondering what catastrophic plans to make for the day. She can take any situation and, within seconds, run it to a hideous tragic conclusion. You only have to tread on a drawing pin and you can see the word 'amputation' hover on her lips. I blame poverty myself. She used to work herself up into a frenzy watching Ma scrabble round the back of the sofa for spare coins to make up our lunch money. 'What if she can't find enough money?' she would whisper, her eyes huge. She was already envisaging the humiliation that would follow at school.

To her surprise, having somehow managed to survive all the way through childhood and past her A levels, she made it her life's mission to find a job that was well paid and secure. Anna can be focused when she wants to be, which comes as a shock when all people see is that docile face, and now she is a partner in a firm of accountants, having come to the conclusion that the world will always need an accountant, so she'll always have a steady income. She is simply raking it in.

I couldn't work out why, with a Waitrose income, she still had a Kwik Save mentality.

'I'm saving up to buy Ma and Pa a mortgage-free flat,' she explained.

'But they don't want to move,' I said.

We were in my bedroom at the time and she looked meaningfully at the buckets. 'One day they might have to.'

I was a bit worried about Anna just then. She seemed to have got even more accident-prone than usual and I thought she'd got something on her mind. She'd recently got her hair stuck in the photocopier at work. Then she was reaching for a tin of beans in the super-market and it fell on her head. And she was distracted. The other night, she was clearing up after dinner and she put the salt and pepper in the fridge and the butter in the cupboard with the ketchup. But why wasn't she talking to me about it? We told each other everything.

Pa took a biscuit and dunked it in his tea, where it instantly crumbled and sank to the bottom.

'Oh, blast to buggery all stupid biscuits! Get me a spoon, there's a love.'

'Pa, don't you remember the conversation we had recently about the sort of language we should use in front of Emma?' Will said.

'There was never a conversation. I do, however, dimly recall a lecture of excruciating dullness along the lines of damaging influences on pre-verbal infants, to which I think I remarked, "Stop talking nonsense," and walked off. Anything similar you have to say on the subject will elicit an identical response.'

'Don't fret, Will. If Emma does grow up to be mentally or morally unhinged, at least she won't have to go far for her therapy,' I said consolingly, putting a fresh cup of tea in front of Pa. I emptied the biscuits into a tin and drew a quick sketch of Emma in her pushchair looking thoughtful while Sigmund Freud chatted to her.

'Stop winding your brother up and don't for a minute think that you can buy me off with hot beverages,' said Pa, sounding stern, which we all knew was just a pose. In this house, Ma is the one you don't cross. 'Soon after your precipitous return from the States you announced you were going to get a job and move to London – "as soon as I get myself sorted," were your exact words. Do you have a date or a plan in mind, given that there are no unmarried men left in the village?'

Will snorted with laughter and I opened my mouth to say something in my defence, though I couldn't think of anything, when the kitchen door was flung open, bringing with it an icy gust of English spring air and my sister-in-law, Sophia. It was probably the first time in my life I was glad to see her.

Actually that's not true. I was pleased to see her the first time we met. I was so excited at the thought of welcoming her into the family and was already imagining cosy late night gossip sessions and sharing clothes and giving each other manicures. But then she asked Anna what diet she was on, just as Anna was reaching out her hand for her third scone. Sophia had a silly smirk on her face as she said it and you could almost see her mentally patting her own twenty-three-inch waist.

Now, even I couldn't describe Anna as skinny or slender or thin. But why would I want to? Anna is voluptuous and gorgeous, and easily the sexiest woman I know. In fact, everyone knows that, apart from Anna, which is why she says things like this.

Anna: 'Oh, Lila, I asked a shop assistant if my bum looked big in these jeans, and she said yes, it did!'

Me: 'She was just jealous of you, probably because the shop manager, who was actually quite fit, was staring at you with his mouth open.'

Anna: 'Yes, but only because he'd never set eyes on someone as fat as me. But thank you for trying to make me feel better. Oh, why don't I have a figure like yours?'

Me: 'Like me? Like Ms Bag of Bones Barton? You might as well just say I've got a great personality and be done with it.'

I don't want to be skinny, I want to be curvy and beautiful, like Anna. Anna is a peach, a really luscious ripe one. But me, I'm a stick of rhubarb, and Sophia, well, she's just a lemon.

Anyway, Sophia doesn't understand either of us. In fact, I think she secretly hoped Will was snatched from his real family at birth, and one day soon they would come for him and take him back to their nice dull house in Suburbanville – a place where the *Telegraph* got delivered each day because the paper bill was always paid on time, and if you got cold you just put the heating on, and everyone had a normal job, but no one was quite as important or as thin and pulled-together as she was.

Sophia has a well-paid job and this evening she was wearing co-ordinating navy and white, which had an underlying theme of extreme dullness. I think it would be fair to say that the mannequin in our local charity shop was dressed more boldly than Sophia. There was also a smudge of lipstick on one of her teeth, something that, I regret to say, caused me great satisfaction.

Her eyes did a quick scan of the room, checking that we hadn't been up to anything she could disapprove of, and she sank into a chair like she was God and it was Saturday evening.

'Long day, darling?' asked Will.

'Shattering.'

I went to the sink to refill the kettle. 'Would you like a cup of tea?' I asked hospitably, hoping to focus attention in the room on anyone but me.

'Oh, I suppose so, but please make sure it is caffeine-free, herbal, and would you take care to rinse the cup properly this time? I could taste soap suds the last time you made me a drink.' She shuddered.

'Go on, be a devil, have some caffeine. You look like you could do with it,' said Will. But she just looked at him like he was offering her a bag of heroin.

Emma held out her arms for her mother and Will stood up to pass her over. Sophia owned thirty-five books on child-rearing – at least that was the figure the last time I counted. She knows the right way to hold a baby, dress a baby, feed a baby, talk to a baby and play with a baby – and we do as well because she has lectured us at length on the subject. So Pa and I couldn't help grinning at each other as she bent over and whispered nonsense into Emma's ear and let Emma see how hard she could pull on her ear – both of which were expressly forbidden, according to her favourite manual. 'Who's my gorgeous snooky-nookums?' she burbled. 'No, darling, you can't eat Mummy-wummy's ear, can you, but you are very clever for trying.' She looked up proudly. Though I was loath to admit it, she really was a great mother.

'She is easily the cleverest baby ever,' I agreed, smiling at Sophia. I made her a cup of something caffeine-free, herbal, vegan, flavourless and disgusting, which didn't have a single molecule in common with a tea-leaf. She then took it, and Emma, upstairs instead of staying in the kitchen and acting as my human attention shield.

Pa and Will were sitting at either end of the table and launched a two-pronged attack.

Will: 'I believe you said, when you left for the States, that this was to be the start of your new life as a responsible adult, did you not?'

Pa: 'Which you have to admit is pretty funny, because you said exactly the same thing when you came – sorry – were sent back!'

Me: 'Well, I lied both times then, didn't I?' I slumped down at the table and put my head in my hands in what, in any other family, would be seen as a theatrical gesture. But my family were always doing it, and meaning it. 'All I want to do is to be left alone with a few pencils and some paper. I could sit by the side of the road drawing portraits of passers-by, or their pets.

I could earn enough to live a humble life on the profits. I am quite fond of cabbage and cheap biscuits. Oh, and not get engaged again for a while, of course. Is that too much to ask?'

'You've never sold a single thing, though, have you?' pointed out Will with brotherly brutality. 'Your art doesn't pay enough to rent out a dog kennel, or keep you in cabbages.'

'How many sessions do your patients put up with before they want to punch you?' I asked through clenched teeth.

Will sighed with exaggerated patience. 'I'm not saying you are no good at art. I love those drawings you did of Emma, and I think –'

'Hah! Well, that just proves you know nothing, because they were awful!' I said in triumph, and then felt confused. Why couldn't I just accept the compliment gracefully?

'Just listen! I certainly wouldn't advise you to give up drawing, or painting, or whatever medium you choose. It's part of who you are. But be realistic, Lila. You've got to get yourself a proper job to keep yourself on that unwholesome and unpleasant-sounding diet.'

I gulped. He was quite right, of course. I had to stop wasting time and living in a dream world. It was time to settle down and do something sensible with my life. It was time to grow up. Now I felt really depressed. 'I did try, when I went to America,' I offered.

'I told you to look up the word "realtor" in a

dictionary before you went off, but did you? No,' said Will, answering his own question.

Of course I hadn't. All I knew was that Aunt Lily, from the kindness of her heart, was paying my fare and then offering what seemed like a fortune in wages for me to go out to California and help her in her business. With the money, I could finally buy some more oil paints – it is impossible to paint anything without red – and maybe some new brushes . . .

I just knew it was all going to work out when Mitch Clayton's latest blockbuster action film was the in-flight entertainment. I have had a thing for Mitch ever since I was old enough to have a thing for anyone, and I was going to live in the same state as him, and be a 'realtor', whatever that was. My optimism proved short-lived. Maybe if I had bothered to find out that 'realtor' and estate agent mean the same thing I would have known that this wasn't going to turn out much fun. Two days into my new career and already I hated it. Short of cleaning toilets, this had to be the worst job in the world. Everyone in England knows you only ever get to buy a house despite the estate agent, not because of her, and it was no different out here. I didn't want to be like the, admittedly few, estate agents I knew in England: their clothes were always shiny and their smiles were stuck on.

To be fair, Aunt Lily wasn't shiny at all, except in the right places. She was fashionable, trim, smart and sassy, and simply rolling in paint-buying dollars. She was very kind to me and desperate for me to succeed, but by the end of the first month, she was also desperate for me to leave.

'It is not part of your job to point out the deficiencies of a property. The buyer will find them for himself, later.'

'Well, I don't know how you can say that, after all you went through, growing up at Barton Willow. You spend hours with that therapist and he still can't help you get over the night your bed nearly fell through the floor!'

'I simply refuse to discuss with you the issues I have regarding that incident,' she stuttered, going pale.

'Oh, for the thousandth time! The floor did not collapse because you were fat. It was caused by wood-worm, not calories! It was because you had the bad luck to grow up in a house that should have been demolished years ago!' I said, exasperated.

'Don't talk about Barton Willow like that!' hissed Aunt Lily, incandescent with rage. Then she sacked me.

I had brought it on myself, of course. I had mentioned her weight, which was an absolute no-no, and I had used the dreaded 'd' word about our house. Will, Anna and I had had many conversations about how it would be better for all of us if Barton Willow fell down or was demolished and then we could all get on with our lives. But the older generation didn't share this view.

I paid for my own ticket home. It was the least I could do. And since then, all I had done was get engaged (again) and unengaged (again). In no way could serial engagements be construed as a career, could they?

'Of course, your career problems are hereditary. Clearly you take after me,' said Pa, and Will looked up in horror.

'That's absolute rubbish –' he began, but Pa ignored him.

'We obviously both like championing lost causes. Look at all the things I have done to try and make this house a going concern. None of them has worked. Whereas you, well, I don't think there's anyone left for you to try and get engaged to. You have no career or even a job, and we all know you are broke. My dear girl, I think we can safely say you have reached rock bottom.'

'Well, that's great news!' I said triumphantly. 'Every step I take from now on has got to be up!'

No one, not even Will, who was still shaking his head over Pa's speech, looked convinced by this.

'Anyway, I have been thinking – and I have come up with a plan,' announced Pa.

I looked over at Will. 'Please tell him to stop,' I begged, but he shrugged his shoulders apologetically. 'Nothing to do with me, sis. The first rule of psychotherapy is – don't interfere.'

'Is it really?'

'No, but I would get no peace in this family otherwise,' he whispered.

'So, what is this plan then?' I asked resignedly. But I was destined not to find out, because there was a loud bang and all the lights went out.

Chapter Two

Johnny

'So, how many people have bought tickets for tonight's performance?'

Stella groaned. 'Twenty.'

'Well, that's five more than last night,' I said, determined to look on the bright side, and we both laughed, because we both knew this play was destined to go down the pan commercially, even if the theatre sold out tonight.

Stella was sitting on the stage with her feet dangling over the edge. She is a tiny woman and this afternoon she looked older than her forty-odd years. I sat down next to her and tried soundlessly to communicate sympathy.

'You've worked harder than anyone – well, apart from me – to make this play a success and I should have damn well known better it wasn't commercial enough to work in this town, so I don't deserve your sympathy,' she said.

'I reckon LA doesn't deserve you – or cutting-edge

drama,' I said fiercely. Stella was one of the bravest and most daring directors I had met. In her company I didn't mind that I couldn't be on stage. I was happy doing anything, however menial, as long as I could be a part of this production. 'So who cares if only a few dozen people see this show – they will have had their minds blown,' I continued, trying to cheer her up. But deep down I wondered what was the use of working your guts out to put on a play if the cast couldn't even scrape a living from it. And then I squirmed uncomfortably because of course I was always going to be all right, wasn't I?

Stella could tell where my thoughts were going. 'There's nothing wrong with the commercially successful stuff the rest of your family do, Johnny. Hell, half the crew went to see your brother's last film!'

'What she means is that tortured look you wear sometimes just makes you more sexy!' said a voice, and we looked round. It was Mary, Stella's partner, who was bankrolling this production of Brecht that hardly anyone would see. But then she knew that would happen when she bought the theatre. She kissed us both and sat down between us, with an arm round each of us. 'So, how are my two favourite head-in-the-clouds theatre junkies?'

'Much better now you're here,' I grinned. 'Whatever happens to Stella, I know she's gotten the love of a great woman, so she'll always be OK.'

'And you? Did you end up going out with that girl from the restaurant, the one who was so into you?'

'The waitress who wants to be an actress who guessed I was Mitch Clayton's younger brother? I don't think so!'

'You've got such a chip on your shoulder about your family. So she was a little star-struck – this is Hollywood! She seemed genuinely into you, not Mitch,' protested Mary.

My phone beeped a message. 'Well, speak of the devil and his family,' I drawled, and listened to it. 'I know you think I'm a little crazy – well, this is why,' and I played the message back to them. It was Dirk, my stepfather.

'Got you another appointment with that shrink Dr Lawson. Get to it this time. Four thirty, corner of Woodville and East,' and he hung up without saying goodbye, or hello even, or indulging in any of the small chat normal families are supposed to do, because of course he was far too busy and important to be polite. But I, on the other hand, was not. In fact, being polite was part of my DNA. I would have to go this time. I couldn't blow her off a second time just because I thought she and all her ilk were charlatans.

'What my family doesn't get is that if they weren't my family, I wouldn't need a shrink,' I said gloomily.

'But you *don't* need one! What you need is a shot of self-confidence,' said Stella.

'Well, this is America – I'll just run out to Wal-Mart

and buy one,' I said, and they both laughed. I looked down at my watch. 'I'd better get going. See you both at tonight's performance.'

I gave the theatre an affectionate glance before setting off. I had been working there for the last four years and some weeks. Getting paid in peanuts would've been a luxury. Stella and I had pretty much kept it standing by sheer willpower recently. It was one of the oldest theatres in LA and easily the most run down. The problem was, someone wanted to buy it and turn it into a casino, so unless we kept it going, its days of contributing to the arts were numbered. But we were determined to keep going until the bitter end, producing quality drama even if we were on our knees in the rubble. I grinned to myself as I thought this. Put that way, I did sound a little off the loop. Oh well, I could have a nice little chat to Dr Lawson about it.

I parked, went inside and looked around in annoy-ance. This was a very exclusive clinic and all the doctors had their own suites so clients were assured complete privacy. There was no general waiting room, so I couldn't even kill time trying to guess how much cosmetic surgery everyone had had done. I was greeted by a softly spoken woman who ushered me to Dr Lawson's suite.

'Can I get you anything to drink?'

'Water would be nice.'

'Still or sparkling?'

'Um, still, please.'

'Ice?'

'Thank you, no.'

'Lemon?'

I gritted my teeth. 'No, thank you – just as it comes, please.'

'You mean out of a tap?' said the woman slowly, as if she didn't know that was where it came from.

'Yeah. Why not?' I smiled at her and then the devil in me prompted me to ask: 'Have you got any coffee?'

'Of course. Filter, espresso, cappuccino?'

'Cappuccino.'

'Skinny, full-fat, soy, extra foam, any flavourings?'

'Never mind. I'm fine with just water. Is there anything to read?' I asked, overwhelmed by the beverage choices.

'Of course. Paper or magazine? We have the *Times*, *Variety* –' she began.

'It's OK, I've changed my mind about reading,' I said hastily before she had time to finish what I knew would be an exhaustive list of most of the reading matter available in LA.

'Well, would you prefer to watch something instead?' she offered, pulling open a cupboard that housed an enormous screen. 'We have two hundred and seventy-five channels, Mr Clayton.'

'Wow. Actually, you know what, I'm fine. I am just going to sit here and think,' I said, and she looked horrified, as if people who came here never did anything like that.

39

Then Dr Lawson came out and ushered me in.

'I am so glad to finally meet you,' she said, sitting down in one of the two comfortable chairs and then she glanced at me sharply. 'Are you OK?'

I realised I was scowling. For some reason I thought she was going to be maybe four or five years older than me. But she wasn't. She was in her fifties, comfortable-looking, with a motherly air. I explained this to her.

'Try and relax, Mr Clayton. I don't mother any of my clients,' she said.

'Good, because other shrinks have and –'

'Are you more comfortable talking about other people than talking about yourself?' she asked, and I groaned.

'I'm sorry, I should never have come. In fact, I only came to get my stepfather off my back –'

'Do you always do things to please other people?'

'No! I didn't mean that!'

'Do you always make a point of calling him your stepfather even though you've lived with the Claytons since you were three years old?' she asked, glancing down at her notes.

I took a deep breath. It was important to stay calm until I could get the hell out of here. 'My family and I have a thriving, dysfunctional relationship, as I am sure you are aware, if you've ever read a magazine or watched TV.'

Dr Lawson laughed. 'Actually, you'd be surprised

how many families have a "thriving dysfunctional" relationship, as you so neatly put it.'

'Actually, I'm not sure it is doing me much good,' I confessed. 'Everyone in my family is hugely successful, apart from me. There's my stepfather, the successful producer; my stepbrother Mitch, the successful actor; my other stepbrother Bradley, the successful –'

'Are you saying you can only be happy if you are successful?'

'No! Of course not! It's just hard, that's all . . .' I really didn't want to get into all this. But there was one of those long silences that practically force you to say something. 'I know I need to find a career – something that has nothing to do with the entertainment industry, obviously . . .' I tailed off.

Dr Lawson stared at her notes for a minute, then she looked up. 'I had a phone call after you didn't turn up for that first appointment. From a friend of yours. She said something very interesting about you. She said, "He's the most talented of the lot of them, but he's trapped. He needs to be set free and fixed."' She gazed at me, blandly. 'Why would she say that, do you think? How do you feel about that?'

I swallowed hard. Then I stood up. I was so angry I was shaking. 'I am not broken!' I said furiously, and walked out. But that didn't make me feel any better. Because I had lied. Stella – I was sure that was who had called – was right. I did need fixing.

Chapter Three

Lila

Bongo started barking furiously. He hates the dark and we always have to leave a light on for him in the kitchen at night. Figures shuffled past me in the blackout and I screamed when one of them trod on my foot.

'Sorry dear,' said Pa's voice out of the gloom.

'I told you to wait a moment – there!' said Will triumphantly, switching a torch on, while I kneeled down to reassure our anxious Labrador. 'I suppose the problem is the fuse box again. Don't tell me you were going to try and get down those steps in the dark, you silly old man?' They went down to the cellar together, arguing amicably.

By this time Ma was already lighting candles from the emergency stock in the kitchen drawer and I went over to the Aga and put the kettle on.

'I expect we are in for a long wait, as usual,' I said.

'Without a doubt,' said Ma placidly, getting out her knitting. She was making a sweater for Emma to wear the next winter, from the same pattern she used when

Will was a baby, then again for Anna and me and countless small relatives, so she could probably knit the whole garment in the dark anyway.

I drank tea and drew a sketch of Ma knitting a sweater that went on for ever, so that she was sitting in a sea of wool, while listening to the faint sounds of Pa and Will tinkering with things and occasionally emitting curses. Whenever something went wrong in this house, it was never a simple job to put it right. The wiring was put in ages ago and of course it had never been updated, checked or tested for safety since. We were probably sitting in the equivalent of a giant, faultily wired powder keg, and one day we would all be burned to a crisp in our beds. Which would be one way out of our pecuniary troubles, I supposed.

The cellar is even colder and damper than the rest of the house, and Pa and Will both looked rather blue round the lips when they finally emerged. They staggered into the kitchen, teeth chattering and demanding vats of tea, and I could tell that the lecture was over, for the time being, anyway.

'You didn't find any wine then?' I asked, though without any real hope.

Will removed several large cobwebs from his person and shook his head regretfully. 'It's hard to believe it was once stocked to the ceiling with dozens of vintages. If only our forebears hadn't been such a boozy lot!'

'If only I had been born a hundred years ago. I wouldn't have been allowed to get a job and would have been positively encouraged to spend all day sitting around drawing,' I continued, warming to my theme and then looking round puzzled. 'Why aren't the lights back on?'

'Because they are buggered,' said Will succinctly. 'We'll have to wait until tomorrow when the shops are open and I can get some bits and pieces.'

I eyed him suspiciously. 'Please remember you are a psychotherapist, not an electrician,' I said uneasily.

'Don't be silly! Of course I know what I'm doing!' said Will, with typical elder brother smugness.

It could have been worse. Thanks to the Blessed Aga, we had a hot meal and an inexhaustible supply of hot drinks, though that didn't stop Sophia shivering exaggeratedly all night and wrapping Emma up so she looked like a huge woollen parcel. Poor Sophia – how her dreams of glory had dwindled. She was practically orgasmic with lust the first time she clapped eyes on the house. As I watched her face quivering with greed, I could tell exactly what she was thinking – that Will was the eldest and that one day all this would be his. Of course, once she got to know the house better she was stunned at how awful it is to live in. They have their own, sensible, centrally heated house down the road, but were staying with us while a new bathroom and kitchen were put in. Every day new aspects of the awfulness of Barton Willow were made clear to Sophia. Then she made it obvious to everyone when Will wasn't around that she laid the blame for this fairly and squarely on Ma and Pa's miserably inefficient shoulders. The subtext was that once she was in charge everything would change for the better. Obviously I don't want anything to happen to Ma and Pa, ever, but sometimes I yearn for the day she and Will inherit Barton Willow and she realises how utterly wrong she was. This house is unfixable.

I went to bed early because there wasn't enough light to draw by without bringing on a headache, and spent a fitful night dreaming about money. First, I dreamed that I found a suitcase of cash in the attic and then decided to count it in the garden, where the wind blew it all away. Then I got a job painting the Queen's head onto fifty-pound notes in a building that looked awfully like the *Big Brother* house. In fact, I think my dream boss was that woman who won Series Six.

My heart was beating like a tom-tom when I woke and, although it was early, I decided to get up. I ran downstairs but tiptoed into the kitchen in case Sophia was down there, having got up early with Emma. But the kitchen was empty and silent. I made tea and then went off to find some wellies, which were in the boot room. I shook them out (in case of spiders), borrowed Will's jacket, which was much too big, but warmer than mine, and got Bongo to his unwilling paws by pulling on his collar until he started sliding across the kitchen floor.

Bongo is the laziest Labrador in the world and probably the most stupid, which is saying a lot. Shout 'walkies' at him and he lies down and pretends to be asleep. But once you've actually dragged him outside he behaves like he has escaped from doggie Alcatraz and charges about like a Labrador possessed. He absolutely loves being outside. He just can't remember that when he's inside.

The air was full of mist, but I knew it would clear later. After yesterday's rain, I was yearning for some blue sky. I was desperate for summer, even though I had lived in England all my life and should have known better. The grass seemed to crackle with greenness and the birds were working themselves into a positive frenzy of song. I walked over to the pond (only Sophia is daft enough to call it a lake) and threw stones for Bongo, who ran around barking madly but refusing to go in, which was sensible, I suppose, as it isn't very deep but is very muddy.

The mist hovering over the water gave a spooky feeling, which reminded me of our resident ghost. Her name was Beatrice and was about my age when, in a torment over some Regency cad, she threw herself out of a window. She howled like a banshee all the way down until her cries were stopped by a hideous crunch and her blood spattered all over the library windows . . .

I'm sorry, I made that up as well. There is no ghost at Barton Willow, though there jolly well should be. It looks like that sort of house: sort of normal on the surface, but subtly sliding off the edge of reality into something slightly fey and witchy. People have lived here for hundreds of years and you'd think someone would have left a ghostly imprint on the place. But as far as I can tell, the entire clan of Bartons have led quiet lives, utterly devoid of any drama at all, so you can see why I feel the need to make things up every now and again. Sometimes I get the strangest feeling that the house itself is slightly disappointed in us for being so, well, tepid.

Although the sun was out, it was still cold and I shuffled my feet together to keep them warm. Then I realised I was getting so cold because one of the wellies had a hole in the bottom. I bent down to take a closer look at the damage and the way the light was hitting the grass and then I saw it, gleaming faintly in the wet grass – a penny.

'This is a sign – our luck will change!' I said out loud. I picked it up and threw it as far as I could into the middle of the misty, mysterious pond, like it was an offering to a god. This was just ridiculous – and clutching at superstitious straws. As Will's sister I could certainly do better than that. I remembered something he had once said about making your own luck. I had to think my way out of my predicament.

To this end I decided to walk round the pond until I had come up with a very organised and highly effective Four-point Plan. I'm not sure why the plan had to have four points in it – it just sounded more impressive that way. After half an hour, I had it sorted.

I would definitely not get engaged again for at least a year.

I would most certainly not let myself fall in love either.

I would not even think about men at all.

I would get a sensible job, by the end of this week. Probably.

I blew out my cheeks in a slightly forlorn sigh. No one could say that this wasn't an eminently *sensible* plan, it just didn't leave much room for fun.

My stomach was really rumbling by now – time for breakfast. As I walked back to the house I realised there were ramifications to my organised and efficient Four-point Plan. It wouldn't happen by itself. I had to be proactive (one of Will's favourite words) and make it happen. Looking down to watch where I was walking (the hole in my boot was getting bigger) I said aloud: 'I solemnly swear I will stick to my Four-point Plan!'

'Maybe you should be careful about making promises you might not keep,' said a rather sharp voice, and I looked up, startled. Tony's mother was standing in front of me. Blimey, she was up early.

'Oh, SylviahellohowareyouandIwantyoutoknowhow sorryIam!' Then I drew a deep breath and felt awful, because of course this wasn't enough to convey how truly terrible I felt about breaking up with poor, blameless Tony. Sylvia might be a vicar's wife and the stalwart of every committee the county had, but I bet she wanted to box my ears and, really, I deserved to have them boxed. In fact, it was my duty to stand firm and take my punishment. 'I quite understand if you want to say you hate me,' I said miserably.

'I couldn't sleep, so I thought I would make an early start with delivering the parish magazine,' said Sylvia briskly. 'Don't be silly, dear, of course I don't hate you.' She fell silent and I could see her struggling to say something polite. 'I expect this will all work out for the best anyway,' she said finally.

'Oh, yes. I think I would have made an awful vicar's daughter-in-law,' I said, and she nodded in agreement, a bit too quickly.

The silence became deafening.

'How is Tony?' I ventured at last, and could have kicked myself for my stupidity. How was a newly jilted fiancé going to be?

'I have never seen him so depressed. His father and I are really quite worried about him,' said Sylvia, not pulling any punches, and why should she?

I hung my head in shame, but she carried on, remorselessly.

'However, he has an extremely well-balanced temperament, as a rule, and I have no doubt he will get through.'

'I feel so bad about all this.'

'Well, really you should, dear, because it's not the first time it's happened, is it? Maybe, a resolution to be less impetuous in future, perhaps?'

'I am *so* not going to do anything like that again,' I hastened to assure her, and then couldn't think of anything else to say. I think it was a relief to both of us when Bongo farted very loudly and unpleasantly, after which it was impossible to do anything but go our separate ways. I trudged into the yard and saw Sophia about to get into her car on her way to an early morning mother and baby class. The 'first day of the rest of my life' wasn't really turning out very well.

'Good morning! How is my gorgeous niece?'

But Sophia was in a lecturing mode.

'Was that Sylvia? That poor woman. I do hope you weren't rude to her, Lila – she probably has enough to deal with at the moment. Maybe you need to leave her alone for a while and not bother her.'

'Of course I wasn't rude to her! And I wasn't "bothering" her. We just met by chance. Anyway, what do you take me for?' I said, through gritted teeth.

'Don't be harbouring any hopes that Tony is pining for you. I expect he will get over you very quickly,' she said, and gave an irritating little laugh.

I tried to smile, but I knew I wasn't fooling anyone. Of course I wanted Tony to get over me but it was a bit disconcerting to learn that everyone was convinced he would in such short order. I ran into the house, pulled my wellies off and threw them violently against the wall to relieve my feelings. Quite a bit of plaster fell off, but I felt better so I reckoned it was worth it.

I gave Bongo his breakfast, made a pile of toast, because people round here had a habit of helping themselves to the piece you had just buttered, sat down with the paper and turned to the jobs section. It was rather unnerving to discover there was a long list of jobs I wasn't remotely qualified for. I couldn't nurse; drive a lorry; plumb; I certainly couldn't cook well enough to be let loose in a proper restaurant kitchen and I could add up only a very simple set of figures. Hmm, my organised, efficient Four-point Plan seemed to have hit a snag already. Then I saw an ad saying: 'Personal assistant required'. Yes, I was fairly sure I could do that. In the margin I started a picture of myself in a smart skirt and a pair of stilettos. I sketched in a laptop and an air of efficient helpfulness. Unfortunately, though, on closer examination, the job required a high level of competence in Office, Excel and Powerpoint, but all I could realistically offer them was a high level of *in*competence. Barton Willow didn't boast anything as technologically up to date as a toaster, let alone a computer, though my siblings had laptops, of course, and Will had paid for an Internet connection. Anyway, I had a suspicion that the advert was just being pretentious. I bet they were just looking for a skivvy.

I folded the paper over quickly as Pa walked in, but I needn't have bothered – he looked deeply preoccupied with the contents of the post. Brown envelopes usually induce fear and loathing but then I noticed that his long and distinguished nose was deep in an airmail letter.

'Oh, good! That must be from Uncle Julian. About time – he hasn't written to us for ages,' I said.

'Well, by the sound of this, he has been rather busy.'

I wrinkled my nose. 'Hang on – the last time he wrote he said he was taking some time off because he was sick to death of actors.'

'Well, he must have got better then.' Pa sat down. He seemed at a loss for words.

'He's all right, isn't he?' I said anxiously.

'Oh, yes, he's absolutely fine. No, it's, er . . . well, he wants . . .' Pa gave up trying to talk. He was staring at me, but I could tell he was miles away.

'Spit it out, Pa. What does he want?'

'Oh, you know what Julian's like – full of barmy ideas.'

'Er, no, I don't, actually.'

Julian wasn't like that at all, as Pa knew full well, seeing as they had been friends for ever. They had met on their first day at prep school. Julian was small, weedy and desperately homesick. On the first night two boys had just drowned his teddy in the toilet and were about to do the same thing to Julian, when Pa stepped in – also rather weedy, but full of rage at having to leave Barton Willow. He always claimed that he was ready to fight anyone, and Julian's tormentors just happened to be in the right place, but we never believed him. Pa hates bullies. Julian, when he tells the story, always describes it as a thrilling display of manly temper, which caused him to fall in love with Pa there and then. This didn't hinder their friendship at all.

Julian was gay long before it became fashionable, and

Pa says that made him the brave one, and really, any fool could punch a couple of noses if they felt like it. Although they don't see each other very often any more, what with Julian being so famous and in demand as an actor and director, they still have an unbreakable bond.

Their career paths had been slightly different, though. While Pa was desperately trying one scheme after another to pay even some of his mountain of bills, Julian went on to become a very famous Hollywood heavy. Apparently he had been the definitive Romeo, Hamlet and Lear, so much so that there's practically no point in anyone else having a go. Lately, he had got very into directing and had directed some amazing plays, including a comedy by a Greek playwright, about frogs, which everyone said couldn't possibly be funny any more. But under Julian's guidance it became the hit of the West End. Recently, he had also done a couple of films. His last one, a brilliant adaptation of *Tartuffe*, set in South America, nearly got him an Oscar.

I loved it when he wrote to us – his world was so different from ours, it was always exciting to hear what he'd been up to. 'So, what does he say?' I prompted, eager for a distraction from my really very ambitious Four-point Plan.

Pa still hesitated, for some reason – usually he needed no encouragement to read out the letters. Then Ma and Will came in and he looked relieved. 'I have a letter from Julian,' he began ponderously.

Ma sat down and took his hand. She always knows

when something is bothering him. 'Go on, then,' was all she said.

'Well . . . do you remember that awful earthquake in Peru?'

How could we forget? I watched it on the news and then looked round thinking that, actually, things weren't really that bad here. Obviously, Ma and Pa didn't have any spare cash to donate, so they found some hideous ornaments that were a wedding present from a great-great-aunt and took them to the Oxfam shop. Apparently, they made a ridiculous amount of money. Will and Anna donated money, of course, and I followed Ma and Pa's example and donated my easel. A month later, to my chagrin, Oxfam still hadn't sold it. I really wanted to ask for it back, but didn't quite dare.

'Yes, but what has that got to do with Julian's letter?'

'I will read it out,' said Pa, and cleared his throat.

'I fell in love with Peru when we were filming there. Everyone was so welcoming and interested in what we were doing and they were so kind. I want to do something to repay those wonderfully hospitable people who now desperately need our help. I have an idea to do something like Live Aid, only involving actors rather than musicians.'

Pa put down the letter and looked at us. 'He wants to direct a production of *A Midsummer Night's Dream* – here, at Barton Willow.'

We all looked round our shabby kitchen, gobsmacked and baffled. 'More like *A Midsummer Night's Nightmare*,' said Will drily. 'Even Julian couldn't pull that off in this house!'

'Let me see – oh, yes, here it is.

'Ever since I got into directing, I've wanted to do this. In fact, do you remember that first time you invited me to your home for the hols? One night I read the play and knew your house was the perfect setting. I think I've been planning a production of it, secretly, ever since. How amazing would it be to fulfil a lifelong dream and raise some desperately needed money at the same time? I can't go into too much detail yet, but I envisage the action taking place on several different locations, with the audience following on – imagine – they will actually follow the actors into an enchanted wood! Obviously, everyone involved will do the job for nothing and most of the people I want are free this summer. I've already checked. I have a few locations in mind, but, William, it's *got* to be Barton Willow!'

'Well, that's it – Uncle Julian has finally lost his marbles,' I said gloomily.

'That's what everyone said when he did that film of *Julius Caesar* set in the Stock Exchange, and then it ended up being nominated for a Bafta,' Will pointed out thoughtfully.

'But . . . well, look around, everyone – this place is a crumbling wreck!'

'That's just it. He says,' looking down at the letter –

'I want this to be an edgy production, pagan and sinister, and certainly not smart and polished and, well, ordinary. This is going to be about the things that hover on the edge of our reality. I want it set somewhere beautiful and odd at the same time. I know this would be a major intrusion into your lives, especially yours, William. Obviously we need to keep as much money as we can for the cause, but we will be able to give you a fee to cover the inconvenience and the inevitable damage that even a careful crew can inflict on a place.'

We were all silent, no doubt trying to imagine how anyone could possibly do anything that would make Barton Willow look any worse.

'How much?' said Will rather hoarsely.

Pa named the sum. It hung in the air above us, as tantalising as a whiff of expensive perfume. It wasn't a huge amount by normal standards, but then I think I have adequately demonstrated that we aren't normal. It would mean that Pa could shore up some of the defences against the ever-encroaching dilapidation. For a minute I was lost in dreams of central heating, a new roof, some new rugs and fewer buckets – definitely fewer buckets. Then I saw Pa's face and came down to earth with a thud.

'We don't have to do it. There are plenty of other places he could use,' said Ma firmly. Pa's hand closed round hers and though I was furious with disappointment, I could see why they, compared to most of their contemporaries, had stayed married.

You see, Pa isn't very good round people. He's fine with us, but he doesn't like crowds or strangers. I suppose he is a bit people-phobic. This is one of the reasons we are so poor.

When they were just married and Ma was full of energy and Pa had just been fired from his job as a Hoover salesman, a stopgap until he had decided what to do with the estate, she had the idea of turning this place into a hotel. To test the water, she opened up a few rooms for bed and breakfast. Pa was so upset when he came across a bearded stranger in the corridor searching for a loo that he took to sleeping in the stables – and they've hardly got any roof at all.

Then Pa decided to organise fishing weekends on our stretch of river, which apparently is chock-full of trout. He was working on the sound principle that fishing was a quiet pastime, so no one would want to talk. That backfired. The fishermen *did* want to talk, non-stop, about what it was like living in such an amazing house. They wouldn't shut up. One or two of them even made advances to Ma. In the end,

Pa barricaded himself in the pantry and Ma had to see them off – and give them their money back.

'I don't know what Julian was thinking about – of course it's impossible,' said Ma staunchly. Will said nothing, but I saw him frown.

I quietly said goodbye to a fleeting dream of maybe meeting a famous actor or two and said bracingly, 'Of course we can't let strangers take over the house. Think of the damage they might do.'

We all stared silently at a mushroom that was growing on the kitchen wall (I made a mental note to get rid of it before Sophia saw it and took Emma away for ever) and I could tell we were all thinking about money.

'I think . . . I will consider this,' said Pa carefully, and I could see what an effort this had cost him.

'That would be good, Pa,' said Will, just as carefully. He was obviously itching to say more, but restraining himself in a professional way. He got up. 'I think I need to stretch my legs.'

Left alone, I unfolded the paper again. I was going to apply for at least five jobs, if it killed me.

An hour later I had sent applications expressing a burning ambition to become: a barmaid at the Dog and Duck; a domestic operative for the council (what did that mean, exactly?); a library assistant (then I could spend all day reading art books); and a dinner lady (once I'd worked out I would only be serving, not cooking the poor mites' dinner). Then I had to screw up the classified page so no one would see I had done a really quite good sketch of Bongo asleep in his basket.

I was just leaning back, quite pleased with myself – surely something would come of one of these applications at least – when Will appeared at the back door, looking grim.

'Get Pa and come outside, all of you,' he said curtly.

Wordlessly we all trooped out to the back of the house, past the kitchen garden and the stables. Then Will turned and pointed up at the back of the house. There, where once there had been tiles, was now a gaping hole. No wonder we had a mushroom farm in the kitchen.

Chapter Four

Johnny

'*El idiota!*' said the woman furiously, trying to push Mitch away, but he was at least a foot taller than she, and much stronger.

'Why don't you just leave her alone?' I said.

He turned round to glare at me briefly. 'Three's a crowd, Johnny, so do me a favour and fuck off.'

I took hold of his arm and it jerked back – into my nose. Oh crap. Now I was bleeding onto our very new, very expensive, white carpet.

'*Aah! Menudo lío!*' cried the woman, and freed herself without any help from me by kicking Mitch in the crotch. She gave us each a look of disgust and kneeled down to try to clean up the blood.

'Is she calling me names?' asked Mitch suspiciously.

'She's complaining about the mess,' I said over my shoulder as I went to the bathroom to find some tissue. I could see Consuela had given up on the stain and was now rapidly retreating to the safety of the

60

household quarters or, if she was really sensible, the sidewalk and the next bus out of town.

'She was coming on to me, you know,' said Mitch defensively, leaning against the door and watching in a detached way as I applied pressure to my nose.

'No she wasn't,' I replied firmly, and banged my head gently against the mirror in frustration. 'How many times do I have to explain, there are some women in the world who don't want to screw you, and Consuela is one of them.'

Mitch's teeth gleamed as he burst into disbelieving laughter. I looked up into his merry, handsome, stupid face. Somewhere, under layers of skin as thick as the Great Wall of China, there had to lurk a tiny glimmer of self-awareness, surely?

'Sorry for nearly knocking you out, Johnny,' I muttered to myself, knowing that Mitch would die before he apologised.

He instantly looked contrite, but I wasn't fooled. It just meant he wanted a short cut out of a lecture. But before either of us could say any more, a door slammed downstairs, footsteps sounded, and we could hear Dirk bellowing for his boys and for someone to get him a goddamned drink. Mitch instantly turned and bounded downstairs like the good son he was and I stayed put, like the rebellious stepson I was.

'Jesus, Johnny! What the hell happened to you?'

I looked up. It was Bradley, my other stepbrother, and,

relatively speaking, the sane one. 'Mitch's fist,' I said, dabbing at my nose. 'I caught the wrong end of his temper. I took a punch while defending the honour of a lady.'

Brad erupted in fury. 'How many times have I told you not to make stupid jokes like that! You know what people in this town are like. They take everything literally and you never know when someone might hear you. You need to be on your guard at all times.'

I looked blankly round the bathroom. 'As far as I know, we're the only two in here, but I can check the shower, if you like,' I said obligingly.

Brad hissed in impatience as he pulled up the blind, pushed open the window and pointed. Outside, on the lawn below us, at least two dozen people were scurrying round like ants, setting up tables and tents in our backyard.

I clapped my hand to my forehead. 'Dammit! Another party!'

'What the hell do you mean? It's been at least two weeks since the last one,' said Brad. He looked at me sternly through his horn-rimmed spectacles. He didn't need them – he just thought they made him look clever.

He got a towel, ran it under the cold tap and shoved it in my face. I stepped back with a muffled yelp of pain. Brad didn't apologise. 'Get cleaned up.'

'I've got somewhere else to be,' I began sulkily.

Brad gave a snort of derision because he knew I wasn't

going anywhere. He looked at his watch. He always did this. I once conducted an experiment to see how long he could talk to me before looking at his watch and realising he had somewhere far more important to be. His personal best was ten minutes and forty-five seconds. But that had been a long time ago, before he became Mitch's ultra-important manager.

'OK, I gotta shoot. Dad wants us all downstairs by eight thirty. Don't be late,' he said, and disappeared.

'I need to move out of this crazy place,' I promised the face in the mirror, which looked back at me with contempt and doubt. My reflection was right, of course. Every time I said I was going, there was a 'major fucking crisis' and I was somehow suckered into staying. I sighed with regret for my inability to say no, opened the bathroom door carefully – I didn't want an encounter with another member of this godawful family – and padded noiselessly along the thickly carpeted corridor to my bedroom, my refuge.

Except that it was a refuge no longer. Outside the window, completely blocking off the light, was an enormous catering truck, offloading tray after tray of exquisitely prepared delicacies that cost more than the entire budget for Stella's last play. I was tempted to lean out of the window and tell them not to bother because no one at these parties ate anything anyway.

I threw myself onto my bed and thought about doing some reading, but I knew this would be a waste of time. I was in far too bad a mood to concentrate. Also, if I was being honest, the events of the last few days had left me a bit shook up. Stella's play had ended a few days after my visit to the shrink. The papers had been full of praise, but the bank account was full of, well, nothing. Stella couldn't afford to pay anyone and refused to ask Mary for any more money. It had been a critical success and a commercial failure, again. It was all very well pouring scorn on Hollywood for equating success with money, but how long could I kid myself that I was having some sort of career, working backstage on plays that hardly anyone ever saw? How long would this keep me reasonably contented, given that my dreams were so much bigger? Dreams that would never come true, as my family had pointed out many times.

I went back to the bathroom, took a quick shower, then changed into a clean pair of jeans.

Dirk, Mitch and Brad were on the terrace, their faces united in shock at the fact that I was actually on time, and in outrage that I wasn't dressed better.

'What the fuck are you wearing?' hissed Dirk.

'Well, I didn't want to upstage Mitch,' I said with a grin, but of course they didn't laugh.

'You see, it's this sort of crap that gets me really stressed,' whined Mitch.

'It was a *joke*,' I explained patiently. 'Come on, Mitch, you know perfectly well no one ever notices me when you are around.' This had been a truth for my entire life and I had long ago stopped letting it bother me.

'How many times have I told you not to try to be funny at one of our parties?' Dirk demanded, turning on me.

'Sorry,' I remarked, and then scowled, angry at myself for not standing up to them.

'We're not here to have fun,' Dirk reminded us, motioning one of the waiters to bring him some water. He would have had at least two large Jack Daniel's before coming out. Dirk never drank in public. He wanted to show the world – well, LA, but then that was the only town that mattered – that he was always in control and on the ball. Brad, who was really a mini Dirk in the making, copied him, of course. Mitch was allowed to be seen with a bottle of Bud, in keeping with his macho onscreen image, as long as he didn't actually drink from it in public. But, seeing as I was the stepson from the wrong side of the tracks, I grabbed a glass of wine and downed it in one. I was going to need some Dutch courage if I was going to survive the night.

'Mmm, this is good,' I murmured.

'Well, of course it's good,' said my stepfather, and he began telling me how much the wine had cost. Then followed an in-depth analysis of how much the food had cost, how much the flowers had cost, how much the lighting had cost . . .

'So, a ballpark figure?' I said, swallowing a yawn.

He was practically salivating with eagerness to tell me. I slumped, imagining the magic Stella could create in her theatre on half that amount.

Stars surged up the terrace in a relentless tide of bling. 'I see our guest list as usual only includes either power or beauty,' I remarked.

Mitch looked puzzled. 'Well, who else should we have invited?'

I sighed and tried to tell myself I was in the middle of an F. Scott Fitzgerald novel, but they were better read than lived. There was something quite disturbing about the fact that everyone looked, essentially, the same. I imagined a department store full of shop dummies come to life and gliding towards me, with one dark purpose . . .

'Mingle,' said Dirk tersely, cutting short this horror film fantasy.

I gritted my teeth and sallied forth. I tried to talk to people but most of them, men and women, had had Botox so it was pointless trying to make them laugh or look surprised, because they couldn't. In despair, I grabbed a tray of drinks.

'It's not that sort of party, darling. We are here to network, not have a good time,' whispered one woman. She leaned forward and I thought she was giving me one of those non-contact kisses. Then I jumped in surprise as her tongue licked my earlobe. 'Of course, if you want to meet me later at my apartment, we could have a really fun party,' she whispered.

'Will your husband be there?' I said in mock innocence.

'Don't be dumb, kid,' she hissed, and stalked off.

I had my own set of rules, different from Hollywood's. My rules included not talking bullshit and not sleeping with other men's wives. 'This is why you are never going to make anything of your life, little brother,' said Mitch sadly when I told him. He often used to talk to me like this, as if he was an older and wiser brother – until he hit thirty, that is. Now of course 'older' isn't a role he plays.

I glanced around, wondering where he was. Despite the fact that I am younger than him, looking out for him was second nature to me now. He really was so dumb that he couldn't be trusted in too many situations on his own. But he was talking to Carly, his flavour of the week, a newcomer to town and a nice girl.

I looked round at the glittering crowd and realised there wasn't a single person I wanted to talk to. But then no one here wanted to talk to anyone either – they talked because they had to. This party was about work, not play. This was how most of the casting of a film was decided, well before a proposed film was made public. Still, no one was going to offer me a part in any of their films so my being here was pointless. Anyway, I would rather have been over at Stella's, drinking beer with her and Mary on her rickety balcony and talking about plays and actors.

'You sad fool, always the third wheel,' I reproached myself, and set off, slightly unsteadily, because I, for one, had enjoyed the wine, back to my room.

OK, I was drunk. I lay down on the bed and fell instantly asleep.

I was woken by Mitch barging in. 'What a crap night. I've had it up to here with people talking about how great I am, how hot I am and how they just loved my last movie. You are the only person I know who can keep it real, Johnny.'

I sat up, groggily. What the hell was he on about? He loved those sorts of conversations.

Mitch slumped on the bed. He wore the ruminative look he had used to such great effect in his last film, *Ranch*. Casually I covered the book of Greek plays I had been reading earlier with a cushion. If he saw it, he would make a joke about my acting and I was feeling too fragile for that.

'What time is it?'

'About four thirty.'

'Oh. Everyone's gone?'

'Of course – they'll be at work in half an hour.' Mitch put his head in his hands. I sighed quietly to myself. I wanted to go back to sleep, but it was clear he wanted to talk and whatever Mitch wants, Mitch gets.

'What's the matter? You seem down,' I remarked.

'Women!' said Mitch in exactly the tone he had used to equal effect in his film *Dirt*. 'They always let you down, man! You think you can trust 'em, then bam!' He smacked his hand on his knee and I jumped. What the hell was he talking about? It was he who let women down. In fact, he'd practically made a career out of it.

I shook my head, trying to clear it. He and Carly had looked fine the last time I saw them, hadn't they? OK, Carly was looking a bit pale, but she'd just done two films back to back.

'God, wouldn't it be great if we could just get out of this goddamn town, just the two of us, have an adventure, y'know?'

'Wow, that sounds great! What a great idea! I'm surprised no one's made a film of it – oh, yeah, they have,' I said, confident that all this would be lost on Mitch.

He stood up and yawned. 'Well, you never know, do you?'

No, I didn't. Something was going on here, but I couldn't get a handle on it. The wine must still be fogging my brain.

'Right, I'm gonna take a shower and a swim. See ya later. What's that? Ancient geek plays – what the hell would anyone wanna do that for? You're not starting this acting crap up again, are you, Johnny? I thought we'd cured you of that. Please tell me we don't have to go through all that again?' he demanded, rolling his eyes theatrically.

'No, you are not going to have to go through "all that" again,' I said obediently, and watched him go.

I looked down at my play scripts and sighed. Of course I wasn't cured of acting. I never would be.

Chapter Five

Lila

Just outside our front door there was very showy cherry blossom – the sort you see absolutely everywhere at this time of year. But this one was growing against the peeling and crumbling wreck of our house and I thought that made it look more interesting, so I got out my watercolours.

Fast forward three hours. 'Face it, Lila,' I said to myself severely, 'this is just a rather poor picture of some pink flowers and a door with a hole where the handle should be. No one is ever going to want to buy it.'

I stood up and stretched to get rid of the stiffness. What a waste of time! The trouble with having one day off a week was that I felt compelled to cram as much art as I could into it. The rest of the week, I barely managed to stagger home, shove food in my mouth and crawl into bed.

Pa had put his foot down about me becoming a dustbin person – which is what a domestic operative turned out to be.

'I would be anxious all the time about the sort of people you would be working with,' he said.

Will heard this and grinned. 'I would be worried *for* them, not about them. Lila would probably try to marry one and he wouldn't deserve that.' I smiled at him pityingly, because he didn't know about my organised and efficient Four-point Plan. I had told Anna, of course. She was terribly impressed and promised to back me all the way.

'What a brilliant plan. I just know you are going to make the most tremendous success of it,' she had said admiringly.

I hugged her. 'I knew you would support me. But I'm not going to tell anyone else about it just yet,' I warned her.

'Of course! You want to wait until you have your successful new life and then you can go – "It's all because of this, my Plan!"' and she mimed a magician pulling a rabbit out of a hat.

'Yes, something like that,' I agreed a bit doubt-fully. Anna had certainly run all the way with my Plan. Now I felt I owed it to her faith in me to make it work.

So at lunchtimes I served lunch to the children at the village school, then shivered on the playground while they threw things at me and I attempted to keep order, rather unconvincingly. As soon as the whistle blew for the start of afternoon lessons, I raced to the loo, did a lightning change and became Lila the lovely barmaid, a brassy blonde, with huge knockers and a heart of gold.

Actually, I made that last bit up. The Dog and Duck is quite posh. It has a huge wine list and serves things like sage-infused fillet of cod and olive oil-sautéed potatoes, which looked just like a plate of fish and chips to me, but who was I to argue? They loved the fact that I was the daughter of the lord of the manor (their description, not mine), and I soon got the hang of things. The only thing frowned upon was the state of my hands; they didn't really understand when I said the ink would come off eventually.

Although this was all quite tiring and I was getting slightly worried that my school job was fostering a growing dislike of young children, in many ways it was a relief to be out of the house.

We were all trying to put a brave face on things, but it wasn't good. We were all dead keen to pretend that we didn't want/need/care about Julian's cash, but our desperation for it was so loud, it was becoming almost deafening. This was partly why Will had gone home. Before he left he told me that, as a professional, he understood why Pa couldn't agree to the scheme but, as a son, he just wanted to yell with frustration and bang his head against a wall. Except then it would probably fall down and make the situation even worse. Also Sophia kept putting forward inane and patronising solutions to the problem, and she had to be distracted before someone tried to give her mouldy mushroom pie for dinner.

By now, we had all used up our reserves of optimism about life. Pa knew this and was avoiding us. Ma didn't say anything to me, but I knew he had taken to sleeping in the stables again.

I looked at my watch. Thank goodness, it was time to go to the pub. The harder I worked, the less chance there was that I would lie awake at night having panic attacks about life in general. The extra shifts I was doing certainly helped. Last night I had got only as far as, 'Oh my God, oh God, what are we going to do about . . . ?' before crashing into unconsciousness. Today I was going to work on what was supposed to be a whole day off because Mike, the barman, wanted to go to a concert. I think it says everything about my current state of mind that, even though he was straight, good-looking, single and nice-natured, I wasn't even remotely tempted to become engaged to him. The Plan was working!

Due to my abortive attempt at cherry blossom painting, I was a bit late and had to pedal furiously along the winding country roads to the pub. Damn, I thought, as I flung myself off my bike and leaned it against a tree outside – trust me, no one was going to nick it – I had forgotten lunch again and was probably starting to look like I was made out of pipe cleaners. Any hopes of nipping to the kitchen to beg for some chips vanished when I walked into the bar.

It looked like three coach-loads of people had been in and Mike had barely started on the clearing up.

I metamorphosed into a whirling dervish and raced round, clearing tables, moving chairs and throwing rubbish into a bin bag. We had just about restored order when a car pulled up and the horn blared.

'That's my lift,' said Mike, looking round worriedly.

'Well, go on before I change my mind,' I grinned. Left alone I bent down to load the glass washer and got a huge rush of blood to the head when I stood up. I had to eat something, anything, now.

I was just helping myself to one of those giant Mars bars when I heard the door open. I sighed. More customers, and just when we had got the place straight. I turned round with a rather false smile pinned to my face and found myself looking down the barrel of a gun.

For a split second I thought I was having a hunger-induced hallucination, so I blinked hard and looked again. No, it really was a gun. Not a very big one, but I had a feeling that size didn't really matter in this situation.

'Open the till and hand the cash over,' said a voice rather muffled by a nylon stocking. The thief was smaller than I am and I couldn't help noticing that he was wearing quite an expensive jacket and the latest jeans.

Now I was sort of thinking two things at the same time. The first was along these lines: Ohmigod – ohmigod – he's got a gun and I'm going to die – help,

help! The second went like this: Hang on a mo! This person is way better dressed than I am! He's not needy, he's just greedy! Mike and I haven't worked our fingers to the bone to make cash so he can nick it and go shopping!

It was probably a combination of low blood sugar, too much exercise (all that cycling), stress and just anger in general that propelled the Mars bar squarely between his eyes, while I yelled at the top of my voice, 'Fuck off and get a job like the rest of us if you need cash!'

Then there was a loud crack and everything went black.

No, I hadn't been shot. It wasn't even a real gun.

Everyone said later that yes, it did look like one and they would have been completely taken in too. What they probably wouldn't have done was try to defend themselves with a piece of confectionery. But then I pointed out quite fiercely that they hadn't been there so they couldn't possibly know.

The crack was the sound of the toy gun falling on the floor, after which I fainted, apparently, because I'd had a large dose of adrenalin on an empty stomach, which is not a good mixture. Luckily, the kitchen staff were still about and, on hearing the commotion, one of them called the police.

The fake-gun man ran off but was later found by the police at his mum's house (he obviously wasn't destined for a successful career in crime) and I was picked up, dusted down, given a bowl of soup and sent home.

Pa went quite apoplectic with rage and fear when he found out what had happened. The fact that it was a plastic gun made no difference to the quality and range of the ranting. As far as we could all make out, I had escaped death by a whisker and this was somehow all his fault.

Mind you, everyone was overreacting, so much so that the drawing room was opened.

I think it was years since anyone had last been there. We used to go in after Christmas lunch, but in recent years everyone just ended up lounging around in the kitchen, too full to want to move. Somehow, the drawing room, with its lovely faded Chinese wallpaper, the (possibly) Adam fireplace and the (very) faded Aubusson carpet became just a bother because we had to light another fire to be able to sit in comfort and no one wanted the corner near the broken window. I was last in there one January afternoon, reading a very old copy of *The Lion, the Witch and the Wardrobe*, and all of a sudden I felt snowflakes on my face. I was thrilled and thought I had somehow been transported to Narnia, but a closer examination revealed a hole in the window, which was letting the weather in.

But it was formally decided that the squashy and slightly smelly sofa in the kitchen was nowhere near good enough for me in my present state and I had to lie down somewhere better, but close enough to be kept an eye on.

I was about to argue with all this when I realised what a fool I would be to pass up the chance of molly-coddling, so I pressed a hand to my forehead and allowed myself to be led inside.

A huge fire was lit and I was ensconced on the very best sofa (which smelled only slightly mouldy) and covered tenderly with blankets. Will and Anna were summoned and I was offered tea, brandy, biscuits, a cold flannel for my forehead, a hot-water bottle for my feet, Ma's cologne in case I felt faint again, and a small handbell to summon help, though it didn't look like I was going to be left alone for a minute. Even Bongo came and sat near me, but he had to be sent out because he'd been rolling in sheep poo again.

Anna arrived before Will came down. She had simply downed tools, or laptop, and raced over. She looked in a worse state than I did, to be honest, and I felt guilty and slightly fraudulent. Her eyes were huge in her white and frightened face and she was shivering because she had come out without her coat. She was also limping.

'Here, get under these blankets before you freeze to death, and what on earth have you done to yourself?' I said anxiously, shifting over to make room.

'Nothing – heel fell off shoe,' she said tersely. 'I won't hurt you, will I?'

'No, because there is absolutely nothing wrong with me. Honestly, it's just Ma and Pa going a bit mental.'

'But they said –'

'I'm sure they did, but they were exaggerating. OK, for a tiny, tiny second I did wonder if I was going to be shot but then I wasn't.' I chuckled. 'The Mars bar turned out to be a more effective weapon than the fake gun!'

'What a nightmare,' she said, snuggling down next to me.

'Oh, it was. What was really awful was looking at his jacket and realising he was probably better off than I am, and that was why I saw red and threw the Mars bar. Do you know, if it had hurt him I might be sitting in a cell right now on a charge of assault?'

'It's a very unfair world,' said Anna, and her bottom lip wobbled.

'Oh, don't you start! Pa had to go out and blow his nose just now.'

'I'm sorry! It's just that I can't stop thinking of all the awful ways it could have ended! All the way here I kept expecting a phone call telling me to go to the hospital because you'd ended up in a coma. I could see us all sitting round your bed in a vigil that lasted for months. And then, of course, I got to thinking of what hymns you might want at your funeral.'

'What did you pick?' I asked with interest.

'Well, definitely "All Things Bright and Beautiful" because it makes me think of you!'

78

'A brilliant choice,' I lied heartily. Damn. I would have much preferred 'Jerusalem', but it seemed churlish to object. 'Well, the worst didn't even come close to happening,' I assured her. 'Oh, goody – here's our tea!'

The doctor had said I was a bit hypoglycaemic, which Ma took to mean seriously malnourished and on the verge of dying of starvation before her very eyes, so even though I'd had soup at the pub she had put together a small meal of boiled eggs and toast soldiers, sardines on toast, toast and jam and drop scones made on the Blessed Aga.

'I insist you help me eat this otherwise Ma will get upset,' I said.

'Oh, bother – then I'll have to start the diet tomorrow,' said Anna as she daintily dipped a toast finger in yolk. Anna was always starting diets and it was true she was curvy, but only in the places that made men's eyes stand out on stalks when they saw her. 'I wonder if there is someone you could sue – you know, for trauma.'

'But who? Did Pa tell you that the gunman turned out to be Danny Wilkins from the village?'

'Oh blast. Well, you won't get a penny then. The milkman's been trying for years.'

Will arrived just as we were finishing the last scone. 'Pa says I've got to stay until you've had a debriefing and been pronounced psychologically fit and well. I said I couldn't have said that about you before this incident, so what hope have I now – ow!'

I kicked him in a friendly way and stretched back to undo the belt of my jeans. 'Ooh, I think I've overeaten! Have you got Emma with you?'

'No. Sophia has taken her to an accelerated learning baby club.'

'What on earth is that?'

'Dunno.'

'It better hadn't do her any harm,' I said threateningly. I took my duties as an aunt very seriously.

'As far as I can tell, the babies just lie round and gurgle while someone reads them *Ulysses* or *A Brief History of Time*. Last week someone took them through the theory of quantum physics. Next week I believe it's the Cubist movement. Emma usually just has a nice nap and comes home ready for her tea.'

'Does Sophia believe any of this will actually do some good?' I asked cautiously.

'Well, it doesn't seem to do her any harm,' Will replied, which I thought was avoiding the issue.

It was getting dark outside, so Will went over and carefully pulled the curtains shut, and then Ma and Pa came in and told him to sit down.

'But I've still got an hour's work to do on my thesis, and I've left my laptop on in my room. I've got to do a thousand words a day and I'm nowhere near that amount. Besides, it's obvious stick insect's still in one piece and perfectly fit to return to work.'

'No wonder I have issues,' I said darkly to no one in particular.

'This won't take long,' said Pa firmly. 'Now, as you all know, Lila narrowly escaped death today – no – do be quiet, everyone. I will have my say. She was only doing that awful job –'

'You all thought it was a great job until I got shot!' I protested.

'She was only there because of my selfishness and reluctance to tackle a simple problem.'

'Actually, I don't think your problems are that simple, and Lila needed a job anyway,' began Will, but he didn't stand a chance now Pa was in full flow.

'Shush. Now, where was I? Oh, yes. Today was the catalyst that brought me to my senses. I simply cannot carry on being selfish and irresponsible and putting my family in danger. I rang Julian an hour ago. The deal, as it were, is on.'

'Oh, Pa!' I jumped up, shedding Anna, a blanket and a piece of stray sardine. I was completely over-whelmed. He was being so brave. Also, as far as I could tell, it was a pointless sacrifice, as I would still have to go back to work at the pub. I gave him a hug anyway, in recognition of his tremendous gesture. Boy, did we need some cash. His jumper was so full of holes, it was hard to tell where the garment actually began.

'Pa, you can't do this just for me. I am going back to work at the pub tomorrow. And let's be sensible – how many times can I get shot at in one job? The odds of it happening again must be, well, impossible!'

'Your great-uncle Herbert got struck by lightning twice,' said Pa, stubbornly.

'That was only because he . . . well . . . how the hell did he get hit twice?'

'Well, it's quite interesting really,' began Ma.

'Oh, for God's sake – he's been dead for years! Tell them the story some other time! The thing is, you won't be going back to the pub or the school. In return for complete access to the house and grounds Julian has agreed to give you a job, as his assistant or something,' said Pa with a satisfied gleam in his eye.

I was furious. Didn't he realise I was old enough to make decisions for myself? I wasn't a child any more, whose future needed sorting out for me! Julian's assistant – pah! It wouldn't be a real job – it would be something cobbled together just to please Pa, his best pal. I would be patted on the head (metaphorically, because I was at least three inches taller than Julian) and told to fetch his glasses or a coffee or something else useless. There was no way I was going to be patronised like that.

I pointed all this out, rather heatedly, but Pa simply talked over me and carried on. 'I think it's very good of Julian. He wants only one thing in return – a written promise that you are not to fall in love with any of the cast.'

Everyone laughed. I stuck my chin out. 'Fall in love with an actor?' I invested the question with as much sarcasm as I could muster. Really! I've got better things to do than waste my time with a bunch of arty-farty, self-obsessed, vanity-driven show-offs. It is never going to happen anyway, because of the Plan,' I added quietly.

'I wouldn't know what all actors are like; I've only ever known Julian,' said Pa mildly. 'What plan? Anyway, I must warn you. Julian has told me that even sensible and level-headed people have been known to fall in love with, er . . . oh, whatsisname . . .'

'Well, spit it out – what is his name?' asked Anna.

'Oh blast – it's gone right out of my head. Begins with M, I think . . .' Pa wasn't winding us up – he just never went to the pictures. 'Mike – no, that's your friend at the pub . . . something like that, though. Oh! Got it! Mitch – Mitch Clayton! Have you girls heard of him?'

Anna and I clutched each other for support. It took a while for the news to sink in. Mitch Clayton! Practically every woman in the country wanted to sleep with him, marry him, have his babies. And he was coming here. We were going to meet him, talk to him – maybe even touch him. No wonder I hadn't been able to stay engaged! God had been saving me for Mitch Clayton! Bugger the Plan!

Chapter Six

Johnny

All my life I have wanted to be other people. Yeah, yeah, I know what you are thinking, because one of the shrinks I saw said the same thing. 'You are unhappy – you hate your life – you feel trapped – of course you want to be someone else.'

I nodded in agreement because it was easier that way, and got the hell out of there. I wasn't prepared to hang around while a complete stranger picked my dreams to pieces in one of those calm, reasonable, 'this is going to hurt but you'll feel better afterwards' little scenes. I didn't have to listen to someone else saying what I had already told myself a thousand times.

I was about ten years old when I caught the acting bug and I haven't really been right in the head since. I had played hookey from school and was loafing around the house on my own – everyone else was hard at work. Well, it was great at first and then I began to feel bored and lonely. I was on the sofa, flicking through the channels in a desultory way, and I looked up and there was Laurence Olivier in an old, grainy, black-and-white film, playing Hamlet, and I was transfixed. I couldn't quite understand what he was saying but after a while I relaxed into the rhythm of the language and watched the way he moved and how he spoke. I think someone put a spell on me that day. I sat cross-legged in front of the screen until the very last word, utterly rapt.

'I want to do that,' I said aloud to myself when it was all over.

Well, sure I did. That's what everyone did in this town, Mitch better than anyone. But I didn't want to do what he did. Mitch just played himself on screen. Well, he played the charismatic person he can be when he wants to please. Mitch is always the hero on film, never the villain. It's a shame he can't do that in real life. He just has to stand there on screen and there will be a collective intake of breath from practically everyone at the cinema. It's like he puts a spell on us all. No one would ever do that for me, obviously, but I didn't want them to. I didn't want to show me to an audience, I wanted to show them other people – like Olivier had.

And I could do it, I knew I could. But here's the funny thing – I was so screwed up I couldn't do it in front of an audience. Every time I got anywhere near a camera and lights – especially lights – terror would grip me so tightly it was like I was turned to stone. I would start to shake uncontrollably and I swear I would hear someone screaming, though I was sure it wasn't me.

My family thought it was hilarious. 'Imagine being a Clayton and having stage fright!' said Mitch, roaring with laughter. 'He's made goddamn fools of us!' fumed Dirk after my first screen test. He actually punched a wall after the second and yelled that if he ever saw me in front of a camera again he'd have me run out of town. Later, when he had calmed down he said: 'Pick a new career. You're embarrassing our family.' So I did find work, backstage, but always with off-the-grid companies like Stella's, the sort Dirk was barely aware even existed.

The thing was, I only pretended to give up my dream. I was an acting junkie; I was like a dog with a disgusting old bone. I watched plays obsessively, I read plays aloud to myself, I thought myself into every role ever written and made up a few more besides. Of course, I was the only person to inhabit this secret world. I was too scared to let anyone else in. I schooled my face to a blank expression that gave nothing away, but there were always hundreds of people in my head and I wanted to be them all.

It might have been better to run away. The world was a big place, even if Mitch's face seemed to be on a billboard in every corner of it. But I was tethered here, tied to these bloody people with invisible cords. I owed them something, you see, for taking me in after my mother died, when no one else would. Though Stella considered any debt was well and truly paid.

'They were known as "the fighting Claytons" when you were younger, and then something strange happened after you moved in. They all calmed down, especially Mitch. You have this amazing ability to soothe people's tempers.'

'You mean I'm a doormat,' I said crossly.

'You have an excellent aura,' she retorted. She was into things like that. That's why we got on – we were both a little crazy. But if I was delusional, why was I also so despairing? Surely delusions were supposed to keep people happy? Maybe the despair would ease if I finally decided to give up on my dreams?

I was lounging in my room, thinking all this when Consuela tapped on my door to tell me a woman wanted to see me. I went downstairs. It was Carly Cookson, Mitch's girlfriend. What did she want to speak to me about?

We exchanged pleasantries and I offered her a drink, which she refused. 'How are you?' I asked finally, completely at a loss.

'Oh, fine, thank you,' she replied immediately.

Clearly that meant I was supposed to ignore the fact that tears had made train tracks of mascara down her cheeks and she looked like she hadn't slept much in the last few weeks.

'Here, sit down,' I said, scooping scripts, magazines and books off the only comfortable chair in the room. 'Are you sure I can't get you anything?'

'Actually, some water would be great, please.'

'Sure.' I busied myself with glasses and ice and darted quick glances at her when she wasn't looking. She didn't sit down, she slumped, as if she'd come to the last of her options. I handed her the glass and she gave me one of those smiles that everyone does round here, a smile that said nothing.

I pulled over a chair and leaned my arms on the backrest in a casual, unthreatening way. 'So, what can I do for you?'

'You could tell me why the fuck Mitch hasn't been answering my calls for the last ten days since the party! Oh, I'm sorry, I didn't mean to snap. After all, it's not your fault.'

'That's OK,' I said gently.

'I'm pregnant!' she blurted out bitterly, then clamped a hand to her mouth. 'I don't believe I just told you that!'

'I won't bother congratulating you then,' I said drily.

Yeah, she had major problems. I knew she was due to start work on a gruelling adventure film set in the Mexican desert in a few weeks and if word of this got out she would be screwed. Also she'd just become pregnant by the biggest commitment-phobe in the States.

'Carly, look at me. I swear I will not tell anyone about this,' I said slowly, so she could take it in. Then I paused. 'Mitch is the father, right? You told him and he's fucked off? Oh, I'm sorry, I didn't mean to make you cry again.' I found the tissues.

She took one and blew her nose in a businesslike

manner. 'Yes. That's it in a nutshell. I told Mitch ten days ago and since then he hasn't returned any of my calls.' She gave a sobbing sigh. 'I don't want to marry him. I don't want to start a family with him – I just thought he might stick by me while I made some tough decisions, you know. Well, what do you know? Now that we're not having sex or photo shoots, he's suddenly harder to get hold of than the Pope!'

'And you want me to try and talk to him?'

'Well, you could pass on a short message to the effect that he's a slimy piece of shit and I never want to see him again. Oh, and you can give him these back!' She opened her bag and dumped an impressive pile of jewellery on the floor.

'I'll do all that and more,' I promised and then paused. 'I'll find him and talk to him, but I can't promise I'll get him to see sense. He's as stubborn as a mule and the thought of becoming a father absolutely terrifies him –' I stopped. Shit, I'd said too much.

'He's done this before, hasn't he?' she said slowly. 'Oh, I've been such a bloody idiot! It's this town – all the flashbulbs going off all the time blinded me to the truth. I should have known – I did know, really, when I started dating him. But he can be so utterly charming when he wants. I remember his first lead. It was in that film *Robot* and he was only ten years old. "Kid Saves World" was the line on the poster. I was ten too, and I had that poster on my wall for two years and, oh God, I've been so stupid!'

'Are you from England originally?' I asked, noticing a slight accent.

'Yes. I revert to my roots when I get stressed. I've lived here since I was three, but my dad and I are from Yorkshire originally.' She shuddered. 'Oh, my God, if Dad ever found out . . .'

'Well, your secret's safe with me. Have you got a girl-friend, a friend you can really trust, because you're gonna need someone around if you don't want to tell your folks?'

'No, not really. I haven't got any close friends here.' She looked at me and gave a wry smile. 'I was obviously looking in the wrong places. I'm sorry to dump all this on you.' She stood up. I knew she was feeling better – her accent was back in place.

'I'll talk to him, I promise,' I said.

This meant I had to hang around waiting for him to show – for two days. I wasn't surprised. When Mitch is scared or in trouble, he'll take off somewhere discreet and screw around to take his mind off it, while someone, usually me, sorts the mess out. But this time I was really mad at him.

I hate our house. It's full of stuff that some interior designer picked out for Dirk whose only stipulation was that everything should look very expensive. It has far too many rooms, some of which I'm sure have never ever been used, and it's redecorated from top to bottom every year so it is as glossy and impersonal as a hotel.

I wandered into the music room and lifted the lid

on the Steinway, which had never been played. I remembered the day it was delivered. 'Why the hell did you buy this – none of us is musical?' I said.

'Trust you to completely miss the point!' said Dirk, and of course they all roared with laughter. It was the craze at that time to have musical instruments in your home. One day I fully expected to walk in and find an elephant in the sitting room, because 'everyone else has one'.

It was hard to chill out here because it was full of people trying to do things for you. I know this was supposed to be relaxing, but it just made me more wound up. If I went into the kitchen to fix myself a snack, I made the kitchen staff nervous because they thought it meant they weren't doing their job properly. So I had to ask them to do it and wait for it to arrive, which made me really antsy. Clearly Dirk, Mitch and Brad are right when they say I belong on the trailer park where my mother grew up, and not in the middle of all this luxury.

Mary had taken Stella away for a few days and all my other friends from the show were working, so it was pointless picking up the phone. I had no one to talk to. I tried to read, but I was too distracted. I kept thinking about Carly and how nice she was and how she'd ended up with my dumb brother. A girl like that should be with a guy like me, I brooded, but Mitch was so dazzling, the rest of us became shadows. Sometimes I thought that if I didn't do something drastic, I would fade away altogether.

When Mitch finally turned up I could tell he'd been partying solidly for the last two days. His eyes were still glittering with whatever he'd taken so as to stay awake. I sighed. This was going to be bad, but I liked Carly and felt sorry for her.

'Your girlfriend's been looking for you,' I remarked.

'Well, she's been looking for the wrong man then, because I'm the most single man in Hollywood.'

I started to say something, but he cut across me. 'How about spending some time in England, little brother? It's time for that adventure!'

I was completely thrown.

'Oh, come on! You're always saying how you want to go there and now I'm giving you the chance!'

'Whoa! OK, firstly, when did you tell Carly the relationship was off, and secondly, *England*? When you said you wanted an adventure, I thought you meant Vegas or something.'

This was now seriously crazy. Mitch hated travelling anywhere out of his own country. 'What's the point? Everything abroad is just half as good as it is here, isn't it?' he'd said once.

'I've been asked to become part of something really special,' he said, putting on his caring face, the one that didn't fool me for an instant. 'Julian MacDonald is putting on a play in England to raise money for . . . well, it's a good cause, whatever it is.' He wrinkled his brow. 'He wants me to take one of the roles. Well, how could I say no?'

I looked at him levelly for a moment and then the truth dawned. 'Of course! Carly's pregnant and you're running away!'

Mitch sat down and put his head in his hands. 'The bitch!' he muttered. 'She trapped me. Hell, I'm not even sure the brat's mine. She's been all round town, if you know what I mean.' He lifted his head, his eyes wide in innocent outrage.

I stared back silently until he got the message that I wasn't going to buy this crap. 'I'm certain Carly's not like that,' I said. I started to say something about his responsibility towards her, but Mitch wasn't listening.

His face grew cunning. 'Of course, if I go to England you could come with me. It's a Shakespeare play. You love that shit. And you could meet Julian. Isn't he one of your heroes?' His lip curled in scorn, and then he remembered he was supposed to win me over and swiftly changed it to one of his famous megawatt grins.

I took a deep breath. Mitch really was a shit. Of course I wanted to go to England and meet Julian MacDonald! To be breathing the same air as the man who had given the definitive Hamlet? I'd heard about the Peruvian earthquake project and had been wondering from what unique angle Julian planned to approach the play. Of course, even if I hadn't wanted to go, Dirk would have made me, since Mitch would be screwed without me. I'm pretty sure Mitch has never read an entire book in his life. He says reading gives him wrinkles and so this is why his films are short on dialogue. So there was no way he was going to read and understand a play by a playwright who wrote in blank verse. I grinned at the thought of this. Mitch wanted me there because he needed me to translate and explain every goddamned word.

Then I remembered Carly's tear-stained face. He was just going to fuck off and leave her. Well, she was definitely better off without him, but I could do one small thing for her first.

'I'll go – but there's one condition.'

He looked outraged. It wasn't my role in life to set conditions.

'I'm not setting foot on a plane until you've had a face-to-face conversation with Carly.' I folded my arms and stared at him implacably.

'Fine,' he snarled, sounding like a sulky kid. 'But you'd better be on that plane,' he warned.

I nodded curtly and left.

As soon as I was out of earshot, I ran outside, let out a whoop of glee and turned three somersaults, right into one of our pools. 'Woo-hoo! England, here I come!' I said, when I had bobbed to the surface.

Chapter Seven

Lila

People must feel like this when they win the lottery.

Anna was far too excited to be allowed to go home. Ma was worried her head would be so full of stars, she might drive into a ditch. Will took one look at us jumping up and down like a pair of excited puppies, Pa now taking in the consequences of what he had done and Ma looking like she usually does – harassed and anxious – and said it was clearly a mercy he was around to inject some sanity into this situation.

Anna told him to shut up and stop being a spoilsport and Pa told him to go out for fish and chips because he wasn't letting Ma cook after the day she'd had, and I told him he had to go online first and print out every article about the Claytons he could find.

To his credit he grinned and agreed and told Pa to put his wallet away, because we all knew there wasn't anything in it.

Supper was riotous, due to Will having stopped off for several bottles of sparkling wine. Ma went for the glasses but shrieked when she found a dead mouse in the first one she picked up, so we drank out of mugs and ate dinner straight out of the paper.

I told Anna she could share my bed, not just for warmth, but because there was so much to talk about. Pa was still in recovery from my date with death, so as a special treat we were allowed to take the paraffin heater with us, as Anna could be trusted not to fall asleep with it on.

'When I told Mike we still had one of these, he said did our family know the twentieth century had not only come, but gone,' I said, lighting the flame.

'Well, we'll certainly be bang up to date when all these play people arrive,' Anna said soberly, from somewhere under my bed.

'What on earth are you doing?' I asked.

She emerged with a shout of triumph and a cobweb attached to her left ear. 'Looking for Mr Wiggins, of course!'

Oh dear. This meant she was very stressed. 'I didn't know I still had him,' I said, staring at the teddy bear that had started life as Anna's Christmas present, the year I had measles and wouldn't stop crying because my eyes hurt. Anna had said I should keep them shut because the bear would look out for me until I was better. Since then he has gone between the two of us whenever a crisis has occurred.

'Something has been bothering you for a while, hasn't it?' I said slowly.

Anna stared at my room blankly, almost as if she was looking for inspiration. I hoped she wouldn't notice, amidst all the tubes of paint, sketchpads and other artistic debris, that I'd borrowed her mascara and forgotten to give it back. 'It's all very exciting but . . . I'm not certain we are going to be the same after all this is over,' she said finally.

I wasn't convinced that was the only thing she was bothered about, but I let it go for now. 'Surely change is a good thing!' I said, thumping a pillow to make it more comfy.

'Change never seems to be for the better, as far as I am concerned,' she said, but before I could question her further she rushed on, 'Don't you see, a whole other world is going to collide with ours? Ma and Pa and this house – they are all like fragile objects from the past. They should be in a glass case or they might get broken!' Her bottom lip started to wobble. She was very emotional at the moment.

'Well, I don't think we can go on like this, helping Pa not go out and face the world, helping Ma run herself into the ground with work and worry,' I said gently.

'Oh, I expect you're right.'

'If you think of all the awful things that might happen, you'll never get out of this bed,' I said bracingly.

Anna wriggled. 'I can barely get in, actually. What on earth are Pa's old walking boots doing under the sheet?'

'I was drawing them and fell asleep,' I said absently.

My attention was then distracted by the articles Will had printed out. 'Look at all these lovely pictures of Mitch Clayton,' I sighed.

Anna looked at me expectantly and I hastened to reassure her. 'Don't worry, even Mitch isn't going to make me stray from my Plan. I was tempted for a minute, but I'm back on the straight and narrow,' I finished triumphantly.

'I never doubted you for a minute,' Anna said staunchly.

We looked at the pictures and articles anyway, for research.

Mitch didn't come on his own – he was part of a package, an incredibly ambitious package that, according to one paper, had every intention of being to Hollywood what the Kennedys had been to Washington. The family had a single aim: to dominate the film world, both in front of and behind the scenes. They were like an unstoppable force of nature, but with charisma. Head of the clan was Dirk, the most powerful producer in the world at the moment. He was assisted by his second son, Bradley, who was a godlike genius with money, but it was Mitch, son number one, who, it was predicted, would make the whole empire possible.

Oh, Mitch! I could still remember the sigh the entire cinema audience – man, woman and child – gave as he strode out of the saloon in the opening minutes of *Dirt*, the film that single-handedly resurrected the ailing western genre, apparently. But Mitch could probably resurrect a corpse if he put his mind to it, such was the power of those brilliant light blue eyes, the firm, yet humorous mouth . . . And his hands! There aren't many film stars who are as well known for their hands as for their acting – there aren't any, in fact. But Mitch's hands were now famous. They were manly hands, with long fingers, strong but gentle . . . I could never decide what I wanted to do more – touch them or draw them. Soon I might get the chance to do both! Also, he had a way of looking at you, right out of the screen – honest, open, teasing . . . I realised I had just gone into a Mitch-induced trance and that it probably wasn't a good look – mouth open, slightly glazed eyes, I might even have been dribbling. I pulled myself together. Despite that moment of weakness earlier, I meant what I had said to Anna. I was determined to stick to my Four-point Plan with the same dedication a nun has for her vows.

Anna was gazing at a photograph with a dreamy expression on her face. I took a closer look. There they were, the Claytons in all their glory. The picture had been taken against the stunning backdrop of their second home, a ranch in Wyoming (think *Dallas* rather than *Little House on the Prairie*). There they all were, as tall as trees and shiny-looking, as if they had never in their entire lives suffered from anything so mundane as indigestion or boils. That was the power of money and success, I thought.

'So, who is that?' said Anna, pointing to a young guy leaning against the wall and looking like he didn't want to be part of the picture.

'Oh, that's Dirk's other son, I think. He's Mitch's stepbrother and the black sheep of the family.'

'Why do they call him that?'

'I don't know,' I admitted, 'but that's how everyone seems to describe him.'

'Mitch will probably take one look at you and fall madly in love. He doesn't know about the Plan. You are so clever and talented and interesting, and you have a fantastic figure, whereas I am just a fat accountant. I bet he doesn't even notice I'm there,' said Anna, slumping against her pillow.

'One of my fiancés, I forget which, said I was so thin and bony it was like going to bed with a piece of cutlery,' I said to cheer her up. 'Fashion magazines might like skinny women but *men* like women like you. You look like a younger version of Marilyn Monroe and you are as brainy as that guy she married – you know, the really clever one. I only call you fatty all the time because I'm jealous.'

'That reminds me – I really *must* start a new diet tomorrow.'

'Be quick then. Soon we will be awash with maple syrup pancakes and chocolate chip muffins and Hershey Bars and a funny sort of marshmallow spread that comes in jars . . .'

'But they won't actually be staying with us, so we

won't have to feed them,' Anna reminded me. This was quite a relief. I wouldn't have to rush out and buy a new dressing gown. The one I was wearing was sporting so many holes it was almost indecent.

'Oh, here's that rather good-looking Clayton black sheep again.' She pointed to another photograph.

He was coming out of a bookshop and he looked absolutely furious at being papped. He wasn't quite as tall as Mitch, or as broad, nor did he share Mitch's chunky good looks. But there was something about his face that made me want to go on looking at him. Even in a photograph, I could feel the power of his eyes. I knew instantly that he would have interesting things to say. 'Remember the Plan,' I said very quietly to myself.

'Can you believe Mitch will be arriving soon?' said Anna, and we stared at each other in horror as this finally sank in.

'The first thing he'll see is the sign telling everyone to go round the back because no one can manage to get the front door open any more.'

'But when he does go round the back Bongo will rush out and breathe all over him!'

'And have you noticed that the smell in the passage has got worse?'

'Yes! That rat died years ago – how come the smell hasn't?'

'Anna, I bet Mitch falls in love with Ma. She still looks pretty amazing, you know. Then she'll have some mad crisis or other and run off with him, and Pa will start fading away because of a broken heart, and Will, well, he will feel obliged to go after them with a shotgun to uphold the family honour and –'

'Er, do you think we may have been inhaling too many paraffin fumes?'

'Crikey, yes! Look, the flame's gone yellow!'

I jumped out of bed and fell over a box of papers. 'Ow!' I cried, clutching a very stubbed toe, while Anna switched the heater off.

'Are you going to have a tidy-up before our visitors arrive?'

'Why? This room isn't due to be cleaned until Christmas!' I giggled, jumping back into bed. But I was slightly worried. Barton Willow was charming to look at, but it was also uncomfortable, inconvenient and probably, in places, unsanitary. Americans weren't used to their feet going through broken floorboards; they weren't used to ducking their heads to avoid the leaks. I had a suspicion that although they were all tall, fit and bristling with muscles, they wouldn't have our stiff-upper-lipped attitude to things like draughts, dust, woodworm and dead rodents cropping up in unlikely places. Heaven only knew what they would make of the Barton Willow air conditioning system, which was basically about putting up with whatever climatic conditions were currently blowing through the cracks in the windows.

Now the heater was off, the only way we could carry

on reading in comfort was to burrow under the covers with a torch, and mine had run out of batteries, so we decided to give up and go to sleep. But first I needed some of Anna's own brand of reassurance.

'I am going to make the Plan work, aren't I?'

'Of course,' she replied without a moment's hesitation. 'But it's going to be very difficult, like asking me to give up chocolate. I mean, we both know that's never going to happen, however much I want to be thin.'

'Do you think I might give in and end up engaged again?' I said gloomily.

'No, but you might need a tiny bit of encouragement now and then, and that's what I'll be there for,' said Anna encouragingly.

'I have a feeling about the next few weeks. I am going to stay single and you are going to fall in love,' I said portentously. Next to me, in the dark, I could hear Anna sigh.

'My love life is just a figment of our imagination,' said Anna sadly.

'Anna, heaps of men keep throwing longing glances your way! You're just too shy to look up and notice them. You're right: things are going to change and that is one of them,' I said confidently. 'Someone out there is going to see your great beauty and fabulous personality and fall head over heels in love. And I'm going to make sure you are in the right place when that happens.'

But she just sighed again, and then she fell asleep.

I lay awake for a long time, thinking. I couldn't get rid of the feeling that this was somehow our last chance – Barton Willow's, Ma and Pa's, mine – which was ridiculous, really. But I felt it was up to me to make sure nothing went wrong. At least if I was going to be so busy this summer saving the family, I wouldn't have time even to be tempted to get engaged again.

Anna went back to her own flat the next day, but only briefly, just to pack her best clothes and her fancy hair straighteners, and then she moved into the room next to mine.

'I can get to work just as easily from here and it means I won't miss out on any of the excitement, and you might need me for encouragement, you know,' she said in a low voice, and winked at me meaningfully. I was delighted. It would be so much easier for me to organise her love life, in return for her support over the Plan, if she was on the premises. She insisted on giving Ma a huge sum of money for 'rent'.

'But this is your home, darling. You are always welcome here; you don't have to pay us,' protested Ma, puzzled.

'But don't you see, it's very important to me to keep my independence,' said Anna, jumping up and banging her head on a shelf. By the time Ma had found the arnica, Anna had put the cheque in her purse.

All the main players would be staying in huge trailers

in the grounds and less important people were being put up in the village.

Sophia promised to help entertain. 'Our visitors will probably appreciate my cosmopolitan company. Having been to the States several times I am *au fait* with their culture. You haven't travelled much, Lila, have you, apart from that disastrous trip to California? Such a homebody! Well, some people find it difficult to be adventurous.

'Obviously there is something wrong with Mitch Clayton – over thirty and not married,' she continued. Sophia thinks that just because she is married to a psychotherapist, some of the training will automatically rub off on her.

'Of course he's not married – he hasn't met me yet!' I said, but quietly, after she'd gone, and then I remembered my Plan. I had to be constantly vigilant.

Every day after this, more people turned up, firstly with clipboards and harried expressions and then with equipment and harried expressions. Lorries lined the drive and disgorged props and people. And questions. They were continually asking where things were, and could they put things there, and how many sockets did we have in the drawing room, and would we mind if they rebuilt the balcony? It turned out to be my job to answer these questions, which was fine, but the minute my back was turned dealing with one query, someone would pop up with another. Everyone was terribly polite, but very insistent, and I was sure there were at least two more lines on Pa's forehead than there were a month ago.

Then Julian sent Pa an email.

William, I know what you are thinking and you are right, it is a nightmare. I no longer have any idea why I agreed to do this bloody stupid play or why I thought it would be a good idea to involve you – I am so sorry. I feel like a train driver who's just found out that the brakes don't work! I arrive tomorrow – please, please tell me you still like me, just a bit. I couldn't bear it if our friendship was threatened because I've been an overambitious idiot.

'Right. Listen everyone. Julian's in one of his states. You are going to have to leave him alone until I've got him calmed down,' said Pa, rushing off to check there was plenty of camomile tea.

'What a clever man Julian is,' said Will admiringly. 'Pa will be far too busy looking after him to worry about much else.'

At the bottom of the drive there used to be a very imposing set of gates, guarded on either side by two stone lions on pillars. The gates have long gone and the pounding of all the lorries up and down the drive with equipment and props had knocked the left-hand lion off his perch. I was inspecting the damage the following afternoon when Julian rang my mobile to say he was arriving shortly, so I decided to wait for him. There was nothing I could do for the lion. He was lying on his side in a forlorn way, and now sported a crack right down his middle. He had a resigned expression, as if he knew it was pointless expecting repairs. I patted him gently on the cheek and used him as a seat. It was nice to have a rest for a few minutes. Idly I took out a pen and drew a quick sketch of the lion. I started daydreaming.

'Mitch turned suddenly and saw the slender, dark-eyed, not beautiful but interesting-looking girl who had been haunting his waking and sleeping thoughts since he had first glimpsed her. She was sitting alone and, unlike all the other women fawning over him, she was unaware of his presence, so immersed was she in her work.' I made a mental note never to take up novel writing if the best I could come up with was this drivel, but it was like eating chocolate – I couldn't stop. 'He went over, oblivious to the other women, and saw that she was working on a sketch. It was breathtakingly beautiful and precise. The pencil strokes were few, yet she had captured the scene with accuracy and a gentle humour.

'"You are a brilliant artist," he said and was rewarded by her shy, but sexy smile. There were hundreds of people in the room, yet suddenly they could only see each other. They gazed at each other with joy – they were soul mates and would always have –'

'Foot rot.'

I looked up, dazed.

'I said, there is a good article on sheep diseases in this week's farming paper,' said the postman, holding up a bundle of post. 'Will you take these up to the house for me and save my suspension then?'

'Of course.'

'Good. There's no hurry. You get back to your daydreaming! You're as bad as the wife,' he chuckled.

I was about to deny this indignantly, but then realised he was right. No, I was worse, unless the postman's wife also had a Four-point Plan. Honestly, if I couldn't be trusted to be sensible in the absence of temptation, what would I be like when Mitch and all the others arrived? I stood up and stared at the lion. 'I'm going to stay single if it's the last thing I do,' I said through gritted teeth.

It was time to expand on my mental makeover, I decided. Out with gossip magazines and in with serious literature, the sort that featured articles about the economy rather than horoscopes. I would read a sensible newspaper every day and become familiar with the Dow Jones index rather than who was currently hot. At the moment, all I knew about Dow was that he had something to do with stocks and shares, a subject on which I was completely ignorant. Then a car horn hooted. It was Julian.

I leaned in through the open window to give him a kiss and inhale the seductive, subtle scent of expensive leather upholstery, and then ran round to the passenger door.

'It's lovely to see you again,' I beamed.

'And you. How are you?'

'Oh, the same as ever. So, on a scale of one to ten, just how much are you looking forward to the next few weeks then?' I asked innocently.

Julian groaned and put his head in his hands. 'I can't remember a time when I looked forward to anything less. This is starting to feel like a project of unparalleled madness. To even think of gathering together a bunch of ego-driven, snivelling, feeble-minded, "think they are only one step below God" actors and take them to a leaky, draughty, "watch out that rafter's falling on your head" mausoleum – and then expect them to pay to work their socks off on a production that may – no, *will*, given this miserable climate – fail utterly in a welter of colds, damaged sensitivities, sodden feet and lines unheard due to the howls of malicious laughter coming from that pack of miserable hounds who call themselves critics – to – damn, where was I?'

'Getting it all off your chest. There, don't you feel better now?' I asked soothingly.

Julian frowned, looking even more like Indiana Jones than ever, then he threw back his head and laughed. 'I do feel a bit, a tiny bit better, though I dare say I shall still lie awake shivering in fear half the night. I do, in my saner moments, know that with a gargantuan amount of work and just the tiniest smidgen of luck, I can pull this off quite creditably; but at this stage of the project, doom-mongering Julian keeps popping up now and again, like a demon jack-in-the-box.'

We set off carefully up the drive in the sports car that Julian had had for years now, and which he claimed to love more than anyone he had so far met. We had to stop to let a rabbit bound across, back home to its burrow. Julian looked over and I realised I had got my sketchpad out. Quickly I shoved it back in my bag. I intended to show him what a focused and hard-working assistant I would be.

'Still drawing then?' he commented.

'I can't seem to stop,' I confessed.

'Why should you? How are your parents?'

'If you mean Pa, he's just about managing to totter along, with Ma's help,' I said gloomily.

'And there was you, worried he was going to keel over completely!'

'There's still time,' I said darkly. 'You've been a bit cagey about the people who are going to be in this play. We don't yet know everyone's name and they are arriving soon,' I complained.

'I know, but you are still going to have to wait until dinner,' he said.

At home, after a flurry of greetings and Will pretending to get a hernia while carrying Julian's bags upstairs, Julian and Pa disappeared into the study and only came out at dinnertime. Julian was very experienced at being a guest at Barton Willow. His figure looked as elegant as ever, but I knew he was wearing the best thermal underwear money could buy.

As soon as we were sitting down to dinner I picked up one of Emma's dummies and held it out like a microphone. 'OK, spill.'

Julian helped himself to a large portion of shepherd's pie first. 'I must say, I was thrilled that so many people offered to join me in this venture. Cinnamon Jones, for instance, is going to be Titania.'

I pondered on this while helping myself to spinach. Cinnamon, born in poverty in Jamaica, was now one of the world's top models. Just to prove that the gods really are unfair when dishing out talent, she had decided to branch out into acting and had recently got rave reviews for her first film. I was sure she was going to be capricious and demanding.

'Paige and Piper Watson are going to be Helena and Hermia,' Julian continued. They need to be different heights but I've got some unscripted jokes to solve that.

The Watson twins were the stars of a long-running television series in America and were wildly popular.

'They've been famous for ever. Didn't *Girl Talk* start when they were ten?' asked Anna.

'Yes, and they are rumoured to be terribly chilly and aloof when they're working, according to *heat*,' I said.

'Their show goes out twice a week so they have a very heavy workload,' explained Julian. 'I didn't want to have to do this, but my Oberon has gone into hospital to have a hernia operation, so I've taken the role.'

'That's going to be a lot of work – acting and directing,' said Will, thoughtfully.

Julian shrugged. 'I know, but I've done it before. Gary Marsden is taking a break from *EastEnders* to be Demetrius.' Oh, and Andy Sloan will take the part of Puck.'

'He won that reality show on television, didn't he? I didn't know he was an actor,' I said.

'Well, we're going to find out,' said Julian. He bit his lip and I knew he was anxious about this, but then he quickly changed the subject. 'I'm still reeling at my own good fortune in getting Guy Fox and Pauline Fanshawe on board for Theseus and Hippolyta.'

'That's fantastic!' I said.

'I've never heard of them,' whispered Anna.

'Neither have I, but if it makes Julian happy . . .' I replied out of the corner of my mouth.

'Yes, having such highly respected theatre actors is a real boon,' agreed Will, shaking his head at us.

'And last, but not least, the wonderful Mitch Clayton!' said Julian.

Everyone female at the table sighed in unison, though ones without Plans had a perfect right to.

Julian told us how much money the Claytons had donated to the fund and we all sighed this time. It was more than I had ever earned.

'The trailers are arriving tomorrow,' he continued.

'They are those luxury caravans, aren't they?' Anna said.

'Yes – Mitch's is so big it has its own swimming pool!' I explained.

'Really?' Anna's eyes widened.

'You never can tell when your leg is being pulled, can you?' I grinned.

'Well, I've never met a film star, so how should I know?' she countered.

'American film stars certainly have money, but they don't always come with bigger brains or better personalities. Once you have got over your swimming pool complex you will find that they are just like us – sometimes nice, sometimes not,' said Julian.

'But, in Mitch's case, infinitely better to look at,' I sighed.

'That's it. I now declare an official ban on any more drooling. You two are like cats on heat – it's not pretty,' said Will, glaring at Anna and me.

Chapter Eight

Johnny

Brad had decided it was bad form to go to a charity event in our private jet, so he decreed we would have to slum it with the rest of the world and use a scheduled flight. Mitch was in such a foul mood that when we got to the airport I checked myself into economy just to be shot of him for a few hours. The rest of the world ended up crammed in with me, not in First Class with Mitch, but I didn't care because it was peaceful.

Once settled in, I took out my battered copy of the play – I've had this particular version since I was eleven – and spent a happy couple of hours imagining what I would do with each part if it were mine. Then I took out some stuff I had printed off the Internet about Barton Willow. Apparently it had been built just because Queen Elizabeth planned to visit that neck of the woods. I considered this to be a very Hollywood-type thing to do. But then she didn't turn up anyway. The house then nearly fell down again, because no one had the cash to live in it, but eventually it was inherited by someone in the eighteenth century who was loaded. Well, he was for a while. He spent it all on the house, renovating and adding extensively to it and then died, of exhaustion and penury. A number of Bartons had tried money-making schemes down the years, but these had never come to anything. You could hardly see anything of the house in the most recent picture, because everything was so overgrown.

I was stiff and tired by the time we touched down, but it was Mitch, who had slept, dined and drunk his way across the Atlantic, who was in a foul mood. It was very unlike Mitch, but he was actually nervous. I had warned him that Julian expected his actors actually to think about their roles and, being totally unfamiliar territory to him, this had really freaked him out. What Mitch was good at was doing as he was told. He only ran into problems when it came to dusting his brain off and trying to use it. But then, this was where I would come in. It would be my job to break down his role for him and explain what I thought Julian might expect as a director and fellow Shakespeare buff.

'What's my motivation in Act Two?' he kept saying.

'Not to be a complete dumbass,' I was tempted to reply, but to be fair, he had a point. His motivation for all his previous films was to make as much money as possible. But this role wasn't about making money. It was about doing something for other people. He was in alien territory and I could tell he was disoriented.

'Brad said this would be great PR, but I don't get it,' he grumbled.

'He thinks it will help you be taken more seriously,' I explained.

Mitch puffed out his chest. 'Goddammit – everyone does take me seriously!'

'And it will be a tax write-off,' I said hurriedly, and he nodded. Mitch is very astute with money.

The part he was going to play wasn't helping either. The two male romantic leads in the *Dream*, of which he was one, weren't that bright either. In fact, they spent the whole play making fools of themselves. Now, Mitch wasn't the brightest bulb in the box but he never played stupid – that wasn't good for his image. I wondered if any of my family had really thought this through, though anyone associated with one of Julian's projects usually came up smelling of roses, so maybe they had. Also, it was quite possible to make Lysander a charming idiot and I began to think of all the ways I – or rather, Mitch – could make him so.

Mitch had finally gone to see Carly at the very last minute. I can't imagine the visit was a comfort to her in any way, but at least he would have had to break up with her face to face. She was already at work on her new film, and I'd heard talk that she'd had a miscarriage. I hoped she was doing OK. She probably wasn't.

Rumours about their relationship and the break-up were everywhere, and Mitch was coming off as the asshole, so Dirk ordered him to show his big handsome face as much as possible while in England. He was told in no uncertain terms to play nice with the crew and the locals, but not *too* nice. We saw where that had gone with Carly.

Mitch's car was waiting at the airport. I would have preferred to have gone on separately, with the luggage, but he told me to get in. I was so excited I kept sticking my head out of the window to take great gulps of the fabulous English air. It was so fresh and clean, it was almost intoxicating, especially after the stale, recycled air on the plane. The sticky, green leaves seemed to be almost coy about the way they unfurled themselves – as if they half expected winter to come roaring back with an icy blast and screw them over.

Everything was coloured so vividly and the light was so intense I was just fumbling for my shades when Mitch said grumpily, 'Shut the window – what the hell do you think air conditioning is for? And where the hell are we? All these goddamn roads look alike!'

Shit. My job as navigator was to understand just how a map actually worked and it would have been a good start not to let it fall off my lap somewhere outside London. I gazed out of the window blankly, wondering where we were, while Mitch whipped us round a bend. We were so close to the edge of the road we were skimming off the hedgerows and – 'Hey!' I yelled in alarm, but Mitch had already seen the girl in front of us. We screeched to a halt – and she jumped backwards in alarm and fell into the ditch.

'Well, get out, dumbass, and help her up,' hissed Mitch. I glared at him and got out.

She was sprawled very inelegantly on her back and I could see at least two holes in her tights. She had very dark hair and very pale skin, no make-up and slightly crooked teeth. I liked the look of her already – she was so un-Californian.

'Oh, brave new world.' I muttered Shakespeare's words under my breath and then said louder, 'Are you all right?'

'No . . . I mean yes, I don't think anything's broken.'

I held out my hand. 'In that case, allow me to help you up.'

She squinted up at me through the sunlight. 'I would be delighted if you would.'

I reached down, took hold of her hand and pulled her to her feet, and we stood there, smiling at each other. She had her head to one side, as if she was learning the shape of my face and I was more than happy to look back. Neither of us said anything for a moment or two, but the silence was easy.

Then the spell was broken.

'Are you OK?' It was Mitch. He came across and put both hands on her shoulders and was looking at her in a concerned way and suddenly there I was again, on the outside looking in. 'We just didn't see you – I am so sorry!' he said. You had to give it to the guy, he had a way of creating an exclusive space round himself and women that was very powerful. Usually I just watched with interest, but this time, for some reason, I was furious.

'Yeah – he's kinda worried about a possible lawsuit,' I remarked nastily, but she wasn't listening. I could see her eyes widen as she took in who Mitch was. His face broke into his famous grin and hers took on that soppy glazed look women get round him.

Then she jumped back as if she had been bitten.

'Now, please tell me you are OK? You still look shook up. Here, let me brush that mud off your coat,' said Mitch.

'Thank you, but it's not worth the bother,' she said, and lifted her arm to show a large hole.

'How useful, with the warmer weather approaching,' I said, deadpan, and she laughed and noticed me again and it was very nice, and then suddenly she jumped back as if she had been bitten. I wasn't certain, but I thought she muttered something about a plan under her breath and I glanced round to see if she had dropped any papers or a file. When I looked back, Mitch had muscled in again.

'You see, we were so busy keeping a lookout for a house called –'

'Barton Willow,' I supplied, knowing it wasn't the sort of detail Mitch would have bothered to remember.

'I know. You're here for the play,' she said with a charming directness. 'I live there and I'm one of the assistants. I can show you the way.'

'Of course!' Mitch said, seemingly astonished at his

own stupidity (I don't know why – you'd think he'd be used to it by now) and carried on, 'Julian told us there was a beautiful daughter!'

'Yes, that's my sister, Anna,' she explained with perfect seriousness. 'I am the older one, Lila.'

'What a beautiful and unusual name,' said Mitch, and a feeling of foreboding crept over me. He was all over her already, like that weed that was sticking to the back of her coat. And as per usual, I was sure her falling for him was only a matter of time. Every girl did and why would she be different? Oh well, another one bites the dust, I thought glumly, slouching back to the car as Mitch offered her a lift.

This meant I had to fold myself into the back – not easy when you are as tall as I am.

She gave me an appraising glance while she waited, a sort of 'What's your story?' look, but before I could introduce myself, she said, 'I know who you are. You're Mitch's brother, aren't you?'

I nodded. She writhed round in the seat so she could smile at me, but then Mitch started to help her with the seat belt and her attention returned to him and I sat back, resigned to the fact that he intended to be centre stage in this little scene. He was on his post-Carly charm offensive and I knew from bitter experience that I could only hold her attention for as long as he didn't want it.

'Blah, blah, blah . . .' they went on and on. I really couldn't be bothered to listen to their nonsense. I sulked for a few minutes, which was pointless because she had probably forgotten I was even there. God, how I hated the way so many women seemed to care only about fame – Mitch's fame in particular.

But then we turned into a driveway that was pitted with holes and lined on both sides by huge oak trees. Mitch roared over the holes. With every bump I hit my head on the roof so by the time we pulled up and I got out I was convinced I was concussed or dreaming. The house – well, it was amazing. It was built out of the most beautiful, soft, weathered grey stone and arched up out of the earth like it was meant to be part of the landscape, as much as the trees and the lake that lay in front of it like a jewel. I stared and stared and completely forgot my frustration with Mitch and his newest admirer.

No wonder Julian wanted – no, had – to film the play here. It was the most wonderful building I had ever seen in my life, even though it looked like there were holes in the roof and weeds were threatening to take over the garden. It made our house look cheap and nasty.

Mitch's arrival started the hoo-ha it always did. He couldn't go anywhere quietly and of course, he didn't want to. Dozens of people appeared out of nowhere and clustered round him like he was a magnet. Some of them were crew members. Others looked like Lila's family and were all very shabbily dressed. They stood on the worn steps smiling stiffly, like hosts at a party they weren't sure they still wanted to give. I left them to it – they wouldn't be interested in me anyway – and walked round the corner and through a gateway into a courtyard. A very old and fat black Labrador waddled over. I bent down, gave him my hand to sniff and scratched his ear gently. There was creeper growing up the side of the house and through a hole in the window. I pulled it back gently – there was some major pruning to be done here – and then I noticed a man hovering in a doorway. He looked a bit like one of the horses we had on the ranch for a while: nervous and ready to run.

I smiled at him, but didn't say anything. He gave me a small smile. We introduced ourselves briefly and then, I couldn't help it, I just had to keep looking up, but he didn't seem to mind.

'This is practically perfect,' I said finally, more to myself than him, but he looked pleased.

'Of course I am biased because I live here, but I do agree with you,' he said, but then Lila walked over and I couldn't help but notice again she was rather cute. It was just too bad that Mitch had already marked her as his.

'Oh dear, there's been some sort of mix-up. No one's given you a trailer, apparently,' she said, looking worried.

'Well, why don't you stay with us?' the man suggested, and then looked a bit surprised at himself for having said it.

'Pa –' began Lila, doubtfully, but he interrupted her before she could say any more.

'No. Julian said this was my project too, not just his. I'm not entirely sure what he meant by that, but really, we do have plenty of rooms . . .' he tailed off.

'Yes, we do,' agreed Lila, though she didn't sound very confident.

'The hunting bedroom, for instance!'

I looked a bit taken aback so she explained: 'It's full of pictures of people with guns and things, charging after poor animals. My sister and I collected them up from all over the house ages ago, when we were going through a vegetarian phase, and shoved them in there. It's like a gallery of horror.'

'Well, what about the green bedroom?'

'Green because of mould, Pa,' she hissed.

'The one at the back with the bay window?'

'No floorboards.'

'The one at the front?'

'No windows.'

'The four-poster then!' he said triumphantly, as if he had just given the winning answer in a game show.

Lila considered this and I was quite happy to just stand there and watch her thinking. 'I can't think of anything wrong with that room,' she began cautiously, 'but I'm sure something will hit us, probably literally, when we go in.'

'Well, so glad to have got that sorted,' said Mr Barton, relieved. He smiled at me. 'I'll leave you two young people to, er, get on with it then,' and he ambled away.

Lila went a fiery red. 'You have no idea what you're letting yourself in for. Are you absolutely certain you don't want me to find you a lovely room in a hotel somewhere?'

I thought of the shiny, but boring anonymity of a hotel room and shuddered. 'No, thank you, I'll take my chances here.'

We went inside.

'It's a pity – I was going to ask you to pinch all those little pots of jam and marmalade they give out at breakfast,' she said.

'Do you have a jam shortage here?'

She laughed. 'No, I just like them – and the little bars of soap and shampoo and stuff.'

'Next time I'm in a hotel I'll raid the chambermaid's trolley for you,' I promised, and then I had to stop talking to properly take in my surroundings. 'OK, I know I sound like a tourist now, but – wow!' I said eventually. 'Everything looks like it's been here for years!'

'It has. That's why it's so dusty and tattered.'

'No, that's not what I meant. It's full of the memories of all the people who have put their mark on this place. You could never get lonely here,' I commented.

'Well, I'd never really thought of it like that. But when we were children we used to make up stories about the people who used to live here.'

'Sounds like fun,' I said, though I couldn't imagine ever doing that with Mitch or Brad.

'Of course, it ended up getting competitive. We used to spend hours in the library checking to make sure we got our facts right. You know the sort of thing – what did people during the Regency have for breakfast, or when were umbrellas invented?'

'In the library, of course,' I said dreamily. 'I suppose you all read books there?'

'No, we used to eat them, of course! What do you think we did with them?' she giggled.

'You'd be surprised,' I said, thinking of all the unread books with their embossed leather covers in our library at home, which were there just to make the place look good. As we talked I realised we'd hit it off and become friends. Too bad Mitch and his all-consuming need to be the centre of attention wouldn't allow me ever to see if we could be more than that.

'Now, where shall I put you?' she continued, as if I were a piece of spare crockery that wouldn't fit in a cupboard with all the other pieces.

We were standing in a long corridor with an arched window at the end. Sunlight was streaming through and I could see the dust dancing in the air. There were doors opening off all the way down it and patches on the wall where pictures, probably those hunting ones, had once hung.

'You talked about a four-poster,' I reminded her.

'Yes, I did,' she agreed, 'but there was something about that room . . .'

'It lacks walls? A ceiling?' I offered helpfully.

'I wouldn't joke like that if I were you. Oh, well, here goes.'

Tentatively she tried a door. It creaked in a way that would have done Hitchcock proud and I followed her in. The floorboards were bare apart from a rug, and there was no furniture apart from a black and ancient chest of drawers, a rickety chair and the bed, which was enormous and covered in drapes. There was a scuffling under the bed that could only have meant mice, but I didn't care. Entranced, I put my hand out to the drapes.

Definitely a mistake.

The whole thing collapsed just as she shouted, 'Don't touch that!'

It took ages to get out from under all that ancient velvet because I was sneezing and coughing so much with all the dust.

'It's a good thing I'm not asthmatic,' I spluttered eventually.

'Yes, you've got to be tough to live here,' Lila said.

A tassel from one of the drapes had wound itself round my wrist, as if the house was claiming ownership of me. 'Oh, I can look after myself, don't worry about that.'

'Hmm, I'm still not sure. I should have compiled a questionnaire for you to fill in before letting you stay

– you know, like the ones they give you when you start a new job?'

I lay on my back and looked up at the ceiling. Actually, I think I was looking through some of it. 'OK, fire away.'

'Well, to start with, do you have an aversion to wildlife?'

'No.'

'Good. Then you won't mind me doing this.' She leaned forward to pull a spider out of my hair.

'Hey, that's not fair! You didn't mention that the wildlife might actually be on me!' I cried, turning to look at the little creature as it scurried through a hole in the floorboards. I didn't want her to see my face and read what was so plainly written there, that I had wanted suddenly to kiss her.

'It doesn't happen often. Though a mouse did run up Pa's leg once. Anyway, I think we can assume you're not claustrophobic either, since you didn't completely freak out when the bed hangings collapsed on your head, did you? There was just an oof of surprise from you, before you disappeared.' She laughed.

Oh God, she was adorable. I hated Mitch. Amazing how those two thoughts always followed each other.

'So, tell me, how comfortable are you with extremes of temperature?' she asked.

Get a grip, I told myself. She wants to be your friend, but she's gonna fall for Mitch – just like any other girl on earth. I considered her question carefully, to take my mind off the freckles that danced across her nose. 'I've survived a Californian summer and a Wyoming winter, so no worries there.'

She ticked an imaginary box. 'Hot or cold baths?'

'Generally, somewhere in between,' I offered cautiously.

'Oh dear, wrong answer, I'm afraid. Baths here are either scalding, leading you to resemble a lobster, or icy cold, so you get out feeling like you've just jumped into the Atlantic. Let's hope you do better on the next question. What about sprains, fractures, torn muscles, bruising or scars?'

'None the last time I looked.'

'No, failed again, though you may not have understood the question. What I meant was, will you be bothered by the fact that you will probably be suffering from at least one of these by the end of the week, and nearly all of them if you stay longer? Floorboards will leap up and smack you on the shins; panes of glass will break when you try to open a window; draughts sharper than a chef's knife will slice through your bones – oh, I forgot – how averse are you to the sight of blood?'

I bared my teeth. 'Not at all, on other people!' I said, in a Dracula voice and she giggled.

'You are not taking this seriously! I think we already know you are no good at dodging falling objects, but will you be able to find your way to the loo in the pitch-dark? And how good are you at mending fuses? Have you by any chance got a plumbing qualification? Emergency joinery experience?'

'And to think I passed up the option of a relaxing trek to the North Pole!'

'You're nothing like your brother, are you?' she said suddenly.

This made me laugh to myself. The last time he did a movie, he demanded, amongst other things, that the carpet in his trailer contained no yellow fibres and that it always smelled like fresh laundry. So no, he's nothing like me.

'I suppose film actors are different from us, aren't they?' she said indulgently. I looked up sharply. She didn't seem to have that look on her face that girls get when they've met Mitch. Could she actually be different than every other girl?

'Yeah, they come with a licence so they don't have to behave like decent human beings,' I said, more aggressively than I should have.

She looked a bit taken aback. 'I just meant that . . . I thought . . . you see . . .' she tailed off, confused.

'No worries,' I said flatly, and as we both awkwardly stood there in silence, I thought, give it up, Johnny. She's a girl – all girls fall for Mitch. This is how it's always gonna be. I've seen this happen all my life and usually it doesn't bother me, but I thought you were different, I said to her silently. I wanted you to be different, but I guess you're not. Deal with it. 'You'd need a ton of servants to keep this place comfortable, wouldn't you?' I said, out loud.

'Well, we used to,' she replied quickly, pleased to

change the subject. 'Unfortunately that was a long time ago. There's a list of their jobs in a book downstairs. They included the steward, the chaplain, the gentlemen of the horse, the usher, the auditor, the secretary, two pages and my lord's favourite.'

'My father has one of those,' I said. I tried, but failed, to stifle a huge yawn. The jet lag was really starting to catch up with me.

'You must be exhausted,' she said.

'I'm beat,' I admitted. 'I would love some coffee.'

'I'll get you some,' she said, brushing dust off me as we stood up. She was so close I could smell an apply scent on her hair and see the veins running under her milky white skin. I cleared my throat. 'Are there any other bedrooms not awaiting demolition?'

'Yes, but a couple are so bad even the mice have moved out. There is the small one at the back. It will overlook the trailer your brother is staying in.'

I shuddered. I didn't want to have to lay eyes on Mitch any more than I absolutely had to. 'Here will be fine. If you could lend me some cleaning materials I could fix this place up real neat.' I was lying, it needed knocking down and rebuilding, but I was already beginning to picture in my head a scene out of *Macbeth*. When I was on my own here, I could try out some speeches.

I hesitated for a moment, watching her. She was picking up the drapes, bending over from the waist, like a dancer.

'Do me a favour – stay away from Mitch – he's not

good for you,' I said abruptly, and then cursed myself quietly. Now she would just think I was jealous.

'What – like cigarettes or alcohol?' she said lightly. 'And where did that come from?' she asked, laughing. 'Don't worry, I'm not into men right now. You see, I have a . . .' Then she tailed off, spotting another spider and chasing after it.

Utterly confused now, I asked, 'Where's that coffee?' Maybe a shot of caffeine would help me understand this strange duck.

A tall, distinguished-looking man was in the kitchen, a huge room with a deep window, looking over what I guessed was a kitchen garden. I stopped dead and looked round with pleasure. The kitchen had once been painted white, but a long time ago. Now the walls were the colour of that thick cream that is bad for you. There were huge hooks hanging from the smoke-blackened ceiling. One still had a Christmas bauble tied to it. There was a very odd contraption suspended over the range. It looked like it was for drying clothes. Three dressers bulging with junk lined the walls in various places. Mismatched cups and saucers sat on the shelves, full of pens and old feathers and straws, and littered around them were pairs of glasses, some missing any glass, torches, bits of torches, pine cones, stubs of candles and a drawing of a baby. In the middle was a round table, etched with ancient grooves and big enough for Noah and his family to eat at, and in the corner a huge squashy sofa with bits of stuffing escaping from various seams.

There were piles of magazines going brown at the edges and drawers crammed full of so much stuff no one could shut them any more.

'This is my brother, Will. He's a therapist. He's in the middle of writing a very important thesis, which is why he's got that glassy-eyed look – or have you been at the sherry again?'

I grinned, but by now I was utterly exhausted. I accepted a cup of coffee. Lila and Will were chatting, but by now I felt incapable of pleasant conversation, so I took my coffee out to the back patio.

It was very peaceful out here. The sun was setting and the fact that the world was going about its usual stuff had a calming effect on me. These walls had been here long before me and would still be standing long after I had gone. It was a very humbling moment. The Labrador came round the corner and his ears pricked up when he saw me. He came over, sniffed my shoes with great interest and sat down on them, looking pleased with himself. It was good to know that somebody cared, but I was just starting to lose all sensation in my feet when Will wandered out.

'That is a perfectly disgraceful dog. Please don't feel obliged to make friends with it.'

'I don't mind, I like dogs,' I said. The coffee had revived me, a little.

'Oh, so do I. I'm just not very keen on that one. Budge, Bongo!'

There was another Hitchcockian creaking sound

above us. It was Lila, opening a window and waving a cloth, like a white flag of surrender. Above the duster her eyes were anxious. 'I've brought the Hoover up as well. It really does need a good clean.'

'Blimey, I never thought I would hear Lila say that about anywhere. Generally she sees dust as her friend. Clearly she is pulling out all the stops for you. No, don't go up and help – it will do her good. In fact, when you get to know my family a little better, you will realise that you should have run away while you had the chance,' said Will.

'But I guess you could say that about a lot of families,' I pointed out, and he laughed. 'Lila said you were writing a thesis?'

'Well, it started off like that but it will end up as a book, probably. It's on the neuropsychology of attachment.'

'That sounds interesting. Is it based on your experiences of family life?'

'You did that very well,' said Will admiringly. 'I would almost swear you not only know what I'm talking about but you are genuinely interested in it.'

'It's a talent I have, but don't let it fool you,' I said with a grin, and went indoors to find Lila. For a shrink he was actually all right, I guess.

Chapter Nine

Lila

I was sick with nerves on the morning of the press conference in the library, although, looking at the list Cara had given me, all I was really doing was acting as a glorified cloakroom attendant. Cara was Julian's most important assistant and very nice, in a brisk way.

'I won't go into much detail about our different roles, except to say I am the only one who can make decisions. You, on the other hand, can't decide anything until I give you permission. Basically, what's going to happen is that Julian will keep giving you jobs to do, until you are ready to drop dead with tiredness. I'm sorry if I sound abrupt, but there is a lot to do and very little time to do it in.' She gave me a friendly grin but I knew she was thinking Julian had only hired me because I was his goddaughter. Well she was probably right, I thought, uncomfortably. But I was determined to prove that I deserved the job, however menial it was.

This was the only time the press were allowed up

the drive and access to the actors until the night of the play, and as I stood on the steps watching about a dozen assorted vehicles come screeching to a halt, I looked up and saw Pa at the window upstairs. He gave a visible shudder and backed off. I shivered in sympathy for him, but now I had to concentrate.

I was confident that my dinner lady experience of marshalling groups of noisy children would come in very useful here. But the press were much, much worse. For a start, they simply refused to listen to me and as soon as they got out of their cars, began wandering off, clearly trying to get into places they shouldn't. Others gave me a cursory glance and began gossiping and boasting about recent scoops, ignoring me completely. If I raised my voice any higher, only dogs would be able to hear me. But I had a trick up my sleeve – well, in my pocket actually.

I took the whistle out and blew it hard. The noise scorched into people's eardrums and they all jumped. 'I am going to do that every time you stop listening, or fail to follow my rules,' I remarked pleasantly. Well, at least I had got their attention. 'Listen up, everyone. There is no access through the door or gates or anywhere marked "No Access". You will follow me into the house and to the library, where there will be every opportunity to take all the pictures you want and ask all the questions you need answers to. Then, without hesitation or deviation to anywhere in the grounds, you will leave and not return until the performance.'

I held my breath. Had I come on too strong? After all, Julian needed the media to be on his side. Had I made a mess of things already?

But then one of the photographers looked at me admiringly and said: 'OK, Miss Bossy Boots, if you say so. Don't suppose there's any chance of a spanking later?' My face went flame red as they all burst into raucous laughter, but it seemed to work and they followed me into the house without further ado.

Now my second ordeal began, but this time my nerves were on behalf of Barton Willow itself. The house was making its first appearance to the world for a very long time and it was a bit like watching a friend, one who didn't get out much, prepare for her first party. I kept twitching nervous glances into corners, checking for dust or cobwebs, or bits of plaster that might fall off, and when I saw all the photographers and reporters looking round, I found I was shaking.

'Bloody nice, living in a place like this,' grumbled a reporter, looking round with disapproval.

'Only in the summer when you can sit down for a few minutes without worrying you are going to freeze to death,' I snapped. I was fed up with people thinking that because we lived in such a large house, we were rich.

'You could fit the whole of my flat into this room,' said the photographer who had called me bossy.

'Sometimes I yearn for a place like that – warm, and

where the carpet doesn't go mouldy with damp and the wallpaper stays on the wall,' I sighed.

'So, you have a love-hate relationship with this place?' asked another, looking at me sharply.

'Yes! That's it exactly!' I said eagerly, and began telling them about the buckets and the mushrooms and the rotten floorboards, and how you couldn't ever get into a temper and slam a door because all the plaster would fall off the wall, and at some point they stopped looking envious and started looking sympathetic.

'Well, this has been quite an eye-opener to how the other half lives,' someone said.

'If by other half you mean people who are still using their great-grandmother's blankets,' I pointed out bleakly, and they all laughed.

Then, like hyperactive children, their attention was completely diverted when Mitch, Cinnamon, the Watson twins and the rest of the cast walked in. Involuntarily, I took a step back in awe. I couldn't help myself. These were people who, up to now, I had seen only in magazines and on television. Mitch, of course, I had already met, but the women! They were so, so . . . perfect, I just had to stand there and gape. Oh, how I itched for a sketchpad to capture the contrast between the tiny, porcelain twins and Cinnamon's statuesque beauty, and then I glanced down and saw that I was absent-mindedly drawing on the back of my list of press attendees.

The actors stood in front of the chairs I had provided, but didn't sit down. Then I realised why and got my second shock of the morning. They were standing to applaud Julian as he entered the room.

I knew Julian was famous – of course I did. It was just that to me, he had always been Uncle Julian first and foremost. He had been coming and going in our lives for as long as I could remember. He was part of the fabric of Barton Willow, really, and usually he wandered around in very nice casual clothes, including at least three sweaters. Well, today I saw the other Julian MacDonald, the man who was so looked up to by the great and good of Hollywood that they stood up as a mark of respect when he walked in. He looked different too. He was wearing a very smart suit, and shoes so highly polished I could see the lights reflected in them. Suddenly he wasn't Uncle Julian at all, but a handsome and powerful stranger. He stood in the doorway, smiling at everyone genially, accepting the applause with style and grace, and I thought to myself suddenly, this is his world as well. He knows all these famous people and is comfortable around them and he's not a bit bothered by all the cameras clicking and whirring, and people shouting questions. It was rather disconcerting and I wondered suddenly if I would ever see him the same way again. I watched as, with impeccable timing, he waited for the applause – which was coming from the whole room – to die down before striding forwards. Then, smiling, he held up his hand for silence and everyone leaned forward, rapt.

'We are doing this now in the hopes that after this question-and-answer orgy you will bugger off while we get down to some very hard work. This will be a play about journeying – literally, from the real world of the Duke's court into a world of magic. Two pairs of quarrelling lovers run away from reality into an enchanted wood. Strange magical creatures live there. The fairies, who are sly and beautiful and dangerous, add to the mischief. The lovers have spells laid on them and quarrel more. A group of workmen, rehearsing a play to celebrate the Duke's forthcoming wedding, get included in the enchantment. Anyone who enters the wood leaves common sense and logic behind. Anything can happen and probably will. People will be changed because of it, and maybe that will include some of the audience – who knows?' he added, and everyone laughed. 'Now, I know you've heard that the tickets for this play are ridiculously expensive –' he paused – 'and you heard right – they are. That's because this is going to be a brilliant one-off production the like of which no one has seen before and will ever see again. Isn't that right, my dears?' And he smiled at his cast.

'Actors have been around for about the last two and a half thousand years. But someone only invented the job of director about eighty years ago, so I intend to relax and leave it pretty much up to them.' He yawned and stretched, like he was going to have a nice sit down and everyone laughed, apart from Mitch, who looked confused.

'This is going to be a completely different perform-ance for you, Mitch. How do you think you'll handle it?' asked a reporter.

'I'm really excited to be here and honoured to have been asked,' said Mitch, exuding charm effortlessly. 'I'd just like to say that I am just a small part of a scarily talented group of people. Hey, it's a good thing I thrive on challenge, huh?'

'Some people are saying this is perfect timing for you, what with your latest romantic crisis back home. Have you any comment on that?'

'I am so unlucky in love,' mourned Mitch, looking so handsomely, openly miserable, every woman in the room wanted to take him home and comfort him. 'You know, guys, I'm such a jerk when it comes to women. I just can't seem to get it right.' We all sighed, long-ingly. Then his face broke out into a cheeky grin. 'But I'm gonna keep on trying!'

'You can experiment with me any time,' murmured one of the female reporters, but audibly – and everyone laughed. There was something so honest about the way Mitch admitted his failures, it just made us all like him more, if that was possible.

Someone asked Cinnamon a question that amused her. When she threw back her head and laughed it was infectious. She didn't seem diva-like at all. I was fascinated by the way the Watson twins looked at each other before answering a question, as if they were communicating telepathically.

Pauline and Guy talked for a while about various productions of *Dream*. Apparently Pauline had once played Titania in the nude, covered with silver and gold body-paint.

Dylan Bailey, the leader of the mini orchestra, stood up and played a short piece on his violin and we all shivered. It was unearthly, like nothing I'd ever heard before. 'This is the moonlit madness music for the fairy scenes,' he explained. 'The other stuff we'll be doing, for Theseus and his court, will be more conventional. There's only a few of us but we're gonna rock!'

Everyone clapped and then a reporter brought the attention back to Mitch.

'You've brought your younger brother along with you. We've all been wondering if he's going to follow in your footsteps, you seem like such a close family?'

Mitch sighed in mock frustration, the perfect picture of the caring older brother. 'Family – don't they drive you nuts? He hasn't the faintest idea what he wants to do with his life so I said he could tag along to England with me. His opinion is that there are enough actors already in this family without him as well.'

'Of course, he might be competition for you?' commented one reporter.

'Bring it on, I say! Seriously, there isn't anyone I'd rather have fighting me for roles, but he just doesn't want to have any part in this game.' Mitch's face became serious now. 'This is a big deal for me and, I guess, for all my new friends here,' and he waved an arm at the rest of the cast. 'There is no room here for the half-hearted. We are all deeply committed to working our asses off to raise money for a cause very dear to our hearts. I think I can speak for everyone when I say that we are here to give everything to this project.' He stopped, as if overcome with emotion.

'Mitch is right,' said Julian, giving him a polished smile that didn't quite seem to reach his eyes. 'The months I spent in Peru were among the happiest of my life. It is an incredibly beautiful part of the world and the people who live there deserve beauty, because they were the most friendly and hospitable people a film crew has ever foisted itself on to. This earthquake has devastated their already slender resources and I will not rest until I have done my utmost to give something back.'

His beautiful voice rang out across the room and everyone burst into spontaneous applause. I was so excited and moved by his words, I joined in myself. It seemed to me that with people like Mitch and Julian around there was no way this play wouldn't be a storming success – I hugged myself with secret glee – and I was going to be part of it!

Chapter Ten

Johnny

'This is a different performance for you, Mitch. How will you handle it?'

'Pretty much the way I always handle a challenge – by getting my younger stepbrother to do all the work,' I said, in perfect imitation of Mitch's voice. I looked up to see the Bartons' Labrador looking at me.

'OK, I know it's not that funny, but I'm doing the best I can with the material I've got. Give me a break,' I begged it. The dog stared, unmoved.

I bent down, picked up a stone and threw it across the lawn. Bongo followed its path and then turned his attention to me again, as if to say, 'Don't hold your breath, sonny. I know that isn't a piece of bacon, so I'm not going after it.'

'We have to get out of here,' I hissed. There was no way I wanted anyone to come across me skulking outside the library window like an intruder. Hardly anyone knew who the hell I was and Mitch would probably find it a huge joke to watch me being hauled off the premises like a thief. I wound my fingers round Bongo's collar and dragged the unwilling hound down the path and into the woods. He immediately started snuffling around in the undergrowth. I watched him and sighed with longing for Onatah, my hound and best friend at the ranch in Wyoming. My mother was a native American and I named Onatah in memory of her. It's an Iroquois word, meaning 'of the earth', and it was literally true. Onatah was only happy when she was outside, running through the grass, her long ears flapping. Onatah was not a good-looking dog, but everyone loved her and she loved them right back. One night she ran over to welcome Mitch home. But Mitch was drunk and too busy fondling a girl to look at the road. He ran right into her. She died in my arms, trying to lick my hand. I lay in the dust next to her until her eyes clouded over. Mitch had gone from happy drunk to maudlin in a second and wanted to drive me into town that minute to get me a new dog. As if she could ever be replaced, I raged at him bitterly, but he really didn't get it. Mitch really did think his money could buy anything and he couldn't understand why, at that moment, I hated him for it.

'I never meant for this to happen. I'll get you another damned dog right now!' he yelled, tears of self-pity creeping down his cheek because I was refusing to play ball and cheer him up.

There was a clunk as Bongo dropped an incredibly

ancient golf ball at my feet and looked at me as if to say, 'Let's play.'

I kneeled down and ruffled his fur, and my cellphone fell out of my pocket just as it started ringing. It was Brad. I stared at it. I could just leave it here for ever, to get buried by the undergrowth, and I had a sudden picture of Brad, stuck for ever on the other end of the line, with a beard growing down to his knees. Grinning, I answered the call.

'You sound very upbeat,' he said accusingly, as if I wasn't allowed to have a good time.

'Hi, Brad. Yeah, I'm fine, thanks for asking,' I laughed. 'By the way, you completely forgot to find me somewhere to sleep, Luckily, the family have put me up in a very . . . well, interesting bedroom.'

'Shit! Blame my new PA. She went out for Botox in her lunchtime and they must have frozen her brain at the same time. Quit whining. You got a room eventually, didn't you? How's Mitch?' he asked, moving on to more important things.

'You mean, how is he going to cope with the first rehearsal?' I said, deducing that was what he was worried about.

'Yeah.'

'He should be fine,' I promised him. 'Before we left, I read up on everything I could find about how Julian rehearses. If it goes according to form, he'll get everyone in for a general chat about the play and what they think about their characters. He'll then tell them what *he* thinks about the play and what he thinks about their characters. This is where it could get tricky. Julian likes it when people disagree with him, but only when they say something intelligent.'

There was a long silence. 'Warn Mitch to keep his mouth shut in that case, or we're screwed,' said Brad gloomily. 'We need some positive PR from this thing or else it will have been a waste of time and money. And make sure he keeps his dick in his pants until he's home.'

An image of Lila flashed across my mind and I shivered. 'I'll do what I can but I'm not camping outside his trailer to keep watch on who he brings back for the night. I'll warn him to keep away from anyone that looks . . . vulnerable.'

'Listen, I've got to go. Ring me at any time if you've got a problem,' he said, and hung up.

I was tempted to ring him back immediately: 'You see, Brad, the thing is, I thought this would be the most fantastic opportunity and it probably is – for everyone but me. I don't quite know how I'm going to survive being around all this . . . this acting stuff and not being able to take part. I want to run over to Julian now and tell him that I know exactly how Puck should be played and what relationship he will have with Oberon. And Julian will say, "Are you saying it will be a sort of father-son relationship, the sort you don't have with your own father?" And I'll say, "Yeah, of course! Because using your own life experience is partly what acting should be about." And we'll talk for hours about the different ways you can approach a role. Except, of course, Julian doesn't even know I exist and if he did he probably wouldn't care because he's got much more important things on his mind. So that's the problem I want to talk about with you, Brad. But of course you don't give a damn either, so this conversation will never take place. You will only swing into action if the problem concerns Mitch.'

Bongo looked at me with deep sympathy, as if to say, 'So the golf ball isn't doing it for you, then?'

We walked back to the house just as the press were leaving, so I stood behind a tree to watch them go. OK, I wanted to watch Lila, unobserved.

'First, thank you so much for coming today and please give as much coverage as you can to this project. I know you think it's as important as we do. Secondly, I am going to watch you get into your cars and set off and then my assistant at the end of the drive will make sure you leave. We don't want anyone getting lost on the way.'

I knew she was lying. Everyone laughed good-humouredly, but I wasn't fooled by them either. Ever since I've lived with the Claytons I've had to live with the paparazzi. I pretty much know every trick up their very long sleeves. I turned and took a short cut through the trees to the corner just before the end of the drive, Bongo loping along after me.

Sure enough, the very last car dawdled until the

others were out of sight and then stopped. I was at the door before the driver, a woman, could get out.

'Can I help you? Are you lost?' I said, putting on my best British accent.

'Who's asking?' she demanded.

'I am Miss Barton's assistant,' I said smoothly.

'I was just stopping to make a call,' she said, trying to get out.

'The hell you are!' I retorted, slamming the door shut again.

She wound the window down and glared at me. 'Where have I seen you before? Your face is very familiar.'

'Awfully pleased to hear it. The exit is that way,' I said.

'I've got it! Stop talking British, you charlatan. You're Mitch Clayton's little stepbrother and as American as they come!'

'I'm almost as tall as him and only a few years younger,' I said glaring back. OK, I hadn't done much with my life, but I wasn't a kid.

'It's those cheekbones, they're the gift of eternal youth,' she said, smiling now. 'You need to relax more. I was trying to pay you a compliment.'

I folded my arms and stood like I was ready for trouble and looking forward to smacking it on the nose. 'I'm sorry, ma'am, but I've got to ask you to keep moving, that way,' I said implacably, and pointed to the gates. I seemed to have morphed into an American bodyguard, but she didn't care.

She patted the passenger seat invitingly. 'Tell you what, can I give you a lift somewhere? We could get to know each other better.' She smiled at me. She was very pretty.

I couldn't help grinning back. 'Thanks for the offer. Another time maybe.'

She leaned out of the window and wrote something on my hand with her pen. 'That's my number, if you change your mind,' she said, and drove off.

'I think I scored,' I said to Bongo, as we strolled back to the house. OK, she was only doing it to get a story out of me, but maybe not every woman wanted only Mitch.

I stayed quite upbeat until I bumped into Mitch. He took my arm and dragged me over to the privacy of his trailer.

'What the hell . . . ? Julian just asked me if I was a method actor or an improviser! Don't just stand there – what am I?'

'You are definitely not an improviser,' I said, with a shudder at the thought of how that would turn out if Mitch ever tried it. He thrust a sheaf of papers at me.

'He's given us all notes and we haven't even started rehearsing yet!' said Mitch, aggrieved.

'OK, OK. When's your first rehearsal?'

'Tomorrow. There's a welcoming party in the house this afternoon so we can all get to know each other.'

'Great. That's plenty of time for me to look through

these and then go over them with you,' I said soothingly. Actually, I wished I could've looked through
everyone else's as well. It would have made fascinating
reading.

Mitch was looking at himself in a mirror. He had
already lost interest. 'I cannot believe there is no pool
here,' he grumbled. 'I've had to get Phil over so I can
keep working on this.' He patted his six-pack. Phil was
his personal trainer back in LA. It was good to know
that the Claytons were only increasing their carbon
footprint over really important issues like Mitch's abs.

I took the notes and wandered outside to find somewhere peaceful to read them. I should have stayed in
Mitch's trailer. It was crazy out here. The place was full
of vehicles unloading equipment and people. I stood
still for a moment and breathed in the chaos like it
was a perfume. But there was something so exciting
about the start of a production. Everyone was so full
of hope and ideas and enthusiasm, and, unlike the last
few plays I had worked on back in LA, a lot of people
were going to see this one. This was going to make a
splash, I was sure of it.

Resolutely, I turned my back on the scene and went
indoors. I was looking down at the notes and chuckling at the idea of anyone thinking Mitch was clever
enough to improvise when I ran smack into Julian on
the stairs.

'Oh! I'm sorry,' I muttered, standing aside to let him
pass. He walked on, but then turned round. He had

changed out of the smart clothes into more casual gear. It suited him but then he would look good in anything.

'Haven't we met?'

'No, that's not something I would forget,' I assured him.

He looked closer. 'You are wrong. You introduced me to your dog, a beautiful lurcher that could run like the wind. But I don't blame you for forgetting – you were only three at the time.'

Eventually I remembered to shut my mouth. He carried on, obviously adept at dealing with awkward people.

'You are Johnny Clayton and I think your mother and I should have become great friends, but tragically she died soon after I met her. I have never forgotten her, though. She was a most remarkable woman.'

I nodded, totally speechless.

'So, are you a friend of the family here?'

'I certainly hope to be, when I get to know them better. I've tagged along with Mitch to . . . er . . . to keep him company.'

Julian frowned as if this wasn't the right answer, but it was the only one I had. 'You're a friend of Stella Southern's, aren't you?'

Christ, he knew everything.

'She's doing some very interesting work at the moment. I was so sorry I couldn't get to see her last play, but I was already organising this little caper.

Yes, when this is all over, Stella and I must get together and have a talk about things,' he ruminated, then pulled himself together. 'Ah, well, better get this one finished first. I am so pleased to have met you again,' he said, looking as if he really was. But then he was famous for his charm and courtesy.

I ran up the stairs, texting Stella with the news.

She texted back immediately. 'You doofus! You meet the great Julian MacDonald and you have a conversation about *me*? Consider yourself shaken! Call me when you are doing something for yourself for a change!'

Chapter Eleven

Lila

'A party?' I said, with horror, looking round the kitchen. It was certainly big enough for a party, but I could think of better places to hold one. The *Titanic*, for example. I had only popped indoors for a reviving cup of tea and now Ma had thrown this . . . this . . . nightmare at me.

'It's not really a party, it's just an informal get-together for the cast,' she said, comfortingly. 'Julian said he couldn't think of a better way for everyone to get to know each other than over a cup of tea and a bit of cake round this table. So you see, it isn't a proper party,' repeated Ma firmly, twisting the tea towel into such knots it would soon be unusable.

'Oh God, what are we going to do!' we both cried out in unison and clung onto each other for dear life, like drowning people.

'Right, we must meet this head on,' said Ma, becoming businesslike, and I was full of admiration for her courage. 'There is simply nothing we can do about the state of the kitchen – they will have to take it or leave it.'

'But anyone in their right mind would leave it – and head straight for the nearest hotel!' I said in desperation.

'Well, they'll jolly well have to put up with it. Now, we can certainly tidy up, starting here for –'

'Don't move those papers!' I cried, but it was too late.

'When did that crack appear?'

'Just before that one, underneath it.'

'Are there any more I should know about?' asked Ma, grimly.

'Not just now,' I told her firmly and looked down at my list. 'I've only got one more job to do and then I'm free. I will come back and tidy up and that will leave you free to get started on the biscuits and scones.'

'Americans like cookies, don't they? I don't know how to make those,' she mourned.

'They will eat your home-made custard creams or lump it,' I said with a firmness I didn't feel; drank my tea in one go, which was a mistake because it was still scalding hot, and dashed off. Honestly, until now I had always felt there was more than enough of me to go round. Now, there was never enough. Luckily, my last job, delivering some material to Abby, the wardrobe mistress, was quickly done and soon I was back in the kitchen. I dived into the cupboard for the feather duster.

'No. Use the Hoover. The duster will just move the grime around,' said Ma, hoarsely, busy on her umpteenth batch of scones.

Pa walked in. Ma waved the rolling pin at him. 'Jam. Two pots, one damson, one pear and apple. The best tablecloth – you know, the one Aunt Lily sent us – and round up every teacup, saucer and plate you can find. Well, what are you waiting for?' Pa looked at the rolling pin and vanished.

'There probably isn't a single matching teacup and saucer in the entire house,' she said.

'They will think it's part of our famous British charm and eccentricity. It will probably be all the rage in LA after they go home,' I said consolingly, vacuuming up cobwebs and a piece of paper that Will had made notes on. I prayed they weren't important; there wasn't time to retrieve them.

Thanks to our combined efforts, two hours later, the cakes were made, the table was laid and two ancient kettles were on the Aga, boiling enough water to quench the thirst of a small army.

'I think we might pull this off,' said Ma.

'You've got flour on your cheek,' said Pa, kissing it off.

'Go and change,' I ordered her.

'Is there enough time? And what about you?' she said, looking at my pale pink shirt, which was now covered in grey streaks.

'You are the lady of the house. You deserve to look

your best. I'll stay and repel boarders – I mean, let our guests in,' I said, and she gave me a look of gratitude before dashing off.

She had just come back in when there was a knock and Cinnamon put her gorgeous head round the door. 'Oh, wow! That sink is nearly big enough to have a bath in!'

'Lila did when she was little,' said Pa, and I groaned because now I had no credibility. But Cinnamon was laughing like he had made the best joke ever, and when I saw him relax a little I thought, oh, well, dignity's never really been my thing.

Cinnamon said she was dying for a cup of tea, and stood up to drink it so she could gossip to Ma, who was busy putting the last touches to a sponge. The pair of them were talking and laughing so animatedly that by the time the others started coming in, it looked like the party had already started and they surged forward, anxious to join in. I had to completely revise my opinion of Cinnamon. She was such an easy, unaffected person, without a trace of vanity.

Pa still looked a bit grim, but then one of the Watson twins began admiring a teacup. 'This is so beautiful. Spode, isn't it? Yes, I thought so. This is one of my favourite designs.' It turned out she was a keen collector of porcelain and knew quite a bit about it, so Pa took her off to look at a broken coffee cup, which she seemed to be incredibly enthusiastic about. 'I've been longing to get my hands on one of those, but they come on the market so rarely,' she said as they left the room. Well, she'd come to the right place then.

Mitch came in, followed by his brother, and both walked in my direction.

'Hiya, Lucy, do you have anything to drink aside from tea?' Mitch asked, rather presumptuously.

'It's Lila, actually. There's coffee but I'm afraid it's only instant. Or there's some beer!' I said, inspired, remembering that Will kept some in the fridge. 'Oh dear, there's only one left.'

'You only want one, don't you, what with having to start work early tomorrow,' said Johnny, meaningfully, darting a quick glance at Julian, who was talking to the girl who was playing Peaseblossom.

'So, how are you settling in?' I asked them both. Mitch's eyes were sky blue and very bright, I thought dreamily, and pulled myself together as I remembered the Plan.

'Mitch can settle anywhere, as long as he has his luxury trailer with him,' muttered Johnny, looking down at his cup of tea and grinning to himself.

'I'm loving it! The countryside is so beautiful and the air so fresh,' Mitch said, leaning back against a dresser and dislodging a pile of dusty books.

'I'll get you some water,' I said in concern as he started coughing.

When he'd recovered – Johnny seemed particularly to enjoy slapping him on the back – I asked him if there was anything he especially wanted to see while he was here, but although he talked enthusiastically about how wonderful it all was, he was quite vague.

I looked over at Johnny. 'How long have you got?' he grinned. 'The Globe, of course; Stonehenge; Canterbury Cathedral; the Lake District; Loch Lomond . . .'

'Oh, well, can I come with you? I'm ashamed to admit it, but I haven't been to Stonehenge either,' I laughed.

'Well, tourists always know more about a place than the natives,' he said tolerantly.

'That's nice of you, but I'm afraid I'm just ignorant,' I said.

He looked down at my ink-stained fingers. 'I'm sure that's not true. You've obviously been busy doing other things.'

I beamed at him, but then Ma called me over to serve up more scones. The noise in the kitchen escalated, fuelled by tea and animated conversation. I handed round scones and cake, and refilled cups. Everyone was talking to someone and scoffing the delicious food, some of them both at the same time. Everyone except Johnny, who was now leaning against a wall, his dark blue eyes veiled. And Julian, who, in a rare moment when no one wanted his attention, was looking at Johnny in a very thoughtful way. I went over to him and he dragged his gaze away.

'Sorry, am I disturbing you?' I said, aware that he was now my boss.

'I was wondering . . .' he said, vaguely, then shook

his head, as if to clear it. 'Well, how did your first day go?' he said, linking his arm through mine.

'Terrifying,' I said honestly.

'Well, you survived, didn't you, so that's a great start?'

'And what about you?' I said anxiously.

'Do you know, when I talked about everyone going on a journey, I thought I already knew my way clear and straight. But I think this project has still got some detours to make.'

'And is that a good thing?'

He laughed. 'Don't look so worried. Things never entirely turn out the way you plan them and that's usually a good thing.'

By the time the tea party was over I was quite desperate for Anna to come home – I couldn't believe she had missed this – but Will had mentioned before everyone arrived that she had gone to the pub with Tony.

'She was driving home when she nearly ran into him. He was trudging down the road in a very dispirited sort of way – he should have been jogging – and when he asked if she wanted a drink she said she hardly dared refuse in case it drove him to the brink,' he explained.

To say I was surprised would be quite an understatement. 'Brink of what?'

'She didn't say. She imparted all this information on her mobile in a whisper from the ladies' loo. I didn't like to ask anything else.'

'Should I go and rescue her?' I asked.

Pa peered out from behind the paper. 'Why would she need rescuing? From what Will says, she didn't sound in any real distress.'

'Well, you know . . . Tony and all that . . .' I said doubtfully.

'Just because you don't want him,' he pointed out reasonably. 'Anyway, it's your turn to cook supper.'

I groaned. 'I never want to see food again.'

'Only because you ate three scones and four of those amazing cookies with cream in them,' said Johnny, coming back into the kitchen with his arms full of laundry. 'I saw these hanging up and it's starting to rain,' he said.

'Oh, I had forgotten all about the washing. Thank you,' said Ma, taking it from him. 'Don't go, Johnny. Aren't you going to stay for dinner?'

'I was just going to try and walk to the nearest pub. I thought maybe you'd want some peace,' he said, looking awkward and backing off, like he was used to not being wanted.

'Only from Lila, because she never shuts up,' said Will, grinning and moving up to make room for him so he had to sit down.

Ma made an enormous lasagne. She was hungry because she had been too nervous to eat scones, and Pa was hungry because he had been too busy talking, for once. 'My throat is actually quite sore,' he said, slightly astonished. Once I smelled the lasagne I was hungry again anyway and we had a riotous supper. Even Emma stuffed herself and then fell asleep instantly, like infants do, head down in the cold pasta. She didn't even stir when Will lifted her out of the high chair.

'Bedtime, I think. Crikey, Emma, you weigh a ton. I think you must have eaten your own body weight tonight,' Sophia tutted in admonishment, as she took her off to bed.

Emma had left Wol behind, so I picked it up off the floor before Bongo ate it, and took it upstairs. Wol was a knitted owl, a present from one of Ma's great-aunts, a knitting freak, who for some reason had decided to do it in yellow and green stripes. Sophia had had hysterics when she clapped eyes on it and tried to chuck it straight into the bin on the grounds that it didn't have a health and safety label. But Emma had already seen it and had given a shriek, the sort that when she got older, would mean, 'I need those shoes, now!' Will shoved Wol in his mouth and tried to pull bits off with his teeth, which made Emma shriek even harder, but he explained that if he couldn't pull a bit off and choke on it, then Emma and her two baby teeth certainly couldn't either. Sophia started to make noises about harmful dyes in the wool but when she saw how much Emma loved Wol, she knew she was defeated.

When I came back downstairs, Johnny had disappeared. His phone, which he'd left on the table, started ringing.

'He went that way,' said Pa, pointing outside. He was reading the paper again.

Johnny was standing looking at the stars.

'Your phone was ringing.'

'Thanks,' he said, putting it in his pocket without looking.

'It might be important.'

'It isn't,' he said firmly. 'Well, not as important as checking up on Orion.'

'What?' Then I looked to where he was pointing. 'Oh. Astronomy. Are you interested in it?'

'A bit. I used to do a bit of star-gazing with my grandfather.'

'I thought everyone did, in Hollywood.'

He laughed and I tried to imagine Johnny as a small boy, sitting out under the stars, cooking a fish that his grandfather, a grizzled and wise old man, had caught. Or maybe they had been hunting with a bow and –

'I said I was interested in astronomy to stop him drinking,' he said flatly. 'Dirk used to leave me with him, but he always dropped me off outside the trailer park. They didn't know he had a problem.'

OK – maybe not quite such an idyllic life then.

'But your stepfather – your brothers – why didn't you tell them? They would have been able to help and they certainly wouldn't have left you alone with him if they'd known!'

He shrugged. 'Yeah, I did tell them, eventually. But then I wasn't allowed to go back, which sucked.

He was all right, my grandfather, when he was sober and he was, most of the time. He just had bad episodes. I missed him after that.' He bit his lip and stared straight ahead.

We looked at each other. I didn't know what to say and wanted to reach out and give him a hug, but I wasn't entirely sure where hugs lay on my Four-point Plan so I hung back.

Then he yawned. 'Well, it's been a long day. I think I'll turn in.'

'Oh God, I've got to do all this again tomorrow!' I wailed.

'Oh, well, being an assistant is the first rung of the ladder in the acting industry.'

'Is it?'

'No, not really. Once a drudge, always a drudge!' he laughed. 'Good night.'

I went upstairs to my room and got into bed with Mr Wiggins with a weary sigh.

When I heard Anna coming up the stairs, I called out to her, 'Come here this instant, missy! Where have you been all this time?'

'Listening to Tony's woes while stuffing my face.' She leaned against the wall and dislodged a poster of Robbie Williams that had been there ever since I was a teenager. 'Oh dear, I am too full to bend down and pick it up.' She walked over and lay down on my bed and groaned. 'I have heard too much and have definitely eaten too much. I had garlic mushrooms to start, then steak and kidney pie with proper, home-made chips, and sticky toffee pudding for afters. I couldn't decide whether to have it with custard, cream or ice cream, so Tony ordered all three. Wasn't that nice of him?'

'Well, that's even more piggy than usual, even for you,' I laughed.

She pulled a face. 'I know, but I thought I should keep quiet while he got you out of his system.'

'Oh dear. What was he saying?' Just because I didn't love him any more, it didn't mean I wasn't interested in what he thought of me.

'Just that he was still sad,' said Anna, staring up at the ceiling. 'After dinner he was telling me about a team-building course he is taking, and I told him about one of my colleagues who keeps pestering me, and Tony told me exactly how to deal with him. I had a lovely time, actually.' She burped loudly. 'Anyway, give me the lowdown on Mitch.'

'Well, we did chat for a while . . .' I tried to recall what we had discussed but could only remember Johnny talking about all the things he wanted to see. 'I am sticking to my Plan,' I said firmly, 'and to be perfectly honest, he doesn't seem so irresistible now I've met him. But he really does look as good in real life as he does in his films,' I finished off.

Anna burped again. Then she got off, or rather rolled off, my bed and waddled over to the door. 'That's it – I simply have to go to bed. Night-night.'

When she had gone I picked up my favourite pencil and drew her as a bride in a fabulous meringue dress. I had done this for her several times already – she wanted to see what she would look like in various wedding dress styles. Just for a joke, I put Johnny next to her as a bridegroom. I smiled because they made a beautiful couple. OK, Johnny clearly had a number of issues, as Will would have put it, but who better to help him sort them out than my empathic and patient sister? Well, me, actually. The thought popped into my head entirely unbidden and I realised with horror that I had forgotten my Four-point Plan. I was just going to have to work on it until it became second nature, a sort of reflex action. Johnny and I were just friends, that was all, even if he was rather endearing.

Chapter Twelve

Johnny

I dreamed I was standing on stage. Just beyond the lights I could see the audience – rows and rows of them – all waiting for me to deliver my first line. There was a weight of expectation hanging over me. It felt so heavy I could hardly breathe under it. But what was my line? I opened my mouth to say something, anything. Everyone was staring at me. I was in a cold sweat of panic and my mouth was so dry I was incapable of uttering a word. And the silence grew louder and louder . . .

I came to into soft, velvety darkness with a sob of terror, and relief washed over me when I realised I was safe. I lay back on the lumpy pillow Lila had lent me. I hated that stage, but I yearned for it at the same time and as the fear from my nightmare receded, the emptiness grew.

I sat up, rubbed my eyes and cursed quietly. It didn't matter what time it was, I knew there was no way I would be able to go back to sleep. I got up, pulled some clothes on and crept noiselessly through the silent house to the warm kitchen.

It was a little after four and getting light. I wasn't too surprised to find Mrs Barton already up and about. She'd been getting up earlier and earlier since the production started. I wondered if she too had dreams bad enough to chase her from sleep.

She smiled at me and nodded to where the kettle was bubbling away on the stove. I loved everything about England, but I couldn't get used to this family's habit of drinking pallid, weak tea when any sensible person knew that what you needed in the morning was a gallon of really strong coffee.

We had our first drink of the day in companionable silence and then when we'd poured the second cup, we started a conversation. Actually, I tried to get her to tell me stories about living here. I couldn't get enough of them. Everything about the Bartons' way of life seemed fascinating to me.

Several hours later found Mrs B telling me about getting snowed in a few winters ago. Of course, it snows at our place in Wyoming, but we don't have to creep around with candles when it does. It's just normal life with snow.

'We were completely blocked in for a week in the end and neither Will nor Anna could get any signals on their phones so they couldn't get in touch with work. Lila said Will's patients would just have to stay mad for a few more days then, so he locked her in the attic – not her bedroom – the one with all the junk. When he let her out she was wearing some absolutely ancient clothes she'd found in a trunk. She looked like something out of a Victorian melodrama. Then we played charades all evening. Well, we weren't very good. Poor Will had a bit of a tantrum when, after three-quarters of an hour, nobody could guess he was doing *War and Peace*. Actually, Lila said later she knew what it was immediately, because she'd seen him reading it, but she decided to pay him back for locking her in.'

I sighed enviously. It all sounded like so much fun.

We had moved on to toast and jam, and the birds were singing furiously when Anna walked in. She was wearing a smart black suit and her hair was pulled back from her face in a very severe style. She looked good, but slightly uneasy, like she was dressed up to play a role for which she had forgotten the lines. She sat down at the table and one of her earrings fell into the butter dish.

'You look very . . . er . . . efficient,' I said, removing it and handing it back to her.

'Oh? Where did that come from? Yes, dull but efficient was the look I was going for,' she said, pleased. 'I'm going to a conference today. It will be full of men in shiny suits. They will talk about projections, and leer.'

'I could come with you as your bodyguard,' I offered, and turned into one of those faceless people that hover round the president. I got up and stood behind her, ultra casual, muttering into my cuff, and she laughed.

Will came down with Emma and Sophia. I sat down and started reading Emma a story about a dog called Spot. She kept laughing and pointing at Bongo. Then Lila walked in, clutching her face in a rather melodramatic way.

'Oh, no! It isn't –' began Mrs B, looking upset.

'Oh, Lila!' cried Anna. She looked ready to burst into tears of sympathy. I was mystified.

Lila nodded and sat down at the table. 'Yes, it's my wisdom tooth again,' she said out of the corner of her mouth.

'Oh, Lila, how awful! And there's no way I can go with you to the dentist today!' said Anna.

'If you need to see a dentist I could go with you,' I offered. Mitch had thrown his script at me last night and told me to fuck off, so I decided I would. I intended to stay well away from him until he had relearned how to be polite. I had nothing else to do today but watch people acting parts that I knew I could do much better myself.

Lila tried to smile at me. She got up and tottered to the sofa. I thought she was way over-acting but now probably wasn't a good time to tell her that.

'You have a problem with the dentist?' I ventured, and Will groaned.

'Yes, you could say that she does have a bit of a phobia,' he agreed.

Lila came back to life. 'That's not fair, or accurate,'

she managed to mumble. 'A phobia is an unreasonable fear of something, isn't it? Well, my terror of dentists is perfectly reasonable, given the circumstances.'

'And they are?' I asked, intrigued.

'Post-traumatic stress,' said Anna, grimly. 'You see, Pa's uncle had this friend who was a dentist and he always did our check-ups for free.'

'Which we all thought was very kind of him,' put in Mrs B.

'He certainly meant well,' agreed Will. 'Unfortunately, soon after he started treating us his life took a downward spiral: his wife ran off with the bank manager. Mr Hudson took to consoling himself with gin.'

'Yes, even at nine thirty in the morning!' said Lila. 'I was in there, having a filling, and he passed out. He dropped the drill and it very nearly took my eye out! I have had a horror of dentists ever since.'

'I don't know about having a horror – you certainly have hysterics,' said Will disapprovingly. 'The last time you went with Anna you gripped her hand so tightly you drew blood.'

'I still have two tiny scars,' said Anna, rather proudly.

'Well, I am up to date on all my shots and I've got nothing else to do,' I offered.

'It is a far, far better thing you do, you poor sap, than any of us would be prepared to,' said Will.

'Yes, you are positively heroic, isn't he, Lila?' said Anna.

'Yes, whatever. It's me that actually has to sit in the chair and relive the nightmare!'

Everyone went their respective ways. Will and Anna sped off in their cars and when I went outside I found I had been left with the family car. Apparently, in England, people call their old cars bangers. Personally, I would have just called this one a piece of crap. It was so old and decrepit I had to walk round it to check it still had four wheels. With a flourish I opened the passenger door to let Lila in. She huddled in her seat, deathly pale – even paler than was usual for her. I got in behind the wheel and turned the key, really with more hope than expectation. Nothing. I tried again. On the fifth go, it was making a noise, but we still weren't going anywhere. I was about to give up when Lila's father ambled out.

'Don't worry, it always does this at first. If you could just, er, hop out and go round the back and on my signal give it just a small push. That should probably do the trick.'

I got out and braced myself against the car. Flakes of rust came off and stuck to my jumper. I hoped this wasn't going to take long since it had started to rain and every so often a really annoying little gust of wind would blow the rainy rust flakes right in my face. The car made its reluctant groaning sound again, Mr B called out and I pushed. Nothing happened, so I pushed harder and it suddenly surged forward, unfortunately without me. I ended up face down in a mixture of mud and gravel. It was at this moment, in a perfect piece of timing – for him, anyway – that Mitch swung round the bend in his car.

Lila wound the window down and was looking round at me in a concerned way, but then her head swivelled back towards Mitch. At that moment the depth of my dislike for him surprised even me.

'What are you doing down there, Johnny?' Without waiting for an answer, because he was only pretending to care, he turned to Lila. 'Hi, Laura! You're obviously having trouble there! How about I give you a lift? I was just taking the car out for a spin,' he said amiably.

'Her name is Lila,' I said, through gritted teeth.

'Johnny was taking me to the dentist, but the car won't start,' she explained.

'Oh, you poor thing,' Mitch purred, slipping easily into caring mode. 'Look, I can take you, if you promise to show me round the area afterwards. I have a couple of hours off and really want to soak myself in this fabulous countryside – you know, get a feel for the place that Shakespeare was writing about. It would be a real favour,' and he smiled winningly.

I scrabbled back to my feet and started brushing bits of the Bartons' drive off me, head bent so they wouldn't see my face. Mitch could only do two roles, caring or brave, but he did them both brilliantly. Lila got into Mitch's car. She even managed a wonky smile before they drove off, without a backwards look.

Perhaps I had read her all wrong. She really was just the same as every other girl.

Chapter Thirteen

Lila

Carefully, so that Mitch didn't notice, I pinched myself hard. It was probably a good thing I had toothache, otherwise I'd be grinning hugely, like a complete idiot. This was a story to dine out on for the rest of my life. I hoped my mobile phone was well charged because I was going to be making a lot of calls tonight.

'Oh, hi,' I would say to one of my friends, deceptively casual. 'No, I haven't been up to much, had toothache; Mitch Clayton took me to the dentist, yes, Mitch Clayton the Hollywood heart-throb.' I felt like I had already moved up in the world and my imagination was spinning off into over-drive. No longer was I just a lowly assistant, I was now the girlfr –

Somewhere in my head a set of imaginary brakes started squealing. I couldn't believe I had just thought of myself, even in a fantasy, as someone's girlfriend. How long before the forbidden word fiancée followed? Maybe I should start carrying my Four-point Plan around written down for me wherever I went, to consult in times of need? I am not getting engaged to anyone for at least a year I said, over and over again. That was better. My head cleared and I felt calm. So what if Mitch was a film star – he was just a man. I stole a quick glance – OK, an incredibly fit man, so hot, in fact, that I could feel my cheeks going red.

His head turned and he threw over a swift but penetrating glance. 'How're you doing?'

'Fine, thanks,' I croaked, and could feel my blush going deeper. Pull yourself together, I said sternly. OK, so I was resolutely single. But that needn't stop me becoming Mitch's new best friend. How fantastic would that be? I picked up an imaginary phone. 'Yes, Mitch and I are really good mates. I am going to LA next week, just to hang out,' I could hear myself saying airily. Yes, that would still be amazing, but perfectly safe and my Plan would stay intact.

'Er, the dentist is just round this corner, thanks.'

I was going to have to come up with some better lines than that, I mused as I positively flung myself into the dentist's chair.

'Hmm, I think we are going to have to think about removing this troublesome tooth if this happens again,' began the dentist as gently as he could. He knew all about my problem.

'Yeah, whatever,' I said impatiently, and he blinked, startled. Usually, there was a ten-minute wait while he tried to coax open my mouth. But I was so excited at the thought of becoming Mitch Clayton's new best friend, I was practically handing him the instruments. He fiddled around for what seemed like ages while my fingers drummed an impatient tattoo on the armrest. Finally he was finished.

'I wouldn't eat for a couple of hours,' he warned me, but I was already halfway out of the door.

'OK, painkillers – prescription – another appointment for next month – got that – marvellous, thanks – see you soon!'

I ran into the loo. I had a sneaking suspicion that even though I only planned to be a 'friend' I was going to have to look my best. I sniffed. The room smelled of dental disinfectant; I hoped it wasn't going to permeate my clothes. I stared hard in the mirror. Did my face look weirdly lopsided or was it my imagination? I scrabbled around in my bag – oh, why hadn't I known when I left the house that I was going to need one or two essential aids to beauty? My hand closed round something disgustingly soft and crumbly and I yelped with fright. It was a rusk. Of course – I had given Emma my bag to play with the other day. She adored rootling around in it and it had deflected an approaching tantrum. Please God, I will do anything, but please let there be a lip gloss somewhere, and obviously I know you are busy, but if you wouldn't mind, while you're at it, some mascara and a bit of scent wouldn't go amiss.

I knew a hairbrush was too much to ask for so I didn't even bother. I ran my hands through my hair to flatten it down, gave myself a quick spritz with something that had come free with a magazine – hmm, not really much better than the disinfectant, but it would have to do now – and tried to sashay out like a film star's friend would.

'OK, I've been thinking,' I began, determined to suggest some civilised sightseeing, despite my numb mouth. 'There are some very nice stately homes – proper ones, not like ours – or a cathedral not too far away. There's a very good museum of Kentish history in the next town, or, if you don't mind the drive, a really fabulous ruined castle with a moat and dungeons.'

He stared at me blankly, like I had suggested a day out in a sewer. 'I was thinking about lunch,' he said. 'You know, somewhere quiet and peaceful, where we can have a good talk and get to know each other better,' he added, looking deep into my eyes. My heart did a triple flip. I invoked the Plan. This was a bit like that time Will had given up smoking. Every time he felt the urge, he popped a piece of chewing gum into his mouth. Eventually, he lost the craving and didn't even need the gum. Eventually it would be like that for me and staying unengaged, but now it was only early days, I consoled myself.

We drove out of town, into the countryside and pulled up outside a gorgeous little pub with flowers adorning every windowsill and a dog asleep in the porch. But Mitch didn't like it, for some reason. So we drove on. Then we found another with a river and a garden at the back, but he didn't like that either. Finally we stopped outside the Olde Oake, which was a lie because there were no oaks any more, no trees of any sort. They'd pulled them all down to make room for a massive car park on which three coaches and an assortment of vehicles were parked. I had been inside once before. It was full of fake beams and plastic flowers, and had a fake log fire at one end. The food called itself 'homestyle' but was actually bought in frozen and reheated in a microwave.

Mitch looked round in satisfaction at the crowded car park. 'This looks great.'

'Does it?' I said doubtfully. At least I hope I said that. My mouth was so numb from the dentist, I wasn't sure what I was saying, or, hellish thought, dribbling. I was certainly in no condition to argue, so we got out of the car and went inside.

The place was packed. Almost every table was occupied. Everyone looked up and of course they recognised Mitch. I suddenly realised that I hadn't thought this 'best friend' thing through very well. I hate being stared at. I had to get up in assembly once and describe a picture I had painted. I stood there in silence for what felt like hours, with my jaw clenched and my knees turning to jelly. When I did manage to speak, it came out as a high-pitched squeak, like an animal in pain. Afterwards I had to go to the first-aid room for a lie-down. Mitch, on the other hand, looked pleased at the sight of all these people.

'Just going to the loo,' I said, but he wasn't listening. He was gazing happily at the excited crowd. In fact, I don't think he noticed I'd gone. In the ladies, I stood in front of the mirror and practised talking. 'The rain in Spain falls mainly into Barton Willow,' I intoned. A woman cleaning the loos stared at me. 'A film star's just walked in,' I informed her and she scurried off to have a look, leaving me in peace. I tried all the vowels and although I couldn't feel myself saying them, they sounded and looked OK and they came out without dribbling.

Back in the bar, Mitch was sitting at a table surrounded by three waitresses and a queue of people wanting his autograph. I went to the bar and ordered a beer and an orange juice from the barmaid, who served me, took my money and gave me the wrong change without even looking at me. She was too busy drooling over Mitch. I was about to tell her she had given me change for a twenty-pound note when I had only given her a tenner, but she had already whipped her phone out and was gabbling into it. 'You'll never guess who's just walked in!' I left her to it.

'Get to the back of the line,' said someone shrilly as I edged past, a drink in each hand.

'I am with him,' I said, equally shrilly, and she looked amazed. I sat down, with difficulty.

'Yes, I'm over here for a while. I'm just loving being in your beautiful country,' Mitch was saying, signing autographs at speed and giving everyone the same intense look he had given me.

'Is this your girlfriend?' someone asked, looking at me disbelievingly.

'Liz's just a friend, unfortunately,' said Mitch, pressing my hand warmly and stroking a finger. My heart flipped again, but I invoked the Plan and it settled down, grumbling.

Eventually the waitresses shooed everyone away, but only so they could have Mitch to themselves. I didn't think it needed three of them to take down a simple order for burger and chips.

Damn, I couldn't eat for at least another hour. 'I'm not having anything,' I said.

'I think Lydia is on a diet,' Mitch told the waitress with a grin.

I tried to remind him who I was, but he wasn't listening because one of the waitresses was thrusting the menu and her breasts into his face. 'We've got a very large range of toppings to go on your burger,' she said.

'You never told us that,' complained an elderly couple at the next table.

At last the waitresses took themselves off and left us in peace, sort of, though I could feel their stares like a hail of bullets on my back. It was horrible. I would hate to be famous. Mitch smiled at me. I smiled back, a bit distractedly, and cast around feverishly in my mind for something to say. I couldn't commiserate with him about the fame thing because he clearly loved every minute of it. What else would he want to talk about? The play? No, he was probably still studying his role, thinking about it and having long talks with Julian about his motivation. He wouldn't want to be pumped for gossip about Hollywood – that would be in bad taste and definitely not the sort of thing a best friend would do. What hobbies did he have? Surely one of the articles I had read would have mentioned his interests?

'So, how are you liking England?' I said lamely.

But it didn't matter. I was rewarded by another of those intense warm looks. Was it my imagination, or did he just bring them out whatever the occasion?

'I think England's great!' said Mitch, fixing me with his eyes and then darting a quick look round the room. 'Everyone is so cool and, you know, relaxed here. You folks are so good at, you know, keeping it real.'

Were we? And how could one keep it any other way?

'So, are you hoping to get a career in the film industry after this?' he asked.

'Oh, no!' I laughed. 'I'm just doing this to help Julian out – and stay out of trouble,' I added quietly to myself.

'So what's your career plan then?'

I was flummoxed. 'I don't think I've got one,' I said at last, and he looked shocked. 'I'm trying a few things out. I haven't settled on anything yet,' I explained hastily, but I could see he wasn't impressed.

'Back home we'd think you were completely washed up if you weren't successful in your career by the time you were thirty,' he explained. 'It's all about being focused and driven, you know? I knew I had to earn as much as Clooney by the time I was thirty or I wasn't gonna make it. You've got to have goals in your life.'

I looked down. I had torn the back off a beer mat and was doing a quick sketch of an old woman at the bar. She had a raddled but interesting face. 'I don't know about goals, but I do have a dream,' I murmured, but he wasn't listening.

'My father and I put together a career plan when I was seventeen and we've stuck to it since,' said Mitch.

'Pa and I put together a greenhouse when I was seventeen. We were going to grow tomatoes and sell them, but it blew down in a gale,' I reminisced. Mitch stared at me blankly.

Food arrived. The chef sidled out. 'Man, this looks great!' said Mitch. 'Sure, you can have a picture!' He stood up and put an arm round two of the waitresses and smiled at the cameras. He really was very nice, I thought. He was so patient and obliging with his fans.

'I think this has gone cold,' I said, looking down at the chips after everyone had gone.

'I wasn't going to eat it anyway: too many carbs,' said Mitch dismissively.

So what the hell are we doing here? I thought sulkily. Because of my sore mouth I couldn't eat anything, even if I had wanted to. I wasn't enjoying being the subject of so many stares and whispered conversations. I was bored and I wanted to go home. I put my hand over my mouth in horror. Bored? In the company of Mitch Clayton, the most lusted-after man on the planet? Here I was, with the biggest celebrity in the whole world, and I was actually having to stifle a yawn.

'What do you do when you're not working?' I said, desperate to keep some conversation flowing if neither of us was going to eat.

Mitch looked thoughtful. 'Well, Lindy, I usually get up at about six and go for a swim,' he began.

A day in the life of a film star. Concentrate, Lila, you will be able to tell your grandchildren about this. Even if he has got your name wrong again. Best friend? Pah!

'I'll have an early breakfast, usually cereal and fruit, and then have a session with my trainer . . .'

'How interesting.' Try and look interested, Lila. Nod your head or something.

'. . . at least a two-hour session, including weights and ten miles on the treadmill. Then I'd do another session in the pool.'

This place would look a lot better if they painted it white and got rid of these horribly uncomfortable seats.

'. . . some kind of protein, with vegetables for lunch . . .'

I know what I haven't done for ages – dyed my hair! I could go purple this time, perhaps.

'. . . meet with my agent . . .'

Maybe I should go veggie this week – have a bit of a health kick. No, I didn't want to miss one of Ma's roasts.

'. . . teeth whitened . . .'

I hadn't been this bored since the day I'd waited at the bus stop for two hours because I'd forgotten the timetable had changed.

Then his phone rang.

'Sorry, but I have to take this,' he said, in exactly the same drawl he had used in *Family*.

I busied myself putting sauces on the burger he wasn't going to eat so he would know I wasn't listening in, though it was impossible not to hear snatches.

Mitch's face darkened as he listened. 'Goddammit! No, how the hell was I supposed to know that would happen! How much is it gonna cost to keep this under wraps? Well, sure it's worth it!'

My gossip radar flicked into action. Something was going on here and it sounded interesting, I thought, absent-mindedly adding relish and mustard and mayo to a rather wizened burger.

He clicked the phone shut. 'Sorry about that. Women trouble,' and he grinned at me wryly.

'Oh dear,' I said politely.

'You have no idea how hard it is always being in the public eye,' he said. He began telling me about how women were always pestering him. People always wanted a piece of him and sometimes it felt like there just wasn't enough of him to go round. He glanced down complacently at his perfect abs as he said this. Really, the only time he ever got any privacy was doing laps in the pool.

'People don't understand the pressure I'm under, never having any "me" time. Of course I'm not complaining. Being famous is part of my destiny,' he said, a solemn expression on his big, handsome, stupid face.

All I had to do was nod and smile in an understanding way. I nodded so hard my head nearly fell off, and smiled until I remembered only one side of my mouth was working. This reminded me that he had never once asked how I was. I made a little tower of tomato and cucumber slices and wondered what Johnny was doing.

Chapter Fourteen

Johnny

Mr B got out of the car. He scratched his head in a puzzled way.

'Oh dear. How did that happen? I thought Lila was going with you? I am sorry, that was very discourteous of her.'

'It's OK. It's the Mitch Clayton effect. I see it all the time,' I said gloomily.

I could tell he didn't understand this, so when he said, 'Shall I put the kettle on?' I nodded politely. After all, it wasn't his fault. When he had gone in I vented my frustration that Lila was as bad as the rest of them (women, I mean) by kicking the damned car, which was probably a mistake, because something fell off it. I was totally wet and miserable by now, so I didn't really mind lying on the ground and peering underneath to see if I could put the bit back.

Will returned. 'Oh, hello? What happened?'

'Nothing,' I said bitterly. 'We were busy going

nowhere, but luckily Mitch swept up and offered Lila a lift. His car never lets him down.'

'Ungrateful woman, my sister. I thought she'd sworn off men,' he said. The sympathy in his voice made me feel a bit better. 'Anything I can do?'

'Well, you could bring me a toolbox, if you've got one.'

He returned a couple of minutes later, his arms full. 'I found this oil cloth for you to lie on. It'll stop you getting, well, wetter, I suppose. You know you don't have to do this.' He looked up at the house and sighed. 'You start off doing the odd job and suddenly you are a Canute – up to your knees in the brine and the waves are rising. One day we will look up and there will be a tidal wave on the horizon and we'll all have to run for our lives.'

'Yeah, but until then . . . Anyway, I like lost causes,' I said stubbornly.

'Do you?' he asked in a vague sort of a way, and ambled off.

I thought about this. Of course he was right. I didn't really enjoy lost causes. I just always seemed to want things I couldn't have, for example, an acting career and now Lila. I seemed inadvertently to have developed a crush on her, even though I knew I didn't stand a chance, with Mitch being around. Barton Willow had seduced me but it didn't look like Lila was going to, unfortunately. What was Mitch playing at? She just wasn't his type, but maybe she did seem just the tiniest bit disinterested, I thought hopefully. Maybe *he* just wanted what he thought he couldn't have. Mitch liked cute Californian blondes. Lila was tall and dark and pale, like a lily at night, I decided, and rootled around in the toolbox for a spanner.

There was the sound of another car pulling up. I could hear someone get out and knock on the door.

'Why, Tony! How . . . er, lovely to see you!' said Mrs Barton, obviously perplexed but polite as always.

'Anna and I passed each other in the lane. She was having a bit of a panic because she suddenly thought the car might not start or, if it did, the brakes would fail and then Lila would end up in an awful crash and then miss her dentist's appointment. Or something like that. She was a bit garbled, but quite distressed, so I came along to see if I could lend a hand.'

Tony had a deep, pleasant-sounding voice. So this was Lila's ex-fiancé. He wasn't what I had been expecting.

'Well, the car didn't start at all, but she managed to get a lift with someone else. How kind of you to come and check, given the circumstances,' said Mrs Barton warmly.

'I didn't like the thought of either of your girls getting stranded somewhere. I've got the day off, nothing planned. Thought I would pop along, see if I could fix things – it – the car, I mean,' he added hurriedly.

'One of our American friends, Johnny, is doing the same thing, but I am sure he'd be glad of a hand.'

'How do you do?' said Tony, bouncing over and giving me his strong, dependable hand to shake. I stood up and offered mine, curious to find out more. This morning, Mrs B had filled me in on Lila and Anna's love lives. I think worrying about them both was what woke her up so early in the first place and she needed to vent. It turned out that Lila had far too many men, and Anna, not nearly enough. This Tony guy was the latest of Lila's beaux and he seemed like a regular guy.

'Well, I'll leave you to it,' said Mrs B, a bit doubtfully.

'So what's the problem?' asked Tony, sounding like he was in for a real treat. I eyed him beadily. I lived in LA so I was used to forced enthusiasm, but hell, we were standing in the rain, trying to mend a crappy old car. What was there to get excited about?

Tony dived into his car and pulled out a watertight jacket and trousers, which he put on. Then he lifted a huge toolbox onto the bonnet as easily as if it weighed nothing. I could tell he worked out a lot. Maybe that was the sort of guy Lila went for. He was quite similar in build to Mitch. I sighed. No wonder Mitch got all the girls. I had gone into our gym at home once, but got so bored I almost fell asleep on the exercise bike. In build I was probably closer to Johnny Depp than Daniel Craig. Maybe all women preferred muscles to intellect? Instead of reading obscure Greek plays, I should have been using weights; instead of Pinter I should have been thinking of my pectorals; built up my biceps rather than my knowledge of Beckett.

Tony walked round the car like a doctor doing his rounds. 'Hmm, tyre pressures certainly need checking. Goodness knows what the spare one looks like, eh, Johnny? And I wouldn't like to put money on anyone knowing what the oil level in the engines is like, would you?'

'Actually, I do and it's fine. It was the first thing I looked at,' I said, lying through gritted teeth. I knew he was trying to be helpful but there was something about his manner that was starting to grate on me.

'Marvellous! Well done!'

Oh dear. I could just tell he was going to spend all morning being hearty.

'Well, I suppose it's time to get dirty.' He rubbed his hands as if he was in for a real treat. He really needed to get out more.

'Be my guest,' I said politely. Tony's toolbox was immaculately organised. Everything was where you would expect it to be and in pristine condition. There was even a packet of wipes for cleaning up afterwards. My lips curled in scorn, but I pinched one anyway.

'Yes, I see the problem. If you could just pass me the – oh, you have – excellent. Right, won't be a mo!'

'Be as many mos as you like,' I muttered. I wasn't in any hurry for him to emerge from under the bonnet and start up another conversation, though it would have taken my mind off worrying about what Mitch was up to.

Unfortunately, it took him only a minute. Then I cheered up. That would mean he would have a quick cup of tea and be gone.

'Now, I really think we should bleed the car brakes, just to be on the safe side. Anna seemed particularly concerned about that.'

'I was going to ask Will to do that later,' I said firmly, but there was no stopping this insanely driven Good Samaritan.

'Why bother him? He's busy writing his thesis, you know, and we are already out here with the car. I don't believe in hesitation or procrastination.' He laughed heartily. I wished he wouldn't. He was starting to drain all the energy out of me. 'Now, I'm sure you won't mind acting as my assistant?'

What are you, a goddamned magic act? I thought to myself, unkindly, because I knew he meant well.

Tony got up and went over to the toolbox. 'So, you are with this acting lot then?'

'Yeah, sort of, I just came along for the ride,' I said without thinking.

He darted me a sharp look. 'It must be nice to have the opportunity to do that,' he remarked.

I opened my mouth to say something, and then I shut it again. Probably everyone thought I was tagging along because I didn't have anything better, or more important, to do – and whose fault was that? Mine. I didn't go round telling the world that I had to be the brains to Mitch's brawn because he couldn't help it if he was a dumbass. I also couldn't explain how ultimately I had no choice in the matter. Dirk told me to come, so I came.

'I never seem to have time to go to plays. I suppose you're really into it, aren't you?'

'You'll be really into it if you step one inch to the left. Oh dear, you have!' I commented.

'Bother! Oh well, I'll just have to remember to take my shoes off before I go inside.'

'So, you're not rushing off then?'

'No, thought I should stay for a bit – show there's no hard feelings, that sort of thing. I . . . um . . . well, Lila and I were an item for a while, you know,' he confided, looking forlorn.

'I'm sorry,' I said gently.

'Still, I suppose it's for the best, you know.' He stared morosely at a spanner. 'I must be a complete chump but I didn't realise anything was wrong until she said it was over.'

'Women can be very puzzling,' I said helpfully.

He seized on this like it was the most profound thing he'd ever heard. 'Yes! They never tell you what's wrong until it's too late to fix it!'

I smiled to myself. Clearly Tony was the sort of man who thought anything was fixable. He was completely at a loss when faced with something that wasn't.

'Right. Here's the brake-bleeding kit. I always carry one, just in case.'

Sure he did. He was the sort that would always carry a knife for getting the stones out of horses' hoofs, a torch in case of a blackout, a roll of bandages in case of emergencies . . .

'We'll start at the back, shall we? OK. Now, what I want you to do is to jump in and pump the brake three times and then hold the pedal down firmly. Got that?'

Well, I wasn't an idiot, so I nodded to show that I had.

'Three times and then press on the pedal,' repeated Tony slowly, who clearly thought I was.

If he was going to repeat everything, this was going to take twice as long. I wanted to bang my head on the steering wheel in frustration, but I felt sure he would insist on taking me to hospital in case I had concussion.

'Now, I need to get the bleed-screw open, so, on my command, take your foot off the brake pedal, but don't do a thing until I say so.'

'OK,' I said resignedly.

I did as he said, but then we had to repeat the process. For each wheel. Including the spare. Tony probably had sex like this, methodically. He was bound to have a checklist: erogenous zones 1–4, tick. Passionate kissing – five minutes minimum, tick. Hand on thigh for at least two minutes before moving upwards, tick. Suddenly I felt quite mutinous. I was starting to get very fed up with always being obliging.

'Right. I think we're done. I say, I hope you don't mind if I just jump in and check these dratted brakes for myself, do you? Bit of a control freak, as I'm sure Will would describe me, but I do get quite concerned that these girls are safe when they go out and about.'

At last even Tony had to concede there wasn't anything else he could think of to check. 'Brilliant. Couldn't have done it without you,' I said heartily, shaking him by the hand again and trying to edge him towards the car. Surely Lila would be finished at the dentist by now? What was Mitch doing with her?

'I'll just pop in and say hello,' said Tony, edging back again and of course he remembered to leave his dirty boots by the door. We were just standing in the kitchen when Anna came in.

'Goodness! I wasn't expecting you for hours,' said Mrs Barton in alarm.

'Oh, the man who was doing the presentation this afternoon got food poisoning, so he cancelled and there wasn't anyone to replace him, so we all got to go early,' said Anna. 'What's for lunch? I'm starving. Why don't you both stay – there's enough, isn't there?' she added, meaning Tony and me, though she was looking at Tony as she spoke.

'It's stew and it will be ready in five minutes. There's more than enough,' said Mrs B, smiling at us.

'I need a bath, but I can take it later,' I said.

Tony shuffled his feet and looked awkward. 'I would love to stay, but Lila might come back and it would look odd, you know?'

'Oh, Lila's gone off for the day with a handsome film star. She won't be back for hours!' said Mrs Barton, and then clapped a hand over her mouth. 'Oh, Tony, that came out all wrong. I didn't mean . . . well, of course she wouldn't have found someone else already.' Then she stopped, confused.

'It's all right. I've got to go anyway. Nice to see you, and good to meet you, Johnny,' he said, giving my hand a hearty shake before leaving.

'Oh dear. I really put my foot in it there,' said Mrs B, putting plates on the table. I followed her with knives and forks.

'Where are you going?' she said, as Anna disappeared.

'Just to change my shoes.' Her voice sounded flat. When she came back, she had changed into tracksuit bottoms and a pair of slippers that looked like rabbits. 'Isn't Lila back yet?'

'She must have gone out for lunch with Mitch,' I said glumly.

'Oh, I'm so envious,' said Anna, helping to dish out beans. 'Lila's such a lucky person – she was bound to end up with Mitch,' she said, with a certain amount of pride. 'You've got to admit it, they do look good together. Lila just seems to attract men whether she wants to or not.' Then she clapped a hand over her mouth. 'Oh dear, the . . .' but the rest of the sentence was garbled.

Her parents looked like they were waiting for her to explain what she meant, but she didn't so we carried on eating lunch in silence. I brooded a bit on the unfairness of Mitch always getting nice women. He should really come with a warning sign, like on the freeway when they warn you there's ice ahead. With Mitch it could be something like, 'Warning! Danger of Heartbreak Ahead!'

After lunch, Anna and I helped clear up and then I went to get cleaned up.

There was a bathroom on my floor and one on the floor above, where Anna and Lila slept, but only one bath plug, I had discovered. Apparently we had to share it and the girls must have used it last. I went up to retrieve it. I was just about to go back down when there was a wail of anguish from Anna's room.

'Are you all right?' I said, running in.

'Oh yes. I just stubbed my toe on the bed.' She sat down on it and began rubbing her foot.

'Ouch,' I said in sympathy, sitting down next to her and removing two paperclips, which for some reason were stuck in her hair.

'Thank you. A whole box of them fell on my head this morning. I thought I'd got them all out,' she said, and sniffed.

'You're not sniffing over your sore toe, are you?'

'No. Oh, I'm all right really. I'm just a bit fed up.'

'Are you imagining Lila having fun without you?' I asked, but really it was me feeling left out.

'No, not at all. I'm thrilled for her.' There was a short silence. Then, 'Do you know, sometimes I feel like I'm invisible! Have you ever felt like that?'

'Yeah, once or twice,' I said drily.

'I mean, I don't feel invisible. But some people just don't seem to notice I'm there.'

'You're not talking about Mitch, are you?' I asked uneasily.

'Oh, no!' she assured me. 'I think he's lovely, of course. But he's someone to dream about when you go to the pictures. I think it might spoil it if I got to know him in real life. No offence.'

'None taken,' I assured her with a grin. 'So who's ignoring you then?'

'No one, really,' she said and then started going on about the awful irony of being Lila's sister, which didn't make any sense. But women often do that when they are venting some strong feelings. It's usually better to be patient and try to work it out later. 'You're so easy to talk to, Johnny. That's what Tony says about me.' She ground to a halt and suddenly I got the picture. 'The other night when Tony took me for supper, he went on and on about Lila.'

'Well, was that the only thing you talked about?'

Anna shook her head. 'No. Then we had a really nice chat. He wanted to know all about my job and he seemed really interested. I don't think he was just being polite.'

'Well, that's a good sign.'

'Yes. Now you mention it, we had to order fresh coffee because ours had gone cold while we were talking.'

It seemed to me that Tony and Anna were perfect for each other. Tony was strong and dependable, just the man to remove her heel from a grate or a splinter from a finger. He would love searching for a lost contact lens in her soup or the right glue to stick her handbag back together. Tony was born for the challenge of ensuring that Anna got through life unscathed. He just had to be made to see that.

'I reckon you have got to stop being so polite and obliging for a start,' I began, stifling the thought that I could have been talking about myself. 'Obviously, you've got to spend time with him whenever you can, so he can find out how great you are, but he's got to stop using you just to kick off about Lila,' I said.

'But how do I do that?' I could tell she was intrigued. This was encouraging.

'When he starts getting dreary about Lila, you've got to start looking polite but a bit bored at the same time – like this.' I showed her and she giggled.

'That's brilliant! But what do I do next?'

'Change the subject as soon as you can without it looking too obvious. Start talking about yourself.'

'But if I don't let him talk about Lila, he'll lose interest in me and leave.'

'Now, that's the sort of attitude that's bound to end in disaster! You are convincing yourself there's no hope for you before you've even begun. You've got to change your attitude from a hopeless one to a hopeful one. Visualise an outcome where things turn out how you want them to. That way you really increase your chance of success,' I said, getting into my stride.

'Yes, I see what you mean. I never realised that was the way I was looking at things. Well, it's worth a try. Thank you. How clever you are!' she said, looking at me admiringly.

I smiled at her, but inwardly I was cringing. Because, of course, these were exactly the sorts of things *I* should be doing. They applied as much to me as they did to Anna. In fact, I was guiltier than anyone of thinking that things would never get any better. I dragged my mind away from my own problems and concentrated on helping Anna.

'It might be a good idea if I flirted with you a little. Maybe Tony's gotten used to seeing you as Lila's sister. He needs to realise that you are an attractive and desirable woman.'

But where the hell were Lila and Mitch?

Chapter Fifteen

Lila

'Portable toilets,' said Cara briskly, handing me a list of addresses, then bustled off at a pace that was closer to a run than a walk. Everyone on The Dream Company, as they were known, walked like this. I barely had time to nod before she moved on to her next victim – sorry, job.

Toilets it was then. After all, I had promised Julian I would do anything, however menial. Why on earth had I promised that?

I went back to the house to use Will's laptop. At breakfast this morning he announced that the incessant noise of hammering from the stage carpenters was getting on his nerves, so he was going into town to the British Library, to spend a peaceful day in the company of Carl Jung. It then became clear how stressed we all were by the influx of people into our quiet lives, because Ma said, 'Well, please let me know well in advance if you are bringing this Carl person back for supper because I will have to get another chop out of the freezer,' and looked rather startled when we all laughed.

'Jung has been dead for a while now. I shall be reading about him, not chatting to him,' explained Will.

I had laughed, though it was a bit of an effort. When I finally got home from my monumentally boring 'date' with Mitch, it was to find Johnny and Anna in the kitchen, getting a crossword outrageously wrong. And laughing. And joking. This made me feel even more depressed.

The thing was, it was all too easy to stick to my organised and efficient Four-point Plan around Mitch, and it shouldn't have been. He was a film star – there should have been temptation. But there wasn't. I was about as tempted by him as you are by the prospect of an ice lolly on a freezing cold day in January. And to make things worse, my lack of interest in Mitch seemed to be spurring him on. 'We must do this again soon, Latoya,' he said when he dropped me off.

'Did you have a lovely time?' said Anna, as I sat down at the table.

'It was so dull I had to keep slapping my leg to stay awake,' I admitted.

Johnny and Anna looked surprised.

'You were bored?' Johnny said, as if he couldn't believe it. Suddenly he looked even more cheerful.

'Yes,' I said simply. 'We didn't have anything to talk about really. If you can't talk to each other, it's never going to work,' I finished off. Come to think of it, Tony and I had never really been able to talk much either, I thought as I plodded upstairs a bit gloomily.

I thought I would have cheered up the next day, but I didn't. Maybe this play was getting to me. It had seemed like such a brilliant idea at first, but I hadn't spotted the sting in the tail. As more and more people descended on Barton Willow and began sawing and banging and hammering and wandering round muttering blank verse under their breath, and playing music at all sorts of odd hours, I could see that Pa's face had taken on a haunted look. So, of course, Ma got anxious. And Will couldn't work in peace on his thesis, even though I knew he was getting up at four in the morning. Sophia said Emma wasn't getting her afternoon naps, and Anna – well, I didn't have a clue what was going on with her. We needed another late night sisterly chat. And Julian's forehead had developed an ever deepening crease.

I went into the kitchen for the laptop and stopped dead on the threshold. One of the Watson twins was sitting at our table, sobbing. Was she rehearsing? If she was, I wished she would go and do it somewhere else. The kitchen was one of the few places we had to ourselves at the moment.

'Er, can I help?' I began, thinking that the tears looked awfully real.

'It's all right, she's with me,' said a firm voice, and I wheeled round in astonishment. It was Pa and he was carrying one of the enormous white handkerchiefs he insisted on still using, even though everyone else had long gone on to paper tissues. 'Here, this is a proper hanky and much better for you. Those tissues are just sawdust, you know. Are you going to be long?'

I suddenly realised this was addressed to me. 'Um, well, I need Will's laptop, but I can take it somewhere else.'

'Oh my gosh, I don't want to disturb anyone,' said Paige. 'We can sit on the step, if that's all right?' Paige looked at Pa and he nodded. She smiled politely at me and went to get the teacups, her hair swinging perfectly.

I stopped goggling and started googling toilets. Pa made tea.

'Don't tell me – you won't take sugar because you are on a diet,' he said to Paige.

'Well, yes, but actually, I don't take dairy either,' she replied, with a ghost of a smile.

'Have you thought of the importance of a good toilet when planning your party?' boomed a voice from the Internet video site. Pa and Paige turned round in astonishment. I clicked it off hurriedly and mumbled, 'Sorry.'

They went outside with their tea. The fresh air would do Pa good, I thought – he hadn't been out for the last couple of days.

'Nowadays people expect the same high standard of toilet facilities that they get at home,' I read. That meant everyone that didn't live at Barton Willow then.

'Of course I know they are going to take pictures of me – it comes with the job,' I could hear Paige saying. I was really trying not to eavesdrop, but they had left the door open.

Did I want flushing no mains and hot hand washing? I wasn't sure, so I ticked yes to both, to be on the safe side.

'Being photographed all the time – well, it's like a dripping tap. You don't really notice it for ages and then suddenly it drives you crazy,' said Paige. 'I had had this really awful day and I walked outside the gates and about fifty flashbulbs went off and they started shouting questions at me all at once. It was like they were sticking red-hot needles into me. Oh, you must think I'm completely spoiled and ungrateful – or just crazy.'

'No, I don't. If it's any consolation, you are not the only one who feels like that. I feel like that nearly all the time about everyone, even people without cameras,' replied Pa, and Paige laughed.

'Do you want the ability to discharge into a main drain?' Absolutely. Timber or anti-vandal steel? Someone might possibly feel the urge to pen a Shakespearean couplet on the wall, I supposed, but I doubted it. The Poseidon was blue, but the Jupiter was bigger. The Juno, on the other hand, came in a wood-panelled cubicle with pictures on the walls, fresh flowers in little vases, a proper window with a blind and a CD player, with a choice of classical or easy-listening pop. I didn't want to rent it, I wanted to live in it. My hand hovered over the mouse, but then reality set in. More than four hundred people would have to use this little baby – she'd never take the strain. For the same price I could buy ten Minervas (fully skirted and chrome taps). Rather regretfully, I put in my order and while I was waiting for it to process, I drew a portable toilet coming to life and chasing Paige. I was giggling to myself when Pa came in and began washing mugs. Paige was going – I could see her hair swinging perfectly from side to side again as she walked away.

'So, have you made a new friend?' I asked.

'Yes, she's a nice girl. I asked her to lunch but she had to go and rehearse.'

'Fancy you hobnobbing with television stars!'

'To be honest, I didn't think of her like that,' said Pa vaguely.

'Well, I still think you made an odd couple. Talk about having nothing in common,' I said.

Pa turned round, smiling. 'Lila, I am surrounded in this house by women of all types. I can confidently say your gender is no longer a mystery to me.'

'Yes, I feel the same way about toilets now,' I said. While I had been talking, I was doodling. Now I looked down and squealed in horror. Next to the toilet sketch I had absent-mindedly drawn Mitch looking insuffer-ably smug and totally oblivious to the fact that I was sitting next to him fast asleep, with my mouth open. I tore it into little pieces before anyone could see it.

'What was that?'

I jumped. Johnny was beside me, hands in pockets. He was as quiet as a cat sometimes.

'Oh, nothing,' I said casually, looking down at my list of jobs, covered in doodles. 'I've got to go up to the wood to give one of the assistant stage managers a note about blocking. Do you want to come?'

'Yeah, sure.'

We went outside. Behind the wall, near the trailers, I could hear someone making the most awful wailing noises, like they'd got their finger stuck in the door or something. I clutched Johnny's arm. 'My God! What the hell has happened?'

'Nothing. It's just someone doing their vocal exercises,' he said calmly.

I steadied my breathing. I would really have to stop imagining a disaster round every corner, or I would be a wreck before the play began.

We walked up the woods. I found Liz, the ASM, and gave her the note.

'The brilliant thing about doing the play like this is that the actors have a real wood to work in,' said Johnny dreamily, looking round with pleasure.

'What is Liz doing?' I asked. She was on her hands and knees, like she had just dropped a contact lens.

'She's putting markers down so the actors know where to stand so they are completely in the spotlight,' he explained.

'You do know a lot about this sort of thing, don't you?' I said, glad he was around.

'Yeah, it's kind of a hobby of mine,' he said casually, but I suddenly sensed there was more to it than that, but that he didn't want to say any more.

'Whenever I come here it reminds me of Carl,' I said, to change the subject.

'And he is?'

'An ex-boyfriend. He was one of the bad boys at our school – a bit of a hellraiser. I was having a bad time with some of the other kids until he asked me out. My reputation soared. Unfortunately it had the opposite effect on my grades. We used to sneak out early and come up here and snog. He was such a good kisser, I didn't care I had just failed my exams.'

'So, how many boys have you kissed in these woods?' demanded Johnny, sternly.

I started to tick them off on my fingers and then stopped when Julian suddenly appeared through the trees. I bent my head and pretended to be busy looking at my list. I didn't want him to think I was fooling around when I should be working.

Julian nodded hello to Liz, who looked up and smiled briefly. I peeped up at him from under my lashes. Yes, there was definitely a new line on his forehead. I could feel myself growing cold at the thought of something going wrong with the production. It probably still wasn't too late for the company to pack their bags and find a proper theatre to act in. He turned to me. 'Sandwich, anyone? They're good,' he said, holding out a paper plate.

'What did Ma tell you about sitting down and having a proper lunch?' I said sternly. Honestly, how did he think he could do a proper day's work on an empty stomach? Then I went from cold to hot – I hadn't said that out loud, had I?

'She said that walking around with a plate of sandwiches wasn't nearly as nutritious as actually eating them,' he said, with a vague smile. Liz finished what she was doing and went off. Julian leaned against a tree in an abstracted way. I signalled to Johnny that we should leave him in peace. But he saw us going.

'No. Stay where you are. Seeing as you are here, I could use a couple of bodies,' he said.

'Where do you want us?' asked Johnny, obligingly.

Julian stared at the trees. He looked distracted. 'The problem is Puck,' he said, more to himself than us.

I was fairly sure Andy Sloan wasn't working out too well. I had happened to catch a few minutes of him rehearsing the other day, and even I, who knew nothing about plays, could tell he was a bit wooden. I looked hopefully at Johnny, willing him to say something helpful. He reminded me a bit of Julian, actually. They always had their noses in books and seemed to know quite a lot of poetry.

'Do me a favour, Lila, and be a fairy,' said Julian suddenly.

'What?' I squeaked in alarm.

'I have an idea about something and I need you to stand in during Puck's first scene, you know the one.

Johnny, you can be Puck, obviously. Now if you would be so kind as to go over there . . .'

I stood up stiffly and followed Johnny obediently, but I was sure my face was turning positively purple with panic. Obviously, as Julian's assistant, I existed only to follow orders, but not these ones, please. I should have realised when I woke up this morning that today was the day I would be exposed as a total idiot. There should have been a warning of some kind and then I could have pretended I had come down with something. Oh, how I yearned for my dear, safe bed!

'What's the matter? You look like you're having an awfully premature hot flush,' hissed Johnny.

I wished I was. Anything would be better than this torture. I wanted, with every fibre of my being, to be helpful. If Julian wanted me to stand on my head, I would do it. If he wanted me up a tree, I'd be up there in a flash. Though why he would ever want either of those things was beyond me. The point was, I would do anything to please him. There was just one tiny problem – anyone normal who found out that they had been given a job assisting on the production of a play would probably have prepared themselves for the whole experience by, um . . . well, reading it, probably. They wouldn't have contented themselves with a nodding acquaintance of the last half-hour of a film version that they had happened to catch one rainy Saturday afternoon several years before when they'd had nothing better to do. No, they would have made absolutely certain they had a comprehensive knowledge of the entire text. Goodness, they might even have gone in for a thorough revision of all the versions available in Folios One, Two and Three. With notes. And appendices. Especially people who had resolved to improve the *heat*-dominated quality of their reading matter.

But in my defence, I had been reading a lot recently. It just wasn't Shakespeare. It was *Movie Monthly* magazine, the one with the article about Mitch Clayton in a feature called 'Hot', and all those lovely photos of him with his shirt off. What this boiled down to was the painful reality that I hadn't actually read the blessed play at all. Ever. The contents of the script Julian had just handed me were as mysterious and impenetrable as an Amazonian rainforest might be to an Eskimo. It was horribly obvious to me now that I was bound to be exposed in all my ignorance. What a fool I was!

I stood there with the script in my hand and gulped. I would have to come clean. I would be sacked, of course, probably banished from the premises altogether, exposed, ridiculed, villified. I would have to move, to another country probably, change my name, dye my hair . . .

'I've got stage fright!' I blurted out the first thing that came into my head.

Johnny gave me a wry grin. 'Tell me about it. What you've got to do is breathe, in through the nose and out through the mouth,' he said, riffling through the pages. 'Here. Also, you only have one line.' His navy-blue eyes were looking at me anxiously and he gave my arm a reassuring squeeze. 'And don't worry. Julian just wants to move us around like pieces of scenery – he's not going to actually listen to us.'

Julian stood up. 'Yes, stand there, Lila. And Puck would enter from the left. How do you see him?' he asked Johnny.

'He'd be swaggering through the woods like he owned them. He's probably on an errand for Oberon, but he's easily distracted. He's quite hyperactive, I guess. As soon as he saw the fairy, he'd be up for a little flirting, anyway,' said Johnny instantly. I stared at him in astonishment. He had forgotten all about me and was talking like the character of Puck was a real person that he knew well.

'Yes, that makes sense . . . I can see that might work,' said Julian, thoughtfully. 'Show me what you mean.'

Johnny walked off a few paces, turned round and came back as a complete stranger. I was so taken aback by this I think I just stood there with my mouth open and forgot I had a line to say until Julian nudged me. But it didn't matter, he wasn't listening to me. I completely forgot about my pretend stage fright because I was so taken up with watching the scene. For a minute I forgot everything except this magical wood and this magical creature.

This Puck was a swaggering show-off and just a bit scary. He was a creature on the wrong side of every-thing – of reality, law, and morals; you would never know where you were with him. He was dangerously confident, but he made you shiver slightly. Actually, he was hot. Why had I never noticed that about Johnny before? I fanned myself with the script. Suddenly I imagined what it would be like to kiss Johnny. I fanned harder. Pull yourself together, I told myself crossly. You will never stick to the Plan if you behave so foolishly.

I was brought back to reality with a crunch when Julian said he wanted to go through another scene, and I had another panic about which scene he was talking about, but then he said he didn't need me.

Weak with relief at my reprieve, I sat down and said helpfully that I would be the audience. But they barely heard me. They were both engrossed, talking about the play and then acting bits of it. Johnny seemed to know it off by heart – oh, how I wished I did. But then I forgot about my ignorance, because it was so brilliant watching them together. If Johnny was this talented, why wasn't he doing it properly, as a professional?

'Yes, I like that, but why did you move away just then?' said Julian, and Johnny started explaining and I might as well have not been there. I didn't mind, though. I started drawing the two of them on the back of my copy of the script – the way they were standing, the way they were looking at each other. I couldn't explain it in words but I knew I could in pencil.

I was just finishing when the alarm on Johnny's watch began to beep. 'Oh, dammit. I've got to go and show

– I mean talk to Mitch about something. See you later!' and he darted off.

This would have been an excellent moment to make my exit as well, before Julian found out that I was a complete stranger to iambic pentameter. But I had a tremendous urge to interfere on Johnny's behalf.

'That was amazing! I didn't know Johnny could act. He was brilliant, wasn't he? Why on earth isn't he an actor?'

'Stage fright,' Julian said tersely.

I was stunned. And then I blushed with shame, remembering how I had pretended to have it. 'How bad is it that it's keeping him from something he's so good at?' I asked soberly. 'How long has he had it? Why hasn't anyone tried to cure it? Surely they could do something!'

'He is paralysed by it – literally,' said Julian gloomily. 'I talked to a friend of his recently. Stella told me that as soon as the spotlights go on, he becomes utterly unable to move or speak. It's like he's in a trance. If you say something to bring him out of it, he just stares at you, white-faced and shivering. And of course what makes it particularly awful is that, as you just saw, he can really act.'

I shivered in empathy, because I was imagining what it would be like if I suddenly found myself unable to move my pencil when I wanted to draw something. I might be a rubbish artist but at least I could keep on grafting away at it, whereas Johnny . . . Well, it was like the gods had given him this great gift and then snatched it away. 'Obviously Mitch has tried to help him, right?'

'Obviously,' agreed Julian non-committally. But then I remembered some of the things Johnny had told me about his childhood and I realised they probably hadn't tried to help him at all.

'He seems lonely sometimes, but it must be awful to lose your mother when you are still only a child,' I said. 'Did you ever meet her? What was she like?'

'Astonishing.'

'Was she beautiful?'

'No, not really. But when she laughed – and she did that a lot – she had a way of throwing her head back and half closing her eyes . . . Well, she was one of those people you always want to be around, because they seem to make life more fun.'

'I can imagine her riding bareback across the Californian plains, her black hair whipping out behind her,' I said dreamily.

'Now don't go all *Dances with Wolves* on me! The reality was that she lived on a trailer park and probably never rode anything but the bus until she met Dirk. Her childhood was just poor and tacky – a lifestyle of cheap burgers and clothes from K-Mart.'

'But she doesn't sound like Dirk's type at all,' I protested, recalling a picture of him with the beautiful, highly polished blonde who was his first wife.

'She wasn't. Johnny's mother was Dirk's mid-life crisis

marriage – every powerful man in Hollywood has to have one. And she was so sexy and sparky and fun. She might have started out as trailer trash but she was intensely alive, and that's a powerful aphrodisiac to a jaded and spoiled man like Dirk. He was so enchanted, he didn't mind that she already had a kid.'

'Wasn't there some talk that she was going to leave him, just before she died in that car crash?' I asked, a bit uneasily. I wasn't at all sure Johnny would like the thought of us talking like this but I was very curious.

'Things began going downhill for them as a couple after a few years. There were some quite spectacular fights. One party I went to, she saw him flirting with another woman and so she pushed him into the swimming pool. I remember once she said to me, "I would have married the devil himself to get out of that trailer park – actually, I think I have!" I knew at the time she wasn't joking. But Johnny was the reason she stayed. She wanted him to have the things she missed out on in her own childhood. And anyway, she wasn't a quitter. And Dirk was in pieces after she died. I think in his own way he really loved her.'

'What a mess people make of their lives.' I thought about Ma and how tough things were for her but how awful it would be if she wasn't still there for us. 'Johnny hasn't got over it, has he?'

'Every time Dirk looks at Johnny he is reminded of her. He deals with his grief and regret by taking it out on Johnny,' said Julian.

'Well, at least Johnny has his stepbrothers to look out for him.'

'Hmm, the trouble is, he's not like the rest of the family, who measure their success by their bank balance. Dirk used to tell this story at parties about Johnny at fifteen saying: "We've got enough money now. Why can't we just stop and do something more interesting instead?" Dirk said this was the dumbest thing he'd ever heard. The Claytons have the casual cruelty that comes from being insensitive and super-ficial. Underneath, Johnny is the toughest of them all because he's managed to survive all that.'

'I don't know why he doesn't just leave them to it!'

'Well, funnily enough, I think Johnny is the glue that holds that family together. He has this immense charm, which is all the more powerful because he is unaware of it and because it comes from him being a genuinely nice person. They may seem tough, those Claytons, and that's certainly the image they like to put about, but the moment anything goes wrong, they forget how badly they treat him and call on him for some emotional rescue.'

'You like Johnny, don't you?' I said curiously.

'Yes. There are many layers to him. He's quite a mystery. I don't know him that well, but I've heard loads about him from my friend Stella, and I like what I've seen thus far. Some woman is going to find him an enthralling challenge.'

Mitch was about as deep as clingfilm, I thought.

'Right. That's enough gossip for one day. I must be off. Are you going to leave those bits of paper there?'

'Certainly not!' I said indignantly. 'I was brought up to put rubbish into a bin, which is more than I can say for everyone round here at the moment. I found half a sausage roll and a banana skin in the urn at the bottom of the steps. I know the urn is hideously cracked but it is two hundred years old and –'

'Why are you going to put them in a bin?'

I looked down at the drawing rather doubtfully. 'It is just a scribble, though I suppose I might be able to improve it with a bit more work.'

'Do you really need to?' said Julian, rather obscurely, and he walked off briskly.

That evening, I marched up to bed with a sense of resolution, a piece of fruit cake and a copy of the play. I was going to read the damned thing if it took me all night. Skimming through the pages, I realised it probably would take all night, so I went back downstairs and filled a large Thermos full of coffee to keep me going. And maybe another, larger slice of cake? Or a cheese sandwich? Or a ham sandwich? Oh goodness, I was already trying to find other things to do and I hadn't even got past the first line! I swiped Will's laptop on the way past. If I managed to get through – sorry – read the whole play tonight, I could go on the Internet afterwards as a reward and look up pictures of Johnny's mum.

Back in bed, I plumped up the pillows, which was

difficult because they were so old, there wasn't much of the insides left to plump. I put on my dressing gown – no, too hot – and took it off. OK. Ready now. Act One, Scene One, line one . . . how many pages did I have to get through? I flipped over to the end and then something occurred to me. I got up again and went down to the library. There was a collected works of Shakespeare somewhere – yes, there it was. In this edition, the play was only twenty pages long, though obviously the print was a bit small. But twenty pages! Why, I could get through that easily! I took a thoughtful sip of coffee but it wasn't easy balancing such a heavy book on my knee at the same time as holding hot coffee. Right. List of characters. There was Johnny – or Puck, rather. I wriggled my toes in pleasure at the memory of how good he had been . . . how attractive he had looked when he gave that crooked smile . . . I could suddenly recall with intense clarity the way his dark blond hair curled into the back of his neck – hair that I wanted to put my fingers through before pulling his face towards mine and . . . I pulled myself together and returned to singledom reality. OK, focus. Athens, the palace of Theseus . . . I'd always wanted to go to Greece. I thought about going there with . . . oh, someone like Johnny, perhaps. We could live really cheaply; pitch up a tent on the beach or just go to sleep under the stars, snuggled together in a sleeping bag. It would be hot, so we wouldn't be wearing many clothes – in fact, we wouldn't need any . . . I shook my watch disbelievingly. It couldn't be half-past two already? I had been up here for hours, daydreaming about things I shouldn't, and I still hadn't got past the first page in any edition.

Then I had another idea, and this was one that would really work. I got up again and went back to the library. Somewhere on the bottom shelf I could distinctly recall seeing . . . yes, there it was! A rather tattered copy but intact. York Notes on Shakespeare's *A Midsummer Night's Dream*. And the synopsis was only half a page long! I read through it quickly. Duke – marriage – wood – lovers – magic potion – misunderstandings – happy ever after. There, I had done it. OK, maybe it wasn't quite enough to go on *Mastermind*, and I wasn't sure of the exact times characters came and went, but at least I now had a vague idea of what and who everyone would be talking about.

I went back to bed, delighted in my ability to problem-solve and was asleep before I could even switch the laptop off.

Chapter Sixteen

Johnny

I strode out of the woods and back down the hill, hands in pockets. Various people looked up from what they were doing to smile at me and I smiled back absent-mindedly. I was too busy thinking about what had just happened. That moment when Puck had sat down – that was all wrong. He should have been wandering around, touching things and darting quick looks over to Oberon. And his head should be tilted, like a bird perhaps, but definitely not like a human . . . Then I stopped dead. What a jerk I was. None of this was ever going to matter. I was never going to play Puck, was I? But then I had never, even in my wildest dreams, imagined that I would get to talk shop with the great Julian MacDonald.

'Where the hell have you been?' said Mitch irritably when I wandered into the trailer, stars still in my eyes. Then I was bumped back to reality. There was a woman with him, holding armfuls of clothes, but at least she was still wearing hers.

'Are you with Wardrobe?' I said curiously. I am a quick study and I thought I knew everyone who was working on this production. She giggled.

'No, this is Susan, she's from a shop in London. I called them up – I needed more shirts,' said Mitch impatiently. He flung his script at me. 'Come on! Let's get this over with.'

'I can wait for you to finish trying shirts on first,' I explained patiently.

'Finish? I haven't even started yet! I am going to multitask,' he said importantly.

'You are kidding, aren't you? It takes him all his time and concentration to single-task,' I remarked to the girl, but of course she wasn't listening. She was gazing at Mitch with adoration.

'Where art thou, proud Demetrius? Speak thou now,' said Mitch in a deep voice.

'Here, villain, drawn and ready,' I said, obediently, playing my part.

Mitch grabbed the script. 'Yeah, what the hell is this? I don't get it. Why does it say that Puck's speaking that line?'

'Because he's pretending to be Demetrius.'

'OK, OK, I see.' Mitch threw down the script and his shirt and took his time getting a new one from the girl, so she had ample opportunity to admire his washboard stomach. She also took her time, kneeling down to pick up the discarded one, so he could get a clear look down the front of her dress. I sighed and tried to recapture my good mood from talking to Julian. But Mitch had killed it. Then we wasted more time because he got distracted by his reflection and stood there preening himself, until I was so bored I started to nod off. I lay back on the sofa that was better and more expensive than anything the Bartons had in their home and recited a scene from *Hamlet* to try and keep awake. Mitch continued to try on shirts he didn't need.

'Which looks better, honey?'

'Oh, you look lovely in both of them, but better in nothing at all,' she sighed.

I sat up. 'Right. I think that is my cue to leave.'

'Sit tight, I'm nearly done,' said Mitch, and winked at the girl. 'Maybe you've got something there that might help my brother get a girl.'

'No, thanks. I've got to run!' I protested, but she had already zeroed in on me. She had probably figured out she could use me as an excuse to hang around a little longer.

'This is pure silk and is exactly the same colour as your eyes,' she began.

I took the shirt from her and counted to ten. 'OK, Susan, you can have Mitch all to yourself if you give us an hour, please.' I pushed her gently out through the door, shut it and leaned on it. 'What's your next line?' I asked sternly.

Mitch grinned. 'Well, it was going to be something like – why don't we have a drink to get us in the mood, darling, but she can't hear from out there!'

'Focus, Mitch,' I said, but I was thinking furiously. There had to be some way to get my idiot brother to concentrate. Then I got it. 'I hear Finn McGuigan is flying over to see this play,' I said casually, examining a nail.

Mitch stiffened. If Finn was on board for a future movie, it would be an even bigger success. Finn was one of the hottest directors in town just now.

'Still, if you can't be bothered . . .' I said, making out I was leaving.

'Siddown,' he said, suddenly businesslike and grabbing the script. 'OK, I've got it. I say – "I will be with thee straight."'

'He means, I'll be with you right away. He's angry – he wants to catch up with Demetrius and start a fight.'

'So, does he know it's Puck speaking?'

'No. He's under a spell.'

Mitch looked up, suspicious. 'You mean he's being tricked by those fucking fairies?'

'Yeah, in a nutshell,' I said cautiously.

'I'm not being made to look a complete dumbass and that's final,' said Mitch.

'What? The man who wrote this play has been dead for four hundred years.'

'Well, it's time for a rewrite then!' yelled Mitch.

'Nobody rewrites Shakespeare!' I yelled back, losing all patience. Oh God, why the hell was I here? This was going to be such a drag. I was going to have to work my butt off to make Mitch a success and for what? No one would know I had contributed anything to this play and even if I took credit where credit was due, who would believe me? I would be ridiculed or, worse, pitied. Suddenly I was sick to death of being a doormat. I stood up, ready to get the hell out of here. Then I remembered how it felt when I was with Julian today. And in my rapidly improving mood, I thought of Lila. Since her lunch with Mitch she'd seemed to be avoiding him. She did seem different from most girls. I started to feel less angry and more hopeful. Yeah, there were a few things worth staying here for, I thought.

'Everyone gets tricks played on them, even Cinnamon. She ends up falling in love with a donkey,' I pointed out to Mitch.

'Is that so?' he said, thoughtfully.

'Don't worry. As usual you get the girl in the end,' I said, smiling.

'Of course I do!' said Mitch. He sat down and looked like he meant business.

'Right, this is how we are going to do it. We are going through every one of your lines and I will show you how to say them. If you do it exactly the way I show you, you'll be brilliant, I swear,' I promised.

And he was.

Chapter Seventeen

Lila

'I'm looking for Lola,' said the man when Will answered the doorbell.

'What key do you want that in?' asked Will. 'Well, a phrase like that is just begging to be set to music,' he added, grinning.

I gave him a repressive glance, indicative of my status as a responsible working woman, and pushed past him. 'How do you do? You must be Mr Todd. I'm Lola – I mean Lila,' I said hurriedly. 'You're here for the health and safety check, aren't you?'

'Yes, that's me. I'm responsible for seeing that your audience goes away with the same number of limbs they came in with.' He looked up at the crack in the kitchen wall with great interest.

'Obviously no members of the public will be coming in here,' I said, and put a helping hand under his elbow to usher him outside.

I'd practically fallen into hysterics when the production manager had announced this visit. 'It's just a formality really, and all you have to do is show him round quickly. But for God's sake don't let him see that patch of dry rot on the library floor,' Tom had concluded, chuckling at his own wit.

I'd stared at him stonily. 'The last time someone made a joke like that round here, a chandelier fell on his head and killed him stone dead,' I remarked. Tom had looked up, anxiously. 'That was in 1843,' I admitted.

'It's not as posh as I imagined it would be before we arrived,' Tom had said. 'I was thinking *Brideshead Revisited* until I spotted a very scruffy man weeding the vegetables and then someone introduced him as your dad.' Then he smacked his hand confidently against the banister. 'But, don't worry, this house is staying put. You'll be fine. Just tell this safety guy loads of stories about your swashbuckling ancestors and he'll be eating out of your hand.'

I'd given him a wan smile, and then, when he'd gone, pushed back the piece of wood he had dislodged from the banister with his slap and which was probably the only thing keeping it up. I just knew this man would find something awful and shut us down, and then it would all be my fault. Mind you, I had taken to seeing doom round every corner recently. Even though you couldn't go anywhere without coming across someone humming tunelessly while measuring a bit of wood, or a group of fairies practising a song, or Bottom wearing nothing but a pair of jeans and his ass's head (Bongo took one horrified look and ran off howling), despite all this clamour and disruption, the whole thing had an insubstantial feel, as if all I had to do was blink hard or say the wrong thing and they would all vanish and I would be back in reality, with no job and no prospects. I knew this was ridiculous, but I had taken to carrying my lucky pencil around with me wherever I went.

Now I hadn't even got Mr Todd out through the door and already he had found something nasty.

'Now, that's very interesting, that crack.'

'Is it?' I said doubtfully. It had been there for years and I had never found it the slightest bit diverting.

'It doesn't look like much, does it?'

I agreed heartily with that. 'Though if you look at it with your eyes half shut, it's exactly the same shape as the Mississippi, isn't it?'

'I wouldn't know about that. But I do know it's creeping down the wall, isn't it? Well, when it eventually meets that second crack that's busy creeping slyly up – well!' Mr Todd blew out his lips in a sigh that was full of foreboding.

So that was another thing I could put in my diary to worry about in the future, then. I urged him outside before he could get started on the rickety hinges on the larder door. We walked round to the terrace, where two stagehands were leaning out of an upstairs window at a precarious angle, working out the best way to suspend a backcloth.

Mr Todd watched them and said, 'Now then – that will never do!'

'What won't?' I asked in alarm. Terry, the stage manager, was a gimlet-eyed man with muscles of steel and a terrible temper. If he wanted his crew to perform cartwheels up and down Ma's washing line, I wasn't going to say anything.

'That ivy. You've let it grow too far, you see, and it's going to become a big problem.' He blew out his cheeks again in a way I just knew I was going to become awfully familiar with.

'So, will we have to take it all down?' I asked miserably. Everyone here was tight on budget and short on time. They wouldn't be pleased at all if they had to factor in a day of ivy removal. I knew they were over budget on the costumes already, and behind schedule on the rehearsals because Julian was still having problems with the scene he had practised with Johnny in the woods.

'Oh, no, it isn't a safety hazard, just a terrible nuisance. Mark my words, you'll be wishing you had done something about it in a year's time.' He looked down at his list. 'Now then, are people going to be walking up and down those steps?'

'Well, yes, if by people, you mean actors,' I said cautiously.

'Oh, well, that's all right then.'

'So they don't count?'

'Nope. Nothing to do with me. I'm here on behalf of the paying public.'

Surreptitiously I swallowed a couple of herbal Keep Calm tablets and pulled a face. I think they only worked because they tasted so disgusting they took your mind off whatever had been worrying you in the first place.

Mr Todd was looking at his list and frowning. 'Now, it says here that this play is going to move from one place to another?'

'Yes. Promenade performances are terribly popular nowadays,' I said glibly, though really I had no idea if that was true or not.

'So that means the audience, supposing you get one – sorry, just my little joke; I'm sure you'll be packed out – they have to walk up that hill to the woods? What about wheelchair access?'

'Well, my mother used to push us up there in a massive pram when we were babies, though not all of us at once, so I don't think there would be a problem.'

'Lights?'

'Erm . . .' My attention was wandering slightly, to a figure loitering outside the drawing-room window as if he was waiting for something. I went over, and when he saw me he held up a piece of wood.

'Have you seen Terry? He needs this, now.'

I couldn't see why Terry, the carpenter, or anyone, for that matter, would want what looked like half a sawn-off chair leg, but it really wasn't my place to say so. My place was just to run around and follow orders.

'He's in there,' I said, pointing towards the library.

'Now, that will have to stop right away. I cannot

possibly give you permission for that,' said Mr Todd sternly, and instantly I forgot all about the man with the chair leg.

I went cold with fear. Nothing could stop, not even for a minute. We were on far too tight a schedule for that. 'What?' I asked with foreboding.

'Flirting with the men, that's what! You have to fill out at least eight forms – in triplicate – before you can do that! Sorry, just another of my little jokes. Don't mind me!'

'Oh, well, I won't then.' Hang on a sec, Mr Todd, while I catch my breath from laughing so hard at all your fabulous jokes. You should really be on the stage with all the other bloody comedians – or bound and gagged somewhere until all this is over. I took deep, calming breaths.

'Ah, well, back to business. About the lights – how are you planning to get your audience up the hill at night in the dark?'

I didn't like the way he called them 'my audience'. I could feel the imaginary weight of all these people weighing me down. 'The extras are going to carry lanterns and there will be fairy lights strung up in all the trees,' I said, consulting my notes.

'Oh.'

Dammit, he was doing that lip-blowing thing again. I couldn't bear it. 'The lantern-bearers have all completed a three-week course in lantern-bearing and are sitting their final test as we speak. They will also have to sign a contract beforehand stipulating that any lantern swinging will not exceed two inches in either direction.'

There was a long silence.

'Sorry. Just my little joke,' I said feebly. 'They're not real lanterns. They are torches, made up to look like lanterns. Couldn't be safer.'

'Right then. Ah, now that will have to go.'

'What? The whole tree?' I said in alarm, looking to where he was pointing to a massive and gnarled old chestnut that had been peacefully minding its own business for hundreds of years, probably. 'It's a protected monument,' I improvised madly. 'King Charles hid in that tree on his way back from . . .' Oh, why had I not concentrated more on history and less on kissing boys when I was at school?

'I meant the root. People could trip over that.'

'Oh, that.' I sagged with relief. 'It will be covered by a mat and will signify the journey from the real world to the magical one.'

'It would take a bit more than a carpet to get me to believe that. I hope you've got a few other tricks up your sleeve otherwise your audience will be off home pronto. Now, tell me, have you seen the long-term forecast for June?'

'No, but I've got four hundred umbrellas on order,' I said, just in case my remit included controlling the elements.

'It doesn't matter to me one way or the other.

Just thought you'd like to know there are terrible storms predicted for June.'

'But . . . I thought we were in for a heatwave?'

'Ah, but you always get a terrible drop of rain after a spell of good weather, don't you? Mark my words, this path could be knee-deep in mud next month. Blimey, the rehearsals don't half look lifelike!'

I looked up, bewildered. What was he talking about? Then I saw Terry. He was dragging the man with the wood down the steps, with no regard for his safety or comfort at all. Terry looked grim. The man looked purple and was trying to free his windpipe from the vicelike grip of Terry's huge, sausage-like fingers.

'Bloody reporters! How the hell did you get in, you little weasel?' yelled Terry.

Oh dear. This wasn't good – not good at all. It was me. I had let him in, though of course I didn't know he was from the press. Oh God, I should have made sure I'd known exactly who he was.

Then Paige rushed out, in tears, her sister in hot pursuit. 'I knew something like this would happen. I should have taken a break this summer, instead of cramming in more work. I just can't do this! It's not like back in LA – there's security there. There could be one of them lurking under every bush, for all I know!' Paige cried out. I could hear every awful word and I shivered with foreboding.

Suddenly there was a crowd of actors and crew milling about on the terrace and talking excitedly.

They were followed by Julian, who was doing his best to restore calm. I could hear his deep measured voice as I raced back down the hill. 'OK, everyone, calm down. Tom and Liz are making sure no one else from the press is lurking anywhere. We'll all take a break now and let Paige have some time out, and recover her nerve, and then we'll get back to work.'

'You'll be having a hell of a long break then. She's just said she wants to go home,' said Piper, returning and looking grim.

Julian went very pale. 'Clearly she can't,' he said.

'Do you think I don't already know that?' snapped Piper, who looked very stressed out as well.

Julian began pacing the terrace as he worked out how to rectify the situation. I wanted to help, but didn't know how. I had done enough by letting the man in.

'I told you we should have done *The Comedy of Errors* instead, or even that Scottish play,' said someone, no doubt trying to lighten the mood.

'Which one? *Mac* –' I began, and everyone hissed in alarm, except Mitch, who looked blank. They stared at me as if I had suddenly gone completely mad.

'Surely you know never to mention the name of that play out loud?' said Guy reprovingly, whilst Eric, one of the rude mechanicals, shook his head at the folly of staging a play surrounded by greenhorns.

'Why not?' I stuttered.

'It's bad luck,' explained Cinnamon, kindly.

I swallowed. Had I just brought the whole production

crashing to its knees? But I hadn't meant to! How was anyone sane supposed to know you couldn't mention the name of a famous play out loud? It was just daft. Imagine if every time I wanted a particular coloured pencil I had to say, that one that looks just like grass? And anyway, what was going on?

'If I ever find the idiot who let that hack in . . .' said Julian.

'Er . . . the idiot . . . well, that would be me,' I said miserably. 'I thought he was part of the stage crew, so I let him be. I'm really terribly sorry.'

'Well, journalists can be very cunning and devious, and you've never had to deal with them before,' said Julian, managing a small smile for me, which was much more than I deserved. He went and sat on the terrace wall to consult with Cara. 'It won't happen, but if the worst should come to the worst,' I heard him saying.

'Well, we'll bring the understudy in. She's perfectly competent.'

'But Paige and Piper have this incredible relationship, which works so perfectly for the play. I absolutely refuse to even contemplate losing that,' he said.

'She'll probably come round soon,' said Felicity, one of the fairies, hopefully.

'Paige has been hurtling towards the end of her tether for a while now. She looks to me like she has finally reached it,' said Piper, miserably.

I wanted to run far, far away from all this. Every shred of common sense I possessed told me that this was exactly what I should do. After all, I had already caused a huge amount of damage without even trying. And even to me, my plan sounded absurd and implausible. I briefly touched my lucky pencil for comfort, walked over to Julian and put my hand rather timidly on his shoulder to get his attention.

'I'm sorry for interrupting, but I have an idea. I think we should get Pa to talk to her, calm her down. I know it sounds odd, but I think it might work,' I said in a rush because Julian was looking at me as if I had just offered to paint the front of the house with a toothbrush. 'You see, he has seen more than his fair share of tethers. It's worth a try, isn't it?' I finished lamely.

'Of course it is,' said Julian kindly, as if humouring a child.

I promised myself a good cry later and went off to find Pa.

I didn't want to go back to Mr Todd, but I was determined to finish possibly my last day of work in a professional manner.

We plodded up to the wood. 'We have removed all stones, branches, roots and assorted greenery that might in any way prove a danger to health. However, it's quite likely that someone could walk into that tree and knock himself out. Or trip over a daisy. Or a bird could fly over and drop a twig into someone's eye.' Good heavens, now I had got into my stride, I could go on for hours listing all the possible dangers to safety. 'In fact, I'm not happy with anyone even getting out of bed without a certificate to prove they've considered all the risks beforehand,' I said gloomily.

'Now cheer up. I've never met anyone more prone to look on the bad side. I'm going to sign this bit of paper, giving you lot the go-ahead.'

'You are?' I said, spotting a glimmer of light at the end of an extremely long tunnel.

'Now, just one more thing. It's not really my remit, but I'm wondering if you've thought hard about your toilets?'

'You bet I have. I looked into them thoroughly – I mean, I researched them and have decided to go for the Minervas,' I said confidently. That would blind him with lavatorial science.

But he scratched his chin. 'Yes, well, that's a shame.'

I might have guessed that wouldn't please him. 'What's wrong with them?'

'Minervas are terribly prone to leakage. No, you should have gone for a Jupiter. Now that's a sturdy little loo for you, and a very nice enamel finish too.'

It hardly mattered – we were well up poo creek without a paddle if Paige went home. I walked Mr Todd down the drive to where his car was parked and was outraged to discover the wood-bearing hack still lurking in the undergrowth.

'Haven't you done enough damage for one day? Why are you still here? Don't you ever give up?' I shouted.

'No, of course I don't. It's my job,' he said, in surprise.

'I can't believe you had the gall to pass yourself off as one of the stage crew,' I continued bitterly.

'I can't believe you fell for it. Did I really look like I knew what I was doing with that chair leg?'

'Not really,' I admitted. 'But I hope you are ashamed of yourself now. We are in so much trouble. Paige may leave the play and goodness knows what will happen,' I said, too upset to think straight.

'Blimey,' he said, and whipped out his notebook. 'Television Totty in Tantrum Trauma,' he mused. 'When's she leaving? What did she say? Is she on medication? Does she drink?'

'Go away!' I howled and ran back up the drive with my fingers in my ears.

I wandered around aimlessly for a while. I found myself looking for Johnny so I could talk to him about my mad day, but I couldn't find him anywhere. Anyway, I would have to face the music sooner or later. When I went into the kitchen, Julian was there with Will.

'No news then?' I asked.

Julian shook his head. 'Apparently she once locked herself in her dressing room on set for two days. Her mother got her out eventually, but she's in rehab at the moment and so we can't contact her.'

'Oh, poor girl,' I said, my heart going out to her.

'I will be able to replace her, I think, but it won't be the same. They were just so good together, those two, perfect really, and exactly what I envisaged for their roles,' he sighed.

I knew just what he meant. He didn't want anything less than the best for this play. We drank tea in a glum silence.

We were so deep in thought we all jumped when Pa walked in. 'Oh, there you are. They are all waiting for you,' he said to Julian.

'All?' said Julian, a glimmer of hope dawning on his face.

'Yes, Paige too. A little fragile, but quite willing to get back to work and very sorry about letting you down earlier. I said I was sure you would understand.'

'I understand you've performed some sort of miracle,' said Julian slowly. 'How on earth did you manage to pull it off?'

'Oh, it was nothing. The women round here are always having crises,' said Pa, peering hopefully into the teapot.

'He means that for the last thirty years or so he has been able to witness the entire range of emotional and psychological issues facing the modern female. Having gathered a deep level of insight into the female psyche, he was able to empathise with Paige in her dilemma by calling upon a highly developed degree of sensitivity. Then he concluded the session by communicating his support for her in a nurturing way,' said Will, laughing.

'Well, I took her a cup of tea and then we chatted,' said Pa, doubtfully.

Julian grabbed his hand and shook it energetically. 'Always the hero to me,' he said.

'We've pulled each other out of a few scrapes before now, haven't we?' smiled Pa.

Julian took a deep breath. 'I'm prepared to admit things were looking quite bad just then. We would have got by, of course, patched something up, but I want this play to be much better than that,' he began, sounding slightly hesitant.

'That performance doesn't fool me,' said Pa firmly, and we all looked up startled. 'I know perfectly well you are absolutely driven to achieving perfection and you won't settle for anything less. It's quite tiring to watch but I am beginning to see why it might be worth it. Well, what are you waiting for? They are all ready for you. Go on and do your magic!'

Chapter Eighteen

Johnny

I spent most of the night tying myself, and the bedclothes, into knots. Part of me sort of enjoyed helping Mitch – as long as I pretended I was a director. Part of me had loved helping Julian out – I was acting, wasn't I, even though there was only an audience of two? But the rest of me was being driven into a frenzy of frustration by it all. I loved being here, yet at the same time I almost hated it. I felt like I was being torn in two. I must have sat up a dozen times and turned the pillow over. I pulled the bedclothes up and then I threw them off. I switched the light on and tried to read, but my unhappiness seeped onto the page and I couldn't concentrate. Eventually I did sleep, fitfully, but woke up more tired than when I went to bed.

Will took one look at me when I came into the kitchen and pushed the coffeepot over wordlessly.

'Thanks. But I should really go and sit in the ashes with this,' I said glumly.

Will raised an eyebrow.

'Isn't that where Cinderella had to sit? I am feeling a kinship with her this morning,' I explained.

'Interesting. Of course, fairytales do illuminate the human condition. My mother, for instance, always claims that she only felt half alive until she met my father.'

'She's certainly got the looks of a Sleeping Beauty,' I agreed, grateful to Will for not laughing at me.

Lila came in and started rummaging through cupboards. 'I need porridge. It's good for the heart, isn't it? Mine's been beating so fast ever since Mitch arrived, I need something to calm me down.' She looked round. Our faces were stony. 'I was only joking,' she said plaintively, surprised I hadn't realised.

'It was a very bad joke,' I said crossly. What did she think I was – some sort of captive audience? Hell, I really was in a bad mood today.

I was just thinking that maybe I should go for a walk, or something, to work off my bad temper, when there was an urgent tapping on the kitchen door and Liz put her head round it. She looked slightly agitated. 'Oh, thank goodness you're in! Your sister is up a tree in the woods and she's asking for you,' she said to Lila.

'Ohmigod! Come with me,' Lila begged, and I nodded.

We set off at a brisk pace up the hill. 'I don't understand. Anna doesn't do tree climbing. She loathes heights.'

'Apparently she doesn't any more,' I said, pointing,

because now I could see her feet dangling from the branches of an enormous oak tree.

'Anna, what on earth is going on?' demanded Lila, but before she could reply, there was a mewing sound. The leaves parted and a cat looked down at us, in an aggrieved way, as if we had disturbed its nap, which Anna probably had. Now the situation was beginning to make sense.

'So, Anna, you climbed up to rescue the cat,' said Lila, and I could hear deep respect for Anna's bravery in her voice. 'I understand now. You thought the cat was in trouble and you didn't think twice.'

'Yes. Unfortunately I have now had ample time to think since I got up here,' remarked Anna.

'Can you pass the cat to me?' I asked.

'No,' said Anna firmly. We could see a leg twitch.

'Well, climb down and I'll go and get it,' I offered.

There was a hollow laugh from the tree.

'When I said Anna doesn't like heights, I should have explained that actually it's more of a phobia than a fear,' hissed Lila.

'How many more members of your family have these irrational fears?' I said, interested. No wonder Will went into psychology. Lila didn't like dentists; Anna didn't like heights; Mr B didn't like people . . .

'I think that's our lot, though come to think of it, Ma can't even bear the smell of sweetcorn –' Lila began.

'I don't want to interrupt this fascinating insight into

our family's problems, but – *HELP!*' said Anna in rather a shrill voice.

'Sit tight, we've got this covered,' I said to her and then quietly, to Lila: 'I could go up after her, but, well, I don't want to worry you, but that branch doesn't look too solid.'

There was a rustling of leaves and the cat jumped with the ease of an acrobat onto an even higher branch, where it started washing its nose. Clearly the cat had no problem with heights.

'I came out and I heard the cat crying. It sounded so terrified and lonely. Tony's mum told me their Tibbles had gone missing a few days ago. I saw it in the tree, starving and scared, and I just rushed up here and now . . .' Anna's voice wavered into silence.

'Now neither of you can get down. There is only one cat up there, isn't there?' I asked, a bit dubiously. This particular cat didn't look like it had missed a snack, let alone a proper meal in the last week.

'Anna, if you just come back the way you came, very slowly, it will be perfectly safe. Johnny and I are here to catch you, anyway,' said Lila coaxingly.

'I am?' I said. I wasn't thrilled at this idea.

Lila grimaced at me and went on. 'Look, you can't just stay up there, can you?' she said in her most reasonable voice. There was a moaning in the leaves.

'Now look what you've done,' I remarked.

'Well, have you got any better ideas?'

'Hmm, let's see – there are only two solutions: she climbs down or I climb up. She doesn't want to do either of them. I'm all out of ideas.'

'Oh dear,' said Lila.

'I don't want to bother anyone, but I have now lost all feeling in my right leg,' said Anna. Then I heard a car pull up. I turned round and saw Tony bounding down the slope towards us.

'What's going on?'

Lila explained.

'Right. Leave this to me,' he said confidently.

'Why? Have you come with a pair of amazing extending arms then?' I muttered under my breath. That was all we needed – Mr Know-it-all Tony Anderson, Barton Willow's answer to Superman. Come to think of it, this was exactly what Anna needed, the perfect knight in shining armour.

'Anna? It's Tony. Can. You. Hear. Me?'

'She's stuck, not deaf,' I said. Lila giggled.

'Oh, hello! How are you, Tony?' enquired Anna, as if this was a casual meeting.

'I'm fine. Now, don't worry, we'll have this sorted in a jiffy.'

'Oh, thanks, but I can't move an inch. I shall have to stay here for ever. Well, until I starve to death. I was only trying to rescue Tibbles since your mother mentioned he'd gone missing and I saw him up here in this tree –' said Anna.

Tony interrupted. 'Anna, listen to me – that is not

going to happen. I am not going to leave you. We are going to get through this and I am going to get you down safely!'

'Again, stuck in a tree, not halfway up Everest!' I remarked quietly, and looked over at Lila, who was cramming her fist in her mouth in case Anna heard her laughing.

'I happen to have done a course on this sort of thing!' said Tony.

'I might have guessed,' I said, but only to myself this time.

Tibbles had spotted Tony and launched into a litany of mewed complaints.

'That cat is lying,' I remarked, but no one was listening.

'OK. I am going to need a ladder,' said Tony, turning to me.

'Why, it's perfectly easy to climb. Even Anna managed it,' I pointed out.

'Yes, but she clearly doesn't want to climb down the same way.'

Good point.

There was a ladder nearby that had been used for the hanging of the fairy lights for the play. I brought it over. 'I'll go up, shall I?' I offered, pausing long enough to allow Tony to jump gallantly over to the tree like I knew he would.

'Hold on, Anna, you'll be safe soon,' said Lila.

'She's fine, just having a little lie-down on this

branch, aren't you? I am quite sure there is no need to grip it that firmly, Anna.'

There was more rustling of leaves and some more moaning from Anna. Tibbles ignored Tony's outstretched arms and jumped lithely from branch to branch, performed what looked like a double somersault in the air and landed neatly on four paws at our feet, yawned and went off in search of better entertainment.

'Now, Anna, what I want you to do is visualise what it is going to feel like when you are safely back on the ground again. Shut your eyes and imagine you are there. Are you doing that?'

'Yes,' said Anna, politely but dubiously.

'Excellent. Imagine how great it is going to feel. You want that feeling, don't you? Well, we are going to make that feeling happen. All you have to do is listen to me and do everything I say. I am going to ask you to do ten things, very slowly, and when you have got to number ten, you will be with us, on the ground.'

I was quite impressed by this. This sounded like a good plan.

'I can't,' said Anna firmly.

'You've got to have faith in me,' began Tony.

'You don't understand. The branch is bre –' yelled Anna and then there was an awful creaking sound, a high-pitched squeal, and Anna and the branch fell out of the tree. She grabbed Tony as she went past and he fell with her. For a horrible split second all I could see was an inert tangle of arms and legs. Then they both moved.

Tony jumped up. 'I'm OK. I've learned how to fall safely. Anna, are you all right?'

'Oh, I'm fine now I'm back on the ground,' said Anna. Then she shuddered. 'Oh, my God! Imagine all of the awful things that could have happened! I thought Tibbles would die up there, but I climbed up without even thinking of myself. I thought we would both die!'

'Yes, you were very brave. Thank you for rescuing Tibbles,' said Tony soothingly.

Anna stood up gingerly and winced. 'Ow. I think I've hurt my ankle!'

Without thinking, I leaped forward to support her, but Tony swept her into his arms with a proprietary air. 'I think I should take you to A&E.'

'Oh, no, I'm sure that's not necessary!' began Anna. I nipped her arm gently. She looked at me, startled, and then got the message. A few hours alone with Tony in casualty would be a great opportunity to get their romance off the ground. 'Well, maybe it would be a good idea after all.'

'That's my girl!' said Tony heartily.

'Do you want me to come with you?' Lila said tenderly. 'Oh blast, I can't. I've got to go to work!'

'I'll be OK. I'm in good hands,' said Anna, who, despite the fact that she had just had an awful experience and now a very swollen ankle, looked rather pleased with herself. She even winked happily at me as Tony carried her to the car and put her in as gently as if she were made out of eggshells. I realised this was just what Tony needed to realise he and Anna were perfect for each other. As they drove off I could see Tibbles looking out over the back seat.

'Oh dear, I hope the cat doesn't get travel sick,' said Lila, giggling, and I grinned.

'I wouldn't worry. Tony's probably packed an emergency cat-sick kit, just in case,' I remarked, and suddenly we were both laughing helplessly.

'Only Anna could think that cat was in trouble,' she said.

'I was positive Tony was going to dart behind a tree and come back with his pants over his tights and a blue cape on,' I said.

'Oh, yes, he does love mending and organising things. Once he tidied all my paints away and washed up my palette halfway through a painting. I never managed to mix the same shade of blue again.'

We started walking back to the house.

'Are you OK? You seemed a bit out of sorts this morning,' Lila asked, after a minute.

'Yeah, I was in a bad mood. I was wondering what the hell I was doing here, actually,' I admitted.

'You're not thinking about leaving, are you?' she asked in alarm.

'Why? Would it matter to you if I did?' We had stopped walking and were staring at each other. For some reason she started blushing. She looked down and started scuffing the earth with her shoe.

'Promise me you won't go,' she mumbled.

'Sorry, I didn't catch that,' I said firmly. I wanted to know how much she wanted me to stay.

She looked me in the eye. 'Please don't go.'

'Well, OK then, I won't,' I smiled at her.

She went off to work and I pretended to go round to the trailers. But as soon as she was out of sight, I slipped stealthily into the library and made myself comfortable on a window seat behind a pair of heavy curtains. Julian was holding a rehearsal in here in half an hour and I wanted to watch. This was going to be a master class in acting. I swallowed the thought that watching how to act was pointless if you weren't going to actually do it and told myself that I could pick up plenty of tips to pass on to Stella.

I hid just in time because Lila came in and started tidying up and putting chairs out. I half thought about offering to help – she wouldn't snitch on me – but suddenly I just wanted to watch her. I liked the way she moved and the way she impatiently blew her hair out of her eyes and the way she counted on her fingers the number of chairs she needed. She was rather adorable and seemed like she might actually be interested in me, not Mitch. I was just wondering uneasily if I was being a bit voyeuristic, when she pulled the curtain aside and we both jumped in shock.

'What are you doing here?' she hissed, and I pulled

her down next to me, because the cast were already starting to come in.

'Watching,' I said tersely. 'You?'

'Snooping,' she giggled and then whispered, 'Julian will be furious if he finds us. He strictly forbade anyone except the cast in this rehearsal.'

'Well, we'll have to make sure he doesn't then,' I remarked, pulling her closer, and feeling her leg pressed against mine. She wriggled and took out a piece of paper and a pencil from her jeans pocket.

Paige and Piper came in. Paige looked a bit better today, still stressed, but resolute. The twins both sat very upright and very still, like two blonde, porcelain dolls, only able to come to life when Julian spoke his magic words. I glanced down and there they were again on Lila's paper. She had captured them perfectly. I must tell her that later.

Andy Sloan came in after them – and somehow he looked more on edge than Paige. He sat down on the front of his seat like he couldn't wait to get away. I felt really sorry for him; I knew what it was like to feel sick with nerves. But then Cinnamon came in and she was so wonderful, so amazing to look at, and her good humour was so obvious, I had to smile. She had to be nearly six foot tall in her stockinged feet, so it was impossible not to notice her. Today she had piled her ebony hair on top of her regal head, adding a few more inches. She had the body of an Amazon warrior princess, skin the colour of treacle toffee and a big, generous mouth made to break into jokes and laughter.

'Hello, everyone. I'm not late, am I? I didn't really want to come – well, I did, but I'm sick with nerves. What the hell has Julian got in store for us, do you think?'

'Oh, it won't be that bad,' said Patrick O'Connor, who was playing Quince.

'That's easy for you to say, darling! You've been acting for ever. Some of us, like me, are new to this game. I'm so out of my comfort zone already!' She sat down and smiled at everyone, radiating such warmth I could almost see the rest of the cast draw closer to warm themselves.

'I don't think she really believes those fantastic reviews she got for her cameo role in that film *The Generation*,' whispered Lila.

'Yes, that's exactly what I was thinking,' I agreed.

When Mitch appeared at the door, he paused and I whispered, 'He's going to wait a second to let everyone notice him before coming in.' Lila grinned back.

When Julian entered, he strolled in as if he had all the time in the world and I realised he was deliberately playing down his powerful position in order to put the cast at their ease. 'Jolly good, you all seem to be here,' he said, as if he half expected a few people not to bother turning up.

He sat down on one of the chairs and I expected him to tell them what he had planned. But he surprised me by saying instead, 'Right, let's be off, literally. We're going to have a bit of fun with this by doing a speed-read through. I want you to say your lines as quickly as possible – it's pace I want, not performance. Think of it as a sort of mental limbering up.' Everyone looked a bit puzzled, but then jumped right in. It was quite funny to watch because everyone had their heads down, trying to keep up. Even Paige seemed a bit more relaxed at the end, though I noticed Andy shrug, as if he was wondering what the hell he was doing here.

'That was great. Thank you. Now let's do it one more time, but this time read the part of the person sitting to your right.'

'Watch and learn, buddy,' said Cinnamon confidently, laughing and nudging Stu, who was playing the role of Bottom.

I noticed Mitch had brought an impressive wad of my notes with him. He looked totally pissed off at the prospect of having to play the part of a fairy queen.

'Mitch looks rather put out,' Lila whispered. 'Do they not have acting classes like this on film sets as well?'

I started to shake with silent laughter.

'What's so funny?'

'How deep do the characters in *Dirt* actually go? Ride into town, look brooding, sleep with girl, shoot man, lose girl, ride out, broodily. Or, what about *Meteor*? Big rock, build spaceship, look brooding, sleep with girl, bomb rock, lose girl, fly off into universe, broodily.

At first Mitch flatly refused to play the fairy queen, though Cinnamon tried to persuade him. 'Listen, honey, I certainly don't want to play the ass either, but if we all do it, I won't tell if you won't.' And she burst into her deep, throaty laugh.

I knew Mitch wouldn't buy it. Then, as if on cue, his phone rang. 'Sorry, I gotta take this,' he said, and walked out.

Julian looked furious. 'Has anyone else forgotten the rule of not bringing a phone to a rehearsal? Good. Well, let's just carry on without him. Andy, you're going to be – where the hell is Andy?' Everyone looked up, startled.

'He's probably just nipped to the loo,' someone said. But if he had, he didn't come back. After ten minutes, Julian sent people to look for him, but he was nowhere to be found.

'Maybe it's nerves. He'll be back,' said Cinnamon.

'I sort of hope he doesn't. He really sucked,' said Piper quietly to her sister, and Paige nodded.

Julian was looking like he was about to lose his temper when out of the corner of my eye, I saw Lila get up. And then it felt like everything was happening in slow motion, or that I was tied to this seat, bound and gagged, able only to watch in horrified fascination as she pulled the curtain aside and bounced into the room like a character in one of those pantomimes the British seem to love.

'Let Andy go! He obviously doesn't want to do it and you don't need him. Johnny can do the part brilliantly. Uncle Julian, you know he can – you've seen him act! You know how good an actor he is!' She moved her arm as if to say – And here he is! She was smiling as if she had just done me the biggest favour in the world and was waiting for applause. But instead, there was only silence.

Julian's face was completely blank, but I knew that underneath he was absolutely furious. 'Why are you two eavesdropping on a private rehearsal?' he asked, quite mildly. Instantly the gravity of what she'd done dawned on Lila and she visibly sagged.

'But, Uncle Julian –' she began.

This was my cue to slouch out of the room quietly and leave her to face the music, which she so richly deserved. But however loudly my head screamed that I should leave, my body wouldn't listen. My stage fright had struck again. I did some deep breathing and it seemed to work. I grabbed Lila's arm and muttered apologies, pulling her across the room with everyone watching us, rapt, as if this was a play and we were the actors. I thought we might just manage to get the hell out of here with minimal damage when I stopped dead, because Mitch was in the doorway.

'Lily, you weren't seriously suggesting my little brother becomes an actor, were you?' he drawled. 'The kid can't do anything under the lights – stage fright. He just stands there like a friggin' stone, making a fool of himself! I thought everyone knew!' Well, they certainly did now.

Mitch looked round smiling to include the rest of the cast in the joke, but I could tell he was genuinely pissed because a muscle was twitching at the corner of his mouth.

Cinnamon shuddered. 'Shut up, Mitch, you're making it worse for the rest of us. We've all got stage fright, especially for a production of this calibre,' she said weakly, smiling at me. I was dimly aware that other people were nodding in agreement.

'This isn't Johnny's fault, Mitch, and my name is – oh, never mind,' said Lila, pulling out of my grasp and turning to Julian.

'Thanks for nothing,' I said, walking out while I still could.

Lila ran out after me. 'Johnny, please stop! Look, I was really stupid. I don't know what came over me. I didn't mean it to go wrong like that. Johnny, I'm sorry!'

I turned round. 'I don't need your pity!' I shouted, incandescent with fury now. 'How dare you stand there feeling sorry for me? Do you know how that makes me feel?'

'I realise I've got it all wrong,' she began, and I could hear her catching her breath on a sob, but I didn't care. It was like she had opened my eyes to the doormat I have been my whole life. I took her by the arms in a vicelike grip.

'I'll tell you how I feel! I'm sick of being patronised and looked down on and taken advantage of. You thought you were being so helpful to poor pathetic

Johnny! You thought you could just make it come right just like that. Did you think I was some sort of Cinderella figure and you were the fairy godmother and all you had to do was wave your magic wand and make all my dreams come true?'

She nodded speechlessly and I loosened my grip a little. She was brave to admit that.

'What makes you think I want your help, anyway?' I demanded.

'Maybe you don't. But I can't just sit back and watch you watch this opportunity sail past!' she cried.

I stared at her.

'Don't try and pretend this isn't killing you,' she said, more quietly.

We were so close I could feel her breath fanning my cheek.

'Now try using that magic wand to keep your job,' I said more calmly, and strode off. I suddenly realised I was feeling, well, OK. How the hell had that happened? I should have been writhing on the floor in agony at being such a useless failure and having a girl trying to force me into the opportunities I was too cowardly to take myself. And while I certainly felt like I had been hit by a huge tidal wave, it hadn't swept me to my death. I was still here, battered and bruised, but alive. 'There's still hope,' I said. Was it really me saying that?

Chapter Nineteen

Lila

Facing Uncle Julian was far worse than being held at (plastic) gunpoint. And I was fairly certain I wouldn't be given tea and sympathy afterwards. Oh, why had I been such an interfering idiot? I ran towards him as he emerged into the hall (better to get this over with quickly) and said: 'I know what you are going to say and I agree with every word. I am so sorry. Even I can't believe what I did in there. Please accept my resignation right now and I promise I'll keep right out of your way until after the play is over.'

Julian looked at me and then said, 'Is Johnny all right?'

I wasn't expecting this. 'Um . . . he was really angry of course, but . . . well, he wasn't quite as furious as I thought he would be,' I said. 'I think he's OK,' I finished off.

Julian went to sit on the steps. I sat down next to him. Was I seeing things, or did he look older and more tired than when he had arrived?

'I haven't ruined everything, have I?' I said in a small voice.

He looked up in surprise, as if he had been thinking of something else entirely. 'That was a terrible perform-ance in there. You were waving your arms like a demented fairy godmother in a pantomime,' he said, laughing.

I cringed. 'That's pretty much how Johnny saw it.'

'And you interrupted me in the middle of a bloody rehearsal!'

I cringed further. 'I know.'

'No one disturbs me when I am at work. I don't take messages. I don't take phone calls, even from your father – my oldest friend – even when he rang up to say you had just been born.'

I gulped, overcome with misery at my stupidity, waiting for the axe to fall. I would have to find another job, quickly, and far away, because I couldn't bear to hang around here if I wasn't involved with the produc-tion in some way. Although I never quite knew what I was doing, or whether I was doing it right, I did love this job. Even more, I loved having the chance to get to know all these eccentric, artistic people, Johnny included. I couldn't be separated from all this now!

'I am not saying I wasn't grateful for the chance to get out of there for a minute or two, though. I was on the verge of a major tantrum about Mitch and Andy.'

I looked up with a tiny glimmer of hope. Was it my imagination, or did he sound just a tiny bit less cross?

'If you give your solemn promise never to do anything like that again, you can keep your job.'

'Really? Are you sure?'

He cocked his head towards the library. There was an awful din in there. I could hear someone talking and then there was a sudden burst of laughter. It sounded like they were having a party.

'I think they are bonding,' said Julian, with a grin.

'And that's a good thing?' I asked, just to be perfectly certain.

'Well, it's what I wanted to happen this morning. You see, that room was filled with scarily talented but very frightened people. Maybe they don't have it as bad as Johnny, but they understand how he feels. Fear is terribly isolating and it doesn't belong on this set. When I left, Cinnamon was telling everyone how she was so terrified she burped during her first screen kiss. From the noise, I imagine other people are trying to cap that. So, in an awful, muddle-headed way, you seem to have broken through everyone's fear and nervousness.'

I let out a huge sigh of relief. 'You still look a bit drained, though, Uncle Julian. Can I get you anything – tea, something to eat?' I said anxiously.

'Are you telling me I'm losing my looks?' he asked, outraged. 'Oh, calm down, I was only joking, though your honesty is most unflattering. Of course I'm worn to a thread – I'm directing a play, for God's sake!' He looked down and started to laugh. I followed his gaze.

I had drawn a picture of Mitch staring down at his notes, a look of complete bafflement on his handsome, stupid face.

'Don't worry, I won't let anyone see this,' I said hurriedly.

'Why not? It's very good, and surely he deserves it after his behaviour back there? Right, back to work. As a punishment, you can help Liz sort out a schedule for the costume fittings.'

'That doesn't sound too bad,' I smiled.

'Ha! You haven't done it yet,' he said, and went back to the rehearsal.

I was tempted to listen in again but I didn't want to push my luck, so I went off to find Liz. She was using a tiny room next to the stables as her office. I had tried to find her somewhere more comfortable inside the house, but she said she was from Cumbria, so she was used to draughts, and here she could have a fag whenever she needed one without having to go outside. From the number of butts in the ashtray, I guessed things weren't going well.

'Oh, thank God, you're here,' she said, looking up from a sheaf of papers.

I assumed my most efficient expression. I loved being a tiny cog in this enterprise.

'Ring all these numbers. Tell them about the costume fitting in the village hall. I started calling an hour ago and I've only got through to three people,' she said, harassed.

I glanced down at the list. 'Oh, yes, Mrs Jenkins. I expect she told you all about her grandson's ear grommets?'

Liz shuddered. 'Worse. Now he's got a discharge!'

'Yes, that would be a nasty conversation,' I agreed. 'Well, with Mrs Jenkins you just have to be ruthless and interrupt – she won't mind. Mrs Thomas, on the other hand, is more tricky –'

'You see! You know all these people and how to handle them! I knew I could leave this with you,' said Liz gratefully, and dashed off.

It took me ages. I had to listen to a lot of ailments and some awful excuses, but I quickly found a method for dealing with them. 'Well, if you are going to be busy hanging your neighbour's curtains/ seeing your chiropodist/ having Rentokil in, I will just have to give your part to someone else . . . No, I'm afraid I can't say who . . . Oh, good, you can make it after all . . . Two o'clock, be prompt. Bye-bye.'

I put the phone down and went back to the house. There was an awful crash from the hall. I raced in. Stu, the actor who was playing Bottom, was sitting on the stairs with a dazed expression and a piece of banister in his hand.

'It just came off while I was walking down and then I tripped.' He bent over his ankle and groaned. I kneeled down beside him and looked. Crikey, it was already the size of a football. Of course, everyone else had heard and come out to see what all the fuss was about.

'I just nipped up to the loo. How was I to know the bloody house would fall apart on my way down and break my ankle?' he said.

'I think it might just be a sprain, but you should get an X-ray, honey,' said Cinnamon, who was much more practical than she looked.

'I'll take him,' said Liz.

'I'll need to check my script. You haven't written any more stunts in there for us, have you, Julian?' grinned Cinnamon, trying to lighten the mood.

Stu's face was twisted with pain. 'I'm sure it's broken. I fractured it twice playing rugby at school and it's been weak ever since. The last time it did this, I couldn't walk for weeks.'

'Fuck,' said Julian quietly and we all jumped. He practically never swore. He helped Stu to Liz's car and came back slowly.

'I'm so sorry,' I said miserably. It seemed to be a week for apologies.

'Why? It wasn't your fault,' he said kindly. 'Right, well, I need to make a contingency phone call just in case Stu's ankle puts him out of action, which I think it will.'

'I suppose this sort of thing happens a lot when you are putting a play on?' I asked hopefully.

'No, not really.'

I went outside, depressed. How could Barton Willow be so ungrateful and sabotage these nice people? I felt awful that Julian had to make contingency phone calls when he already had so much to do. I saw Mitch coming towards me and was tempted to run away because I was still angry at him for being so horrible to Johnny earlier.

I gave him quite a curt smile and started to leave, but he blocked my path. I looked up reluctantly and saw that he was wearing a hangdog expression. 'Lulu, you must be thinking really bad things about me,' he began.

'Actually, I wasn't thinking about you at all,' I said honestly, edging aside. But of course he didn't take the hint – he never listened to a word I said.

'Where are you going? I'll walk with you for a while, if that's OK? I need a break after that rehearsal.'

'All right,' I said reluctantly. He was a guest, of sorts, so it behoved me to be polite. But there was no danger of wavering on my Four-point Plan with him.

Mitch sighed. 'You see, I know I came across badly in rehearsal, but I really do spend a lot of time looking out for my little stepbrother. He's kinda vulnerable, he doesn't really fit in, and I think it's my responsibility to watch his back. But you must know what families are like: sometimes the jokes seem more harsh from the outside.' He looked at me with exactly the same expression he used in the seduction scene in the film

Mountain. I had a bad feeling I knew where this was heading.

'Yes,' I said politely, 'I expect if you could overhear the way we talk to each other in our family you'd be a bit shocked sometimes.' This was true. I called Anna fatty, regularly implied that Will was less clever than he really was – outsiders would probably think we loathed each other. But ultimately it was clear to anyone how much we all cared for each other. Mitch's behaviour had felt nasty and spiteful.

'We've all tried to help Johnny with his problems, but I don't think he really wants to be helped, you know. In the end I think we all know his strengths lie in being in the background, helping me with my roles and running errands for me.'

'You make him sound more like a servant than a stepbrother!' I said, furious on Johnny's behalf, though really, given all the damage I had caused recently, maybe I should just stay out of his affairs.

Just for a second, Mitch scowled. It was so fleeting I wasn't really sure I had read his expression right and then he said: 'Listen, babe, Johnny's doing pretty well, considering he's only my stepbrother. I don't get why you are so interested in him anyway – he's just a nobody. But enough about him, let's talk about you . . . well, you and me,' he finished, with a dangerous gleam in his eye.

'Look, I think I am going to go back in and . . .' I cast around wildly for inspiration but the muse had obviously departed in disgust after today's antics.

'Don't go,' Mitch said, his voice going more soft and growly. 'I don't want you to go and think badly of me. I think we have something special here, Lulu.'

'Lila.'

'Yes, of course. As I was saying, I like you a lot. I've liked you ever since I first met you. Come here,' and he pulled me firmly into his arms.

I pulled just as firmly back and then stopped, confused. I could have sworn he wasn't really that interested in me – he didn't even remember my name – until I'd started to stand up for Johnny. Was he jealous? He was certainly a strange man. I tried to pull away again.

'Now, don't be scared, darling.'

'I'm not!' I said, but it was a bit muffled because his lips were clamped on mine and he had me in a bear-like grip.

Mitch kissed long and slow, like he had all the time in the world and didn't care who saw him. He had a very good technique, I decided. On points like these I felt I was well qualified to make a judgement, though really, if I was capable of being so clinical and detached during the kiss itself, it had to be missing the mark.

Mitch pulled back slightly and I could feel his hot breath on my ear. Looking over his shoulder, I saw someone staring at us out of the window but I was too far away to make out who it was. 'Oh, Lolly,' said Mitch, huskily, just like he had after kissing that gorgeous

Russian spy in *Secret*, though of course she wasn't called Lolly – she was called Natasha – and nor was I, for that matter.

'You are so . . . so . . .' He pulled back even further to get a better look but then his eyes widened more in shock than admiration. 'Oh my God!' he spluttered, and recoiled in horror.

'What do you mean? That's not very nice!' I said, rather crossly. After all, this whole thing was his idea. I stood back rather sharply and hit my head on a branch. My eyes filled with tears of pain and shame. Had I not showered properly? Were my ears full of wax? I was certainly deaf to reason around a man. My Plan did not include becoming repellent to men, even if I didn't want to snog them!

'Your face! It's all – my God – it's horrible!' and he backed off with unseemly haste.

With shaking fingers I touched my face gingerly, though I didn't need to – I could already feel it stinging. 'Listen, Mitch, it's all right. I mean, I know it doesn't look that way, but really – oh, blah, blah blah,' I finished off bitterly, because by now I was talking to myself. Mitch had gone. He had given me one incredulous look and shot off like a champion sprinter. There was nothing else for it but to get indoors while I could still see well enough to walk.

I stumbled across the grass and slipped in through a side door. I was groping my way blindly forwards, with one hand covering my face when the other outstretched hand collided with someone's chest. 'Oops, sorry,' I mumbled, trying to edge past.

'No, excuse me,' said Johnny's voice, polite and distant, as if I was a stranger. But then I could sense him stopping. 'Er . . . are you all right?'

'Yes . . . well, no . . . well, I will be if I could only get upstairs,' I said, covering my face with my hands and hoping he would leave me alone. Though why did he sound so . . . unfriendly all of a sudden? I thought we'd made up after the scary Cinderella incident at rehearsal.

'What is going on?' he demanded.

'I will tell you, but you've got to promise not to laugh,' I begged him.

'Why on earth would I do anything like that?' he said in a bewildered tone.

'Well, the rest of the family usually do in these circumstances. They've seen this a few times now. It's become a bit of a family joke,' I explained.

'Are they nuts? Look, what the hell has happened? What did Mitch do to you?' he asked urgently.

'Nothing, apart from wear the wrong sort of after-shave,' I said. 'And how do you know Mitch did anything to me? Oh! It was you at the window!'

'Yes, well, I was looking at the view and got more than I bargained for,' he said, crossly.

'So did I,' I said quickly. It really mattered to me that he realised I had not enjoyed that kiss. 'This sort of thing has happened before. The doctor said it's just an allergic reaction. Obviously, as you can see, quite a bad one. This hideous sight is just the first stage.'

'What's the second stage?' asked Johnny with interest and, maddeningly, a slight smile on his face.

I sneezed. 'This. Lots of sneezing, during which my eyes will swell up and water uncontrollably. I should recover in a few hours.'

'So, you're allergic to Mitch then?' Johnny sounded positively cheerful.

'No, not really, just the fact that he's rich, I suppose, and I have spent so long being poor and buying really cheap scent, my system can't cope with anything better. I am allergic to quality. It would be ironic if it wasn't so annoying. And uncomfortable.'

During this conversation he had been guiding me upstairs, one hand under my elbow, stopping every so often when the sneezing built in a crescendo. Finally we arrived at my room. I sank down on the bed, lay back and closed my eyes. I was aware that I was bound to look an awful fright, but Johnny didn't seem to mind too much about that. He didn't seem to be searching for an excuse to leave, anyway.

'Shall I close the curtains?'

'Oh, yes, please. The sunlight makes it feel worse.' I heard him moving across the room, then a thump and a muffled curse. 'Sorry, but I wasn't expecting part of your chest of drawers to be on the floor.'

'I should have told you. I took that drawer out to . . .' Why had I done that? Oh, yes. 'I was looking for my lucky knickers; couldn't find them anywhere,' I explained, rather embarrassed now.

Johnny chuckled. 'What happens when you wear them? Do you turn into Wonder Woman?'

'I like to think I've been fairly efficient recently, but I wouldn't go that far,' I added, recalling my gaffes. Well, apart from letting that awful reporter in – oh, and making a fool of myself at that rehearsal – and kissing his stepbrother – apart from all that . . . I could hear him walking off and I didn't blame him – I was a fool.

'Don't worry, I'm not leaving you. I'll be back in a moment.' And he was, with a cold flannel. I put it over my hot, achy face with a sigh of relief. 'Oh, that's lovely.' He was being far nicer than I deserved.

'Johnny, please don't get cross if I bring this up again, but I have simply got to say it. I am so sorry about earlier. I didn't mean to be patronising. I was trying to help. It was a stupid thing to do. I know that now.'

There was a silence, but I could feel him sitting near me, breathing evenly, thinking.

'OK, apology accepted. So, how long have you been allergic?' he said, changing the subject.

'Most of my life, probably, but we didn't find out until Will's wedding when he came downstairs positively awash in aftershave.' I smiled suddenly. 'At first it seemed like the most stupendous piece of luck.'

'Why?'

'Go to the chest of drawers to the right of the window. Second drawer down there's a photo album. Look at page four. Particularly, look at Anna.'

I could hear him shuffling the pages, then: 'Oh my God, what is she wearing?'

'Sophia's idea of a bridesmaid's dress. Isn't it utterly vile?'

'In every way possible. It's hard to know what's worse – the colour or the style.'

'Exactly. And before I ran into Will I was wearing the same dress.'

'In that colour? You must have looked like a giant banana.'

'Thanks for that. Actually, you're right – I did. At least Anna looked like a beautiful banana. Nothing can dim her loveliness. Anyway, our doctor was also going to the wedding. He popped in on his way, said it was just a reaction, probably, but to stay at home and see if it got better. Will got Ma to take a photo of me, to show Sophia to prove I wasn't skiving.'

'And after a while it got better?'

'Funnily enough, I recovered just in time to get changed into something decent for the evening do,' I said with satisfaction. 'Look, you don't have to stay with me, you know.'

He sat down again on the bed next to me. I could feel him shrugging. 'I haven't got anything better to do.'

He passed me tissues, because by now my eyes were

so swollen I couldn't open them at all. He found the pills the doctor had prescribed to lessen the symptoms, even though that meant rooting round in two drawers full of ancient make-up, blunt pencils and odd socks. He even brought me a glass of water with a straw so I could have a drink without spilling it. Then, because I couldn't really speak any more since my throat was so rough, he told me stories about the ranch in Wyoming. He much preferred it to California because it was so wild and beautiful and he could camp out there for days and not see another person.

'Isn't it full of bears?'

'Well, some, but I didn't mind. It's better than LA, which is full of sharks. Anyway, it's not dangerous if you take sensible precautions, like keeping the food well away from your tent.'

'So no midnight snacks in bed then?'

'Not unless you want to become a snack for a hungry grizzly. Do you feel any better, because you are certainly starting to look more normal.'

I sat up and opened my eyes. 'Yes, actually I do, a bit. I told you these episodes don't last very long.'

'OK. I'll be back in a minute. Don't go anywhere.'

'Oh, I'm not quite ready to face the world yet,' I said.

He returned soon with another drink and a straw. 'Here – try this. Oh, hang on, you're not allergic to expensive wine, are you?'

'Certainly not! Oh, this is delicious! But you didn't get this from our fridge, did you?'

'No. I pinched it out of Mitch's trailer. He's got loads of wine, but he prefers beer anyway. I thought this Chablis should go to someone who deserved it. I also return bearing good and bad news.'

'What is it?'

'Don't look so worried. None of it is that terrible. The bad news is that Stu phoned from casualty. His ankle is badly swollen and he's been ordered to rest. But the good news is that Julian has a friend who he was holding back in case of an emergency. This guy is a brilliant character actor and can take over pretty much any role. He was going on holiday to LA, but he's cancelled it and he's coming here.'

'Oh, that's fantastic!'

'And now, for some really good news.' He fed me something with a fork. It was a chocolate cake of such intense velvety deliciousness I must have looked like a greedy chick, opening my mouth for more.

'Did this come from Mitch's trailer as well?'

'No. Mitch wouldn't give houseroom to a carb-laden goody like this. I found it in that funny little room off your kitchen – what do you call it? Oh, yeah, the larder.'

'Oh dear.' I started laughing and spitting crumbs all over the bed.

'What?'

'Well, I am almost certain this is a cake Sophia bought from Fortnum and Mason.'

'So?'

'I would have to sell myself into slavery to be able to afford to buy a cake there. She had it earmarked specially for a coffee morning – you know, to impress the neighbours.'

'Whoops. I probably shouldn't have peeled off some of the icing to give to Bongo then,' said Johnny thoughtfully.

'That's it, we're doomed,' I giggled, making a mental list of all the people I would have to avoid when I re-entered public life. Sophia would probably forgive me, but not before I had suffered one of her lengthy lectures. And Mitch – well, I cringed as I recalled the horrified expression on his face when mine swelled up. He'd probably never seen anything like it in his life before.

By the time I felt able to open my eyes, it was late. Johnny had found and lit a dozen or so candles I had bought and never used. They gave the room such a comfortable, cosy light and we were so full from choc-olate cake we decided not to go down for dinner. Also, we were in the middle of a fierce debate about which of Julian's acting roles was the best. Johnny, naturally, held out for one of the Shakespearean roles, while I staunchly defended his one and only foray into romantic comedy. 'He will never play a part like that again, so it makes it unique – and he was very funny,' I argued.

'I agree, but it can't ever match up to his Lear,' said Johnny, stubbornly.

It was a difficult debate because I had actually fallen asleep during the screening of that particular film and I didn't want him to find out, to think I was an intellectual lightweight. Which I was, but it was far too early in our – our what? Relationship? Friendship? What were we doing? I needed to refocus on my Plan.

I stared at him. He was gazing dreamily at one of the candles. 'There is a moment in the play when he is alone and he is absolutely still, but you just know he's feeling so many things, the silence is almost deafening.' He got up and began pacing up and down my room impatiently, ducking to avoid the rafters. 'I've watched that scene a dozen times and thought of a dozen different ways to play it, but I always come back to that moment of stillness. Only a man as gifted and brave as Julian would have the nerve and the insight to do it like that.'

'Please stop walking up and down. You are very agile, but I'm terrified you are going to knock yourself out,' I begged. 'And *you* could do it,' I said slowly. He turned round and stared at me. 'You've got as much, maybe more talent than anyone here. Why don't you let someone help you?'

He sat down on the bed and began tracing a pattern on my blanket with his finger. 'Don't you think I haven't tried? You can't move in LA without falling over a shrink. Most of them are complete assholes. Do you know, one of them was just pumping me for information about Mitch so he could sell a story to the media? Another was sure it was all down to a bad birth experience. I am just sick of everyone telling me what to do and how to do it. This has to be something I do on my time.'

'Yes, but this is a perfect opportunity! Here you are, having Shakespeare rubbed into your nose every day and you are being forced to watch, and this could be the point when you say, "Enough! Now I am ready to change,"' I finished up. I was sure this was a phrase I had heard Will use before.

'Have you been talking to Will about me behind my back?' said Johnny, sharply.

'No, of course not. But don't you think there's something very significant about the fact that there is a therapist on hand when you might need him?'

'That's funny. I would have assumed that after this morning you would have learned not to stick your neck into other people's affairs!'

'I think you are angry because you are scared, and that's very natural and nothing to be ashamed of, and Will says that the people who take on challenges even though they are terrified are the really brave ones.'

'Well, that obviously doesn't include you, then!' he retorted sharply.

'What are you talking about?' I said, bewildered. I had never seen him behave this way.

He jumped forward and pulled a sketchpad from under my pillow. I had no idea it was even there.

'You just keep on finding one casual job after another instead of getting on with trying to be an artist, which is what you really want to be – or are you too scared of failure to risk it?'

Now I was furious. 'This conversation is about you, not me. You are just trying to deflect attention away from yourself.'

'Oh, yeah? You can hand it out, but you can't take it, can you?' he said mockingly.

I glared at him. This wasn't at all how I meant the conversation to go. 'I'm sorry if I've upset you but I was only trying to help,' I said, folding my arms.

'Oh, don't go and back down now, just when things are starting to become interesting,' he said, his eyes glinting dangerously. I stared at him. There was a spark about him that hadn't been there when he had first arrived. I was suddenly aware of the space between us. I felt hot, as if my allergy had suddenly turned into a fever. We both moved closer together, looking into each other's eyes and then –

Anna crashed in. 'Pa said he thought you had the lurgy again – oh, sorry, am I interrupting?' She started backing out, confused, accompanied by Johnny and me uttering simultaneous inanities along the lines of, 'No, no, absolutely nothing, I mean of course come in,' and then we banged our heads together and came to a merciful silence.

Point Number Two – I am not going to fall in love for a year, I reminded myself. I was suddenly very sad.

'By the way, I saw Mitch a while ago. He was looking for you,' said Anna to Johnny, who hesitated and looked at me.

'Right. OK. Well, I'd better go. I'll . . . er . . . see you tomorrow, then.' He threw me a searching look. I wanted to shout at him to stay, but then he walked slowly out.

'Are you sure you're all right? You look very flushed. You weren't about to break any plans, were you?' said Anna, suspiciously.

'I'm fine,' I said, faking a huge yawn, and she padded off to her room. But I couldn't sleep. Endlessly I rewound the tape of Johnny and me arguing. I couldn't believe he'd had the audacity to turn it around. As if I was the one who was scared of failure! I threw my pillow across the room in frustration. I would have to go downstairs and get some hot milk. In my experience the only immediate effect of hot milk is that I have to use the loo all night, but maybe the walk would tire me out.

The house was hushed and dark and silent – like it had been before the whole cast and crew had descended on us. Part of me wanted it back like that again. It seemed safer that way.

Will was in the kitchen making a cup of herbal tea for Sophia.

My Plan barred me from kissing anyone, but it didn't bar me from interfering in other people's business.

'Will, if someone suffered from something like . . .

oh, I don't know . . .' I pretended to think, 'well, stage fright, for instance, you could cure them quite quickly, couldn't you? I mean, how serious could it be?'

'Lila, I am a therapist not a magician. I would do the same as with any client – which is to talk through any issues they might have and try to work out a solution.'

'That's what I said!'

'Sometimes a consultation can be long and arduous –'

'The conversations you have with me are a bit like that too,' I said, kicking a chair leg gloomily. Johnny needed a solution to his problems quickly. We didn't – he didn't – have time to mess about.

Will paused on his way out. 'Sometimes when people come to me for help they have done a lot of the work already. Unfortunately for my bank balance, it doesn't always take years. But you have to remember one very important thing: I cannot help anyone who doesn't want to help themselves.'

'So if they say they don't want help?'

Will, shrugged.

'Well, that's really annoying.'

'Funnily enough, that's exactly what Freud said!'

'Did he really?'

'Don't be daft!' chortled Will, and went to bed.

Chapter Twenty

Johnny

Whatever Mitch had wanted me for it couldn't have been important because when I got to his trailer all the lights were off and the door was locked. When I moved closer, I could hear faint snores coming from his bedroom. Mr High and Mighty had forgotten all about me. I wandered around for a bit, enjoying the peace and quiet, because it had been a hell of a day. But when I got back to the house, I hit a bit of a snag. They'd locked up and gone to bed without me.

Crap. Now I would have to break in. I tried the windows, but they were all shut fast. Luckily I remembered there were some tools in the stable block. I would use one of them to jemmy a window open and hope that I could repair the damage before anyone noticed. Or I could just give Tony a call. He would be made up if he had to mend a broken window on his day off.

But when I got back, I discovered that there was someone ahead of me in the queue for breaking in and he'd made short work of back door locks already. The burglar looked like he was carrying quite a few extra pounds so I reckoned I could take him. I imagined myself as a cop in one of those television dramas the British were so fond of. It would be good to play the hero.

I tiptoed closer, and grabbed hold of him by the seat of his pants. He grunted and pulled just as hard the other way and we both ended up rolling around on the kitchen floor.

'The game's up. I'm making a citizen's arrest,' I hissed.

'Let go of me. I'm not a bloody burglar!' he retorted in a gargling whisper – I had my hands round his neck by this time.

'Oh, my mistake. You must be just visiting – except it's gone midnight, dumbass!'

'You're a fine one to be calling me names when you were trying to break in yourself. I saw you,' he retorted.

'I live here!'

'Without a key? Why? What's wrong with you?'

'Nothing,' I said irritably. We seemed to be straying from the point. 'You can explain what you were up to, to me or the police.' I fished around in my pocket for my phone.

'Oh, put it away! I've told you, I'm not a burglar. I'm a journalist,' he said, pulling an NUJ card and a wad of notes out of his pocket at the same time.

'You rob people of their peace of mind, so it's the

same thing. Put your money away – you can't buy me,'
I said.

'Everyone says that. There's a hundred quid here.
So, who are you then? Family or friend?'

'None of your business, you lowlife.'

'OK, OK,' he said, rubbing his neck. 'I'm leaving.'
He brushed himself off. 'I'm only doing my job. Do
you think I like spending my nights picking locks? And
you've torn my trousers!'

I stared at him. 'Do you think I care? Where's your
car? I just want to know how far I have to walk to escort
you off the premises.'

'You don't have to come with me. I know where I
bloody parked it,' he said irritably, going back out.

'Do you seriously think I trust you to leave without
my escort?'

'But you look very familiar,' he said, trying to peer
closer in the dark.

I pushed him along towards the drive.

'Touchy fella, aren't you? So can you confirm any
of the rumours I've heard? I heard Mitch Clayton was
in a lot of bother with an ex-girlfriend, and I also heard
he was already going out with another girl who was
living here. I could make any information worth your
while.'

'I told you earlier to put your money away,' I hissed
as we set off down the drive.

'Oh, don't get moralistic with me! Do you think
someone like Mitch Clayton gives a shit about a nobody

like you? He'd sell out his own brother without a second thought.'

'Yeah, don't I know it?' I muttered without thinking, which was a big mistake.

'Wait! I knew I recognised you. You're Mitch's step-brother, aren't you? I've seen your picture somewhere. You're the one who can't act – whoah, sorry, mate! Hey, let go of me – I could have you up on a charge of assault, you know!' By now I had my hands round his throat.

'Everyone would say it was just an act of mercy, like putting down a rabid dog. Tell me what you've got on Mitch and I'll let you go.'

'His ex was spotted in LA a while ago, coming out of a clinic, the sort you only go into when you're pregnant. But he's seeing someone here, isn't he?' The reporter continued with trying to get a quote on the alleged rumours, but I had stopped listening.

Was he? Sure, he'd kissed Lila, but I think she made it fairly clear she wasn't into him. I even sensed she might be into me. But I knew better than anyone that nothing turns Mitch into a predator more than a disinterested girl. The reporter was staring at me avidly, like he wanted to reach into my head and steal my thoughts.

'So, what's it like being Mitch's stepbrother, then? You're a bit of an outsider, aren't you? You must feel under pressure to start making something of your life. I'm sure we'd be able to negotiate an exclusive inter-view. It'd be very sympathetic towards you. What do you think? We'd pay a good sum for insider detail. You're a clever-looking lad – you'll know what I mean.'

'I'm a black belt in karate,' I lied glibly, hoping he would take the hint and just go.

'In my experience, if you were going to hit me, you would have done it already,' said the journalist, having weighed me up.

'I guess you've got a fair bit of experience of people wanting to hurt you then?'

'Happens all the time in this job, mate,' he said gloomily. 'I don't know why. So, Mitch's ex – are the miscarriage rumours true? If not, how does Mitch feel about the prospect of becoming a dad? Isn't he an eternal bachelor boy? I could write you a cheque right now for that interview.'

'Get out of here!' I said as I shoved him towards his car.

'It's your turn to grab a bit of the limelight. Must be bad for your self-esteem, living in the shadow of a famous stepbrother. I know how you feel – my brother always did better than me at school, but it's got me where I am today.'

'Right. You either get in and drive off, or I get security. It's your choice,' I reminded him.

He got in, but continued with his constant barrage of questions. 'Do you see anything of the Watson twins? How are they getting on? Isn't one of them overdoing her medication? And what about that Andy fella – there's definitely some trouble in that camp,

I've heard.' I slammed the door, but he only opened the window and carried on. 'OK, I'm going. Just tell me one thing, though – just answer this – why are you so loyal to a family who don't seem to give a shit about you? I mean, blood might be thicker than water, but I think you deserve a break, mate.'

'Just drive,' I said through gritted teeth, but he was unstoppable, like Niagara Falls.

'If you change your mind, here's my card. How's Cinnamon, by the way? She's an old friend of mine,' he added casually.

'Then ask her yourself,' I pointed out, and watched him reluctantly drive off.

Well, of course I couldn't go to bed after that. I was too churned up. The journalist had gotten under my skin. I paced around for a bit, but I just got more stressed. The guy's questions seemed to have pricked dozens of tiny holes in this production. Everyone would come through, wouldn't they? Of course they would. Actors were often vulnerable – it didn't mean they couldn't get the job done. Was Carly all right? I should ring her and make sure. What was the exact nature of Lila's relationship with Mitch? Come to think of it, what exactly was the nature of her relationship with me? Were we progressing beyond friendship? Sometimes I thought we were and then she seemed to retreat from me. What was she scared of? By this time my restless feet had taken me to the . . . well, Lila called it a pond, but it was too big for that. It was too small to be a lake, however. Whatever it was called, the still silent water looked very inviting. A short swim would get rid of some of this fidgety tension and then, maybe, I could sleep.

Of course, by the time I was halfway across the intensely cold water, it occurred to me that it might be full of pond weed and if I was going to get stuck in it, I would drown because no one would know I was here. I decided to stop kicking so energetically and then I heard a voice.

'Oh my God! I'm coming to get you!'

I turned round in amazement, forgot to paddle and sank. When I surfaced, spluttering, Anna was racing towards me. She was a good swimmer. I opened my mouth to ask her what the hell she was doing, but she had grasped me around the chin and was already heading for the shore. My foot slithered over a bit of pond weed; it would be better to keep still and ask questions in shallow water.

'OK, you can let go of me now. Look, the water is only up to our knees. Er . . . what did you think you were doing?'

'Rescuing you, of course! Oh, Johnny, if things were that bad, why didn't you tell one of us? We are all so fond of you. If you had . . . oh God, I can't bear to think of it!' she said through chattering teeth.

'Anna, did you think I was trying to drown myself?'

'Well, yes.'

I was busy pulling on my jeans. I wrapped my sweater

round her shivering shoulders. 'It was very brave of you – and totally unnecessary. I was going for a midnight swim. If I'd wanted to drown myself, I would have left my shoes on. It would have made the job quicker.'

'Oh.'

'Don't stand still or you will be the one that dies – of cold. Where did you learn to swim like that?'

'At school. It was the last lesson before lunch and I always wanted to get it over with quickly. Are you sure you weren't trying to end it all?'

I made her jog faster before replying. 'I swear solemnly I wasn't. I just couldn't sleep and thought a swim would get me tired. But what were you doing out so late?'

'I c-c-couldn't sleep either,' she said vaguely.

We were at the house now. I stopped and put my hands on her shoulders. 'You are the sweetest person I know, but please promise me you won't try and rescue anyone – anything else – otherwise I will never be able to sleep!'

Anna smiled at me and I hugged her. I liked her so much – it was like having a kooky younger sister – and we tiptoed our separate ways. As I lay down it occurred to me that I liked Will as well. He was a sensible guy and easy to talk to. Maybe I could have a chat with him, a very casual, no-pressure chat about a few things. Like overcoming stage fright.

* * *

After all that, I slept late the next morning. Groggily looking at my watch, I saw it was past ten o'clock.

The kitchen was empty. I grabbed a coffee and stumbled outside. I pulled out my phone and switched it on. It rang instantly.

'What the hell is going on?' demanded Brad's voice down the line.

'Nothing. What do you mean?' I said, confused.

'I've been trying to get through to you for the last thirty-six hours and all I get is voicemail. Don't tell me you've had your goddamn phone switched off?'

'OK, I won't then,' I said obligingly and held the phone away from my head while he shouted. 'Anyway, I'm here now,' I said, hoping my pacifying voice would calm him down.

'So am I,' he growled, and I jumped in fright, because there he was, walking towards me. He looked good. He was sporting new glasses and a new, neatly trimmed beard. Not one whisker was out of place. But then this was Brad – even his facial hairs did as they were told. As usual, his furious pace and look of controlled energy made me feel like a useless dreamer.

'So, how are you doing? Good, that's great,' he answered for me. If I wasn't quick he would conduct the entire conversation for me before I had time to open my mouth.

'I didn't know you were coming over,' I said.

'I wasn't, but things came up,' he replied. I waited,

but he seemed to think this was enough explanation. 'So, where's Mitch?'

'Rehearsing, probably. There was a bit of an accident yesterday. Someone got injured and they've had to call in a replacement,' I explained, but Brad couldn't care less about the play. 'So what's come up?' I had to stall him or he would just burst into the rehearsal like he had every right to be there.

'I'm pretty sure we've got Finn McGuigan on board for Mitch's next film.'

'Wow,' I said. Even I was impressed by this. McGuigan was a notoriously tricky director, who took things on according to whim and not according to the amount of cash on offer. This was definitely a coup.

'Yeah. I need to talk strategy with Mitch,' Brad said.

'You'll have to wait until rehearsal is over,' I told him uneasily. I hoped Brad didn't think that Finn was a bigger priority than the play. Mitch needed all his powers of concentration – and there weren't that many to begin with – focused on *Dream*.

'By the way, Dad wants you on the next plane back,' he added casually.

'Why?' I said, completely thrown.

'I don't know,' said Brad, shrugging. He obviously hadn't bothered to find out.

'I'm not going,' I said flatly. They would have to remove me bodily from this soil because I wasn't going willingly. I had far too many plates spinning in the air at the moment to take my eyes off them for a second.

Brad looked astonished that I had questioned the will of the great and powerful Dirk. I could see him blinking rapidly as he tried to make sense of this. 'I'll tell Dad then, shall I?' he said drily. 'Of course, I'm sure he'll understand.'

'Tell him whatever you like,' I said furiously. 'You and Dirk can't just order me around whenever you feel like it!'

'Why not? It's what we've always done before,' said Brad, genuinely surprised.

'Things are different now,' I said coolly. I felt amazing, standing up to Brad for the first time in my life.

I wished he would stop walking for a moment, turn around and listen to me, but I was way down on his list of priorities – if I ranked at all. He was making for the terrace, where the cast was gathered.

'This isn't one of Dirk's films, Brad. No one will know you or care why you are here.'

'Yeah, right,' he said, but he slowed down. I watched him check out every detail of the place, the people scurrying about on a million errands, the truck unloading portable hygiene cubicles. The recent rain and sunshine had produced a luxuriant crop of weeds in the gravel driveway, and when the sun appeared it illuminated the flaking paint on the windowsills. 'Why's he set this play in a dump?' he muttered, but before I could answer he had turned the corner and was on the terrace.

Julian was just starting to speak. 'OK, we are, of course, short of time, but I must introduce you to my good friend Jim, who has kindly cancelled his holiday for the next few weeks in order to take on the role of Bottom.'

'It's a pleasure to be here,' said Jim, smiling, but I stiffened. There was something wrong with the way he said that. 'Now, I'm not one for speeches, but . . .' He turned round, searching for someone. I followed his eyes as they fixed on Mitch and he moved closer.

'Why hello, Mitch! I think I should introduce myself personally, seeing as how you were responsible for me nearly becoming a grandfather!'

Mitch stood there with his mouth open, not understanding what was going on. I realised, with a horrible churning in the pit of my stomach, that this was Carly's father.

'It's good to know we see eye to eye, son. She's too young to settle down and start a family, what with her career just starting and all. And she's too nice to settle for a bastard like you. Though I'm sure you meant to be there with her while she went through some tough times, didn't you?'

Don't say anything, Mitch, I shouted in my head. You need to keep your mouth shut while he gives you an earful and gets it out of his system. But of course Mitch wasn't great at picking up the subtleties of human interaction.

'I don't know what the hell you're talking about, old man!' he said, but I could see his panicked eyes shifting from person to person.

Julian stepped forward and put his hand on Jim's

arm. But Jim just shrugged it off without a glance. He moved closer, as did Brad and I.

'Am I talking too fast, laddie? Let me make it clear, then. I am Carly's father – the girl you got knocked up and then fucked off, leaving her to deal with the consequences!'

'But Carly's American and you're British,' said Mitch, utterly confused. I groaned at his stupidity. He was busy missing the point when he should have been busy running.

'Yes. I'm from Leeds, but Carly grew up with her mum in the States. She's American; I'm British and *you* are a right little tosser,' said Jim, raising his fist.

There wasn't really time to intervene peacefully, and Brad was nearer to Mitch than I was, so I shoved him in front of Mitch just in time. Jim's fist hit Brad's face squarely. I was pleased at my fast acting, though I didn't expect Brad to appreciate it.

'Sorry,' I said to Brad, who was sitting on the ground nursing a bloody nose and a look of confusion. 'You're expendable – Mitch isn't,' I explained, just in case anyone thought I was saving the person, not the play.

'I'm Johnny, Mitch's stepbrother,' I said to Jim, advancing with my arm outstretched as if we were at some fancy party. He could take a swing at me as well, if he liked.

'Jim, what the hell is going on?' demanded Julian, holding Jim fast with his gaze. 'Did you agree to take the part just so you could rough up another member

of the cast? For God's sake man, where's your profes-
sionalism?'

Jim looked down at his feet. 'I know, mate. But I
wasn't completely lying to you. I'm happy to help out.
But what was I supposed to do? I couldn't keep silent
about the fact that this – this piece of shit has been a
complete bastard to my daughter, could I?'

'You could have come to me first,' said Julian shortly.
'Right, you two –' he nodded at Mitch and Jim – 'we
need to go somewhere private and sort this out. We'll
take a break, everyone, and start again in an hour.'

'No way! I'm not going anywhere with this guy! He
tried to punch me!'

'Under the circumstances, Mr Clayton, I am not a
bit surprised,' said Julian grimly. 'But we do have a
play to put on, so –'

'I don't give a fuck about your play. No one treats me
like this! I'm outta here!' snarled Mitch, and stalked off.

'Now look what you've done!' Brad glared at me.

'Darling, how could this be Johnny's fault?' asked
Cinnamon.

Brad shouted at me a bit and then I took him into
a bathroom to get him cleaned up because, after all,
I was responsible for his bloody nose. On the way out
through the kitchen, we walked straight into an anxious
crowd of cast and crew, who had moved discreetly in
there while Brad was shouting.

'Mitch is refusing to come out of his trailer,' said
Cinnamon, gloomily.

'We've always known he is a complete prick, but we need him, don't we?' said Guy.

Brad bristled. 'Relax, we all know he's only speaking the truth,' I said tiredly. What was going to happen to the play if Mitch left?

Jim stood up, took my hand and shook it vigorously. 'Carly said you were very kind to her. It's a pleasure to meet you,' he said gruffly.

I smiled wanly, but couldn't take my eyes off Julian, who was slumped at the table.

'Come on, man, Mitch must have an understudy?' Jim asked, trying in vain to cheer Julian up.

'Jim, you are a great actor, but you haven't a bloody clue! Like it or not, Mitch is the main reason people are coming to see this play. Celebrity matters nowadays. You might not agree, but that's the way it's played. Just now, I am all out of ideas.'

'You're outta cash as well,' said Brad thickly. 'You can kiss goodbye to the Clayton donation if Mitch goes.'

'But that money was for the earthquake fund! It was about helping people. It has nothing to do with Mitch,' said Julian, bewildered.

'You get Mitch, you get the money. Without him, you get nothing,' said Brad implacably. I wanted the ground to swallow me whole. As if we didn't have enough to be ashamed of.

I leaned forward and looked at Jim. 'I am really sorry about Carly. She had a horrible experience. But she is so much better off without him.'

'Aye, that's what she said. Look, I know I've been a bit . . . hasty. I am prepared to put it behind me for the sake of the play. But I'm not going to apologise.'

'You won't have to because I'm going to make sure he's on the next plane out of here. He doesn't need this crap. We agreed to do this as a favour,' Brad blustered, choosing to ignore the fact that this play was helping Mitch's career as much as vice versa. 'Well, the favour's all used up. Come on, Johnny, we're outta here.'

Brad stood up and made for the door. As far as he was concerned, it was over. Already he would be thinking about the next project. He didn't give a damn that he'd just placed a bomb in the middle of this venture. He got out his phone and started talking to the Clayton PR office. In an hour there would be a press statement out, bigging Mitch up and dissing the play and Julian in a subtle but devastating way. Once the Clayton machine started rolling it would crush anyone in its path. I had to do something and quick.

'Hold up a minute. You are making a big mistake,' I said, jumping between Brad and the door, so he had to stop. He waited. Everyone was looking at me like I was going to save the day. Crap. Come on, birdbrain, think of something, I told myself fiercely. My mind was a blank, but I had to come up with something. I looked hard at Brad. 'If you want to keep Finn you've got to make sure Mitch doesn't walk.'

Brad stopped and I knew I had him hooked. Now I had to reel him in. 'Finn kinda likes people who screw up,' I said slowly. 'He's screwed up himself often enough in the past. But he doesn't like quitters.' I looked round. There was a pile of newspapers and magazines on the sideboard. Wonderful Bartons – they never threw anything away! The interview was in a *Sunday Times* from two weeks ago. I started rifling through them and found the relevant paper. 'Listen to this. "We are all fools, but do you know who I hate the most? People who can't admit it. They are the real losers and I won't have anything to do with them."'

Brad came to a complete halt and I knew I had him.

'If Mitch walks, he won't get Finn. He has to have Finn. Mitch has to stay.'

'I'm still not apologising,' said Jim.

'I don't see how you can make him stay if he doesn't want to,' said Cinnamon.

'Of course he will. Johnny will talk to him,' said Brad simply.

Oh hell. I was so stupid I hadn't seen this coming, even though it had been announcing itself in neon letters a mile high for the last ten minutes. This was always my job, wasn't it? But I couldn't keep doing this. I needed to mutiny. I needed to break out.

I looked at Julian. 'You don't have to do anything,' he said firmly and smiled at me. I smiled back. I would do anything for Julian.

'Sure, we all know about my powers of persuasion,' I said cheerfully. 'I'll give it a go, OK?' And I walked out.

Hold on to this idea that you are gonna save the

day, Johnny, because you're gonna need it, I thought grimly. I tapped on the trailer door and walked in.

This was the last coherent thought I had for a while, because the next moment I was on my knees. My arm was being wrenched so violently behind my back I was robbed of speech. I couldn't have cried out if I'd wanted to. I could barely breathe. Above me I could hear Mitch spit curses into the air. I forced my brain to start working and start a silent countdown. Get from twenty to one and he would've let me go.

Well, I think I had to do it twice. Or I passed out. Not sure which.

Some time later I opened my eyes and I was free. He was sitting across from me on the sofa. 'Fucking play. Fucking bitch. I should never have come here,' he was muttering.

But if you hadn't, I would never have come here either, so screw you, I thought.

'What a fucking mistake,' he said. Then, 'Oh God, Johnny, I'm sorry.' He stood up and pulled me to my feet, which was a kind thought, but I wished he'd used the arm he hadn't strong-armed minutes earlier. He sat down again and put his head in his hands. 'I'm such an idiot. I knew my problems with her weren't over. God, it's been haunting me all this time! And her father – he could have damaged me!' He touched his perfect face tenderly.

'You've had a narrow escape,' I agreed solemnly.

'England is bad for me. I need to go home,' Mitch announced.

'Sure you do, but there's a slight problem with that,' I said and explained the Finn McGuigan thing. This took quite a long time, because Mitch didn't get it the first time or the second. 'Look, what's important is that he will be really pissed if you go and really pleased if you stay,' I said at last, and he got it, finally.

'This play – you're going to be brilliant in it,' I continued. I hated saying this, but it was true. Yes, he needed a lot of coaching, but when he was on the stage, he was so highly polished, he shone. 'Everyone's eyes will be upon you and thinking about how impressed they are that you are still working, despite your issues. It will show the world you are not a quitter.' This was garbage. Mitch was a terrible quitter. The only thing to which he was unequivocally steadfast was his monstrous ego.

'You're right!' he said eagerly and stood up, practising the face of someone who is man enough to deal with deep stuff. 'I'll have to work this out very carefully. I've got to be absolutely word-perfect before I say anything to these fuck – I mean, these wonderful, caring people.'

'Yeah, that's it,' I said, and eased myself out of the door. Mitch didn't notice – he was busy rehearsing remorse in the mirror. Now was maybe not the time to mention that he would have to get himself a new acting coach. I had other things to do.

This had been my last act as a doormat. I went to find Will.

Chapter Twenty-one

Lila

I missed all the excitement because I had my head down a portable toilet.

'There's a technical issue with one of the lavatories,' I was told, which eventually I was able to translate as 'the bloody thing doesn't flush'. When I asked why Liz was telling me this piece of unwelcome news, she replied it was because she thought I was the toilet expert round here. Great. Well, I suppose it was a career, of sorts.

'I knew we shouldn't have gone with a flushing no mains,' I commented, knowledgeably, deciding to show off a little. By the time I had got it sorted, everyone was busy rehearsing, and Will and Johnny were out on a walk and were not to be disturbed, according to Ma.

This was curious, but I was diverted by dealing with the logistics for the impending costume fitting at the village hall for all of the play's extras.

In honour of this event I changed into a clean pair of jeans and whistled as I made my way to the village. When I arrived, it was to find Johnny and Anna sitting on the bench outside, talking and giggling. Well, Anna was giggling.

Taken aback by seeing them alone together, I asked, 'What are you doing here?'

'I said I would keep Tony company,' said Anna, blushing.

'And I said I would keep Anna company while she is waiting to keep Tony company. And now you are here, you can –' began Johnny. He gave me a huge grin, which only confused me further.

'I am here to work, actually,' I said, shuffling papers importantly and dropping the key to the door, so we all ended up scrabbling around on our knees for it.

'Stay where you are – you'll get that gorgeous dress dirty,' said Johnny to Anna. He showed no concern for my jeans, but he was right. Anna was looking extremely lovely in something floaty and golden – a colour that does nothing for me.

As soon as the doors were opened, people began to arrive. They left their bikes outside, but brought their prams and pushchairs in. I drew the line at wheelbarrows, however.

'Gordon, what are you doing with that?' I said sternly.

'Well, I'm off to the allotment, after,' he said.

Why was Mrs Fleetham here? She wasn't in the play. And why was she carrying a small chest of drawers?

'This is the *Antiques Roadshow*, isn't it?' she said.

I ground my teeth silently and ushered her out.

Johnny and Anna put out chairs for the waiting

extras, which was kind of them, and Anna was explaining what a hall monitor was. 'I was classroom leader every year. I had a badge,' she said proudly.

'What was Lila?' Johnny asked.

'School rebel. She had so many detentions, Ma gave her a diary so she could keep track of them . . . Oh, hello, Tony!'

I ticked him off my list, though of course I knew he wouldn't be late. There were supposed to be about thirty extras here, but they had all brought family and friends. And they were all very excited.

'I've heard some of the scenes are going to be in the nude,' said Agatha Jenkins.

'Really? Which ones?' said Fred Fossett, enthusiastically.

'Well, none of them that you're in, Fred, otherwise the audience would think they were at a horror show!' said the woman, and cackled. 'I'm hoping it'll be ones with that Mitch Clayton!'

'The director person said I was going to mingle with the audience,' said Mabel Thomas importantly. 'I'm getting stage fright already.'

'Whatever for? You're not going to have to say anything,' Agatha said scornfully, sitting down and getting out a large Thermos flask and a plastic box of rather smelly egg sandwiches from a carrier bag. Agatha had clearly set herself up as the expert of the group.

I felt like I was in charge of a children's party, one that had already got out of control.

'Bert Williams, you're up next – and didn't I tell you to leave your dog outside?' I said crossly.

'This little thing won't cause no trouble,' protested Bert.

'That "little thing", as you call it, bit me on the ankle when I was working at the pub last month, and if it wees on those costumes I'll be sacked,' I muttered.

'Lila, I thought Bethany Campbell was next?' called out Abby, the wardrobe mistress.

'We sent her outside. The baby's nappy needed changing,' said someone helpfully. I went out, rounded Bethany up and dropped the baby off with her grandmother, who was busy ogling a picture of Mitch in *heat* magazine.

Johnny was sitting next to Anna, but he jumped up as soon as Tony came over.

'Take my seat. I need to stand for a while, stretch my legs. Anna, Tony would probably know why your car is making that clicking noise.'

'Now, where exactly is the clicking coming from – the front or the back? And is it a regular clicking or does it sometimes gain in intensity and then die off?' asked Tony. Johnny leaned against a wall and yawned.

I could only watch in awe as Abby dealt with people with ruthless efficiency. Why couldn't I be like that?

I went over to find Ethel Johnstone, who insisted on telling me about the torch she still carried for Pa. 'He was a lovely boy,' she reminisced. 'Of course, it was only right he married a stunner like your mother. You don't look much like her, do you?'

Bert and Gordon went missing. I found them outside, talking about marrows. When I went back inside I noticed that Johnny was pretending he could read palms. I knew at once he was only pretending but Anna was drinking it all in.

'A lot of native Americans have the skill. It's quite a tradition with our people,' he said. 'Yes, you have a very long love line – that means you have it in you to be totally faithful to the right man, should he get a move on,' he uttered under his breath. Who on earth was he talking about?

'Do you think they'll be able to see my varicose veins in this dress, dear?' said a dubious voice beside me.

'What? Oh, no. They won't see a thing.' I lowered my voice. 'You'd be amazed at what stage lights can do, Mabel. Mitch Clayton is not a day under forty-five in real life, you know. And he has terrible acne.'

'Really?'

I caught Abby's eye and nearly choked. I hoped she wasn't going to sack me. Johnny was really getting into his groove now. 'These little feathery lines here – see – they mean you have many admirers, far too many to count. The man who captures your heart will have to be strong and bold and daring!'

Tony interjected. 'Anna is far too sensible to be taken in by silly superstitions like fortune-telling,' he said, in a tone that used to have me grinding my teeth with frustration. But my sister didn't seem to mind at all.

'Do you agree it's just coincidence then if a horoscope comes out right?' she asked, and they bent their heads closer as they talked. Again, Johnny looked pleased, until he realised he had attracted a slightly wider audience than he wanted. At least three elderly ladies thrust their hands into his. Serves him right, I thought, slightly crossly. He was hardly talking to me at all today.

'Go on, do mine!' said Mabel, who had to be at least eighty.

'Why, you're so old, you've barely got any future left,' said Agatha. 'Here, have my hand. I'm at least five years younger than her!'

'Yes, but only because you've been seventy-five for at least the last ten years, Agatha,' retorted Mabel, quickly. I would have to watch out, or I would have a fight on my hands.

'Settle down, ladies. I can do you all,' said Johnny, who then looked confused when they all cackled in a dirty, knowing way.

'I'm on a diet – I'll have lost at least another six pounds by the time the play is on,' said Bethany to Abby, who looked unconvinced.

'You've been saying that for the last two years. I suppose you won't be wanting these then,' said her mum, pulling out a bag of doughnuts.

'Don't get even a single crumb on your costumes,' I thundered, and everyone jumped.

Johnny gave the three women outrageous fortunes and they were cackling so loudly with mirth, I couldn't hear myself think.

'Could you please keep it down?' I said sharply, and he immediately started looking under the chair.

'Lila's lost her sense of humour. Everyone help her look for it,' he said, and they all laughed. I grinned. He had really come out of his shell recently. Standing up to his family had apparently been a liberating experience.

Tony was busy trying to persuade Anna to join his self-defence class. 'It starts at six thirty on a Wednesday. I could pick you up and drive you home afterwards. The feeling of empowerment you would get from it would do you the world of good, you know,' said Tony.

'I thought we were going to see a movie on Wednesday?' Johnny remarked, winking at Anna. When had they decided that? Why had he not invited me?

'Well, we could go to the pictures the week after, couldn't we?' said Anna vaguely, and asked Tony if she would need to buy a special pair of trainers for the self-defence class.

After an hour, Abby gave us all a tea break. Well, everyone but me, because I was in charge of the tea urn.

'I'm glad to see you're having a good time,' I remarked casually, when Johnny came over.

'I am. Anna's such terrific company,' he said, as if this had only just occurred to him.

'Yes, she is,' I agreed. Did that mean he liked her more than he liked me? Why would that matter? Anna didn't have a Four-point Plan forbidding her to fall in love with anyone. She could do what she liked. Suddenly I hated my Plan.

Johnny started telling a story about how he had pulled a muscle at the gym. I don't know why – it was a very dull story.

'I expect you didn't warm up properly before-hand,' noted Tony, and Johnny nodded humbly. Tony turned to Anna. 'Don't worry, we'll make sure that won't happen to you. Warming up is a terribly important part of any exercise class and I have a very good DVD at home. I will take you through it before my self-defence class.' He went off to have his costume fitted. When he came back, he said, 'I don't feel like I've done much today, but I feel distinctly peckish.'

'Well, why don't you come back for tea with Johnny and me?' suggested Anna, and all three of them went off without a backward glance.

I felt lonely after they had gone, which was silly.

I was so fed up by the time we were nearing the end of work that evening that I even checked my diary to see if my period was due, but my hormones weren't due to kick in for another ten days. My good mood of earlier had vanished, though. I felt cross and fed up and slightly self-pitying. What on earth was the matter with me then?

I gritted my teeth and carried on, but by the time we finished, I hated my job. Why had I ever thought

I would be good at organising other people? I couldn't organise myself, didn't want to – I liked chaos. I knew I was being unreasonable, but when I saw Anna leave with Johnny and Tony I just wanted to drop everything, run after them and insert myself between them.

Eventually, we were done. As we were leaving, Abby turned to me. 'That went really well – and it was all down to you.' I stared at her with my mouth open and she went on: 'To be honest, I did think at first that Julian had given you a job just because you were family, though he's not normally like that, but I was wrong. I couldn't have asked for a more organised and efficient assistant. And that bit about Mitch having acne – hilarious! I didn't know you provided entertainment as well.' She locked the costumes up and gave me a friendly grin. 'You know where the key goes, don't you? Thanks – see you tomorrow.' She got into her car and drove off.

I checked there was no one left in the loos, switched off the lights and locked up, weighed down by guilt. I should be grateful for having a job and thrilled that I was doing it well. My Four-point Plan was turning out to be a brilliant success. I should be pleased. So why did I feel so low? Stop being so wet, Lila, I told myself sternly. Everything is great; everything is working out just as you planned it. But why had Johnny been behaving so peculiarly? He kept talking to Anna, and then turning round and pulling strange faces at me. I brooded on this as I turned the corner into the village hall car park. Everyone had gone without me, leaving me with only a bike for transportation home. Thank God I was wearing jeans. There were no lights on it, so I would have to make do with ringing the bell in warning if I saw another vehicle. But when I tried it, it emitted a hoarse and rusty sound, like a very old man trying to cough. No one would hear until it was too late and I was squashed. I wobbled about madly for a few yards as you do when you have to get your cycling legs again, and set off roughly in a straight line towards home.

Looking down at this pathetic excuse for a bike, I saw it had been cobbled together from bits of other bikes. The person who had done this must have been in a hurry – a bit too much of a hurry, I thought, as I heard something drop off and land in the road. I still seemed to be travelling forwards, so it couldn't have been too important. Six yards on, however, it suddenly felt like I was cycling up a mountain. But the road was still flat. It was like the bike was in another dimension, heading for the Himalayas, perhaps? I hunched over the bike and gritted my teeth. My legs were burning from the effort of pushing the pedals. On another day, I might have thought, in a pleased way, what an excellent way to get fit. Now I just thought swear words. Then it started to rain, the sort of rain that doesn't appear heavy, but creeps silently down the back of your T-shirt. My hair, not terribly bouncy at the best of times, as a hairdresser had once unkindly pointed out, was sticking to my head flatly. It looked like a helmet by the time I got home.

I let the bike fall to the floor of the boot room and trudged through to the kitchen. I wanted tea and sugar, chocolate – lots of chocolate – and a nice, hot bath. But chiefly, I needed to be on my own until I could shake off this awful mood.

I opened the kitchen door. The bloody place was full of bloody people, all bloody shouting and bloody drinking and having a perfectly splendid time. Bloody hell! Someone had even set up their iPod, so there was music as well. It was a party! Ma and Pa were there. Ma was looking quite pink and holding a glass brimming with something alcoholic. I saw Julian, Johnny, Mitch (groan), Tony, Liz, Tom, Guy and Pauline, and Cinnamon standing by the sink. She was chopping pieces of fruit and putting them in a large jug.

'Oh, goody, you're back at last. Sit down – you've got some catching up to do. Cinnamon is making the most fanstatic – oops, I mean fantastic cocktails. What's in them again?' burbled Anna. She was looking very rosy-cheeked and lovely. She was sitting between Tony and Johnny and looked like she was playing the part of most popular girl at the party, a role that used to be mine before I had got myself a Plan.

'I'll tell you tomorrow when I'm round again, making you the hangover cure,' said Cinnamon, flashing us a wicked grin.

'I would have got here earlier if someone had waited and given me a lift,' I said, but no one was listening, so I went off to find a towel for my wet hair. While

I was in the bathroom I gave a quick glance in the mirror. Crikey – when was the last time I had plucked my eyebrows? And surely that wasn't the beginnings of a moustache? I leaned forward in a panic and sighed with relief when I realised I had been drying myself with the dog towel and they were only dog hairs. But now, of course, I smelled strongly of Bongo, which wasn't good on a human being. Well, it wasn't that good on a dog. Any make-up I'd put on in the morning had long since vanished and it was such a long time since I had been to the hairdresser's my bob was now mostly blob – wet blob. I would have to do some serious damage limitation, and darkness would help – then no one would be able to see my face.

I went back into the kitchen and got the candles out. 'They are so much more romantic and party-like,' I explained, as I went round switching off lights, though a party was the last thing I felt like. Anna's bag was lying open on the sideboard. With a skill reminiscent of my schoolgirl shoplifting days, I palmed her make-up bag and scurried into the larder for an emergency spritz of her scent. While I was at it, I applied rather a lot of mascara, too much – now I looked like Morticia Addams – and some lipstick, a huge mistake – now I looked like a clown. I wiped it all off, depressed.

It was at this point that I should have cut my losses and gone to bed. But when did I ever do the sensible thing?

Chapter Twenty-two

Johnny

The party had started out as a retreat from a perfectly hideous rehearsal. Every play has a day or two like that and afterwards you laugh about it, but perspective is always hard to have at the time. And this production had already suffered more than its fair share of crises.

Almost with one mind, cast and crew decided that the Barton Willow kitchen was the perfect place to unwind.

'Oh, dear sweet Lord, everything I did today was bloody stupid,' recalled Cinnamon with a shudder, taking a swig straight from the rum bottle. 'Luckily I wasn't the only idiot. People forgot their lines – they made people laugh when they shouldn't have done. Mitch fluffed up two entrances, though I suppose you can't blame him – he was probably too busy worrying about getting punched. Piper sat on a chair and it broke. She looked horrified at first and then began to giggle because it was obvious the chair was so rickety it would have collapsed if a feather had landed on it.

She laughed a bit too long, however, and got slightly hysterical, so we had to have a break and then someone knocked their tea over Julian's script.'

'And how did Julian cope?'

'Oh, like the pro he is. But we all saw a vein start to throb in his forehead and we all lost our *joie de vivre*. He finished early because he said that he had to go away and work out how we had managed to make a sparkling comedy so bloody dull we wouldn't be able to hear ourselves speak over the audience's snores.' She winced and took another swig. 'So we all drifted here, for comfort. He was right. We were duller than an annual meeting of accountants – oh, my stupid big mouth, I didn't see you there. I –'

'It's perfectly all right. I like dullness. It makes me feel safe,' smiled Anna.

'Honey, you need to get out more.'

'I do – and that's where I feel safe. It's this house that's full of unwelcome surprises. Collapsing chairs are the least of it. It's not comforting at all,' she said, and Tony patted her hand comfortingly. I was very pleased with the results of my work at the costume fitting. They were getting on like a house on fire.

'Right. That does it. We officially need cheering up. I shall make some very special medicine. But I will need more rum, much more rum – and limes – and ice. And tequila,' said Cinnamon.

'I'll pop to the off-licence, shall I?' offered Tony.

I nudged Anna to go with him, but she didn't take the hint until it was too late.

'Oh. I've messed it up again, haven't I?'

'No, of course not. You've been flirting brilliantly. You are really getting the hang of it. He is definitely starting to sit up and take notice,' I said encouragingly.

'Do you think so?' said Anna, brightening up.

'Oh, he's hooked,' butted in Cinnamon, who had been eavesdropping shamelessly. 'He was pretending to talk to your father, but he kept looking over at you. But I think he's a bit confused.'

'He was engaged to Lila for a while,' I explained.

'That makes sense. He has the look of someone who is starting to realise that things might have gone horribly wrong.'

'Really?'

'Trust me, sweetie, I got all three of my sisters husbands,' grinned Cinnamon.

Tony came back with supplies and was sent out again to buy a sensible amount of alcohol – 'and by that I mean at least another two bottles,' said Cinnamon. The kitchen filled up as more people sensed the possibility of a party. Mrs B started preparing supper. Felicity, fairy-like, jumped up. 'Ooh, can I help? I love cooking, especially on an Aga. My cousin Jake is a chef.' She started chopping vegetables with enthusiasm, which let all of us off the hook.

I sent Tony and Anna off to find glasses. They were gone so long, Cinnamon let us take shots straight from the bottle to tide us over. She forced Tony and Anna to have one when they got back, as punishment, and when Anna merely sipped hers, made her take another.

There was a sticky moment when Julian walked in and everyone looked guilty and tried to hide their drinks and pretend they weren't really enjoying themselves.

'Oh, stop it,' he said crossly. 'I see you all, drinking and fooling around, when you should be sitting in your trailers and brooding on how rubbish you were today.' We were all silent. Jim looked sheepish. Liz looked at the floor and Felicity clutched a cabbage to her chest protectively. 'Well, get me a bloody drink, someone, and I might let you off,' he said and we all sighed with relief.

Mrs B went out to pick some herbs and came back with Mitch because she had no idea he wouldn't be welcome. He hadn't either, so he stayed.

We were having a blast by the time Lila got in. She looked tired, cross and wet, and even crosser when she saw us all having fun. She fussed around putting candles out, then filched something from Anna's bag and disappeared. What the hell was she up to? When she came back I shot her a quick glance, but she just scowled at me. Right, if that's the way you want to play it, I thought crossly, and turned to Anna, thinking that perhaps with a little creative flirting, I could make both Lila and Tony jealous.

I had found a pack of cards, so I started some card

tricks. Lila took a huge swig of the drink Cinnamon had given her and choked so hard her eyes started streaming and Will had to get up and pat her on the back, laughing as her face got redder and redder.

'I'm glad you think it's funny,' she spluttered.

'Come on, lightweight, you've got a lot of catching up to do,' he said.

I produced the ace of spades with a flourish.

'But I saw you tear it up!' giggled Anna, who was starting to hiccup. 'Johnny, you are so clever. What else have you got hidden up your sleeve?' She took hold of my arm, glanced at Tony and winked at me. She had had two shots and two cocktails and was warming up nicely.

'Here, have some water,' said Tony, pouring her a glass and leaning closer.

'She doesn't need that,' I said smartly, and gave her some rum.

'OK, boys, I shall have to please you both,' she hiccuped, drank the rum down in one go, took a dainty sip of water and smiled so seductively that if I wasn't in love with her sister, I'd have gone for her myself.

'Watch out – the last time Anna was drunk, Will had to carry her to bed and she was sick all down his back and up the stairs and along the carpet,' said Lila.

Tony shook his head at Lila and then he looked back at Anna, who was blushing. The two of them stared at each other as if there was nobody else in the room. Until Anna hiccuped again. I grinned. Tony was now putty in Anna's fingers. That sorted, there now remained only the question of Lila and me . . .

Mitch was talking to Cinnamon. 'When you've been in as many films as I have, you'll realise what a tough job it is.'

Cinnamon giggled. 'You looked like you were having a ball in *Assault* when you had about four women after you.'

Mitch looked important. 'It may have looked easy, but I had to dig deep to produce that performance.'

'You weren't complaining at the time,' I blurted out, much to the amusement of those within hearing distance.

But Mitch wasn't listening. 'Apparently Adam Archer is going to remake that scene in *Meteor*, the one where I seduce two women in one day,' he said with a smirk.

'That's because most Hollywood big-budget action films, the kind at which you excel, lack the imagination to try anything new,' I said.

Mitch looked surprised, as well he might. He wasn't used to me being openly critical. Then he sneered, anxious to put me back in my place. 'So what are your tips on how to seduce women, little brother?'

'It would start with a conversation,' I said, and glanced at Lila, who was guzzling down her second drink.

'Oh, well spoken! You're a dark horse, Johnny, but a sexy one,' said Cinnamon.

Mitch scowled, and then he sidled over to Lila. 'Layla,

babe, good to catch up with you. How are you doing?'
Without waiting for an answer, he leaned closer and
said, 'I'm not wearing any aftershave, so you and I can
have a real good time.' He pasted on his most seductive
grin.

'Do you know what? I don't think I'll take the risk,
Mick. We wouldn't want a repeat of what happened
the last time, would we, Miguel?' said Lila.

I was extremely heartened by this. She went off
towards the jug of rum, leaving Mitch scratching his
ear in a puzzled way.

'Here we are, everyone,' said Mrs B. She and Felicity
put about four dishes on the table. 'It's all the same
thing – I just didn't have a casserole dish big enough.'

Sophia came in from putting Emma to bed and
started making herself a salad. 'I really don't like to
eat meat more than twice a week, and obviously I'm
not complaining, but we do seem to have had a lot of
it recently,' she said, as everyone else leaped on the
casseroles.

Anna got up to find some napkins and Lila moved
towards Anna's seat. But they both arrived at the chair
at the same time and bumped heads. Anna began
giggling and hiccuping. Lila held on to the chair with
a mutinous look on her face. Mrs B stepped in. 'What
are you doing, girls? There's plenty of room down
here.'

'Yes, go to the other end of the table, Anna. I have
business to dishcush – to talk about with Johnny,' said

Lila. She leaned closer to me and wobbled drunkenly in her seat. 'I need to talk to you about . . . about get-ins and get-outs and strikes. The last thing we want is a strike, isn't it?'

'Well, they are quite a good idea,' I said gently. 'Striking a set means dismantling it after the show is over,' I explained, wondering how she had gotten so drunk so quickly.

'I'm only just getting to grips with it all and it will soon be over and you will go home,' said Anna, sadly.

'Why are you being such a wet blanket?' muttered Lila, refilling her glass.

'Don't fret,' said Tony, patting Anna's hand and looking pleased at the thought of us all going.

'But you can always come and visit,' I patted the other hand and winked at Anna.

'Oh, stop pawing her, the pair of you! She needs a hand free so she can gobble her supper down!' said Lila loudly and crossly. Her father looked over, concerned, but then Julian said something to him and he turned away.

'What's the matter, Lila – is no one paying you any attention?' asked Sophia in a patronising voice. 'Perhaps you should get engaged again,' she continued wickedly.

'I can't, ever,' said Lila, staring morosely into her drink.

I wanted to ask why she had apparently taken a vow of singledom, but Julian called over, 'Lila, Abby tells me you did really well today.'

'Do you hear that? This may be a sign that Lila is actually capable of earning her own living. I think that calls for a toast!' Will raised his glass and stood up. 'To Lila – who may have finally found a career!'

Everyone else laughed and stood up so I think it was only me that could hear Lila swearing softly under her breath. 'Here's to finally being able to afford to get out of this hellhole,' she slurred.

'Oh, I think I've got everything I need right here,' said Anna softly. I nodded and smiled, because there was a look of gratitude in her eyes that only I could see.

'Men are stupid,' said Lila under her breath. 'I except – I mean, I expect you can't wait to get back home, can you?'

'Why do you say that? Do you want me to go?' I asked quietly, but she had got hold of another drink and wasn't listening. I pushed my plate away – the food was delicious but I had no appetite any more.

'What have you got to look glum about?' demanded Lila. She glared at me, and when I started to ask her why, turned away.

Mrs B, who hadn't noticed how much Lila had been drinking, asked her to help serve pudding. Lila got up and threw bowls across the table like she was dealing cards. She banged mine down on the table so hard Anna jumped. Then Lila sat next to Tony. 'How are you doing?' she asked, leaning her chin on her hand and looking into his eyes as if she found him completely fascinating.

She even batted her eyelashes and tried to look flirtatious. Really, she just looked like she might barf. Tony leaned back, looking cornered. 'We've come a long way, haven't we, Tony? We have quite a history, you and I. There are times I wonder how things might have been, had I been a very different person,' she added quickly. 'But we are two civilised people who know how to behave, aren't we? Would you like some jelly?'

'What? Oh. Er, all right then,' he said dubiously and looked even less enthused as Lila practically got into his lap to reach the jelly. She had that look of intense concentration that only very drunk people get.

'You see, I have wanted to tell you for a long time . . . for a long, long time . . . I have wanted to tell you that . . . oh yes, that I would be so happy . . . so, so happy . . . if we could become friends. What do you think?'

'I think you should take your elbow out of the jelly for a start,' he hissed, and I stifled a laugh.

'Spontaneity,' she said, very slowly. 'That's never been your thing, has it, Tony?'

But Tony was looking over at Anna. He seemed distracted. 'Sorry, Lila, what did you say?'

'Nothing,' Lila said sadly, following his gaze. 'Life's hard, isn't it? It's not a laughing matter. Why is my elbow in the jelly? Where was I? Oh, yes. Life. Bloody life – oops mustn't swear in front of guests. Family hold back. Stiff upper lip. I'm the only one who really knows life. I am the only one who has a Plan. Bloody Plan. Did you know that, Tony? Anna thinks she knows what

318

she's doing, but she doesn't. I am the only one with a proper handle on things; only I can see life for what it really is. That is because I am an artist and suffering is an integral part of the artistic life. In my own small way I am part of the noble band of tortured souls, Van Gogh, Beethoven, Amy Winehouse . . . why the hell are you laughing?'

'Oh, Lila, you are as drunk as a skunk! I love it when you talk nonsense like that. You are so funny,' giggled Anna, setting off another round of hiccups.

'I'm not funny, I'm furious,' Lila said coldly. 'I was trying to make a serious point about the nature of art, which obviously you didn't get. But you don't always get the intellectual stuff, do you?'

'No, almost never, and I don't have an artistic bone in my body,' agreed Anna hastily, but it was too late. Lila was in full drunken flow. This wasn't gonna be pretty. I stood up to try and catch her attention, to head her off at the pass, as it were, but I was too late.

'No you don't. You are just a dull accountant. You don't understand me at all. You never have. But then you are far too busy being flirty and stupid with men to really know the real me.' She stood up.

'Oh, darling, shall I take you upstairs for a lie-down?' said Anna tenderly, but Lila brushed her arm off.

'Leave me alone and don't patron . . . patra . . . anyway, did you know that you look really fat in that dress? It's at least two sizes too small. You really will have to start shopping in shops for fat people. But you won't care, because you'll be too busy flirting and rubbing my nose in it that I can't flirt any more,' she said on a sob, and staggered out.

Anna and I stared at each other in horrified silence.

Tony was the only other one who had been listening. He stood up and stared after Lila. I held my breath. He didn't know it, but this was make or break time for him. If he went after Lila, I reckon he would have blown it completely with Anna. Which would he choose?

He turned back and looked at Anna, whose bottom lip was wobbling. 'Oh, darling, come here,' was all he said, but it was enough. He took her arm gently and walked her outside.

'You look very pleased with yourself,' smiled Julian, as I walked past him to get some water. He out of everyone, including me, had drunk the least.

'I am. I have been playing Cupid with great success,' I said, and then I remembered my own loveless state and amended that to, 'Well, a partial success anyway.'

'I sometimes feel that is the best anyone will say about this play,' he confided.

I nodded sympathetically, but didn't say anything. He didn't need anyone to protest; he just needed someone to listen.

By the time he'd summarised all the things that had gone wrong and listed a few things that still could, he seemed more cheerful. There was nothing like facing your demons head on to make them shrink, even slightly, I reflected, thinking of my talk with Will.

When Julian stood up to go, everyone took it as their cue as well. During the goodbyes, I saw Anna slip in, alone, but her eyes were shining. She grabbed my arm and dragged me to a quiet corner.

'We kissed,' she said. 'He said he had no idea he was falling so hard for me until the past few days when he thought you might like me and then the truth hit him right between the eyes. Oh, Johnny, it feels like all my Christmases came early!'

Then her face fell. 'Oh. I've just remembered – Lila. Tony told me not to be too upset. He said some people go very peculiar when they are drunk and, let's face it, Lila can be slightly peculiar when she's sober, sometimes, can't she? Mind you, Tony said he's glad she behaved horribly because it gave him the impetus to tell me how he felt!'

As Anna finally took a breath I told her how pleased I was for her.

The party was breaking up. I said good night and went slowly upstairs. I was thrilled with my success as a matchmaker, but depressed at the failure of my own romantic aspirations. I was tempted to go up to Lila and demand to know what the hell was going on between her and us, but I knew it was better to let her sleep it off. She had said a few things about not getting engaged again. Were those remarks directed at me? Was she hinting that she wanted us to be just friends? I tried to remain optimistic, but it really looked that way.

Chapter Twenty-three

Lila

'Oh my God! Oh my God! I've been buried alive!' I sat up, thrashing about wildly.

'Don't be ridiculous,' someone said, removing the wet flannel from my face. I sat very still, my eyes still tightly shut, and then Johnny said, very slowly and clearly, as if he was talking to an idiot which, frankly, he was, 'Listen to me. You may well wish you were dead – now and certainly later on in the day when your memory returns – but for now I am afraid you are very much still alive.'

Slowly I opened one eye. 'It was all dark and something was covering my face,' I said, as if that explained everything, and because this was Johnny, he nodded as if it did.

'It was dark because you had your eyes shut, you ninny. Look – it's a glorious day!' He went over to the window, pulled back the curtains and opened the window. What seemed like a howling gale shot past him and blew a pile of papers off my dressing table. He turned round and grinned. 'Sorry. I obviously still haven't got the hang of British weather – you know, when it looks like it's a lovely day but actually it's as cold as hell.'

'Hell is usually hot actually,' I said dully. I lay back down and pulled the pillow over my head.

'Now listen up – it's two o'clock in the afternoon. You've been lying here festering for long enough. It's time to get up and face the music.'

I couldn't answer him because I was too busy trying to work out what was worse – the incessant hammering in my head or the parched-to-a-crisp texture of my tongue. Coming up nicely in third place was my stomach, which was protesting violently about last night's intake of hardly any dinner and far too much alcohol.

'Drink some water, you'll feel better in a minute,' said Johnny sounding cheerfully unsympathetic.

'May I have a straw?' I asked feebly.

'No, you're not ill, you're just hung over. You can sit up like a normal person,' he replied briskly.

I managed to sit up, slowly, like a very, very, very old woman, but it was worth it. With the glass of water, the desert in my mouth retreated a bit and the litany of complaints from my stomach subsided to a quiet grumble.

'What happened last night?' My mind was a pounding, painful blank.

'To you? About a whole bottle of Cinnamon's one hundred per cent proof Jamaican rum,' said Johnny, drily.

'Rubbish. I cycled home, I had a drink – I ate jelly . . .'

'No. You had many, many drinks and tried to eat jelly, but I think most of it ended up in Tony's lap.'

'Oh God, oh God,' I said, burying my face in the duvet.

'He must be busy. There's still only me here, I'm afraid.'

'Yes, what *are* you doing here?' I asked cautiously, poking my head out of the duvet.

'Well, Anna was with you all night but then she had to go to work. But she didn't want to leave you on your own so I said I would sit with you.'

'That was nice of her,' I said sleepily. It was in-expressibly comforting to have Johnny here. His very presence was as soothing as a cool breeze on a hot day. Now, if I could just lapse back into unconscious-ness again for a few more hours, things would be so much better when I woke up. Anna would be back from work, would make me tea and –

Suddenly my face felt like it was burning off and my heart was yammering so hard I nearly couldn't get my breath. Bits of last night started to roll in like a big, black cloud of foreboding. OK. Breathe in through the nose, out through the mouth. You got a bit tipsy, Lila, nothing wrong with that – maybe made a few bad jokes, threw jelly around, probably shot your mouth off a bit – Anna would forgive me, I was sure. But why did I suddenly get an awful feeling that I didn't deserve forgiveness? I was almost too scared to find out *what* needed to be forgiven.

'OK, you've got to help me out here,' I said from beneath the pillow. I needed something to cushion me from reality. 'Tell me slowly and clearly, step by step, what happened last night.'

'We were sitting in the kitchen drinking rum cocktails when you got back. You were a bit wet. So you went to dry off. Then you came back and chugged your first cocktail straight off.'

'Rubbish! I would never do that. I sipped it!'

'Whose memory is at fault this afternoon, yours or mine?' asked Johnny.

'OK, OK, go on, but on second thoughts, don't give me a blow-by-blow account. Just skip straight to the bad bit,' I muttered.

'Right. Well, be warned. It is very bad,' he said seriously. 'You got really wasted really quickly. You were in a truly appalling mood. Then you wrestled Anna for a chair so you could sit next to Tony and launch into a monologue about Van Gogh and Amy Winehouse. You need to brace yourself for the next bit. You said some really horrible things to and about Anna.'

I came out from under the pillow. 'I told Anna she was fat?' It wasn't really a question – it was more of a plea for an amended reality. But Johnny couldn't give me one.

'Well, you're always teasing each other about that sort of thing. You call her fatty, she calls you a daddy-longlegs,' he said slowly, though I could tell he was just clutching at a comforting straw, because it hadn't been like that at all.

'Yes, we do that. But I wasn't teasing her, was I? I wasn't larking about. I was mean and hateful, and Anna knows me better than anyone. She would have known immediately that what I said wasn't said in jest.' I spoke with complete certainty, because even now I could still taste the vitriol that overcame me when I had insulted her. The heat ebbed away from my face and a horrible chill of guilt and dread came over me. 'I'm going to be sick,' I said abruptly, and just made it in time to the bathroom.

When I came back, Johnny said reasonably, 'So you had a bit of a spat – it's not the end of the world.'

'When you saw Anna this morning, how was she?'

'Fine.' He had his back to me so I couldn't read his expression.

I sat down on the edge of the bed and put my head in my hands, but not because it hurt. 'What have I done?'

'Nothing that you can't apologise for when she gets home,' said Johnny.

'I'm sorry, would you mind leaving me alone for a bit?'

'No problem. See you later.'

It was amazing how quickly my hangover seemed to improve now I had something much worse to worry about. I got back into bed and thought feverishly. There was no doubt in my mind that I had been seriously horrible to Anna last night and she knew it. I couldn't even hope that I could pass off my insults as the demented ravings of a drunk woman. I had meant to upset her when I called her fat. I am a horrible, mean, terrible sister. Maybe I should add another point to the Plan about grovelling for forgiveness from Anna. For, oh, at least the next ten years. Anna might appear soft and placid to the rest of the world, but to me, she was sturdy and dependable. She never made fun of me, she listened, she soothed, she encouraged. And how did I repay that? With bile.

I turned over and cried for what seemed like hours. The crying made me feel better for a bit, but then it just felt like a complete waste of time because it wasn't doing anything to help repair my relationship with my sister. I tossed and turned for a while, but dread at the thought of confronting Anna with some sort of explanation was making me so uncomfortable I decided I might as well get up. The headache and dizziness that followed would be a well-deserved punishment for my stupid and selfish indulgence.

I tottered to the bathroom – alcohol was so ageing; I felt like I had fast-forwarded to my early seventies – and ran a bath. I lay in it and shivered for a while, but it must have had some healing properties, because when I got out I felt like a new woman, well, one in my late fifties, perhaps, which was a bit of an improvement. I pulled on some clothes and went slowly downstairs.

The kitchen was empty apart from Will, who was reading a very dull-looking journal. He looked up as I came in, but didn't say anything. I suppose his years of experience in psychotherapy meant he could keep silent when most of us would have burst into tactless speech.

'Where's Ma and Pa?'

'They've gone out with Emma and Sophia for lunch with Julian.'

'Pa? Gone out? Out? Those words together just aren't making sense.'

He grinned. 'I know. I think there was a magic potion in that rum last night. He looked a bit shaky just at the last moment, but he made it into the car and they left ages ago so I think it must all be going quite well. I certainly haven't had any calls for me to go and rescue him. Actually, I think he's been getting better for a while now, but we've all been so busy with other things, we haven't really noticed.' He took off his reading glasses. 'I am not, however, going to be so crass as to ask you how you are.'

I sat down opposite him. 'I'm going to tell you anyway.' But then, weirdly, I sort of dried up. I wished I was a million miles away from here, living in a shack somewhere and painting all the time. Then I would be able to stick to my FIVE-point Plan. It would have to be somewhere tropical, because I would eat less if it was hot and then it would be cheaper. I would only need to pack a few sarongs and a bikini or two, and the shack, which I mentally equipped with a tiny kitchen in the corner and a coconut tree by the window, wouldn't require any heating. It was perfectly possible because Robinson Crusoe had managed for years. I could see myself now, sitting outside in front of my easel, wearing some sort of hat to keep off the sun (with my pale skin I suffer terribly from sunburn). Actually, in view of the fact that I am liable to turn into a lobster under our pale English sun, maybe tropical wasn't such a good idea. Maybe it would have to be somewhere northern, a Hebridean island, perhaps. But then I would be buffeted by strong winds and huge hailstones, and I would have to wear at least two pairs of gloves, which would make it very difficult to hold a pencil . . . Coming back to reality I realised Will was watching me patiently. 'Um, yes . . . well . . . oh, Will, I think, no – I know – I've really upset Anna. What on earth can I do?'

'Say you're sorry?'

'That's exactly what Johnny said!'

'Clever chap. I like him a lot.'

'Yes, I do, as well,' I said, and then stopped, confused.

Will said nothing but carried on looking at me in a friendly sort of way. But for some reason I had dried up again. This was possibly because there was a percussion band rehearsing inside my head, which was making it difficult to think properly. I got up, made a huge pot of tea and sat down to rehydrate until Anna got home.

After two cups I felt sufficiently restored to find a sketchpad and do a few quick drawings of Bongo, who was lying in his basket in the corner. He was dreaming and every so often his paws would twitch manically. As the clock ticked away, I grew tense. This was much, much worse even than waiting for a root canal treatment with the dentist.

Ma and Pa, Emma and Sophia came back from lunch in tearingly good spirits. I had never seen Pa so animated. I thought back longingly to those happy days when I was a nice, normal person who wasn't horrible to her sister and thus could enjoy the nice, normal things in life like other people.

I made everyone tea and scones, even though, unsurprisingly, nobody wanted any – mine always come out more like rock cakes – but I had to find something to do to pass the time until Anna returned home.

'Don't you think you're overreacting a bit, darling? Of course, Anna will forgive you if you just apologise to her. She seemed in remarkably good spirits at the end of the night. She can't be too angry,' said Ma eventually.

I just nodded. I couldn't explain to them how confused I felt about Anna, about Johnny, about my Plan. I wasn't sure I knew myself.

At half-past five Anna's car pulled up in the driveway. I knew this to the minute because I had been sitting in the porch waiting for her for the last hour or so. She turned off the engine and I climbed into the passenger seat. I couldn't look at her, but I couldn't think of anything to say either. I gazed numbly at my knees and burst into tears.

Despite having endlessly rehearsed how I would apologise, she ended up comforting me.

'I'm so sorry. I don't know what came over me,' I hiccuped into her shoulder. 'It must have been the drink. You must know I love you and never ever want to hurt you.'

'You did look a bit fed up and damp when you came in,' began Anna cautiously.

'I was in a stonkingly bad mood for some reason,' I said frankly. 'Obviously I know now I should have gone to bed with a nice cup of tea . . .' I tailed off.

'I just don't quite understand why you picked on me,' she said carefully, not looking at me.

I was jealous of you sitting with Johnny. He belongs to me, I wanted to say, but of course I couldn't because it sounded so stupid. Johnny felt like the first man with whom I was really comfortable. I could say absolutely anything to him, and he might laugh, or disagree, or he might even get angry, but it didn't really matter – he would always be there for me. And to top it off, I was upset that the only Clayton brother that seemed to be noticing me was stupid Mitch. And he didn't even know my real name! Not that any of it mattered because I was sticking to my Plan.

But the thing about friends, of course, is that you should be able to share them. I wasn't in love with

Johnny, of course not, and obviously I would know, having been engaged so many times. And if, as evidenced by her and Johnny's flirting yesterday, Anna was, then why wasn't I happy about that? It was awfully confusing. I knew I shouldn't and couldn't want him as a boyfriend, but I didn't want Anna to have him either. Well, that just made me sound stupid, selfish and horrible, so it was clearly something I should keep to myself. What would my family and Johnny think of me? They would think I was a nasty, greedy person and they would be right. Out of the three of us Barton children I had always been the worst at sharing toys as a child, I recalled.

'Once you've made up your mind about something, you always stick to it, don't you?' she said.

'I don't know what you are on about,' I admitted.

'Well, about . . . oh dear . . . you wouldn't say you didn't fancy someone if you didn't mean it, would you?'

Did she mean Johnny? Had I told her I didn't fancy him? I must have. 'Never,' I said firmly, though I suddenly felt on very shaky ground indeed. I knew that I didn't want to fancy Johnny because of my Plan. But somehow, every time I thought of him, I just wanted to fling the bloody Plan out of the window. But when I saw the look of relief and happiness wash over her face it was worth it. Almost. I clenched my hands into fists. I knew that I really should try and explain my complicated and confusing emotions to her. But they didn't seem to make the slightest bit of sense to me, so they certainly wouldn't to anyone else.

'Anyway, at least you had a great evening, until I ruined it. I just wanted to say, I think you two make a great couple.' I kept my voice light. Maybe she hadn't heard me, because she had her head under the dashboard.

'What are you doing?'

'I leaned forward to scratch my knee and now my hair is stuck,' said Anna. Eventually she got free and we started to giggle.

'As long as you're sure I'm forgiven, well, I don't care about anything else,' I said impulsively. That would be my penance for being such a horrible sister. I would be happy for her and Johnny. I would get over my incredibly confusing crush and move to that tropical island to end my days as an old spinster. Because if I couldn't have Johnny, I wouldn't want to get engaged to anyone else, ever, Plan or no Plan.

'Do you fancy starting the car and taking me to the corner shop? I have a sudden need for chocolate.'

'Goody, you must be feeling better.'

'I am,' I lied.

Chapter Twenty-four

Johnny

I woke early, as usual, got up and went for a jog to get rid of some of my pent-up frustration. Even at this early hour, people were at work. Cinnamon was walking up and down the drive muttering her lines under her breath and Liz was sitting on a wall, going over what looked like the running order for the lights technician. I set off at a good pace, but quickly decided that jogging was about the most boring thing you can do, especially when you are running through countryside so beautiful you just want to stop all the time and look at stuff. By the time I got to the wood, I had slowed down to, well, walking, really, and then I saw Julian among the trees.

He had his head down and he was swearing. A lot. I could make out quite a few bloodys, several buggeries, a good handful of fucks and one or two words I wasn't sure I'd heard of. Then he looked up and saw me.

I backed off instantly. 'Sorry, didn't mean to disturb you!'

Julian gave a wry grin. 'You've been here so long, Johnny, you sound like an Englishman.'

'I know. It's awful. I just can't seem to help myself. I sort of pick up other people's accents without trying. Anyway, I'll, er . . . go then.'

'Too late. You've already heard me. Oh, dear Lord.' He sat down abruptly on a tree root and put his head in his hands. Now I clearly couldn't leave, so I sat down next to him.

'I have never, ever been involved in a production like this one, cursed with crises. And as soon as I get one resolved, another pops up like an unstoppable army of demons. OK, there was that time, in *A Passage to Nowhere*, when a girl brought her baby to work and hid it in the dressing room. That was an uproar, though, and not a crisis. One of the Three Sisters lost her voice – on stage – in the middle of a scene, that was definitely a crisis. But then we got a replacement and carried on. But this – this is a conspiracy! I think Lila's mention of that Scottish play which cannot be named has cursed us.' He smiled to show that he was only joking but I wasn't deceived.

I was desperately sorry for him. 'She didn't get the whole word out,' I reminded him reassuringly. 'Is there anything I can do?'

Julian looked up and said, 'Not unless you can persuade Andy Sloan's now ex-girlfriend to go back to him.'

'Oh. So she's gone back to the guy she was with

when she met him, you know, the footballer?' I said confidently and then felt a complete fool. Last night when I couldn't sleep, I had gone downstairs and read every single one of the Barton girls' celebrity magazines – and there were a lot of them. I was now an expert on the tangled fortunes of everyone from Kerry Katona to Heather Mills.

Julian looked amused. 'No. She's run off with one of the members of that new girl band – Apple, I think they call themselves.'

'Wow, major scandal! So he's in a bad way then?' I said, trying to sound sympathetic. I hated Andy's interpretation of Puck. Actually, 'hated' was too strong a word for his colourless performance. He was so lacking in confidence he tended to skitter round the edge of the role like a nervous rabbit. I said this to Julian and he laughed, but quickly relapsed into gloom.

'Well, now he can't even do that. He's gone home to his mother.'

I was shocked. I wasn't expecting that. Death was about the only thing that should stop a serious actor from performing. A broken heart was a really lame excuse. But that was everywhere else – this was Barton Willow.

Julian looked grim. 'Go on, say it.'

'I, er . . .'

'This production is not cursed! I refuse to allow myself to fall into this stupid superstition that is breaking out amongst the crew like a rash.'

'Oh, so you've heard the talk then?' I said uneasily.

'Of course I have! I know everything that goes on in the production – apart from the things that go on behind my back,' he said wryly.

'Well, I'm sure you've come up with a solution,' I said encouragingly.

'I sat up most of last night, and the best I could come up with was Jimmy Lander.'

I stared at Julian in horror. 'It is cursed!' I said without thinking, and winced.

Jimmy had once been a brilliant television actor. But now he had a drinking habit so bad he couldn't be relied upon to even stay conscious for the entire length of a play. I imagined him making an entrance, cross-eyed and hiccuping, and felt sick. Then I felt sick with envy. The spectre of Puck danced before my eyes. Here, now, I could pull him down out of the ether and give him to Julian, but then I had to put my hand in front of my eyes, because those damned lights were dazzling. When I uncovered them again, Julian was looking at me with such a look of loving sympathy I felt quite ill with the shame of having to let him down.

'Never mind,' was all he said. Then, 'Ah, well, I must go and do some damage limitation with the press,' and he wandered off.

Now I really wanted to run, far away from here, but when I looked up, Puck was still there, taunting me. I had a sudden, horrible picture of myself, running for the rest of my life, with him following me, except that now he wasn't a mischievous sprite, he was a demon.

I was walking blindly back to the house when I collided with Lila.

'Hello!' She grabbed me by the hand and pulled me into the empty library. 'I'm glad I bumped into you. I want a quick word.'

'What's the matter?'

'Why do you say that? Nothing's the matter!'

For some reason that made me angry. She was such a terrible liar. I could tell at a glance that there was something up. I don't know how – I just knew.

She started fiddling with some of the books in the bookcase. I could tell this was because she didn't want to look me in the eyes. But I didn't need to see her eyes – I could read her like one of the books she was holding.

'Sorry, I don't know what's wrong with me this morning, I must still be suffering from traces of yesterday's hangover,' she said to the bookshelf. 'Anyway, Anna and I were talking yesterday and I said . . .' She shuddered, and then pulled herself together. 'I said how pleased I was that you two were getting on so well. You do make a lovely couple –'

'Hang on,' I began uneasily, but she wasn't listening to me at all.

'In many ways it'd be so great, with you and me being good friends, but of course sometime soon after the play you'll be going back to the States, I expect, and we might never see each other again, what with me moving to a tropical island and whatnot. Anyway, what could be better than if you and I were really good friends, which we are, of course – I know, I've already said that – and maybe, obviously, sometime long in the future you may well become, I don't know, like my brother?' She gazed earnestly at an ancient volume of poetry.

'Are you ever going to turn round and look at me?' I demanded.

She picked up another book and leafed through it. 'Hmm, how interesting,' she muttered.

I took it from her. 'I wouldn't know – it appears to be in Latin. I didn't know you were familiar with dead languages. Maybe you could translate for me, that and the rest of the rubbish you've been talking?'

She put the book back and made a great show of looking at her watch.

'Bloody hell – is that the time? I promised Uncle Julian I'd be with him – oh, about five minutes ago! He's going to be so cross! Sorry – must dash!' She turned round and ran off.

I waited until she was out of sight before walking round to the back of the house, the only place empty of any cast or crew. I briefly considered banging my head against the stable door until it, or I, fell down. But the stable was in such a state of advanced decay, it was a poor challenge. I had to do something to obliterate my thoughts, so I went into the kitchen garden and pulled up weeds, saying under my breath, 'I don't want to be your bloody friend!' My flirting with Anna had worked with Tony, but it had back-fired horribly with Lila. There were a lot of weeds, so I got quite a lot of venting out of the way but it didn't help the fact that our relationship was stuck in completely the wrong place and there didn't seem a thing I could do about it.

I toyed with my options. Staying here meant I had to deal with the exquisite torture of being around her, but not with her, if you see what I mean. However, if I went back to the States I would probably never see her again and that would just be torture, plain and simple. Besides, what was I going to do with the rest of my life when I got there? Today, the prospect of going back to that empty, pointless existence was almost more than I could bear.

Sometimes it takes a lot of bad things to happen before you can finally put up your hand and say: no – enough – that is as much as I'm going to take. Today was one of those days. There were only two things in my life that I really loved – Lila and acting. Today had shown me that I didn't have either of them. Earlier, I had thought about my options but now I realised what my real choices were. It was simple really. I could either die or I could go down fighting. Well, I've always been a sucker for a lost cause.

I walked back to the house, where I knew I would find Will in the kitchen, reading.

'I am sorry to disturb you, but can we have a final talk? It won't take long,' I said, politely.

'Of course,' he said. Then he looked at me and grinned. 'I can tell by the way you are standing and from that very determined glint in your eye that it won't take long at all. You've done pretty much all the work yourself.'

Later, I went out into the sunshine and stopped dead with shock – it was actually warm. I could feel the sun's heat pulsing through my skin and all of a sudden the air was vibrant with scent – honeysuckle, jasmine. My senses were so alive, I fancied I could actually smell the green of things growing. The air was heavy with the hum of insects and it felt like I was noticing all these things for the very first time. There were sparks of energy coming off my fingertips.

I walked at a furious pace for a while. I needed to expend some of the energy that was coursing through my veins or I might burst. I walked right up to Lila's tree and sat down with my back resting on the trunk. I was so still and silent, a bird hopped onto my outstretched foot.

I stood up. I could go back to the world now, and suddenly it seemed like a day when all things were possible – so I went to see Julian.

He was on the terrace, talking to the carpenter about the stage set. I stood and looked on for a moment, the way I always had – from the outside. But this time it needed to be different. I squared my shoulders and walked over. Act casual, yet confident, I told myself. No, not too casual – I wasn't going to ask him if he fancied a beer, was I?

He saw me coming, looked up and smiled.

'Can I talk with you for a minute, please?'

'Certainly,' said Julian, suddenly looking very cheerful. 'Shall we walk over to the lake? Then we won't be interrupted.'

For a minute my courage ebbed away, and then I squared my shoulders. I was in charge here, not that black dog of terror that was yapping at my heels. 'Down, boy,' I said to myself, but quietly, in case Julian heard.

But Julian had already set off down the lawn at a rapid pace and of course I had to follow him. When he turned to me his voice was as relaxed as if he had all the time in the world. 'So what did you want to say to me, Johnny?'

'I want to ask you a favour, to do with the play.'

Julian suddenly became businesslike. 'When it comes down to work, believe me, I never do favours for anyone. I make decisions purely upon merit.'

My mouth went dry and I stared at the ground. Then I raised my head. If I was going to do this, I would have to look him straight in the eye. 'I've been talking to a friend for a while now about ways to control my stage fright. He says he thinks I'm now ready to stop talking about it and start doing something about it. I am still scared, but this time it's not going to beat me.

I want to audition for the part of Puck.' I finished firmly and waited for the kind words Julian would find with which to reject me.

I waited. Julian regarded me gravely, but with affection. Then he smiled at me. Actually, a huge grin spread across his face. 'But, Johnny, you already have auditioned. You showed me all I wanted to know that afternoon in the woods. I've been waiting ever since – and I must say, you do like to cut things fine – I have been waiting to say that the role is yours as soon as you're ready to take it on.'

I stared at him. He put his hand – in a purely paternalistic gesture – on mine. 'Dear Johnny, I just know you are going to be a very great actor indeed.'

Chapter Twenty-five

Lila

I was in my room, doing yet another wedding sketch of Anna and Johnny, when I realised I had drawn myself instead. Horrified, I ripped up the paper and started again. Unable to concentrate, I looked round my room, trying to find something else to take my mind off, well, everything. There was a heap of discarded clothes on my chair and rows of empty hangers in the wardrobe. The drawers were pulled out and my knickers and socks were flung all around the room, the detritus of my recent search for my lucky pants. I wandered over to the dressing table and wrote my name in the dust. I thought about the last time I had been in Johnny's room – how neat and tidy and organised it was. We had nothing in common. In an effort to tidy up, I picked two mugs and a toothbrush off the chest of drawers and put them down on the floor by the door. I went round the room doing this and soon there was an impressive queue of items waiting to be returned to their proper homes. Then I was overcome by a terrible attack of inertia. Who was I kidding? I couldn't care less if those newspapers stayed on the floor until they too crumbled to the dust that was becoming such a feature of my room. I tried to drum up the energy to put my clothes away and then decided they weren't in the way, they were just airing. You had to do that to clothes every now and again. OK, I was pretty sure that sweater at the bottom had been there for about two months, and as I started putting the lids on bottles of make-up, I noticed the tube of expensive concealer I was convinced I had returned to Sophia. There was a major drawback to tidying up: it did terrible things to my conscience.

I went downstairs and found the whole family sitting round the table. 'You look like you are about to have a séance.'

'Oh, there you are,' said Ma. 'Thank goodness you're not outside anywhere.'

'Why?' I said, peering out of the window in alarm.

'Well, Julian's sent everyone away from the sets. He wants some private time and no one's to disturb him.'

'Have you seen Johnny?' I asked, noticing that other than Anna, he was the only one of us (even though he wasn't officially a member of the family yet) not in the kitchen.

'He's with Julian,' said Will.

'Why?'

'I'm flattered that you think I have the answers to everything, and usually I do, but I can't help you on that one.' I looked at him. I knew he was lying. But as I tried to edge unobtrusively to the door to find out what was going on, he added, 'Exactly what part of "stay inside and out of Julian's way" did you not understand?' So I sat down.

We hadn't been thrown together like this, without outsiders, for a while now, and I don't think we were used to it any more. Even Pa looked . . . well, a bit bored. I stared at him. I had never seen him look like that before.

I was helping Ma sort out the laundry into piles when Anna came home. She looked smudged and smily. Oh! Someone had kissed all her lipstick off. But when I sidled up to her to pump her for details on her and Johnny's snogging session – I didn't want to know, but I had to – she said she had a terrible headache. 'I think I might go and lie down for a while,' she said, taking her coat off. But I didn't believe a word of it and I could hear her humming as she went up the stairs.

Ma made a very sketchy supper and disappeared to another room to do some sewing. With the dress rehearsal tomorrow and the play the evening after that, she had unearthed an old dress from the back of her wardrobe for opening night, which needed taking in. So did Pa's suit, which no one could remember him wearing since 1997, when, with massive grumbling, he'd been forced to go to the funeral of some aged relative he swore he'd never met in his life.

Sophia was at another conference – this one about

children's lunch boxes. Apparently they weren't nutritious enough. This meant that Will had his hands full with Emma, who was crotchety, so he took her off to bed.

I was restless. I went upstairs and tapped gently on Anna's door, but there was no reply so I carried on to my own room. I wasn't in the mood for drawing so I had a go at cutting my fringe, which always sounds easier than it is. Surely all you have to do is cut across your forehead in a straight line? I was an artist – I was supposed to be good at lines. By the time I had finished, it was apparent that I needed to work on perfecting my straight lines, and my fringe made me look as though I was still at school. It would be worth remembering this when I'm in my forties, though.

I started to varnish my nails, but ran out of nail polish halfway through, only to discover I had also run out of nail varnish remover.

Feeling lonely I decided to stay up till Johnny came home. I wanted to talk to him. I wanted him here next to me, looking at me with those amazingly expressive eyes, telling me a joke or disagreeing with me about something, or just not saying anything at all. It was like there was a hole in this room without him. I then felt terrible for lusting after my sister's boyfriend and I lay down on the bed, reminding myself of the Plan and the gallons of sun cream I would need for life on a tropical island. Surely I wasn't such a terrible sister if I was willing to move away so they could be together?

*   *   *

The dress rehearsal was due to start at ten o'clock in the morning, after which there would be another one and possibly even a third if things weren't right, Julian had explained. He was going to be terribly hard to please today.

The weather was perfect and even tattered old Barton Willow looked rather nice. All the creeper growing up the walls covered its imperfections very nicely. I did a quick impersonation of Mr Todd being gloomy, just to cheer myself up, and went to the terrace, where Julian had called a quick meeting.

'Before we start I want to announce the absolutely final change to this play. Johnny Clayton is going to be taking the part of Puck. I think you will find he's word- and foot-perfect, and I am confident you will welcome him.'

'Sure we will,' said Cinnamon, rushing over and kissing him. I was rooted to the ground with shock. I couldn't believe I was hearing this stupendous piece of news in public, with everyone else, like, well, an acquaintance. Everyone was following Cinnamon's lead, so I hung around at the back of the crowd, feeling a bit lost. I noticed that everyone was being very loud and complimentary. Too loud. I overheard one of the fairies say, 'He's lovely, of course, but this isn't exactly a low-key production to have stage fright on, is it?'

'Oh, man, he could die up there!' muttered Paige, and shivered in sympathy.

'Julian believes in him, so that's good enough for me,' said Piper staunchly.

'This is still the curse in action. That girl should never have mentioned that play!' someone else said – I don't know who because I now had my eyes fixed on the ground, ears burning. I was shuffling away as surreptitiously as I could when someone tapped me on the arm. It was Johnny.

'I wanted to tell you first, but we were rehearsing nearly half the night. I came up to see you but you were fast asleep on your bed. Like the hand, by the way – is that a new fashion?' He sounded very calm, relaxed even.

I leaned forward to give him a friendly hug and realised that if he'd been with Julian he couldn't have been snogging Anna. How did her lips get so smudgy then? 'Johnny, I am so pleased for you. I just know you are going to make the most terrific success of the play and this will be only the start. I bet Julian's thrilled to have a protégé. He does like playing the aged, wise counsellor, you know.' I was babbling now, but I couldn't help it. I had suddenly felt very stiff and awkward while I was hugging him, remembering my disloyal unsisterly thoughts last night. Johnny and I knew each other better than anyone. He had seen me swollen up like a balloon; he had seen me drunk; he had seen me in my pyjamas – the ones I wore for comfort rather than style. He had been with me during all my moods and I had seen him from the beginning when he was awkward and angry; when he had found a place within my family, even though he couldn't find one in his own. We were so close. But now I felt like there was a Hadrian's Wall of awkwardness between us.

He pulled away from the embrace suddenly and stood with his hands on my shoulders. He looked deeply into my eyes, his mouth set and determined. I shivered suddenly, though it wasn't cold, and I felt he was about to say something momentous, when Julian called out for him.

'Photograph time. It's obviously too late to change the ones in the programme, but the press have kindly agreed to take a few. Hopefully they will keep everyone interested and that will mean they'll keep topping up the earthquake fund.'

Of course the press were salivating at the prospect of a new angle to the Clayton clan. They wanted pictures of Johnny on his own, Johnny with Mitch, Johnny with the rest of the cast, and they bombarded him with questions. Why had he suddenly taken up acting now? What did Mitch feel about it? Was this just a one-off or the start of a new career? I saw Johnny blink as the flashbulbs went off and for a moment I panicked, but then he seemed to be coping fine. Standing there, with Mitch's arm round his shoulders in casual sibling affection, I thought he looked like he had been doing it all his life.

When they had finished he turned to me and by the

look in his eyes I knew he was burning to tell me something. Maybe he knew who was responsible for Anna's smudgy lips? Had I completely misread the situation? I dared not think it. But then a reporter asked a last question and I felt a hand on my shoulder. It was Tony, in costume and looking very handsome.

'I must say I feel a bit of an idiot in this get-up, but at least half the village is in this too, so we can all be fools together,' he said.

'Well, you don't look silly,' I said firmly, but he wasn't listening to me. I looked closer. He had a soppy smile on his face and an air of being somewhere far away.

'Pull yourself together, Tony, you're only an extra.'

'I know. It's just that . . . well . . . oh, I've got to tell you – I've fallen in love, again,' he said.

'Well, that's great!' I said warmly. Tony deserved someone better than me and I knew it was only a matter of time before he found the right woman. It also meant that I could stop feeling guilty about him.

'It is – it's great. But she's very worried about hurting someone close to her.'

I wasn't really listening that closely since my head was full of Johnny – there was no room for anyone else. 'I'm sure you will sort it out,' I said vaguely.

'Oh, I hope so! I've made such a mess of things recently. I was starting to think I was destined to be a loser in love. Some people are like that. They never get it right and then they have to spend the rest of their lives on their own because they've lost the one person who means something special to them, and after that, of course, no one else will do. They might as well go and live on a deserted island!'

I stared at him. Everything he said made a terrible sort of sense. He could have been talking about me.

'Look, Tony, our break-up had nothing to do with you and everything to do with me being an idiot. Not that I regret stopping the engagement,' I added quickly. 'But the truth is, I should never have got engaged to you in the first place,' I continued, getting into my stride and smiling at Anna, who came out of the house, saw us and suddenly veered away. 'I should never even have gone out with you in the first place,' I explained, watching her rush off. Where was she going in such a hurry? I turned back to him. Illumination filled my mind. 'You see, I really, really liked you, but I was never in love with you. I just wanted to be in love with you. I've spent half my life wanting to be in love with someone,' I said slowly. 'That's why I kept getting engaged. I kept looking in all the wrong places for the sort of relationship Ma and Pa have. Maybe that's why I keep coming home: to try and work out what they've got, so I can have it too.' This psychology stuff that Will did was clearly catching. I pulled myself together. 'It was all my fault and I do hope you can forgive me.'

'Of course I do, Lila, and I hope we'll always be friends. Actually, in a funny way, that makes me feel a lot better, at least about some things. I was very much in love with you at the time, but my feelings – well, they've faded slowly, really ever since . . . I started noticing this other person.'

'Well, I am very happy for you. Who is she, by the way?' I added, curiously.

'She's very different from you. Quiet, but very deep. She's very gentle, but strong too, and so easy to talk to. And of course looks don't matter, but – well, wow! Thanks for listening and good luck with the rest of your life. Er, by the way, did you know you've only put nail varnish on one hand?'

Walking towards the set in the brilliant sunshine, I felt very sad.

My job responsibilities as Julian's assistant now had less to do with the play and more to do with the after-show party. Since Julian had hired caterers all I had to do was open the door at the right time and say, 'This way, please.' It seemed unnecessary to practise to get this right.

I turned the corner and was bombarded.

'Where have you been? I need you to run into town and get some paracetamol – we've run out. Abby wants you to pick up some dry-cleaning while you're there, and these glasses need mending at the optician's. One of the toilet doors is jammed shut and one of the windows on to the terrace is cracked – here's the number for the glazier. Agatha some-body or other has rung to say she can't do the play because she's got to wait in for the washing machine repair man – sort it out, will you?' Cara took a deep breath – was there more? 'When you've done that, Sarah in make-up is having a panic because she's lost the box of glitter for the fairies. I'm sure she hasn't, but go and help her find it, please. Julian has decided the grass in front of the terrace isn't short enough – this guy will mow it if you give him a ring . . . blah, blah, do this . . . blah, blah, this hasn't been done . . . blah blah emergency . . .'

I stared at her aghast. 'What the hell . . . ?' I said brokenly.

Cara stared at me and then giggled. She patted my arm. 'It's always like this on dress rehearsal day. Don't worry, it will all come right in the end.' Then she lowered her voice. 'Though I must say, we are all a bit worried about this latest cast change. Johnny is a great guy – a really great guy; I'd take him home any day – but the question everyone is asking is – can he pull this off?' She pursed her lips and looked doubtful as she went off.

I didn't know either. But I was more scared for him than I had been about anything in my life before. My fear of dentists faded into insignificance. Even my secret night-time terror that I was just a mediocre amateur artist didn't seem so important just now. If this all went wrong for him, how would he deal with the rest of his life? Well, all I could do was send secret waves of support to him while I tackled this list.

I was kept so busy running errands I didn't really see much of the *three* dress rehearsals. Which was a relief, because what I did see looked like a complete shambles. Instead of a smooth run-through, just like it would be on the night, they couldn't seem to get through a page of script without someone calling a halt. People kept running over to Julian and engaging him in brief, intense conversations and then running off again. There was a hiatus of about an hour due to a problem with the lights. Cinnamon and Jim sat down, back to back, and I think she actually dozed off. At one point I saw Johnny sitting on the steps, as still as a cat, his eyes utterly blank, and I was dying to go over and check he was OK, but then one of the extras said she'd laddered her tights, so I had to find her a new pair.

They finally finished around eight o'clock, apparently, though Julian said he wanted to go through a couple of Mitch's scenes one more time. Did that mean Johnny had done well then? I couldn't find him to ask him, so I went into the house, rather disconsolately.

In the hall I met Sophia, – 'You look fantastic!' I said, with maybe a bit too much surprise. But she didn't notice.

'Do you like it?' she said shyly, stroking the folds of a blue dress. 'Will took me shopping today and made me buy it for the party tomorrow night – not that I care what I wear, really. It's not even the sort of thing I would normally get, but . . . well, I couldn't resist trying it on again when we got home.'

'You are going to knock them dead! I think you

should make Will your personal shopper from now on,' I said. Then it hit me. The party! I hadn't given it a thought all day. I had been far too busy. Actually, come to think of it, I hadn't given the party a thought at all, which meant . . . which meant that . . . I didn't have a single thing to wear! Oh my God! Crisis! Emergency! I ran into Anna's room but she wasn't there, and I was in such a state of muddled panic I ran into the other attic room instead of my bedroom. I stood there, panting and looking round in a dazed way. I knew, with utter, horrid certainty, that there wasn't a single thing in my wardrobe that I could wear to a posh, high-profile party because I hadn't ever been to one. I would have to plead a migraine and go to bed instead. But of course, it might be the last chance I would ever have to see Johnny before he went back to the States and maybe into a new life as an actor. Whatever he did, it wouldn't include me.

I sat on the floor miserably and looked at a box full of broken umbrellas. Why had we kept them? Was this irrefutable proof that all Bartons were completely mad? There was another box full of shoes, none of them pairs. Yes, insanity confirmed. Another had 'princess' written on it in shaky handwriting. Inside was a cardboard crown with painted jewels – a child's dressing-up box. The dress had Christmas tinsel tacked onto it to make it more glittery. I pulled it out curiously. Underneath the glitter was the most beautiful, raw silk, deep blue dress – from the fifties, possibly.

It looked like the sort of thing Audrey Hepburn might have worn. A glimmer of hope dawned. I lifted it out gently and stood up, banging my head against a rafter, so I took the dress to my room and stood in front of the mirror. Yes, I was tall enough to pull it off. It smelled slightly musty so I would have to avoid getting too close to anyone. Well, there wasn't anyone I wanted to get close to – they were all taken.

Carefully I unpicked the tinsel and tried the dress on quickly . . . and gasped. How ironic. I was probably going to look better than I had ever done – and I had never felt more single in my life.

I glanced out of the window. The sun had set, but the sky was still a beautiful deep blue, the colour of my frock. It looked as cool and refreshing as a pool of water. I stretched my cricked neck and went downstairs.

The kitchen door was wide open. That's the only trouble with a Blessed Aga, it keeps on heating the kitchen even in the summer. I went outside and sat on the steps. I could feel sweat in my hair and trickling down my neck. Bongo was on the cobbles, fast asleep, still as a stone.

Cinnamon wandered past. 'I've just told Felicity that she's not to jump into your lake to cool down.'

'No, not the night before the performance. We don't want any more dramas,' I smiled.

'Well, my plan for the rest of the night is some soothing music on the iPod and an early night.'

I nodded in agreement. I was exhausted too, but I knew I wouldn't be able to sleep. I said good night and wandered down the path towards the lake. Cinnamon's words had reminded me of my Plan and how it had seemed like the perfect solution to all my problems when I devised it. It didn't feel that way now. In fact, my Plan felt like a ball and chain.

Away from the house and the gentle lights coming from the windows, the darkness felt velvety soft and heavy and actually quite cloying. All the noises of the day had been smothered in a silence as dense as a blanket.

I shrieked loudly.

'Goodness me, Lila! I didn't see you there! You were standing so still I nearly walked into you!'

'I didn't see you either! Well, I did, but for an awful minute – well, you were dark and shadowy, like a ghost. I thought you were a real ghost, Uncle Julian!'

I burst into tears and ran into his arms like a child. He was very patient while I sobbed myself into a calmer state.

'I'm sorry. I'm an absolute idiot!' I said eventually, wiping my eyes.

'Not at all. Carry on if you have to. In fact . . . I am now sure that is exactly what Titania would do at the end of that scene.' He pulled out a notebook and scribbled feverishly, then looked up. 'Sorry.'

'No, I'm sorry. How are you? How did it go?' The play was, after all, far more important than me.

'We'll get through it, I dare say,' he said.

I hardly dared ask, but I had to. 'And Johnny?'

'Brilliant,' said Julian, and smiled as he recalled Johnny's performance. I hadn't seen him smile like that all summer. 'But he said afterwards that he felt like he was just with a group of friends. His real test will come tomorrow, in front of an audience of strangers. Now, what's the matter with you?'

'I hardly know myself,' I began, and then stopped. That was it really, in a nutshell. I had been going round for weeks under a spell of stupidity. I didn't know myself at all. I wasn't in love with an ass, like Titania was, in the play. But I had been steadily falling in love with Johnny, my best friend, all these weeks. The truth hit me like a bombshell.

There had been a spark between us ever since we had met, but instead of fanning it into a great blaze, I had run round, wildly throwing buckets of cold water over it because I was so intent on keeping to my Plan.

'But when I made a Plan for my future and put that bit in about not falling in love, I didn't know what I was talking about,' I said, brokenly. 'Uncle Julian, until now, I'd never been properly in love. Oh, what a fool I've been!'

Chapter Twenty-six

Johnny

I found Anna in the kitchen, hunched miserably over the sink, doing the washing up. 'What am I going to do? I saw the way she looked at Tony earlier today! I'm sure she's not over him. Tony said he almost told her about us, but she didn't want to listen. I will have to leave, because I just can't bear it. Yes, that's a good idea. I'll run away. I'll emigrate. After all, you need accountants everywhere. I will have to find something to keep me occupied when I am not working so there won't be a single minute spare for thinking about how miserable I am. It would have to be something intense, like rock climbing or scuba diving, of course, though they are a bit risky and I am just a tiny bit accident-prone. Something like knitting would be nice and safe – but maybe too safe? And anyway, you can do loads of thinking while you are knitting, which obviously I don't want to do. But maybe I could take up the tango or learn a new language or –'

I put my hand over her mouth in a friendly way.

'It doesn't add up. I am sure she doesn't think about Tony at all. And put that plate down; you've nearly wiped the pattern off it.'

'Are you saying that to make me feel better or you feel better?'

I grinned at her. 'A bit of both, I guess. But Lila can be an idiot at times.'

'How can you say that about her?'

'Because I love her. Because she doesn't have to be perfect for me to love her.' I sighed. 'Because I would still love her to the very last molecule of my being, even if she was a complete idiot, drooling nonsense all the time, instead of just occasionally. She could be crowned Queen of Idiots for all I care – I'd still love her.'

'You are so romantic!' she said, and she meant it.

'You Bartons are all crazy!' I laughed. 'Look, I hate to leave you in your hour of need, but there are one or two things I need to do before the performance . . .'

She was instantly contrite. 'Of course, how selfish I am! Tomorrow is going to be the most important day of your life –' she began.

'Of course, now you've put it like that, I'm not at all nervous,' I said, with a grimace, but then she tried to apologise again.

'Really, it's fine. Go to bed. Get your beauty sleep, not that you need any.'

'Oh, Johnny, I would love to have you for another brother.'

'Well, maybe some of the magic in the play tomorrow

will rub off,' I said, and kissed her good night, thrilled by the compliment.

I walked around for a bit, too wired even to think about sleeping. It had been a hell of a day. Julian and I had worked on our own for a while before the dress rehearsals proper. He wanted to be sure we both had the same idea about the character. Even before this production began, I had read the play so many times I was word-perfect. I pretty much knew the whole thing off by heart. The totally brilliant bit about my part – well, apart from the fact that it was such a great role – was that I got to act a scene with Julian. He'd prob-ably acted the role of Oberon a dozen times during his career, and it wasn't particularly challenging for him, but he didn't let a single word or a single pause slide past him and I was determined to do the same.

Then we joined the others. I knew a moment of heart-stopping terror just before my first cue, but I remembered the series of conversations I had been having with Will on the subject of stage fright.

'You may always feel like you are actually going to die, but if you take a moment to check, you will find that you are still very much alive. I know you can pull this off,' he said at the end of our last session, the one where I told him I was ready to go out and do this, and that if I didn't, life wasn't worth living.

Of course he was right. My heart was still beating and all I had to do was get through the next moment, and then the next and so on. Instead of visualising one enormous suffocating cloud of fear, I tried to imagine it as a series of small parcels, not too big that I couldn't handle them one at a time. Once I had got past the first, awful hurdle, I was so busy being someone else, so busy acting, I didn't have time to be terrified.

The first dress rehearsal was so awful for everyone that I realised I wasn't the only one facing demons. People who had been word-perfect before today suddenly broke off in mid-line with a look of blind panic on their faces. The door that had worked for the last few weeks suddenly stayed shut and refused to budge. Someone tripped over a tree root in the woods and needed a sit-down and an ice-pack.

During one of these enforced lulls, Cinnamon came over and said to me: 'I remember my first day on set. I hadn't really worried too much in advance. After all, I've been in front of cameras since I was fourteen, and I knew my lines. Well, my first word was "but". I got the first letter out and stalled after that.' She chuckled. 'I kept saying "b", "b", "b". I sounded like a bloody car that wouldn't start. Then I burst into tears and locked myself in my dressing room. It took over an hour to coax me out. God, they must have thought they'd taken on a real dumb diva! So, how's your girlfriend, Lila?'

'She's not my girlfriend.'

'But you like her?'

'Well, yes,' I admitted.

'Then go for it, boy! Just tell yourself you can go for anything you want.'

'I'll try that – and thank you.'

'No worries.'

By now, I was walking past Mitch's trailer. Suddenly the door opened. He was talking on his phone. 'Yeah . . . yeah, I know, but I can't wait to leave. Totally. I couldn't stop him. Anyway he's here now – you can tell him yourself.'

Even before I lifted the phone to my ear I could hear my stepfather shouting.

'What the hell is going on?' But he wasn't interested in anything I had to say. 'Christ knows how we are gonna get out of this one. How many times have I got to tell you – stay away from the stage! You will never be an actor!' He continued ranting on and I waited to feel my usual reaction: that he was right. But I didn't feel anything. He was reading from his script. But it wasn't mine any more.

'I'm sorry, I cannot talk to you about this. I have more urgent things to attend to,' I said politely, and pressed a button to end the call.

Mitch gaped at me. 'Oh boy, would I like to stay for your funeral. If you don't die on stage tomorrow, he'll kill you for sure when he flies over. But as soon as I am finished with this shit, I'm outta here. I've so had it with this country!'

'Have you, Mitch?' I said absently, because I wasn't really listening. I was too busy worrying how this fairy-tale was going to end. How could we possibly all finish up happily ever after?

Chapter Twenty-seven

Lila

My alarm woke me at six thirty. I looked at it in complete disbelief for a minute before hurling it across the room. It had been after five before I had finally got to sleep, too late to make much difference really. I risked a sly peek in the mirror – yes, far too late. The bags under my eyes were so big I could have emptied the contents of my wardrobe into them. I looked like I had aged ten years overnight.

I knew I was going to have a bad night, so I'd taken a cup of camomile tea to bed with me. I opened my copy of the play – that would send me to sleep if nothing else would – but then couldn't resist flipping through the pages to read through Johnny's part. He didn't have the most lines and if I had been him I would have gone for one of the bigger roles. I sighed. Once, a long time ago, I would have gone and told him that, just for the pleasure of hearing him laugh and call me an idiot in that way he had that made it sound like an endearment.

Then I had to go to the loo because of the camomile tea. I lay down on my back and stared at the ceiling because I remembered Will once saying that if Emma had to look up at him it made her eyes tired and she fell asleep quicker. It didn't work. I sat up and rearranged the pillows, but whatever I did with them, they remained hard and uncomfortable. I concentrated on relaxing each bit of my body at a time, starting with my toes, but then I discovered a twinge in my knee that had never been there before. I switched the light on and sat up and shook my knee experimentally. The twinge went, but I was more wide awake than ever.

I got up. I would do some exercises, quietly, so as not to wake anyone else up. That would tire me out. Even the thought of exercising made me yawn. I bent down and touched my toes a few times and then ran out of ideas. The floors were far too fragile to risk doing star jumps. I went back to bed and pulled the covers up round my ears. I was too hot, so I threw them off, but then, five minutes later, I was too cold. Eventually, in utter desperation, I crept downstairs, intending to pinch some of Pa's insomnia tablets. But when I got to their room, all I could hear were snores. Pa, who should have been pacing the floorboards with dread at the thought of all these people storming the house tomorrow, seemed to be sleeping like a baby. It wasn't fair, I thought, as I went back to my room, treading on a splinter on the way. Getting the splinter out took up a fair amount of time.

My nerves were jangled and raw and my heart quailed at the thought of the rest of my life, barren of interesting employment and empty of Johnny. This was such a terrible prospect I could feel my breath become hoarse with an incipient panic attack. There was only one way to stop these. I got out my sketchpad. I still had dozens of pictures in my head to do with the play – some of them of rehearsals, some of the cast and crew at other moments. I closed my eyes and there was a snapshot of the make-up girl doing Johnny's face. Her face was rapt with concentration and his was dreamy as he thought about his role. There was one of Cinnamon laughing with intense, greedy pleasure. Another was of Julian looking at a script in his hand like he was a magician and it was a book of spells, which in a way it was, I suppose. There were dozens more, and I had all night . . .

'Bad night, sis?' remarked Will, who had beaten me to the kitchen and was brewing tea. 'Want some?'

'No, thanks. That's not going to be nearly strong enough to keep me going today,' I said, rubbing my gritty eyes and rummaging in the cupboard for the incredibly strong filter coffee we now kept for Johnny. I made a pot black enough to make my hair stand on end. It could only be an improvement on my current hairstyle.

There was an awful clattering noise outside and Will and I rushed to see who had fallen down the stairs. But it was Pa, chucking three bags down.

'What the hell are you doing, you mad old man?' said Will with a rather white face, imagining broken legs or worse.

'I was being a bit over-enthusiastic,' said Pa happily, his voice full of purpose.

Will and I looked at each other speechlessly. 'Well, strap me in a straitjacket and call me an idiot, but you can fling me down the stairs if it's going to put you in such an uncharacteristically sparkling mood,' Will muttered. 'What the hell is in those bloody bags?'

'Well, do you remember that time we tried to do the fishing holidays?' panted Pa.

'Yep.'

'Well, these are all the shooting sticks we bought and never used.'

'Because you didn't actually want anyone to stay,' I finished for him. 'Of course, these would be brilliant for some of the older members of the audience to sit on.'

'Exactly. They'd be just right for those sections of the play when the audience is going to have to stand around a bit.'

'Pa, you're a genius!' I kissed the top of his head as he bent over one of the sacks. The play had already started to work its magic. There was a new determined side to Pa lately that could only be good for him.

But when I said this to Will he pointed out: 'You started it when you got shot. Pa said to me later it would be the last ridiculous catastrophe this family was involved in.'

'Really?'

He grinned. 'Of course, I replied that was an impossible dream, given that it was the Bartons he was talking about. But we have done pretty well ever since, give or take one or two pieces of idiotic stupidity on your part and Anna's.'

I cast my mind back. 'I can't think of anything particularly silly that either of us has done recently.'

'You needn't look at me like that because I am not going to tell you. Your sluggish brain obviously needs the exercise of working it out for itself.'

I made a face as I took a slug of coffee, and was wincing at its bitter strength when Johnny walked in. I started to say something but then I stopped and shut my mouth firmly. He smiled at us vaguely, but I could tell his mind was far away, deep in the thickets of Shakespeare's verse. He was thinking his way into his role so that by this evening it would be no effort at all to stroll out onto the stage as Puck, weaver of mischief. I made him some coffee how he liked it, and put it down on the table so he could sit and drink.

Anna burst in. 'Oh God! I feel like hell! I think I was lucky if I got four hours' sleep last night!'

'Then you were lucky,' I said enviously.

'Tea, anyone? And what about breakfast?' She turned to Johnny. 'You should have a good start to the day by eating something substantial,' she said bossily. 'Bacon and eggs, probably. Or do we have any sausages?'

'Don't be ridiculous,' sniffed Sophia who had come

in with Emma in her arms. 'He needs complex carbs like oatmeal, bananas to keep the energy levels up for hours and a good handful of raisins for the vitamin C.'

'I put all the raisins in the cake I made last week. But if you went out and collected some eggs, Johnny – I know you like doing that . . .' Ma had her head in the cupboard, looking for the eggcups.

'Of course, scrambled eggs and tiny slivers of smoked salmon is the least Johnny deserves on this most auspicious day,' mused Pa, knowing full well we didn't have any.

'Smoked salmon? Think of the salt!' begged Sophia.

'Think of the taste!' added Anna, salivating.

'Oh, quiet, the lot of you!' I yelled, goaded beyond endurance. The coffee had done nothing but awaken my bad temper, it seemed. 'You can all eat what the hell you want. Johnny left the building ages ago.' I pointed to his empty chair. 'No, don't go after him, Ma. He'll come in for food when he needs to. Just leave him be. That's all he needs today – space.'

'And what makes you think you know him so well?' said Sophia sniffily.

'I just do, that's all,' I said firmly and went off to find a way of getting my hair to behave.

The one thing that was working perfectly today was the weather. Maybe that was the only miracle we were going to get. I stood outside and held up my face to the sun for a second. I could see Tom approaching from one direction and Liz from another. Abby was just getting out of her car, with an armful of stuff. She brightened when she saw me.

'Great – Lila – just the person – right, I need you to –' they all said, pretty much in unison. I got out my notepad. 'One at a time, please,' I said.

I had wrongly assumed that caterers could be left to their professional selves, but my first crisis of the day was when their lorry was too big to get through the gates. 'What do you want me to do, knock them down?' I said in exasperation.

'Well, they're half gone already. If I have to go back all the way to Maidstone and find two smaller lorries and another driver, you'll be having this party sometime next week,' the driver explained.

'Knock the gates down,' I said.

When the lorry finally arrived, along with the accompanying chefs and waiters, they all sat down on the grass and had a fag break before lifting out a single chair. The stage area had been cordoned off, but that didn't stop them leaning over it for a glimpse of one of the Watsons or Cinnamon.

We were going to lay out the bar and buffet on the terrace after the play was over, so everything had to be stacked up in the drawing room.

'If you put the chairs there, then we will have to take them out first and really, we need the buffet table out first so we can start putting food on it,' I explained. 'Stack them up in the corner there. Surely you can carry more than one at a time,' I muttered.

Paige came by for camomile tea and empathy from Pa, and Cinnamon popped in to give Ma a good luck hug. They had spent most of my disastrous drunken night talking and were now firm friends.

I put another pot of coffee on. Anna came in. 'Hiya,' I said casually.

There was a loud snuffle and I turned round. I heard, '. . . don't know how to . . . didn't mean it to happen . . . never felt like this before . . . last person to fall in love with . . .' but I couldn't make out the rest for the snuffling and the fact that she was talking into the depths of one of Pa's gigantic handkerchiefs.

'You're going to have to speak more slowly. I can only make out about one word in three,' I said desperately.

She put the hanky down and bravely, stripped of anything to hide behind, looked at me. 'You see, I've never been lucky in love. Up to now I've always felt like I was standing on the other side of happiness,' she whispered and, stricken, I could only nod speechlessly.

Both of us were beyond speech then, so I moved forward and so did she and we hugged. I was glad. It gave me the strength to say what needed to be said. 'Anna, you have to go for this.' I took a deep breath because it felt like I was being stabbed in the heart and I could barely speak for the pain. 'You have to go and be happy together. You deserve it. He deserves it.'

'I don't know what to say!'

I hugged her. 'There's nothing to say. Let's both have a nice cup of coffee.' I certainly required something to zip my mouth shut. All I wanted to do was scream out my misery and stupidity. But probably everyone but me already knew me for a fool. It felt like for the last few weeks I had been playing a part in a pantomime. All the time the audience had been shouting out, 'He's behind you!' But I had been deaf to reason. Love had been following me ever since my first sight of Johnny, but I had been too blinded by fairy dust to see it.

I went up to my room, clutching the coffee for comfort. I stared at the table. There was a half-finished painting on it. The paint had completely dried up. It was a rubbish painting anyway and I couldn't bear to look at it any longer, I decided. I took it off the stand and jumped on it until the paint fell off in dusty flakes. Soon – well, later tonight – this would all be over and the rest of my dull and pointless tropical island life would start. Then I went cold with fright as a perfectly awful thought occurred to me. I was wrong when I thought I would never see him again. Of course I would, and with hideous regularity: at every family do at which I would be forced to make an appearance. There he would be – with Anna. I pictured them together, sharing secret smiles and jokes like Ma and Pa did – Anna pregnant, possibly, and Johnny proudly kissing her stomach, pushing her hair out of her eyes, entwining his fingers with hers – all the things he should have been doing with me! At dinner he would feed her dainty morsels – actually, he wouldn't last long as a lover of Anna's if he didn't – she would help him learn his lines and, obviously, at the end of the day, or maybe even in the middle of it, they would go to bed and – no! I definitely wasn't going there.

Of course there was a part for me in all this too. I would become known as eccentric and slightly scatty Auntie Lila. I could picture myself. I would have long, grey hair, held up with a paintbrush instead of a hairpin. I would have that bony look that thin women sometimes get when they are older. I would probably – no, definitely – drink too much. Well, I had to have something to look forward to, didn't I? Gin probably. I couldn't make up my mind whether I would be living in a ramshackle cottage somewhere, with at least eight cats, or be a perpetual guest at people's houses; then I wouldn't even have to pretend to do any housework. I could imagine Johnny looking at the calendar. 'Oh God, it's that time of the year again! We've got your sister arriving today. Better hide the port. We don't want a repeat of what happened last time, do we?'

'Oh, darling, it's only for two months and she's got no one else!' Anna would reply. They would then share a long and passionate kiss, still deeply in love after all these years, and then hurry off to their important and exciting jobs. I groaned softly, and two big tears squeezed themselves out of my eyes.

Then I looked at my watch. I could not believe how quickly the day had flown by. It was time to get changed and go downstairs to greet the audience. How ironic that I too was playing a part. I was going to have to act my socks off, pretending to be cool and calm, in control. I put my Audrey Hepburn dress on and even in the middle of misery it was a bit nice to see that I looked rather good. I tried to put some mascara on, but my hands were shaking too much so I gave up.

I went downstairs. The house was full of strangers, milling about purposefully, I was glad to see.

'We're in here!' Pa poked his head out of the library. 'Darling, you look amazing!'

'Thanks, but I can't stop. I've got to make sure everyone knows where to go,' I said distractedly going in.

'That's fine. We just wanted to wish you –' began Ma.

I clapped an agonised hand over her mouth. 'Don't say it!' I begged. 'I have already brought devastation to this production by saying the wrong thing. They are the most superstitious bunch of people I have ever met.'

'Not like you then, with your lucky pencil and lucky knickers?' drawled Will pointedly.

There was a whirring sound above us.

'What on earth is that?' asked Ma.

I gulped. 'A helicopter landing in the next field. It's carrying some Hollywood friends of Julian's. I think I'm going to pass out from nerves. How on earth does anyone get used to this sort of thing?'

'Well, you already have, dear,' said Pa.

I took a deep breath and helped myself to someone's coffee, just to keep me topped up. 'Right, I'm going out.'

Then, I nearly forgot to breathe for the next few minutes. Barton Willow had been truly transformed. All the noise and bustle of people hammering and sawing and setting up lighting and shouting and actors rehearsing and arguing and eating and wandering around talking to themselves – it had all gone. Any trace that this was my family home had gone as well – the old chair under the tree that Ma liked to sit in during the summer, Emma's pushchair, Will's car. All the fag ends and inevitable bits of litter had gone. My decrepit old house had gone as well. As the sun slowly sank behind the trees, fairy lights came on, perfectly timed, one at a time. The orchestra was playing, the sort of music suitable for a Duke's entertainment, and people were walking down the drive like they were guests arriving for a party – which was how Julian wanted the audience to feel.

I found myself saying a silent prayer. 'Dear Shakespeare,' I muttered to myself, 'wherever you are, which is bound to be some sort of writer's heaven, complete with all the quill pens you would ever use and a neverending supply of ink, please look down with favour on this performance, and make it a night to remember – for all the right reasons, obviously,' I added quickly.

Chapter Twenty-eight

In his new elevated position as one of the stars, Johnny had been given a trailer to get changed in. He wished they hadn't bothered. If there were other people there, they might take his mind off his terror. His hands were shaking so much he couldn't do his own make-up and had to ask for help from Sarah, who had her hands full with the extras. What a terrible start to the evening.

Staring at his unfamiliar face in the mirror, he wanted to go over his lines one more time, but his mind seemed to have forgotten how words worked – what words were – he couldn't even say his own name if someone asked. He tried to remember Will's advice, which had worked so well yesterday. He felt like a fool. It was like practising to be executed – of course the fateful day wouldn't feel the same as practice.

He wanted to run away, but he didn't think his legs would carry him out of the trailer. He just knew in his heart that he was going to let everyone down.

There was a tap on the door and he jumped like he

had just been bitten. He had been – by an acting bug and he thought it was possible this bug would kill him.

'Need company? Oh hell, I don't care if you need it or not – I do,' said Cinnamon, poking her head round the door. She was carrying a small bottle. 'Now, obviously I am not recommending getting drunk before a performance, but this is medicinal. Drink it down in one.'

For a split second he didn't see her; he saw his mother giving him, a very small boy, medicine. The memory cheered him and a small smile crept on his face. He was also heartened to see she was shaking almost as much as he was. The drink lit a small fire in his stomach and then he was able to grin and say thanks, which wasn't much, but it was a lot better than not being able to speak at all.

'Let us in!' begged a quavery voice outside the door, and Paige and Piper stumbled in. They sat down either side of Johnny and held his hands and trembled. It was like he was sitting between two small terrified birds.

'I'm never doing this again,' muttered Piper.

'Well, it's a fine time to have regrets now, when it was you that got me into this,' said Paige.

'Now I don't want to put anyone off, but there are a helluva lot of people out there,' said Cinnamon, and named names. 'And that's just from across the pond. Apparently the Mayor of London has just arrived, half of the BBC, and crowds of journos, of course.'

'Oh, you're not putting us off. Why would you think

that?' said Piper sarcastically, and everyone managed to laugh, sort of.

'And the Mayor of Vacquitos, the town that was worst hit in the earthquake, is here. Julian paid out of his own pocket to fly him over,' said Jim, lumbering in. He took a drink from Cinnamon and choked. 'That's a grand drop of stuff.' Johnny looked at him in admiration and envy. He seemed his usual calm and imperturbable self, though Johnny hoped Mitch wouldn't turn up.

Having found his voice, Johnny thought he should practise using it. 'How is Carly?' he asked in a low voice.

Jim beamed. 'She's doing fine. Out in the desert making a film with that new Mexican director who's really starting to get noticed, Xav Martinez. He took her out to dinner last night, actually,' he added casually.

'The lucky cow!' said Cinnamon, in such a spot-on imitation of Jim's accent that everyone roared.

Paige walked to the sink and found a jug, pouring them all some water to offset the alcohol. 'Ooh, what a fabulous card! It's a picture of you, rehearsing with Julian.'

'My friend Lila drew it,' explained Johnny, making a mental note that he would have to get used to calling her just his 'friend'.

'No cards from your family then?' she asked, looking sympathetic. 'Well, you don't need them, so to hell with them and here's to us,' she said solemnly, holding

up her glass. 'This has been . . . well, it's been an experience, but on the whole, I'm glad I came.'

'I'll be going home with a few more grey hairs,' said
Cinnamon.

'I think we've all been changed by this play,' said
Piper, sitting next to Cinnamon, putting her hand on
Cinnamon's shoulder.

'Mitch hasn't,' said Johnny gloomily, and blinked
when they all laughed.

'Sweetie, he'll never change. But Paige is right: it's
no longer your problem. I have a feeling you will be
too busy doing your own stuff after this to bother with
him much,' said Cinnamon. 'Anyway, you're part of
our family now, all of us actors,' she smiled.

Johnny looked round at them all with love. Then
he grinned. Now they were all in make-up and
costume, they looked like an extraordinary family to
be part of.

Liz put her head round the door. 'Five minutes,
guys. Break a leg.' She blew them all kisses so as not
to smudge any make-up.

'Right, come on, I don't want to miss a thing,' said
Piper, and they all stood up and filed out, talking
quietly.

Cinnamon was the last to go. She turned and gently
put her hands on Johnny's face. 'What's your first line,
honey?' she whispered and when he opened his mouth,
she put her finger on it. 'Save it for out there. I saw
your face change then. You became your character.

You'll be fine – you'll be better than fine.' She touched his lips briefly with hers and was gone.

Julian was standing inside the drawing room near the doors leading out to the terrace. This was acting as the play's backstage area. Memories flooded back. He was at school, miserable, bullied and homesick, and he had just got a letter from his parents telling him he would have to spend the first two weeks of the summer holidays at school because they were busy.

'Never mind, you can come and stay with me – there's heaps of room,' said his new friend, William, robustly. Actually, William was his only friend, but Julian, stumbling through his own personal hell, knew at once that he had struck gold.

William's house was mad, but magical. It was so big he never got round all the rooms. The curtains crumbled when you touched them; the carpets were so beautiful and fragile you didn't want to stand on them, and he woke one morning to find his pillow sodden with rainwater. But you could slide down the banisters all day if you wanted to, or play football in the front garden, and the kitchen was like a hug – always warm and comforting.

One evening, when the slanting sunlight had banished any hope of sleep, Julian found by his bed a miniature copy of *A Midsummer Night's Dream*, bound in red leather, with a gold clasp. He sat on a windowledge and opened it up. Outside on the grass,

William and his sister, Lily, were playing ball but quietly so their parents would think they were in bed. Julian read, understanding only half, but it didn't matter, because sunshine and laughter and a sort of magic had already mysteriously entered the pages.

As Julian recalled the memory, he smiled. It was those exquisite, beautiful and silly moments that he wanted to recreate tonight in this most fitting of settings. But would he succeed? He watched his cast come over and grinned in delight – they looked amazing. Sarah and Abby had transformed them into fantastical beings from another world. He smiled at them all and put his arms round Paige and Johnny, his two most vulnerable children.

'No last-minute notes, gov?' whispered Cinnamon, tripping daintily over.

Julian considered. 'Take pains; be perfect.'

'Hey, isn't that my line?' grumbled Jim.

'Oh – and have fun,' smiled Julian. He could sense Johnny and Paige shaking like saplings in a strong breeze. Cinnamon had walked a few paces away and was doing breathing exercises. Felicity was talking to herself, going over her lines. Pauline was standing very still, with her eyes tight shut. Mitch was checking his reflection in a mirror.

Tony was almost hopping from one leg to the other, he was so nervous. He caught Johnny's eye and gave him a wry grin. Johnny grinned back abstractedly and watched Anna dart in to give Tony a sneaky kiss.

'People are simply pouring down the drive. Pa says the last time there were that many people here, it was for a ball to celebrate the victory at the Battle of Waterloo,' she whispered.

'It's not fair, there are no curtains to peek through and we're not allowed to show our faces,' grumbled Cinnamon. 'Tell me what's going on,' she asked Will, who had appeared at the door. Will was craning his neck to see who was inside. 'Who are you looking for?'

'I was just checking up on Johnny,' admitted Will.

'He's over there. He's fine,' said Cinnamon. 'What's going on out there?'

'Well, there's a good mix of dressed-up and ostentatiously dressed-down theatregoers. The women's heels are sinking into the grass – it's a good thing we're not fussy about our lawn. One old lady thought we were showing a film and I overheard two blokes talking loudly about how they would rather be at the pub, but they weren't fooling anyone. Everyone is hugely excited. There are so many flashbulbs going off that it feels like Bonfire Night, and everyone is taking pictures on their mobile phones to show off to the people who couldn't get tickets.'

Outside, the conversation swelled as the audience grew and friends caught sight of each other. The orchestra, which had been playing quietly, increased its tempo and volume. All non-actors were politely ushered out of the way by Liz. This was it, this was the moment they had all been working towards. Suddenly all the crises, mishaps, quarrels and terrors seemed unimportant, an insubstantial dream. This was the reality. Johnny felt, rather than heard, everyone take a deep breath. When they exhaled, they weren't their old selves any more. He shivered with excitement as he watched Guy hold out a regal arm for his bride.

What a perfect night for a wedding, thought Johnny/Puck, his mouth twitching in anticipation. What a perfect night for things to go magically wrong if you were a not quite human creature with an inclination for mayhem. I am a lord of misrule and my mischief will send you on a giddy dance of midsummer madness.

To think I might have started all this off, just by giving my sad friend a little book to cheer him up, thought Lila's father, and puffed his chest out with pride and then hoped no one had noticed. Next to him, Mrs Barton slipped her hand into his and smiled.

Mitch wasn't thinking about anything at all. He was doing exactly what Johnny had told him to do.

Lila had been busy. Two people had brought their dogs with them, so she'd had to confiscate them and leave them in the kitchen with Bongo. There probably wouldn't be a kitchen left to speak of after the show, when the owners could retrieve them. One elderly lady refused to use the portaloo, even though Lila explained at length how much better it was than a Barton Willow toilet and then, just as she was about to go and find Johnny to wish him luck, or break a leg, or whatever superstitious theatre people did say, she had to deal with a journalist who claimed he was 'lost' when it only looked like he was trying to creep backstage. Now the performance was beginning. It was probably the most important night of Johnny's life and she hadn't been there for him.

She slipped quietly to the edge of the audience and stood in silent misery for a while, missing the opening scenes. But then the performance caught even her attention, drawing her in bit by bit. Of course, I won't understand a word, she thought at first, but discovered that if she listened carefully to the actors' voices – well, it was like music – eventually you picked up the tune.

The lovers' predicament unfolded. Ooh, there was Tony, standing next to Bethany, who *hadn't* lost the weight and had been told not to turn round because her dress wouldn't do up properly at the back. Lila's hands itched to draw Hermia and Helena; they were just like her and Anna! Then Jim came on, with the rest of the rude mechanicals, and the audience erupted into laughter throughout the entire scene. Oh, that's what it's all about, thought Lila, who had thought it was just nonsense and didn't understand how anyone could possibly make it funny.

A flautist from the orchestra, like a Pied Piper, led the way up to the woods. Lila had worried that people would drift off or stop to chat, but they were all under a spell and followed obediently. She found Anna next to her, grabbed her hand and took a deep breath, because there was Johnny standing in the shadows – except it wasn't him, this was the person she'd met in the woods and she shivered suddenly as the lights in the trees cast an unearthly light on his face. Felicity, as the fairy, entered first, unaware that she was being watched by Puck, who was so still it looked like he wasn't even breathing. Then he swaggered into the scene and the two characters danced round each other, teasing and flirting. Johnny/Puck was captivating, but dangerous. If you went on a journey with him you might never come back. Then he suddenly went still, senses heightened like a wild animal. 'Here comes Oberon,' he warned and you knew this was the only person in the world Puck was in awe of.

'He did it!' whispered Anna.

Lila was puzzled for a moment, then her head cleared. Of course – his stage fright – she'd forgotten all about it. There hadn't been a trace of nerves or hesitation about his performance. From the moment he appeared he was Puck. She glanced round. Under the fairy lights she could make out a huge grin on Will's face. He'd definitely had something to do with all this and he was going to be insufferably smug about it. She grinned back at him happily. Sitting next to Will, from the rapt expression on her face, even Sophia seemed caught up in the moment.

Cinnamon floated rather than walked on stage, shimmering and insubstantial, every inch of her a magical queen. Lila blinked and looked closer. Was that really Mabel Thomas, postmistress and avid reader of romances? Now she looked like she had always been part of Titania's raggle-taggle supernatural retinue. Lila would never buy stamps from her in quite the same way again.

The jealous quarrel began between Titania and Oberon. Lila tensed. It was obvious they loved each other, that this was a ridiculous argument! You've got it all wrong, she wanted to cry. But Titania departed in wrath, and furious and thwarted Oberon planned mischief with Puck. I'll put a spell on her and she will fall in love with the next living creature she sees, even if it's a monkey or an ape, he said, and Puck nodded in delight.

Mitch was giving an excellent performance, though he wasn't the star of the show. There was a brilliant scene between Jim and Cinnamon, as, under a spell, Titania fell in love with Bottom. Lila felt her lower lip trembling. I know what it's like to be under a spell of silliness, she thought wryly, as she recalled the fiancés she imagined she had been in love with.

Those lights are holding up pretty well, thought Mr Todd, but there are far too many people here. Those toilets will never take the strain.

Puck swaggered back on. 'My mistress with a monster is in love,' he said with such sly satisfaction, Lila felt the hairs on her neck prickle. It was a good thing Oberon was around to keep control of him.

In a dream, the audience followed the flautist back to the terrace, the scene of Theseus' palace. 'Lovers and madmen have such seething brains,' complained Theseus, on hearing what had happened. Yes, one could write a whole book about the psychological implications of that, thought Will, inspired.

The last scene belonged to Puck, who looked penitent, though Lila wasn't sure if she believed him. 'If we shadows have offended,' he began, looking round at everyone with a rueful grin on his face, and everyone laughed. Glancing about, Lila saw that he had everyone in the palm of his hand. Julian, off stage now, darting his gaze between Johnny and the audience, saw it too. Barton Willow had done it again – it had acted as midwife to the birth of a stunning new talent. And then he blinked because there was a tidal wave of noise as shooting sticks went flying. The entire audience exploded in cheers, shouts and overwhelming applause.

Johnny jumped with fright as the applause grew louder. For a moment he didn't know who he was, himself or Puck. He had been so caught up with being this other person, he hadn't thought about stage fright at all, or even that he was actually acting in a play. Wow, he thought, and grinned.

Julian marshalled his troupe and they all bowed. 'Don't be silly – this isn't *The X Factor*,' he said, when someone in the audience shouted for an encore. There was a burst of laughter and then everyone settled down expectantly.

'You are right, though. We should do this again, shouldn't we?' he said, and grinned at the roar of agreement.

'I am so pleased you had a good time, because I certainly made you pay, didn't I? The people of Peru thank you for your generosity.'

'It would have been worth ten times that amount,' shouted Tony's mum, quite beside herself with excitement, and everyone around her cheered again.

'Unfortunately, this lot –' Julian gestured behind him at the cast – 'didn't get paid a penny and are now on their beam ends, with barely enough cash for their flights home.'

'Aaww,' said the audience, in delighted mock sympathy.

'That's OK – we don't want to go home,' said Cinnamon, smiling across the crowd at Mrs Barton.

'Yes, we've made friends here,' chipped in Paige. She linked her arm with Johnny, who was coming back to reality. He could feel Puck slipping away from him and he felt an ache of loss, and blinked hard.

'Well, you might be slightly consoled to learn that there are whispers of the possibility of a film. Of course, you'll have to pay again, but before we sweeten the blow with some food and drink, can I just thank our hosts, who – well, I think they've done more than you will ever know to ensure that tonight actually went ahead. Once or twice, there's been just a tiny setback, nothing major, of course, nothing to write home about

– I can't even remember what all the fuss was about,' and he winked, grinning – 'and it's usually been a Barton to the rescue. Hip hip hooray!'

'Last Barton at the champagne stand is a rude mechanical,' yelled Will, and set off at a cracking pace.

In the stampede for the bar, Lila lost sight of Johnny. Maybe he wouldn't come to the party at all, she thought. He and Anna might want to go off somewhere quiet and private. She felt a tidal wave of weariness pour over her, and absent-mindedly ate a plateful of canapés.

Sophia wandered up. 'There's at least ten grams of fat in each of those,' she tutted.

'And I've eaten at least six. How soon will they kill me?' Lila said hopefully.

Sophia frowned. 'That's no way to talk.' She peered at her. 'Are you all right?'

'Oh, definitely not.'

'Maybe I should get your mother,' said Sophia.

'You can't disturb her – she's having too much fun,' said Lila, pointing with a slightly shaky finger. Her parents were dancing under the trees in the moonlight. They looked so romantic she wanted to start crying again. Must save some tears for later, though, when I am alone, she thought.

She wandered off, searching the crowd when, at the far end of the garden, she spotted Anna talking to Tony. She was wearing a white dress and in the moonlight she looked ravishing. In the low-cut dress her breasts were spilling out like melting ice cream. No wonder Tony was looking down at them like that. Hang on. He had no business to be looking at her bosoms in that way! They belonged to someone else. Lila looked round anxiously, but Johnny was now nowhere to be seen. She started walking over to them, her eyes riveted on her shameless hussy of a sister. Tony had pulled Anna closer to him and now they were indulging in what could only be described as a passionate kiss in front of everyone. What was going on? Did she have some sort of score card – kiss all the men and make them cry? Lila rubbed her eyes in case there was grit in them, but no, there they were, still locked together. What on earth was Anna playing at? Lila stepped back as if the appalling behaviour might be catching, but Anna came up for air and spotted her. She whispered something to Tony, then ran over to Lila.

'Oh dear. I am so sorry you had to see that! That was unforgivable of us!' she wailed. 'Oh, Lila, this is too awful – please say you still love me!' She tripped over a chair leg and fell into her sister's arms.

'Of course I do, silly! Why wouldn't I?' said Lila, setting her gently upright. Lila shook her head, desperate to clear it. When had her shy sister become such a loose woman?

'I was afraid you weren't over Tony, but Johnny said he was sure you were and encouraged Tony and I to get together.'

'Johnny knows about this?' Lila asked, utterly confused. 'He was right, though. I stopped thinking about Tony in a romantic way ages ago. But what has that got to do with anything? The real issue is why you were kissing Tony right in front of everyone and not caring if Johnny sees. What is this? Some kind of weird threesome?'

Instantly she regretted this accusation and stepped back nervously. Her dear sweet sister, the not-saying-boo-to-a-goose sister, was glaring at her with a ferocious look in her normally mild eyes. Then Anna lifted up an aggrieved finger and began jabbing her in the arm with it. It was quite painful. 'How dare you mention Johnny, that poor man, after all he's been through? You really will have to stop pairing me off with him like we are a pair of odd socks! The fact is . . .' she stopped and took a deep breath, as if to drum up courage, 'the fact is, Tony and I are in love. You had your chance with him but you blew it. We are a couple now. That's why I've been going round for ages saying I'm sorry, you ninny!'

In the stunned silence that followed, Lila's mind slowly caught up. 'So you are in love with Tony?'

'Who else would I be in love with? Of course I am – have been for ages, actually,' she said, and looked all moony for a minute. Then she pulled herself together and became brisk. 'But surely you knew that?'

'No. I thought you were in love with Johnny,' Lila said

weakly, holding on to her arm for dear life because the garden was spinning madly.

Anna started to giggle. 'We were only fooling around to make Tony jealous, silly. I think it was clear to everyone that he's always been madly in love with you. Even Tony could see that, though he did get worked up enough to come right out and say how he felt about me, so really it was worth it in the end and – are you all right?'

Suddenly Lila's legs wouldn't bear her weight any longer. She sank to the grass. You couldn't blame them really, they had been carrying round an idiot for the last twenty-odd years. A huge grin spread across her face. 'The fireworks are lovely, aren't they?' she said dreamily.

Anna looked round. 'What fireworks?'

'The ones going off in my head. There are huge explosions of colour – reds and blues and glittering gold and silver flashes.'

'Lila – LILA! Stay right where you are. I'm going to get help.'

Anna ran off. Lila got up too, because the grass was rather damp here, and began wandering around with no real idea where she was going, except that she knew she had to find Johnny.

'Hiya, Lucy, did you catch my performance?'

She blinked. It was Mitch. 'What? Oh, yes, quite good. And it's Lila, by the way,' she said, still in a blissful dream and barely taking in that he was there.

'Hey, whatever you're on, I want some.'

'I'm afraid this feeling doesn't come out of a packet.'

'Shame. So how do you think it went? I thought my scenes went really well. Acting in plays isn't anywhere as hard as people make out. My part came real easy to me. I might do it again. I was on the phone to my father and he said . . .'

Lila watched his mouth opening and closing, but someone had turned the sound off.

There was a sudden explosion of colour in the sky. Were they real fireworks, or the ones in her head? Oh well, who cared – they were very pretty. Why was she still here, with this idiot? She had to find Johnny now. She turned round and walked off, leaving Mitch in mid-sentence. She was vaguely aware that he was staring after her, mouth open like a stranded goldfish, but she didn't care.

She pushed her way through the crowd with difficulty because people would keep trying to talk to her.

'Ma says there are two dogs having a fight in the kitchen, and you put them there, so would you please sort it out?' said Will.

'Later,' said Lila impatiently, and shoved him aside.

Liz ran over. 'One of the waiting staff drank two bottles of champagne during the performance. He's lying stone cold on the terrace and people keep falling over him.'

'Do they? That's nice for them, isn't it?' remarked Lila, walking on.

'You've got a bit of a problem. One of the Minervas is backing up something terrible,' said Mr Todd lugubriously, barring her way.

'Have I? How wonderful,' said Lila dreamily, pushing past him. She broke into a run, scanning the crowd anxiously. Everyone was here, milling around and having fun, everyone apart from Johnny. Where on earth could he be? Upstairs in his room, perhaps, or on his way to the airport? Think, Lila, she begged herself.

Of course. She set off at a rapid jog towards the wood. As she approached she could see a lone figure leaning against a tree.

'Oh, thank goodness! I thought I'd never see you again,' said Lila, but she was panting so hard this was mostly unintelligible.

'What did you say? Here, lean against me. You look like you might pass out.'

'I'm fine. Just need to – get my – breath back . . . That's better . . . Oh, Johnny, I don't have to go to that tropical island after all . . . been such a fool . . . couldn't see you were falling in love with me . . . too busy trying to keep to the Plan . . . but I was never really in love with anyone until I met you, so it doesn't count any more. In fact, I am officially declaring the Plan NULL AND VOID!'

'What are you talking about, you darling fool? What is this plan you keep talking about? You can do what you like, as long as I can kiss you,' Johnny said.

Chapter Twenty-nine

Lila

Johnny and I spent all night outside under the midsummer trees. Hours passed in an ecstasy of pleasure. We moved beyond our mortal selves and only returned to the real world when rosy-fingered dawn crept across the dark blue sky . . .

I'm sorry. I made that last bit up.

What really happened was that we were just surfacing from our third kiss – and I think our best so far, though I was fully prepared to go back for more – when we were interrupted. Honestly, you never get any privacy at Barton Willow. It felt like the entire party had followed us up here. Amongst the crowd I saw Julian, Cinnamon, Will and Sophia, and Tony and Anna, holding hands. Apparently Mr Todd had told everyone I was having some sort of breakdown. They all calmed down when they saw I was with Johnny.

Will said loudly: 'Alleluia!' He then insisted on shaking Johnny vigorously by the hand. 'Really, I was beginning to think you two would never come to your senses and that I was going to have to act in a most unprofessional manner and simply order you off to bed together.'

If I wasn't so blissfully happy, I'd have thumped Will for being so crass.

But there was no chance of any blissful privacy. Ma rushed over to hug us both, Pa thumped Johnny on the back, and Will called for Anna and Tony, who were still canoodling away happily in a corner, and forced us all to stand together and be cooed over and have our pictures taken.

Julian added some class to the situation. '"Here come the lovers, full of joy and mirth. Joy, gentle friends, joy and fresh days of love Accompany your hearts!"' he said, again, causing several people to start sniffling, so it was lucky that Cinnamon had brought some bubbly with her.

I think it was that glass of bubbly which was my undoing really. Suddenly I started to go wobbly at the knees. The strain of working so hard on the play and the horribleness of thinking I had lost the first (and only) person I had ever really been in love with, suddenly caught up with me. That or the fact that all the caffeine from my endless cups of coffee wore off. Anyway, everyone said it was the caffeine, but I put it down to an excess of emotion and stress.

We all trooped back to the house, a merry, chattering group. Johnny put his arm round me and I pressed close to him, unable to speak but blissfully happy. He took me into the sitting room. It was lovely and peaceful in here, apart from a distant yapping from the kitchen.

'I'm just going to sit down here for a minute,' I said quietly, and sank onto a sofa, still clutching Johnny's hand tightly. I wasn't quite so relaxed that I was prepared to let him go just yet.

And that was it for five hours. Complete oblivion and some snoring, though I think Johnny made that last bit up.

When I finally opened my eyes again, the party was over, the birds were singing and Johnny and I were lying snugly under a blanket. Well, maybe snug wasn't quite the right word – it did smell rather strongly of mildew.

I lay for a while watching Johnny and smiling madly. He stirred slightly, muttered something and woke up instantly, his dark blue eyes bright and alert.

'I'm sorry. I know we should have spent our first night together having inventive sex, but I think I must have passed out.'

'You did. And don't worry, we've plenty of time to be inventive,' he replied, and I shivered with excitement as I thought of all our future together. I kissed him and stretched and yawned.

'Oh dear, I seem to have missed the party.'

'Only just. Most people left at about two a.m., but the rest of your family and Julian stayed out on the terrace until after four. Your parents did a spectacular tango, and then Will talked about Freud's ideas on love. Tony and Anna didn't say much – they were too busy spooning – and Sophia made everyone nettle tea before they went to bed.'

'What did you do?'

'I lay here and watched you sleep,' he said, kissing me again. Then his brow creased. 'I am glad you are awake, my darling. "My heart unto yours is knit" for ever, without a doubt, but can we just clear a couple of things up? Where is this tropical island you keep mentioning? And this plan – is it some sort of legal document?'

I explained it all and didn't mind a bit that he thought it very funny. 'Love has given me a roaring appetite. Shall we find some breakfast?' I said in conclusion.

'Yeah, now there are no secrets between us any more. Or is there something else?' he said, seeing my expression change.

'Well . . . there is just one tiny thing, hardly worth mentioning,' I said slowly. I could feel my mouth go dry with fright. But it would be better to get it over with, whatever the consequences. 'Johnny, I've got something perfectly dreadful to tell you.'

His eyes narrowed and he glanced round, as if expecting to see another ex-lover come crawling out of the woodwork.

'It's nothing like that,' I hastened to reassure him. 'Though, maybe you will think it's worse.'

'Look, you'd better spit it out.'

'Um. Well, there's no easy way to say this.' I took a deep breath. 'Johnny, I have never read a Shakespeare play in my entire life!' I risked a glance at him. He looked distraught with shock. 'In fact, until last night, I had never seen one all the way through. I only watched this one because you were in it!'

'But why, Lila, why?' he said, sounding like a broken man.

'Oh, I don't know. It was always so incredibly dull the way they taught it at school. The teacher would read out chunks of it at a time, or make us read out chunks – I don't know what was worse. I nearly wasted away with boredom. I really suffered, you know. It was quite traumatic and of course I never wanted to go back to it in case it brought back all those painful memories . . .'

'You poor darling,' said Johnny, after he had stopped laughing. 'Obviously, under normal circumstances, a revelation as shocking as that would be grounds for divorce, though I am aware we are not married, yet. I think it might be worth trying a different approach before we have to resort to desperate measures. For instance, if I were to recite some of the sonnets to you, and do this . . .' he leaned over and nibbled my ear gently.

'Yes, that certainly makes Shakespeare more interesting,' I purred.

There was a tap on the window. 'Wake up, you two

– or do you not want to hear the reviews?' It was Julian.

Johnny sat up so suddenly I fell off the sofa.

'Sorry!'

'I suppose I'd better get used to your work coming first,' I said, pretending to grumble. But now Julian had mentioned it, I couldn't wait to hear what people thought of our play.

We met in the hall and went into the kitchen, which was already full of people. Emma, who had been banging her rattle around, decided there were too many of us and started bawling. Johnny lifted her out. 'I'll take her outside for a bit until she calms down,' he said.

Will was going after him, but Julian stopped him.

'Let him go. He needs a moment to pull himself together.'

'But he must know the reviews are going to be brilliant?' protested Ma.

I followed Johnny outside. We talked to Emma about a duck that flew overhead and quacked to make her laugh. I didn't say anything about the reviews, I just waited with Johnny until he was ready to go back inside.

'Thank God, those papers were burning a hole in the table,' muttered Pa.

I squeezed Johnny's hand as he sat down.

Julian read for a while in silence. Then he smiled. 'OK. I like this critic. He always gets the insults out of the way first. Listen to what he has to say.

'When I heard that Julian MacDonald was going to put on a play in a garden I was seriously upset. One of the greatest actors this country has seen since Olivier has lost the plot, I thought miserably. And to try and outdo Peter Brook! But I am a man of faith so I trekked down to a crumbling mansion in Kent and hoped for the best. I needn't have worried. The evening's performance totally outstripped my hopes. This was a production that epitomised the play's central theme of love gone mad. But Julian gave us a glittering dose of magic to help the madness go down. He also persuaded a most eccentric cast of people to lend their surprising talents to the play, including Paige and Piper Watson, who proved they are capable of far more than the vapid show they present on television; Cinnamon Jones, who has an unfair amount of acting ability as well as beauty, and screen heart-throb Mitch Clayton, who gave a very competent performance as one of the confused lovers. But it was his younger brother, Johnny Clayton, a complete unknown on stage or screen, who, to my mind and, I think, most of the audience's, stole the show as Puck with a performance of such shimmering intensity I was left dry-mouthed and humbled at the end of it. I think there will be a lot more to say about this charismatic young performer when we see him, as undoubtedly we will, in all the great roles.'

'Three cheers!' said Anna. 'I thought you were the best, though,' she whispered to Tony, but not quite quietly enough, and we all laughed.

'So what's going to happen now?' asked Pa curiously, his arm wrapped round Ma's.

'Well,' I began, and then stopped. Good question actually. What was going to happen next?

'There are a couple of things, actually,' interrupted Julian. 'Firstly I should tell you that I believe there are a few people interested in this house as a future location for film shoots. They usually pay quite well, I believe.

'But that's marvellous!' said Pa, while his three children looked at him in disbelief. 'Why are you looking at me like that? It turns out I get on quite well with acting people. I can relate to their eccentricities.'

'Well, who would have thought it?' muttered Will.

Julian continued, 'The other thing is a project that I am rather hoping Johnny will be interested in.'

'Go on.'

'I had a chat with the Mayor of Vacquitos last night and then a few people who had come to see the play. We all like the idea of doing a few plays in the States and then further afield, into South America. There are a number of grants available. But it would be a tour with a difference. We all like the idea of alternative venues and new audiences. So, not theatres, but parks, community centres, that sort of thing, all the way from Canada to Peru!'

403

'Or you could set up a simple stage inside a shopping mall. That would be a real clash of cultures,' said Johnny eagerly, and Julian smiled at him. There would be no stopping Johnny now, I realised.

'Exactly. We want to take Shakespeare to people who may never have even heard of him, or who only think of him as the writer who bored them to death at school. Of course it would have to be a very low-budget affair. There certainly won't be any money to stay in expensive hotels.'

'So no red carpets then?' said Anna, sounding regretful.

'Probably no carpets at all,' said Johnny with relish. He sounded like a child on Christmas Eve.

'How long would you be away?' I asked, a chill of foreboding coming over me.

'Well, North America is a big place. And of course there is South America. Peru needs emergency aid, but it also needs its morale boosted.'

'Months then,' I said faintly. Well, if they thought for a minute they were going without me . . . I pictured with a shudder all those women – fiery Mexicans, southern belles, sexy drawling Texans – Johnny wouldn't be safe for a minute. Now, what could I do? Mentally I ran over my accomplishments. I could make lists and follow them, roughly; I could pull a decent pint; I could marshal people into fairly obedient lines. Was that it? The sum total of my talents? Regretfully I came to the conclusion that it probably was. 'You will need a housekeeper,' I said hopefully, and tried to ignore the burst of laughter from my unimpressed family. 'Well, I suppose I could try to become an estate agent again, especially if Johnny could give me lessons in how to tell better lies.'

'He could, but you might be too busy doing other things. Why don't you take a look at this?' Julian handed over the paper with the review in it.

I stared in disbelief. Next to the text was a drawing of the cast at a rehearsal. Mitch was sitting on a log, moodily picking his nose, Cinnamon was about to tuck into an enormous ham baguette, the width of her arm, and Johnny was leaning against a tree, wistfully looking on. It was one of my drawings and it had my name in the corner.

'What on earth . . . ?' I began.

'I saw your drawings and knew immediately that my friend at the newspaper would like them as much as I did. He printed these and is desperate for more.'

'But they weren't – drawings, I mean! They were just scribbles. I sort of did them without thinking, usually when I should have been doing something else,' I added with a blush.

'Well, they work brilliantly.'

'So all the time I was painting, and throwing pots, and doing those collages . . .'

'They were awful. All those dried beans that kept falling into our dinner,' shuddered Will. I gave him a playful shove.

'Seriously, all those experiments and yet the answer was there all the time, under my very nose. I did those drawings while I was thinking of more important things to do!'

'That's life,' said Will. 'That's my professional opinion, anyway,' and ducked as I threw a napkin at him.

'Anyway, my friend at the paper wants more, especially from our new Shakespeare tour, if it comes off.'

'You mean – he's offering me a job?' I said faintly.

'Yes.'

'Drawing?'

'Yes.'

'With pay?'

'Naturally.'

'A proper job – with pay – doing the thing I love best in the world? Well, almost,' I added, glancing at Johnny from under my eyelashes. I was stunned. The family were stunned. Even Emma was staring at me open-mouthed.

Everyone was looking at me expectantly. Johnny came to my rescue. 'Acting as Ms Barton's interpreter, I would like to say on her behalf that she has, uniquely, run out of words, but will get back to you as soon as the whole thing has sunk in.' His mobile rang. 'Er, Lila, I don't suppose you could come out of your trance, like right now?'

'What's happened?'

'Apparently, Dirk, my stepfather is – oh, there he is right now, pulling up.'

'Oh, Johnny, what do you want to do?'

He was pale but calm. 'I guess I need to go and have a few words with him. Hang around and chuck me a life belt if I look like I'm drowning.'

I went and hovered near the window so I could see them, but not hear them. Mr Clayton was sitting in the back seat of a car that was probably hastening the environmental end of the world by a good couple of months. He just sat there and waited for Johnny to join him – like he was a king and Johnny was some kind of servant. 'Well, have we got news for you, you horrible man. Johnny's been recast – he's everybody's hero now,' I muttered to myself. Had Johnny given me permission to eavesdrop? Yes, he had, I decided, slipping outside.

'I've just been talking to a guy at Fox. They're looking for someone to play opposite Cameron Diaz in her next film. If you get the next flight outta here and don't stuff up you might be in with a chance.'

'Thanks, Dirk. I guess you're trying to tell me I did OK last night. But it's too little, too late. I am not going to audition for a film opposite her. Or Scarlett Johansson. Or Lindsay Lohan. Or anyone else you've lined up in order to control my career as you have Mitch's. I am going to America to play Hamlet in a shopping mall!'

The look on Dirk's face was probably also the one he was going to have when he came face to face with his just deserts down in Hell. I was so pleased to get a sneak preview.

'Like hell you are! I'll stop your allowance!' he blustered.

'Go to the bank, Dirk. They'll tell you I haven't touched that account for years. I've been living off what my mom left me.'

Dirk seemed to shrivel slightly at the mention of her name. 'I know I neglected you for a while after she died. I was so busy building up the business. But I wanted to help you. After all, I took you to one goddamn shrink after another . . .'

'I'm sorry, you've mistaken me for someone who gives a damn,' said Johnny smoothly, and I saw Dirk flinch. 'Look, I haven't got time to stand here talking to you. I've got my life to live. Goodbye. It's been, er, interesting knowing you,' and he walked to where I was waiting for him and pulled me round the corner.

'Now, to the really important stuff. The last few hours have been such a whirlwind – are we actually engaged?'

'Well, the Plan did stipulate I shouldn't get engaged for a year,' I said slowly. 'Anyway, my heart is yours, ring or no ring.'

He nodded. 'So these other guys – the failed fiancés – did *they* propose to *you*?'

I smirked. Well, I know it wasn't anything really to be proud of, but I did get offered an impressive collection of rings. 'Yes, every time.'

'Great. You see, we know this is different, right? We'll show the world this is different. You can propose to me.'

'What? Down on one knee?'

'Yeah. If you want.'

'How undignified,' I grumbled.

Johnny was inflexible. 'Go on, we haven't got all day. Oh, and by the way, do you want to be wed "with pomp, with triumph, and with revelling", because I was thinking of something a bit more low key.'

'So, you're going to say yes, then? Oh, I remember that – that's a line from *Dream*!'

'You'll know all thirty-seven of Shakespeare's plays by the time I've finished,' he threatened.

I gulped. 'He wrote that many, did he?' My education was going to take a long time then.

In the end I didn't go down on one knee. I swept him a curtsy like we were in one of the fairytales I used to love as a child. It was a beautiful curtsy – I had been practising all my life. I looked at him lovingly from under my lashes. 'If you would do me the honour of –'

I didn't get any further. We were too busy kissing.

Acknowledgements

Huge thanks to Anne-Marie for making it all happen and whose advice is always sound.

I consider myself incredibly lucky to have been able to work with Emma Rose, Chrissy Schwartz and Amelia Harvell at Random House.

Nothing might have happened at all if Margaret hadn't talked about life scripts; if Celia hadn't provided technical support and if Carol hadn't been fierce about self-belief.